"For fans who st_____ ___ ___ ___ed White's *Fantastic* magazi___, ___ ___ need to say is that Keith Taylor is Dennis More (the latter being the pseudonym) and the bard is Felimid mac Fal. I will let the Erin rover introduce himself to the rest of you:

> I'm a bard of the old blood, and that is only a lesser degree of Druid. You had them here once. Where I come from, bards have been known to sing armies to defeat or victory and kings off their thrones or onto them. My grandfather Fergus is Chief Bard of Erin. We're descended from Cairbre, the bard of the Tuatha de Danann. My line have been poets and harpers in Erin since the world was new, and magic's in our heart-marrow."

—*Science Fiction Review*

BARD II:

The Return of Felimid mac Fal

Ace Fantasy Books by Keith Taylor

BARD

BARD II

BARD II

KEITH TAYLOR

ACE FANTASY BOOKS
NEW YORK

BARD II

An Ace Fantasy Book/published by arrangement with
the author

PRINTING HISTORY
Ace Original / April 1984

All rights reserved.
Copyright © 1984 by Keith Taylor
Cover art by Don Maitz
This book may not be reproduced in whole or in part,
by mimeograph or any other means, without permission.
For information address: The Berkley Publishing Group,
200 Madison Avenue, New York, N.Y. 10016.

ISBN: 0-441-04909-5

Ace Fantasy Books are published by The Berkley Publishing Group,
200 Madison Avenue, New York, New York 10016.
PRINTED IN THE UNITED STATES OF AMERICA

FOR JANET
AND THE TOADS

"On the sea, the ocean, on the isle of Bouyan, live three brothers, the Winds: one is of the West, the second of the North, the third of the East. Blow, ye winds, blow unbearable sadness to the woman I name, so that she cannot live a single day, a single hour without thinking of me!"

—*Slavic Invocation*

CONTENTS

PART ONE: THE WEST

PART TWO: THE NORTH

PART THREE: THE EAST

PART ONE:
THE WEST

I
Passage Out of Britain

"Satan's arse, with piles like fat acorns! Call yourself a steersman? Or a pilot, God aid me? You'll run us aground yet with all the estuary to choose from!" Pascent ripped the stocking cap from his head and crushed it into a ball in his fist. A temperate breeze blew through his russet hair. There was some need for it. "Take the obscenity tides into account; that's why you are here!"

Pascent watched the result of his tirade, scowling. In a moment he nodded, said, "Better."

His outburst had been justified. Pascent had not been able to find his usual pilot, or any other as skillful. Gossip said they had all shared in some spectacularly rich bit of salvage, and dispersed with the pickings to their water rat villages among the endless reeds. Pascent had had to take the best man he could get, and Thames tides were treacherous.

"If *Briny Kettle* ends as salvage for his brother scavengers, I'll have his guts," Pascent muttered.

"He knows the Thames and her ways as well as any, skipper." Uccol of Vannes, the bo'sun, watched their substitute pilot critically. "You made sure of that. So did I. It's ships like this one he doesn't know."

"Hah. Tell me more. We're not out of sight of the bridge yet."

It's glad I'll be when we are, thought their one passenger, overhearing.

3

Felimid mac Fal, a bard of Erin, had not much relished his days in London. In essence, and in spite of a hundred years' decay, it remained a Roman city, hateful to him. There had been nothing but straight lines and ordered forms wherever he looked. When he had crossed the river and entered the city he had felt his bardic powers fade like smoke, and known that until he left London they would not return.

Well enough; he was leaving now.

He sat contentedly below the high stern, his back against the bulwark, out of the sailors' way, for he was a lubber among lubbers and not displeased with that condition. Lithe and supple, above middle height but not conspicuously so, one leg outstretched and the other bent with his hands clasped around it, he watched the sailors with interest. Felimid always admired experts.

The ship now oaring down the sacred Thames was *Briny Kettle*, a fittingly named merchant tub from Gaul, round of paunch and fully decked. Her design was Mediterranean, but she was sturdy and well adapted to northern waters. London faded from view astern, its bridge, wharves, temples, mansions and the decrepit wall-towers on either side of Lud's Gateway (the gate itself long gone). With satisfaction, the bard watched it all recede.

Taking ship out of Britain seemed a simple plan to have been attended by so many dangers and delays. How long had he been trying now? Two eventful months, for the most part spent in swift thinking and swifter action. The Saxon shore and much of lowland Britain as well had become over-warm for Felimid. It was urgent not for his safety alone, but that of some friends, that he leave—quietly. With luck, the setbacks had done no harm. From his heart, the bard hoped so.

Pascent barked his orders confidently, hiding a certain worry. What he was about called for fine timing. He wanted to clear the estuary between midnight and dawn, when the land breeze blew and friendly darkness covered all. The water must be high and slack for the run. *Briny Kettle*'s draught was too much for peace of mind, otherwise. Pascent hated to think of taking her out in the dark with the tide ebbing, as he would have to do if they arrived late. They could stick on sand that way, and be there for twelve hours. The accursed, piratical Jutes of Kent would find them, helpless. Not that there would be slaughter—in those circumstances. First, the Jutes would laugh. They'd double over the thwarts. Then they would help Pascent refloat *Briny Kettle*, and take his cargo, and send him on his way with much witty advice.

Pascent might have avoided that risk by sailing to Thanet in daylight, and there giving up part of his cargo to the Kentish king as tribute. He had never once considered it. A hard, raffish scoundrel, not above occasional piracy himself, he had his pride. Truckle to the extortions of a gray-bearded pagan? Pascent leaned on the taffrail with a snort of disgust.

The bard sang below him:

> "When little fishes fly,
>   And the rivers run dry,
>   And the hard rocks do melt with the sun."

The captain stared at him. "What?"

He knew the words. They formed the refrain of more than one old song. He blinked because they fitted his thoughts so well.

"You spoke aloud, captain," the bard explained.

"I did, eh?" Pascent's weathered face turned an angry red. "When I need to be chorused by a harp-twanging pretty boy who's done me out of the time I'd promised myself with the most luscious whore in London—"

"And paid his passage to Gaul in silver."

"—by God, I'll ask! As for your silver, you may have it back whenever you like! Stuffed down your throat!"

Uccol of Vannes sucked breath between his teeth. The touchy pride of bards was well known, as was the power of their poetic satires to bring bad luck. Bred in the ports of southern Gaul, Pascent might not know, although he should; he had traded in the waters around Britain for years enough.

The bard stared a moment into Pascent's suffused face. Then he laughed. "I think it's Kentish sea thieves you have on your mind, captain, and though they haven't come near you yet they have robbed you, by stealing your manners. As for Vera, she and I are old friends. I'm sorry you were disappointed there, but not too sorry. And the silver is no longer mine, but yours, so stuffing it down my throat would surely be a waste."

Uccol whispered urgently, "Let be, skipper. He's right—and he's a bard."

Pascent fought his temper, and won, though he found it difficult. A volatile man, the scion of Celtic, Greek and Roman forebears blended for generations in the melting pot of Massilia (not a city that encouraged meekness, least of all in the harbor district) he'd have dealt sharply with such back talk from any mariner in his crew. A passenger who had paid well and also happened to be a bard was different.

The captain gave a curt nod. "Aye, that's so. I will own the Jutes are on my mind. Just remember what we agreed. If it comes to fighting, you fight with us."

"I'll remember, captain."

Remember? I'd even fight without the rest of you. I'd have to! You do not know it, captain, and I'll not be the one to enlighten you, but if you gave me alive to King Oisc of Kent, it's himself would pay you!

Relaxing somewhat, Pascent said, "At least the scum never raid London. Full of superstition about Roman buildings, they are. Thanet's in such a strong trade position that if they don't want to go to London, they need not. But there was always fine trade to be had in London for a man who'd risk it, and to the pit with all Jutes and Saxons!"

The youngest sailor aboard *Briny Kettle* reddened. His name was Rowan, and he was a Saxon, from one of their settlements in Gaul. He kept on with his work.

"True for you, captain," Felimid agreed. "It's not for the timid to ply these seas at all. The Jutes at any rate I'll join you in cursing, but you are welcome to London for me."

He might have added that superstitions about Roman masonry were not all nonsense. The Jutes had it back to front, that was all. The Romans had not used magic to build their roads or stone walls; instead, they had destroyed magic wherever they went, leaving in its place Rome's iron, ordered method. That still held. Some kinds of magic could not flourish, could not even exist, where one Roman stone was yet joined to another. Not in a Roman city, even if it stood deserted; not on a Roman road, although no legion had marched along it in a hundred years; not in the shadow of a Roman wall, however ruined. Magic like Felimid's own.

Now, watching the miles of reed wind-rippled in flowing patterns, he felt his bardic powers come back like an infusion of strength. Tossing back his head, he shouted for joy. Some of the sailors turned and looked at him; he looked back unabashed. Within himself he revelled. Felimid of Erin was himself again, able to sing shy dryads out of their trees and dragons into slumber, and juggle the fixed round of the seasons as a jester tosses balls. And free of that mazy stone graveyard where even the open squares hemmed him in!

Let the seamen tap their heads!

Standing, he gazed down the estuary. Roman London was not the first city to lie dying, here in the ancient west. Others much older were drowned and submerged, like Ys and Caer Sidi, and the four cities of the Tuatha de Danann. Land and water had changed places many times.

For no reason except that playing the harp came as naturally to him as breathing, Felimid took the harp Golden Singer on his knee and ran his hand over her shining strings. A bright note here, another there, sparked under his fingers. Then there was music like the rippling water, plangent, glad, cooling, grave. He fashioned words to match.

> "We row towards the sunrise on a river old as time,
>   Above the bones of ships and men corrupting through the years.
>   They tasted triumph and defeat, their women tasted tears,
>   The sea that beckons us called them where sirens dance and mime;
>   They saw it blue with summer and gray with blowing rime,
>   And plied between lands vanished now as morning disappears.
>   We pass like shadows over them, their glories and their fears,
>   And hear the tide-rung copper bells in sunken towers chime."

Uccol paused to listen. The bard's voice did that. It had a mellow clarity which could take it undistorted through the clamor of a carousing war band. Still, the comment Uccol delivered was not one of praise.

"Little you know of mariners! Or the sea! That is a song to raise ghosts of drowned men if one was ever made. Besides, the last thing the skipper wants is to have the tide at the stage of ringing any sunken bells when we clear the estuary. If it

should be, he'll blame you. And send you down to explore
those sunken towers your own self."

"He'd do better to send the pilot who satisfies him so ill,"
Felimid said. "However, thanks for the warning."

No such trouble came. The captain's intelligence about the
Thames tides was good. He'd gone to time, trouble and expense to make sure it should be. *Briny Kettle* came to the open
sea with the densely forested land of the East Saxons on her
left, poor and miserable behind its coast of quicksands and
treacherous waters, and Kent on her right for an utter contrast. Kent, which dominated the trade of North and Narrow
seas.

The bard remembered his treatment there at the hands of
King Oisc, Hengist's son. A lying accusation and the king's
readiness to believe it had combined almost to kill him, and
Felimid had been lucky to escape. Yet he had avenged himself
in a way.

Twilight came on. The sun flattened on the land-rim, fore-
shortening like the mouth of a crucible tilted to spill fiery
copper across the water behind the trader's ship. The hollow
backs of the sails grew rosy. Pink luster and black shadow
sharply defined crawled on the deck, then merged in a uniform
dusk.

Briny Kettle's ten oars were muffled, her sail clewed up and
a score of men put to rowing. None but Pascent, Uccol, three
crewmen and Felimid remained above deck. Near midnight a
strong land breeze arose, the oars were shipped, and the trader
passed Thanet with her sail bulging.

Someone gestured at the isle and made a comment; someone
else guffawed. The sound burst out across the starlit water.
Breath caught in every throat on *Briny Kettle*. Her captain was
too angry to swear.

He said softly, "The rope's end for you both at sunrise.
You ought to hang from it, not feel it on your backs."

He kept his word, striking the blows fast and hard. Panting
with effort, yet feeling expansive because they were now clear
of Kentish coasts and well out to sea, he tossed his knotted
rope aside.

"Ale all around, even for these two," he ordered. He came,
companionably, to drink his own with the bard, from a beaker
of Rhineland glass. Felimid had a leather-sheathed pewter cup
in his bundle of gear. He filled it to the brim.

Pascent's hairy throat worked as he swallowed. Foam hung on the thick moustaches framing his mouth when he lowered the empty beaker at last.

"Ahh!" he breathed. "By Saint Martin, that's a fine brew. One thing I give the sea wolves. They know good liquor if they don't know anything else good."

He cocked his head to one side, a mannerism of his the bard was learning to know. Pascent's left ear was deaf. He wore a garnet and gold earring in it, as if in the belief that since the organ did not serve its proper function, it might as well be ornamental. The gaud flashed in the sun.

"Praise for the day!" Pascent went on. "I've had soundings taken without pause since the false dawn. We've left the East Saxon banks safe behind us, but there's one great one somewhere about here, and we're sailing into the sun's eye. Be other banks to 'ware of once we turn through the strait, but that's for later. Wind smells all right." As he spoke, it was blowing from the north. The land breeze had died. "It ought to shift around and blow due the way we're to go. Like a wager on't?"

"Why not?" Felimid said ingenuously. "I cannot be losing, even if I forfeit. One way it's coin and the other way a helpful wind. Then you reckon the women of Ratuma will greet your crew on the morrow's eve?"

"The next night after." Pascent chuckled. "For a bard the leaping houses can be gain, not loss. Music and song each go well with the other. The Dolphin is the best place in the city. Use my name with the madam if you like."

Pascent had indeed grown more affable, so much so that Felimid wondered if his advice was wholly well meant. The day before, he had been angrily jealous of the bard's couching with a woman in London. Perhaps the Dolphin was the sort of place where a stranger might have his throat opened. Even if the recommendation was sincere, Felimid was not minded to act upon it. He'd had enough of that sort of arrangement in London to last him awhile.

"The fortress of women, each fairer than the last? You tempt me," he said. "But I am pursuing the dream of Angus Og."

"I never heard of him. What did he dream about that he couldn't find at the Dolphin?"

Felimid laughed. "You may have me changing my mind yet.

I'll remember what you've said.''

The bard stretched out to sleep in the morning sun. His harp lay by his side in her worn leather bag, propped against the bundle of his other belongings. The sword known as Kincaid rested sheathed across Felimid's belly. He lay at his indolent ease, head and shoulders resting against a bulwark and one leg bent. His elbows rested on the deck while his fingers curled lightly about the sheathed weapon. He could lie relaxed and comfortable like that, yet be ready to move quickly.

The captain had predicted the wind aright. Down through the strait ran *Briny Kettle*, with the white cliffs' gleaming buttresses in sight. Dark blue waves marched out to pale blue sky. The bilge gurgled; the ship's timbers groaned and creaked.

As he dozed, Felimid's dreams mixed with half-awake thoughts of the past. Four years he had spent wandering at random through Britain, and for what? His original reason had been to prevent a feud between his tribe and another. He'd agreed to exile himself for three years, and his heart had not broken at the prospect. He had liked the idea of seeing what lay beyond his own coasts. There had been much to see, and still was. He regretted nothing, but he knew it was time to go back.

Once ashore in Ratuma city, he would journey to Rennes, and thence make his way to the tip of Lesser Britain.* Ships for Erin were to be had there.

Home . . .

Then the lookout shrieked, "Sail! Sail! *The White Horse*!''

Felimid seemed to curl smoothly to his feet, rather than to stand or leap. The sea wind combed his hair as he looked about him. His right hand held Kincaid's scabbard, his left the hilt.

A long galley had appeared from behind a point of land. Bigger than any ordinary Saxon war boat, it held eighty men. A fanged serpent head glared above the prow, wickedly lifelike at the end of its curved wooden neck. The great square sail was striped and bore the figure of a white horse. Wind bulged that sail pregnant with menace, ready for bloody birth. *So much for dreams*, the bard thought.

The white horse was the badge of Kent's royal house.

Pascent said harshly, "King Oisc himself. May he rot and

---

* *Brittany.*

fish devour him! It's not my cargo he wants. He can sit at Thanet and grow rich if it suits him. He's after sport.''

A grievous prospect. Jutish ideas of sport were bloody. *Briny Kettle*'s men might have received mercy if the captain had paid King Oisc's extortion at Thanet, but as it was they would be granted none. It consoled Felimid to see that they knew it. Pascent would not try to surrender. The bard thus had a fair chance to die fighting with the crew. He preferred that to being captured alive by Hengist's son.

He wanted even more to escape entirely, but *Briny Kettle* was about as likely to outdistance King Oisc's warship as fire to burn at the bottom of the sea. It all augured disappointment for the girls at the Dolphin.

II
"I'll Slay You, and All With You!"

"That's *Ormungandr*!" a mariner cried. "The Great Serpent itself! King Oisc's damned ship!"

"And well I know that!" Pascent had met pirate attacks before. His orders were decisive. "We run before the wind as long as we can. Uccol, start the men hopping; I want all the advantage each breath of wind can give us, and I want the crew too busy for terror. You, Leo! Let's have some pitch to boiling. Not the cauldron, a small pot, you whoreson! I want it ready by the time they overhaul us, and that won't take them forever."

The white sail fled straining; the striped one with its emblem of a horse pursued. Aboard *Briny Kettle*, war gear was brought forth and stacked ready for use. Pascent put on a stiff leather tunic and casque, both strengthened with iron plates. The striped sail came steadily closer.

Felimid watched it, fascinated. Although he had guested with King Oisc before ill will arose between them, that had been at Yule, when vessels lay at rest in their winter quarters. This was his first view of the king's famous ship.

He'd heard much about it. Few vessels the like of *Ormungandr* rode any sea. Red dwarves in the north had shaped her timbers, pegging and joining them by chanted spells. *Ormungandr*'s prow broke sea rocks when it met them, so the tales declared. *Ormungandr* could be rowed up a cataract. If damaged, she would mend herself, and would

12

never founder or capsize. The softest breeze or a mere half-dozen rowers would drive her through the water like an attacking shark. And more tales, and more . . .

Felimid had been skeptical. He felt less so now.

"Captain, we can't lose 'em in this way," one of the steersmen protested. "Best we give the cargo to Neptune and run free."

"Not yet," Pascent growled. "There is maybe a chance we can buy our lives with it, but I mean to try everything else first. How's your taste for a fight, bard?" he asked Felimid.

"Sharpening by the moment."

He sounded airy. There was little use in speaking the truth, after all, which was that he felt out of place, unfairly put upon, and angry. The limited space on *Briny Kettle*'s deck in the midst of so much glittering dark blue water left him exposed and constricted at once.

Ormungandr rushed on like death.

The ship's carpenter had a small pot of pitch bubbling by now. Nearby, two other men ripped cloth to strips and wrapped it about the heads of arrows. The bard began to see the purpose of Pascent's order. He smiled.

The galley drew inexorably nearer. Although it raced through the water, no foam curled back from the driving bow. Only glass smooth ripples peeled away from the cutwater, as though *Ormungandr* slid through a bath of oil.

Behind the serpent head stood a tall byrnied figure in a boar helm. His thick white beard streamed in the wind. He wasn't yet close enough for his eyes to be seen, but Felimid had looked into them and knew what they were like: pale blue, never showing laughter or mercy.

"Bows here!" Pascent said.

His archers had a fistful of prepared arrows each, with fire pots from which to ignite them. They mounted the high stern. No bowman, Felimid had not foreseen this trick, and he knew the Jutes were no bowmen either. He smiled more broadly. He'd have liked to go to the poop himself and watch, but with the captain, two steersmen and four archers already there, it lacked room for spectators. He leaned over the bulwark instead.

"There is your mark," he heard Pascent say to his bowmen. "The White Horse of Kent! *Master Christi*, if a man misses at this range, I'll toss him overboard to try from closer! Shoot as one man when I say the word."

The arrow tips caught fire.

Between the two ships, the gap of sapphire-hued brine shrank further.

"Look at their king, standing there," one of the bowmen muttered. "I vow I could put a shaft straight through the middle of his beard."

"No!" Pascent barked. "You fool, did we kill their king, the rest would hunt us all the way to Spain if they had to. It's how these heathen are. I want you to slow them, stop them if you can." A breath later he added, "Now!"

Four scarlet comets flew, trailing smoke, and four more, and four. Not until twenty burning arrows had ripped through *Ormungandr*'s sail did Pascent's bowmen stop. The sail blazed from edge to edge. *Briny Kettle*'s men roared, jubilant. Flame charred Kent's white horse to a sorry black nag as they watched.

Swearing Jutes flung water from bailing scoops. When that proved futile, they fought to get the sail down before mast and yard also caught fire. Lines were slashed. The sail slid deckward, crumpling, sagging, scattering whirls of sparks. Scorched men hacked through the collar of heavy rope holding yard to mast, and worked like fiends to manhandle the whole blazing mass into the sea, careless of burns. *Briny Kettle* drew ahead while men danced for glee on her deck, bawling insults at the Jutes.

"Lords of the sea, are you?"

"Go home, and grow back the beards we've burned off you!"

"Good work," Pascent said. "Now they will have to row. If we stay beyond their reach until they weary, we will live. If not, we won't. And they have fifty oars."

Hissing, the sail and half-consumed yard were quenched in the sea behind *Ormungandr*'s stern. The mast stood up naked and useless. It too was afire by now. Little flames danced about it, eating greedily. Near the top, where the wood was slimmest, the wind blew them into long snapping pennants.

Raging, King Oisc had a man bend to every oar, while the mast was unstepped and cast after its tackle. The men who were not rowing picked up their weapons again. Many had seared hands, which added to their ire.

Before the wind and her hunters, *Briny Kettle* fled down the

Narrow Sea. Her wake seethed white, and faded into trackless blue. Assessing his chances, Captain Pascent was not hopeful. He'd deprived the Jutes of sail, but nothing could deprive their ship of half a hundred oars and preternatural speed. Oh, *Briny Kettle* had oars; ten of them, for maneuvering in harbor or cove. Seldom were they useful on the open sea, where *Briny Kettle* depended on sail.

In *Ormungandr*'s bow, Oisc chuckled grimly. "We will have them," he said.

A throbbing drum amidships gave the oars rhythm. Oisc's men would row till arms came out of sockets and hearts burst before they surrendered their prey.

The bard considered what he might do. He had powers. He could bring sorrow, laughter or sleep to men with his harping, but any of the three would affect *Briny Kettle*'s crew long before the marauding Jutes. And when the latter came close enough they would probably be making too much noise to hear his harping.

He could see elementals, and speak to them. His own strongest affinities were with air and earth. Water, in his nature, came a sorry third. Though he could sometimes charm the dwellers in lake, spring or river, he had learned not to depend on it, for water was capricious. With the powers of the wide sea he had no rapport at all, and in any case they would favor Oisc. The old king had given them blood sacrifices enough.

The blue afternoon wore on. Shadows lengthened. Every stroke of Jutish oars brought back a fragment of the distance *Briny Kettle* had gained. King Oisc's implacable figure became distinct again. So close was he that one might judge the workmanship in his boar-tusked helm.

"Felimid of Erin!" he cried across the water. "Felimid the bard, Felimid the treacher! Do you know me, you son of a mare?"

It was as unexpected as a sudden lash of sleet in the spring weather.

He knows I'm here! How did he learn?

Does it matter how?

Despite his astonishment, the bard answered.

"By your ox's lowing and the white beard of your dotage, I know you! What do you want, king? It wouldn't be advice on the matter of bear hunting, would it?"

"Laugh on!" Oisc of Kent roared. "You tricked us finely then! By nightfall the crabs will laugh as they swarm on your corpse! You fool, did you not think I would hear you had been in Cerdic's kingdom, and him a son of mine? You of all men should know that men talk! I made it my business to learn what else you had done. I know how Tosti died. Soon, soon now I will avenge him, and those other comrades I lost in the forest! Cur! I'll slay you, and all with you!"

"Perhaps! It's more within the scope of your talents than conversation, whatever!"

Pascent stared at the bard. "You! This is on your account! Oisc wants *you*! Ten thousand devils, and you kept me ignorant! Now, by God—"

"Your anger's justified, captain, but I'd no knowledge that Oisc knew I was with you. By Cairbre's fingers, until this moment I was sure he believed me dead!"

Turning from Felimid, Pascent shouted, "Oisc, lord of Kent! I owe this dog nothing! He has deceived me! If you allow the rest of us to go unharmed, I'll throw him overboard! You may have him!"

"I'll have him, indeed," Oisc said. "I'll have his blood, and my warriors will have yours. No bargains, fellow; no quarter! That is my word."

Pascent gave Felimid a black look. "I'm glad," he said between his teeth, "that I'll see Heaven while you, a heathen, fare to Hell."

He began barking orders at his crew. Felimid watched *Ormungandr*. It was swiftly drawing level with them, no more than a spear's cast astern on the port quarter.

"*Fool*," Felimid said suddenly, to himself.

He drew his harp from her leather bag. She was Golden Singer, the harp of Cairbre, and her music could change the set round of the seasons. It had not struck Felimid before that this power could help. Jutish reivers would row through any weather, and what they suffered, *Briny Kettle* must suffer. Yet there was a thing subtler than gale or sleet which even a Jutish reiver would not care to face.

Felimid harped autumn. He struck notes clear and sharp as frost in an October dawn, the kind of crisp morning he had loved at home because with the harvest safely in he could lie abed. He harped the mellow, golden afternoons, he struck tones as full as the ripeness of apples and nuts, and what he invoked came.

Spring sunlight has a bright, new quality. Around *Briny Kettle* it changed to a glow like that of yellow wine, properly aged. The air turned crisp as dry leaves and held the same scent. Its coldness stung the lungs. Men gasped, and as they gasped their breath steamed white. The same happened on a greater scale as autumn's air met the warm breath of May. Fog surrounded the merchant ship. Oisc lost sight of his prey.

The strong wind tore Felimid's mist to rags almost at once. That he had expected, and harped more as fast as it dispersed. The Jutish oar stroke sounded ragged, somewhere off there in the veiling fog. They were blundering after what they could no longer see. Nor did they like rushing ahead into blind white mist.

"A miracle!" someone said in awe. "The saints are with us!"

Felimid smiled.

His smile vanished as he heard a drum throb on the far side of the fog. *Tum-tum-a-tum, tum-tum, tum-tum.* He recognized the sound. Worse, he heard the sorcery beating in it like a heart.

Kisumola, King Oisc's Lappish wizard, was with him in *Ormungandr*. The bard had strong cause to remember that wrinkled little man and his drum.

Tum-tum, tum, tum-tum-a-tum.

The fog shrank. As it dwindled it grew denser, taking distinct shape. A gray sac large as a hogshead of wine pulsed among tentacles fathoms long. Eyeless and opaque, it sprawled across the water, and though it moved before the wind in pursuit of *Briny Kettle*, it retained its form.

Felimid ceased his harping. The autumnal cold left the air. If he made more fog, he might only feed that shape to greater size. At best he would make it hard to see while it did its creator's will.

"Stand fast," he said to the frightened crew. "Whatever that thing may be, it's only made of fog. I'll rid us of it."

The monster's saclike body changed as Felimid spoke. A dark purple ovoid formed within it. Felimid thought of an egg, or an immense grape filmed over with whitish bloom. More than either, he thought of the octopus Kisumola's shaping so much resembled, which spurts dye to confuse its enemies. Made of fog, the thing behind them would logically eject vapor, to their dire harm.

"Ah, no," Felimid said. "No, Kisumola. I am having none of that today."

He played his harp again, this time to the air elementals darting in the wind. They changed form freely, now like fine masses of streaming hair, now like dandelion puffs, now like whistling disembodied faces. They could also grow from pleasant sylphs to gale giants in an hour. Although Felimid could not command them, he offered them sport they found pleasing.

A score became like blue and silver birds, trailing lacy feathers yards long. They descended on the fog mass. In moments they had torn it apart with sharply cutting beaks and talons, scattering the remains. As it vanished, Felimid breathed one whiff of the vapor it had distilled within itself. His throat closed; he wept tears of pain.

Pascent and his crew had seen nothing but the fog monster's dissolution, like King Oisc's Jutes. None was an initiated bard. No more was Kisumola, but he was a wizard. He would have seen with the true sight.

Felimid turned his gaze from the sea. The young Saxon named Rowan stood near him.

"Now this is dreary," Felimid said. "We're all back where we were."

"I don't understand." Rowan spoke with some awe. "I know what I saw, yet. . . . Did you raise that fog?"

"I did." Felimid coughed the last of the vapor from his stinging nose. "I did, and the Jutes lost us for a space, but now they come again—and I have no more tricks. I think we'll have to fight."

"So, then." Rowan's people accepted fate without wailing or grovelling before it. With his jaw as yet lightly furred and death impending, he did not complain. "You see I am accoutered for fighting. Some war gear is left. Do you want it?"

"I do. Thanks."

Felimid sorted through the various bits of fighting equipment Gervase carried for emergencies. He found a small round shield of the kind he preferred. There was not so much of it to stay between him and a foeman's edge, which was doubtless why everybody else had left it in favor of larger ones, but it could be shifted to cover different parts of his body more quickly. When he fought, Felimid depended on skill, speed and coordination more than strength.

An ox-leather cap was the best he could find to protect his head. Not that many of Oisc's Jutes were better off. Some had nothing on their heads but their braided hair.

"The king grows careless," Felimid remarked. "He's forgotten to plait his beard. Let's hope it blows into his eyes at the right time."

"Aye," Rowan said. "His rowers are flagging, do you notice?"

"I'd thought I did. I wondered if I was deceived by wishing. See! They are being spelled, ten at a time. And it seems to me that in spite of it they no longer gain."

Then the wind began to drop.

"Obscene coprophagy," Rowan said, in short Saxon words.

"Lir," Felimid swore, "and Manannan mac Lir!"

The wind failed further. *Briny Kettle*'s straining sails grew flaccid.

"They gain once more," Rowan said. "I'll luck to them! I think Oisc has been playing with us while his rowers, those he hasn't spelled, found their second wind."

It was true. *Ormungandr* rushed closer each moment. *Briny Kettle* might as well have been riding at anchor. Even with a strong wind to drive her, she remained a round-bellied merchant tub, while *Ormungandr* was ... *Ormungandr*.

King Oisc laughed, his bare arms raised. "I have you now, bard! Oh, I have you now! You can do nothing against my men; their ears are blocked with wax lest they hear your enchanted harp! I know you too well, and your tricks, you young dog! You shall not live to play more of them on me! What? You have nothing to say? No insolence? No lampooning verses? I thought not! You have sung your last song in more ways than one!"

The last slight hope gone. With black sickness in his soul, Felimid knew he ought to have foreseen this. Oisc had come hunting him, had known he was aboard *Briny Kettle*, and had known something of the bard's powers. They had been acquainted in the Yule weeks, and since then Oisc had sent spies to track Felimid's movements. Some of those agents must have been in London while Felimid bargained with Pascent to ride in his ship. They probably had not been Jutes, but Oisc had British servants also. They would have crossed the river at once, and ridden horses to death if need be to bring Oisc the news.

Oisc laughed again. He was close enough now to see the chagrin in Felimid's face. Sweeping his arm in a half circle, he roared, "Take them!" Oisc had shouted the words in sheer glee. His men did not hear. Nor did they need the command; they knew what to do.

"Shoot until it no longer matters," Pascent said bitterly to his archers. "Be sure to nail that old swine through the heart if you can."

They had been choosing targets and shooting for some time. A few Jutes were dying or dead. Perhaps a dozen had been wounded.

"Captain," Felimid said, "I've an idea that may kill others. The sail's no help now. Send two men to the masthead to cut it down at your signal. Some Jutes will be caught beneath it, if you choose your moment. Or cannot the sail be dropped so suddenly?"

"It can. I'll have it done. Uccol, you heard? I like it. Let's take all the sea wolves we can with us! Huh! They come!"

Javelins rattled among the crewmen. One stuck in the plank by Felimid's foot. He drew it forth, but decided not to throw it at Oisc. The wily old king paid him the compliment of watching him like a wolf, and his shieldmen still protected him. The bard chose a rower and put the javelin through his neck. He toppled from his thwart, madly kicking.

Swiftly then, Felimid took his harp to the captain's cabin. She would be safest there. When he came out, his shield was on his right arm. The sword Kincaid glittered bare.

Pascent did not see Felimid make free with his quarters. He was commanding a pair of sailors to take axes into the hold and break open the vessel's sides.

"No, captain!"

"That'll doom us for certain!"

"Go, damn you!" Pascent snarled. "Oisc will not spare us now! He may have our lives; he shan't have our goods!"

They went.

Oisc's warship ran alongside. A volley of spears and throwing axes hurtled at flesh, and grapnels flew after, their points thudding in timber. Oisc was first over the side. He rammed his shield-boss into a face, caught an axe-blow on the rim, and cut into someone's body with his sword. A howl of "Wotan! *Wotan!*" stretched his mouth into a snarl as he cut a path to the waiting bard.

His companions came hewing after. They thundered "Wotan!" as loudly as their king, despite their wax-shut ears. For eternal seconds they battered the line of resisting seamen, until Uccol the bo'sun roared, "Give way! Retreat!"

Briny Kettle's crew ran pell-mell across the deck. The Jutes charged them with a roar like surf. Men waiting aloft cut cords. The sail dropped clapping from the yard, and eight Jutes were enveloped in it.

Blinded, floundering under the heavy cloth, they were easy to kill, and their own comrades trampled across them to reach the Gaulish sailors.

"Look upon that!" Felimid cried to Oisc. "Some of your best cut down with hardly a blow struck, and that by my advice! The trick is one you taught me. Recall?"

Oisc replied with a blow. Kincaid's blue and silver tongue flickered in reply, speaking with wild shrieks of clashing metal. A sharp tongue he was, none sharper, of edge or point. He licked through the iron rim of Oisc's shield. He crashed and shrilled on Oisc's heavy broadsword and notched the gory edge each time they met, yet was not himself marked.

As the weapons, so the fighters. Though Oisc carried nearly three times Felimid's years, he was the bigger, a seasoned and still mighty warlord. Felimid was quicker, but Oisc was stronger. And the king was far better protected. Not even Kincaid's edge would slash easily through his helm or scale shirt.

They fought near the stern. The battle raged about them and they were neither engulfed nor parted. Oisc hewed with deadly patience; he was too old and knowledgeable to be reckless. Hunting Felimid had cost him dearly before. He laid on his strokes like a game player building a pattern.

Felimid's sword raced faster. He pretended desperation, seeking a way past Oisc's shield to any unarmored spot, arm, throat or knee. His point seemed everywhere, the whole of his attack.

Like all his people, Oisc fought wholly with the edge. The bard's style disturbed him, but if he was too old a dog to adapt readily to so new a trick, he was also too old to fluster. He moved his two-foot shield sufficiently to keep it ever between

him and the bard's leaping point, meanwhile working around
its rim with his own blade.

It was wolf battling cat. The cat might be quicker and
possess sharper claws, but the wolf required only one hard
bite.

In warding against that disconcerting point, Oisc left
himself open to a cut. The area briefly exposed was part of his
armored side. Felimid reached through the gap in Oisc's shield
work with a long steel finger. Skill and timing as much as
strength went into his blow.

Two iron scales parted before Kincaid's edge. A third was
knocked loose. Although Felimid's drawing stroke sliced the
ox-leather beneath the iron, it failed to touch Oisc's skin; yet
the impact made him stagger.

Sucking desperately for breath, he hewed backhanded at
Felimid. The bard caught the blow on his targe. It jarred him
from wrist to heels, and Oisc's sword broke.

Most of the blade flew high in the air. Oisc hurled the
worthless stub at Felimid's face and made a swift retreat
behind his skillfully handled shield. Some of his henchmen
closed protectively around him. Snatching a spear, he returned
to the slaughter.

Glancing about him, Felimid was appalled to see how few of
Pascent's crew remained alive. They clustered by the ladder to
the high stern, losing their stubborn lives one at a time—and
exacting payment.

The bard went to join them. He'd barely eight paces to go,
but no others he'd ever taken were so hard contested or greasy
with gore. He turned aside a lunging spearhead with his targe;
it struck and slid awry, sending pain through Felimid's
forearm though he had no time to notice it. He sent Kincaid's
point leaping over a shield-rim, through his foe's teeth and
through the back of his neck, so that he lurched dead against
two of his comrades before collapsing to the deck. A feint, a
downward cut, and a second man ceased to stand, with a great
wedge of his thigh muscles flapping loose. The wound sprayed
blood at a rate which must shortly cause his death.

A third man rammed his shield against Felimid's smaller
one, forcing the bard back a pace. A spearhead flashed like a
striking viper; Kincaid knocked it upward, clashing. The Jute
drove his knee at Felimid's crotch. Before the knee reached
him, Felimid smashed it with his targe's rim. The Jute stag-

gered; Felimid locked his targe behind the Jute's larger shield
and levered it aside, then ran half a yard of blade into his foe's
exposed belly.

Leaping through a momentary gap in the madness, he
joined what was left of *Briny Kettle*'s crew. Pascent himself
almost cut down his passenger without recognizing him, so
blood-spattered was he. They and five others managed the
backward scramble up the ladder to the high stern. Gaining
it, they fought there tenaciously, seven against sixty, with nowhere else to retreat. In their craving to close with the last of
their victims, the Jutes behind pressed the others forward.
They came, and they slew, and they died.

In the pressure of that wild tangle, King Oisc had been held
back from the fighting. Curse and manhandle as he would, he
could not force a way through his men. It was as though the
stopping of their ears had shrouded all their senses in a
berserker haze. They uttered no battle cries. Only grunts of
effort, snarls of fury, or inadvertent bellows of agony came
from them through the crash and jar of weapon-metal.

Two sailors climbed out of the hold with axes in their hands.
Seeing all the Jutes' attention fixed on the stern, the two made
a rush and cut down three from behind. After that a dozen
Jutes turned on them and hacked them to pieces, but not
before they had killed another man each. Their slayers looked
about, lest there should be more of *Briny Kettle*'s crew surviving forward, and thus they were first to spy the newcomers.

Three fast ships raced over the darkening sea. They were of
the Pictish kind, not large, but ideal for reconnaissance and
sudden raiding, and each held thirty men. Their intention was
plain at a glance. One did not have to be an experienced pirate
to know it. By rowing out of the westering sun while every
Jute's mind was fixed on slaughter, they had come so close unseen.

The Jutes alert to the danger made their comrades aware
by dragging them about bodily, pointing, mouthing, kicking
backsides, belike cursing their king for his whim of stopping
their ears with wax. Meanwhile the strange ships had spread
apart, two grappling to the trader, one to *Ormungandr*. Jutes
sprang howling back into the serpent ship to defend it. Others
turned to fight the newcomers boarding *Briny Kettle*. Under
their feet, the hold was filling.

Despite the lines and rig of their ships, the strangers were

not Picts. They seemed a mixed band; not that the harried few
in the stern were given any respite to gape at them. Some Jutes
continued to press them hard.

Axe and sword made a deafening din. Kincaid whirled and
shrieked, shining darkly wet. The captain at Felimid's right,
and the young Saxon Rowan at his left, did bloody work with
the fierceness of desperation. They were the last three left.

Back they were driven, surrendering each span of deck to
men who stamped over fallen friends to reach them. Their
spines almost brushed the taffrail, and beyond that lay nothing but the sea.

Oisc fought amidships all the while. He met the leader of the
newcomers a little abaft the mast. He saw a bronzed face
laughing under a silvered helm adorned with raven's wings, a
glittering mail shirt behind a shield covered with crimson
leather, and a flashing sword.

"You!" he snarled. "Die, then! *Kennnnt!*"

With the name of his kingdom on his lips for a war cry, he
struck. His spearhead met the red shield. Its point stuck. Oisc
jerked it out at once, meanwhile catching a stroke on the rim
of his own shield. He drove the iron umbo with rib-breaking
force at the newcomer's side. The newcomer straightened one
bent knee and shifted aside like a hawk tilting in flight. Oisc's
side was exposed; the bearer of the crimson shield returned his
blow. Iron scales broke. The thongs holding others snapped.
Ox-leather parted under the sword's edge. Oisc staggered,
wounded through his byrnie, yet although blood flowed, the
wound had not reached his guts. The Kentish king had lost
blood in other murderous fights. His laugh was a bark of
scorn.

"A love bite! I'm even standing yet! Bah! You belong in a
nursery, rocking cradles!"

As he spoke, he jabbed for the throat, then for the side of
the knee, to be thwarted both times by skillful use of shield
and blade. He feinted at his foe's ribs with the shield-boss.
The crimson shield sped between them to protect the other
chieftain. Oisc's spearhead flashed through the opening he
had played for, at the stranger's belly.

He reached his target and yet he failed. The war shirt held
against the concentrated power in his spear's point. Beneath
the mail, a leather sark and sheepskin vest spread the impact
somewhat. Even so, their wearer reeled on legs that had

abruptly lost their youthful springiness. A third smashing blow from Oisc's shield-boss flattened the other leader to the deck.

With a roar of triumph, the king drove down his spear. That thrust would have split breastbone or heart, despite any mail in the way, but again the crimson shield moved quickly enough. With splintering noises, the spear's head went through leather and wood to the socket. The red shield was nailed to the deck.

Its owner slid a bare arm free of grip and bracer, even while hooking a foot behind Oisc's ankle. The king was too well braced to be shaken by that. None the less, using the purchase, his foe curled up from the deck, delivering a two-handed stroke to Oisc's thigh. Landing below the edge of the byrnie, it cut muscles and arteries like butter, reached the thigh bone, and chopped it in two with a butcher's noise. Oisc toppled like a tree, his leg almost severed, his death certain.

The conqueror rose, panting, croaking, hand to midriff.

"Finish me!" Oisc demanded.

"Your knife is to hand. Finish yourself . . . dodderer. I've cradles to rock."

"I'd do the thing for you!"

The silvered helm bent. "That . . . may be true. Have it, then."

A long-fingered hand tore off Oisc's casque. The boar's head glared up in empty menace as it rolled on the deck. Oisc received the mercy blow from his own Kentish knife.

On the stern, Felimid, Pascent and Rowan still performed the brutal labor of staying alive. None had seen King Oisc die. None had glimpsed any moment of his last fight. They were wholly occupied with what they knew by now was their own.

Then the strangers fell upon those last surviving Jutes from behind. They were forced to turn from their prey. Wet with blood and sweat, Felimid, Pascent and Rowan fought on to clear the stern. It was the Jutes' turn now to be hacked man by man to their deaths. The dazed survivors on the stern saw it done.

At last, not one of King Oisc's men was left. From bow to stern *Briny Kettle* resembled a floating butcher's yard. The victors looked upon the weary, bloody men at the taffrail. There was an inexplicable pause. The killing lust remained in most of the strangers, ready to flame out again swiftly. Others

were willing to call the business ended. Many admired the
fight *Briny Kettle*'s survivors had made.

Each of the three had the same thought: Were they to
be spared or not? And Felimid added to that, in his mind:
Where is their leader, the one whose word will decide?

"Wait. Do not kill them."

Felimid wondered if the dizzy soughing in his ears had
warped his hearing. A woman's voice had spoken that order.

She trod with a sailor's gait through the press of men who
suddenly cleared her path. A valkyr beauty was hers, though
to judge by her carriage and manner she did not care one snap
of the fingers about it. Raven's wings lifted from her silvered
helm. One had been sharply clipped in the fighting, and an
escaped curl of hair hung on her cheek, black as the feathers.

Sun and wind had bronzed her face. Square of chin, with
cheeks curving beneath wide cheekbones, long brows that
swept like wave crests and eyes gray as the North Sea, it was a
face the bard felt instantly sure had never been used as a mask,
to disguise anything its wearer felt. No. This one was direct
and sudden as a lightning bolt. Her wide full mouth had never
been shaped by careful subtleties. From ear to ear and including both, none of her features was small.

Neither was her body. Few of the men about her stood taller
than she. Her reddened sword and scarred shield gave proof
that she had fought, and her shirt of silvered mail had blood
clotting darkly among the links.

"Christ's wounds," Pascent muttered. "Gudrun Blackhair!"

The bard had heard of her. She was notorious even on a
stretch of water as pirate-infested as the Narrow Sea. The
stories were interesting, but he had tended to dismiss them.
Some were impossible, others plainly wishful thinking. Now it
looked as though the truth might be more interesting still.

With a gesture that said *stay back*, she climbed to the stern
and surveyed the three men, looking last and longest at the
bard.

"Who are you?"

"A bard, lady, from the west."

"What?" she said, amused. "With red weapon in your
hand? Where is your harp?"

"I stowed her for safety when the fight began," he
answered, taking no offense. Despite the strenuous fighting

he'd done, and the reaction of relief that now assailed him, he spoke from burning lungs in a steady, pleasing voice. The long bardic training had given him such control. "As for the sword, we are taught both where I come from. We think little of poets who cannot fight . . . or for that matter of warriors who cannot make verses."

"You are alive; it seems that you can fight. Are you clever enough to make staves and epic songs?"

"Unequalled."

"I'll test that! Come with me and sing in my hall. Sing of my adventures in words that will live when I am dead, and you will not find me niggard. No man who serves me has found me that."

The language she spoke was so much like the Jutish dialect of Kent that Felimid could readily understand it. He replied:

> "I'll believe that Blackhair's bounty
> Betters kingly birth and rearing;
> Still I've never sung in service,
> But have harped for who would hear me.
> As your guest I'll give you glory
> On the golden strings of Erin,
> All my arts for Blackhair's asking,
> The reward for her to reckon—
> As her guest, and not as captive,
> Conquered in the weapon-clashing."

Gudrun Blackhair laughed harshly; not because she was displeased, but because she had swiftly discovered that the pain of Oisc's spear-thrust remained curled under her ribs like something with a hundred teeth, and that laughing hurt. She had been about to respond with a stave of her own, to show that her birth and nurture had been good. Now it passed from her mind.

"Agreed," she said, repressing a gasp. Her gaze sought Pascent and Rowan. "You too have survived, so you must be strong fighters. I take it you are not poets, so for you I have no concessions. Serve me . . . or be prisoners if you can hope for a ransom worth my while . . . or be slain."

"I'm your man, lady," Pascent said at once. "I'll follow you by land and sea, and maybe gain back my losses in your service."

To Felimid, none of these words rang true save the last. Then the deck gave a sudden heeling lurch. Pascent cried, "By God! We're sinking!"

He had forgotten his own order in the rush of events.

"That gives you my answer, lady." Rowan grinned, sixteen and merry in the dragon's maw. "I'll not stay on this deck if I must swim! Command me!"

Briny Kettle was settling like a pottery bowl with a piece broken out of the bottom. Men at her bulwarks were wrenching grapnels loose. As the woman calmly cleaned and sheathed her sword, she spoke the command Rowan had asked her to give.

"Fetch King Oisc's corpse along. His kinfolk on Thanet shall have it back. He's too great a man . . . to feed fish."

Pascent and Rowan looked at each other, then went about the awkward, distasteful task. Felimid snatched Golden Singer from Pascent's cabin. Gudrun Blackhair had no such errands. Turning about, she crossed the trader's lurching deck to drop lightly into *Ormungandr*'s bow. The three men who owed their lives to her whim followed her. The long serpent ship and the smaller vessels moved away from the foundering trader.

"An ill thing, that," Gudrun murmured, watching *Briny Kettle* belch air and sink. "What was your cargo?"

Pascent told her. "But it'll bring no gain to any now, unless to the sea people in drowned Ys."

"Let them have it!" Gudrun exulted. "I've not come empty-handed out of this. I have a ship, and such a ship! Row, my sea thieves, row and take us home!"

A tattooed, rawboned Frank brought a red mantle to put around her shoulders. The gesture was not a lover's, but an underling's. Gudrun looked forward, proud in her crimson cloak, *Ormungandr*'s serpent head lifting above her.

Pascent was looking back. Dead men floated; sharks moved voraciously among them. Uccol and all the rest, gone, slain, and *Briny Kettle* sunk! It was small consolation that Oisc and all his Jutes had been slain too. Although it gave Pascent a certain grim satisfaction to think of it, he'd far rather have had a ship and crew to command and a merchant venture before him. Instead, he was under command—and the command of a woman, a mad northern pirate.

She had not said who she was. It would have startled her to find that needful. Her name ran the length of the Narrow Sea.

It was known as far west as Erin, as far south as Spain, and as far north as Jutland. Because of her recklessness, no men but the wildest would follow her. That suited her well. They were the only sort she cared to lead. She managed with resource, courage, skill with weapons, quick wits and uncanny weather luck. Nor could her worst enemies say that she was close-fisted.

She turned her head to the sound of a muffled squeal. Amidships, a grinning Frisian had dragged someone from under the oar benches. He held his discovery forth by the scruff of the neck.

"Look what I found grovelling under a thwart!"

What he had found did not look like much. A wizened figure in reindeer skins and feathers, it clutched a round hide-covered drum under one skinny arm.

"I know him!" Felimid said.

"Explain, bard," Gudrun Blackhair demanded.

"That is Kisumola, King Oisc's wizard," he said. "Oisc kept him for his skill in reading omens and divination, but more for his weather magic. He nearly lied my life away when I was in Kent last winter. He told Oisc I was a spy for the British kings, at the urging of a warrior who bore me a grudge. It wasn't thanks to them that I lived and made my escape. Escape I did, though—and then Kisumola used his arts to learn where I had gone, that the same warrior might pursue me.

"What, Kisumola? No greeting for me? You went to trouble enough to harm me."

"So?" Gudrun glanced at the Lappish wizard. "How much of this is true?"

"It is all false, lady," he whined.

"False that you denounced me to King Oisc, after a great show of entering a trance and talking to spirits? False that you lied in your teeth when you said these things?"

The Frisian gripped Kisumola's neck harder.

"Lady!" the little man whined. "I beg you! King Oisc was my master, I owed him life. I foresaw that the bard would cause my master's death if he lived, and so I tried to destroy him first."

"By deceiving Oisc and raising ill will between us? Then the fault is yours, not mine. He'd never have been here to fall in battle today if you had not set him to hunting me. You made

your own vision come true by trying to avert it! Well, well."
Brows lifted, he turned to Gudrun Blackhair. "What do you
think of that, lady?"

"I've heard enough," she said brusquely. "I've little need
of weather magic, and less for one who thinks he knows better
than his master what is good for the master."

She turned swiftly, her mail giving forth a rustling of
silvered iron rings, and spoke a command to the Frisian. With
a chuckle, the rogue swung Kisumola up squealing, and
pitched him into the sea still gripping his drum. A great shrieking and splashing came out of the dusk, to be lost behind them
as *Ormungandr* drove on.

"Now he may drown or survive as he pleases," Gudrun
remarked.

She lifted off her silvered casque to show black hair worn in
a braided coronal around her head. Sighing with pleasure as
the breeze cooled her head, Gudrun unbuckled her jewelled
sword belt. Its gems smoldered hotly even in the dusk. Then
came another belt almost as heavy, attached by studs and
buckles to a sort of double baldric or body harness. This was
important because her mail shirt combined weight with flex-
ibility and tended to run like flowing water in whichever direction she moved. Without the harness, it sagged away from her
torso now, as she stood still; without the harness, it might
have spoiled her balance at a fatal moment.

Bracing her feet with care, she bent forward. The mail shirt
slid and bunched with a soft steely rustling. Gudrun Blackhair
writhed energetically from the waist, flexing her shoulders, the
ebon circlet of her hair level with her knees, hands almost
touching the floor timbers. A final shrug and writhe made the
shirt drop over her head. Sliding down her arms, it thudded at
her feet in a smaller pile than the bard had expected.

"Riccho!" she called. The rawboned Frank came forward.
Seemingly he was her armor-bearer. He carried a drinking
horn and there was froth in his moustache. "Have that clean
by morning; King Oisc is all over it. Send some drink forward,
too. I'm dying of thirst, and I'd guess the bard is also. Are you
not? Sea demons, I've not heard your name yet!"

About to give it, Felimid thought again. He had left Britain
in secret, or tried to, for the sake of some friends who might
have been endangered by too common knowledge that he
lived. Oisc had known, but he had been silenced forever. Pas-

cent and Rowan knew virtually nothing about the bard—but they did know his true name, and they were now Gudrun's men.

"My name is Felimid, lady," he said, "but I'd rather be known to you as Bragi."

He liked the joke. *Bragi* meant poetry. Now, how much more should he say? Lie outright and invent a background for himself? Stay reasonably close to the truth? Although he enjoyed telling colorful, richly detailed stories, he did not think he could spin one at present. Not a very believable one. He was tired, body and brain.

"Use whatever name you please," Gudrun said. "Bragi, ha? A northern name, but you are British, I think. Where did you learn the Jutish tongue?"

"From a Jutish boy and girl who were hostages in the Summer Country, and later in Kent, where I was Oisc's guest for the winter . . . or for enough weeks to grow fluent. Didn't Kisumola say?"

"Yes, you are right, he did. But if Kisumola told me the sun gives light, I'd go to see for myself."

The Frank returned with a brimming jug and two beakers. Bard and pirate captain, equally thirsty, gave their attention to the Kentish ale. Felimid teased himself by savoring one moderate mouthful to begin with; Gudrun emptied her beaker in a long steady draught. Watching her smooth throat move was a pleasure.

"Ahhh!" she said at last. "I wanted that."

He'd seated himself while she remained standing. From the black hair which her helmet had pressed close to her splendidly shaped head to her cowhide shoes, she burned with energy and seemed always on the point of swift motion. Freed from the mail shirt and harness, her other clothing had expanded outward, letting air reach her skin. The odor of fresh sweat came to Felimid on the night breeze. He liked it.

"King Oisc hated you much," Gudrun continued. "I commend your choice of enemies. Tell me, what is your lineage and who are your folk?"

"I'm a son of Erin, the land west of Britain."

"I know where Erin is. I've been there. It's a fair, fertile land, and the men fight well." Her teeth glinted through the dark in a reminiscent smile. "The ones I met did."

"We practice among ourselves," Felimid said, wryly and

with a bare trace of bitterness. "Often. My people are the Corco Baiscinn who live in the west, along the estuary of a river called the Shannon. It's descended they are from the Tuatha de Danann, an ancient and powerful and magical race. My own close family sprang long ago from Ogma the poet and Etan the nourisher, through their son Cairbre, a great harper and satirist . . . and were I to tell of all the generations between then and now, I'd be thickly bearded when I finished."

Felimid, now Bragi, drank more ale and reached bottom. He refilled his beaker.

"My grandsire, my father's father, had become the Chief Bard of Erin before I was born; his name is Fergus. He married Umai, the seeress and poetess of her tribe, and their only son was my father, born under stars of unrest and danger and trouble, surely.

"He was the first of our line in uncounted generations who did not want to be a bard. Oh, he endured the training for three years, to please Fergus, but then he went away and became a reiver, and at last made me with a woman married to someone else. I never knew him. He died less than a month after I was born.

"You have maybe heard of him. His name was Fal."

"Ah!" Gudrun was interested. "In the Hebrides, I heard of him. Yes. If he fathered you, I don't wonder you have talents as a fighter. But never regret not knowing him. It's regret wasted. Did you ever have an urge of your own to take to the sea?"

"Ah, no. The closest I came to that was a liking for mussels and dulse! No, the luck was with me to be educated as a bard. There were signs at my birth. My people are great ones for signs and auguries. Kingdoms have fallen because a Druid, staggering drunk, saw salmon strolling about on their tail fins. But this time the signs were right. I might have attached myself to the retinue of some chieftain, or even a king, but . . . " Felimid made a decision between one word and the next, and told a tiny particle of the truth. "I grew restless," he said with a shrug.

"I took ship for the Hebrides and spent a winter there. Finding one sufficient, I wandered south, and came to Kent in hopes of passage across the Narrow Sea. That wasn't my wisest decision, as you will have gathered, lady. I'm disappointed in Jutish hospitality." He smiled at her. "No offense to you intended."

"Offense? To me?" Gudrun was puzzled. "I am not a Jute. I am a Dane."

"Oh." The bard quenched some more of his thirst. "Sad it is to be ignorant. What is a Dane?"

"By Odin, you're insolent, too! I begin to see why Tosti Fenrir's-get wanted your blood."

"But then I was among Jutes," Felimid said. "Now I am the guest of a Dane."

"You are." Gudrun chuckled. "I'll pity your ignorance and answer you. Danes are the greatest people in the north. We forced the Jutes out of Jutland with sword and spear, so that they had to come to Britain. Yes, and one day we may take Britain, too."

"Maybe. For that you will have to wait your turn. And it's in my mind that the Jutes and their allies may yet fail. The Britons are not surrendering their land meekly."

They harbored that night at the mouth of the Somme. Gudrun had King Oisc's body brought ashore on a bier, to a fishing village where she was known. She told some fishermen to take the slain body to Thanet so that the king's own people might bury him. She gave gold for the service, and said that the men of Kent would probably give more.

"When they ask," she added, "say that Gudrun Blackhair of Sarnia sent you."

In the morning, they continued on their way. *Ormungandr* led, with thirty men and eight on the oar benches. The three Pictish ships followed, each with a crew of eleven; Gudrun had lost about a score of men in the fighting. Even lacking mast and sail, and with less than her full tale of rowers, *Ormungandr* might have left the other ships far behind, but Gudrun dawdled so that they could keep pace, eager though she was to fly her fastest.

Mile upon mile of Frankish Gaul's green coasts they passed, forest and field and the wide mouth of the Seine, which had been Pascent's destination until he saw the White Horse ride out on the waves. Although the former captain kept his mouth shut, he blamed Felimid for bringing that about. Nor did he love Gudrun Blackhair any better. Had Pascent met her ships first, it would have been her men who slaughtered his crew. He owed her nothing as he saw it.

The boy Rowan, young and resilient, was content. He'd
lived through his first hot sea fight. There was adventure to be
looked for, and a captain with a famous name.

They met Frankish warships in the bay of the Seine. These
gave chase. Gudrun hooted with laughter to see them pursue.

"Paddling geese to catch a sea eagle! Look upon them, will
you? Come, let's have sport!"

She called orders to her steersman. *Ormungandr* went in
among the Frankish triremes, sliding and turning like the
Midgard Serpent for which she was named. The old warships,
inherited from Roman flotillas and a sad prey to neglect, had a
hopeless task to trap *Ormungandr*. The three fast little Pictish
ships darted among the lumbering triremes, for they were
meant for scouting and sudden raids, and were almost as agile
as the larger vessel.

Gudrun had a delightful time. At last she ordered the game
ended, and left the Frankish warships slogging through the
waves. Her laughter rang above her men's jeering farewells.

III
The Ramparted Island

On the western side of the bay which received the Seine, a large peninsula pointed at Britain. Rounding the tip of that peninsula, Gudrun's ships headed south to approach the island called Sarnia. There she had her lair.

They came to it late in the afternoon, when the island's shadow reached a long way. Chiefly precipice, its coast reared hundreds of feet high in natural ramparts besieged by the patient sea. An isthmus barely two paces wide joined the larger, northern part of Sarnia to the southern, and cliffs dropped alarmingly on either side of that strait crossing. At the bottom, waves crashed hollow.

"Lir and Manannan mac Lir!" Felimid said. "I've an idea now why none has forced your door. How did your captain ever take it herself? Surely she did not find it deserted, a base so useful?"

"No," a rower with a Cornish accent told him. "A band of wreckers had the isle when Blackhair took it. See yon southern bit? Except by the isthmus, there's no way to reach it but a goat's track twisting up from a tiny cove, and a thousand men could not force the isthmus. Ye can feel the rock quivering, feel it in the soles o' yer feet as ye walk across. Some day the

35

waves 'ull pound it down. When the storms blow, well, we don't trouble to guard it then. Ye'd be whirled off like a leaf.''

"How did she take Sarnia, then?"

"With a shipload o' men from the Frisian lagoons. She lured the wreckers out to their work with a coaster she had taken for bait, and ambushed the maggoty turds. Slew them all. Then she took their boats back to the cove and went up the cliff path at dusk. Her plan, and she led the way. The other wreckers scarce had time to know it wasn't their friends returning, I'm told. I was not with Blackhair then. Ah, would that I had been! I'd delight in killing wreckers.''

With a savage grin, he bent to his oar. Although Felimid had never given the matter thought, he was not amazed to learn that a pirate despised wreckers. Being amazed required effort. Gasping at a lack of consistent moral standards could become a lifetime's hard work.

"She's always first when it's dangerous," the rower added. "We don't take her orders a'cause she's clever only."

Or by reason of the glorious black hair she has, I take it, Felimid said; but to himself. He was learning to know how it was with these wild men of Gudrun Blackhair's. They did not care for aught that approached flippancy on the matter of their being led by a woman. They demanded a respect for her of a kind not always given to kings, because their own self-respect was involved in it, and treated her very nearly as a goddess.

She could not have begun with that kind of worship, though. Felimid wondered how she had begun, and where.

The pirates drew *Ormungandr* ashore on the northern part of the island, her long keel turning the sand like a coulter. Cliffs receded above, terrace by grassy terrace, broken by fissures. Gudrun led the way up, tall in her red mantle, made taller by her helm. The men scrambled after, southern Franks and Goths a majority, Germans from the North Sea coast next in numbers. There was a random sprinkling of men from other nations. The two steersmen, for instance, were brothers from Cornwall. In almost three days, Felimid had not heard one Jutish accent, and he would have recognized one afurlong away.

He wondered why. Jutes were among Gudrun's worst enemies, yet that meant little. All tribes had their renegades;

some would have served her. The lack suggested that *she*
would not have *them*. So much the better. The bard's heart
held no yearning to see any.

Hundreds of feet above the sea, they crossed a green plateau
to the narrow isthmus. Felimid's gossip had not misled him.
The waves crashing so far below did send vibration through
the rock, to quiver in the soles of his feet. He did not mind the
sensation. It excited him, rather. The common giddy terror of
heights was not among his weaknesses.

Gudrun's hall stood on the southern part of her island, easy
to defend, most difficult to take. Her more than ten score
followers and their slaves, attendants and fierce women filled
it from end to end that night, making a jubilant thunder.

The trophies scattered about were more varied than the people, and came from lands more distant. Gaul and Britain were
Gudrun's local pastures only. She had raked the shores of Erin
for gold which now glittered on her chief henchmen, and for
the pups since grown to huge dun and brindle dogs cracking
bones by her hearth. She had sailed further, into the Western
Sea where strange islands wavered between the worlds in a
haze of magic, one day solid footing, the next a mirage re-
ceding ever from view.

Behind her chair, skins of white bear and red ape kept company on the wall between racks of battle spears. There was
ivory from the gross, belligerent walrus. Elephant ivory and
mottled cowries had come in trade from Egypt to Spain,
ultimately to enrich Gudrun. She herself had sailed a long way
south of Spain down unknown coasts to slay the perhaps
unique red ape, and loot the strange volcanic gems shining
hotly on her sword belt. The bard saw matter for songs
wherever his fascinated gaze roved.

Leaving her chair, Gudrun joined her men at one of the
tables. She wore a doe-leather tunic pricked with indigo patterns of woad, worn over a flame-colored shirt, and fawn
breeches cross-gartered with braided black silk. Doe-leather
buskins covered her feet.

The flagons went round. Shining streams curved into horns
rimmed and plated with precious metal. Gudrun received ex-
uberant, boastful pledges and returned them in kind, laughing. Her cup-bearer filled her beaker of purple Rhineland glass
time and again. He was adroit; none the less, once he let the

foam spill, wetting Gudrun's hand. She clapped him lightly on the shoulder and spoke a word. He inclined his head.

To the Goth beside him, Felimid said, "Am I right, now, in thinking the cup-bearer has lost the sight of his eyes?"

"He did not lose it," the Goth replied. "No. A Frankish count had it taken from him, in Blackhair's service. She avenged him by getting the count's whole head and his treasures too. She made Abalaric her cup-bearer later. He was clumsy at first, as you'd expect, but he worked at it until he became deft."

Across the hall, Gudrun lifted her beaker. Wax candles burned before her; shields, hilts and scabbards glittered on the wall behind her. The sea-gray eyes shone.

"All I've done yet is paltry to what I will do, having *Ormungandr!*" she shouted. "I may sail out of this world and harry the folk of Alfheim! Why not? The eyes of that serpent head can see the way! Who'd sail with me?"

They roared their answer so that massive tables vibrated and beam echoed at beam.

"Oisc Hengist's son did nothing with his ship but raid earthly coasts and impress men he had cowed as it was." Gudrun continued. "For that it was hardly worth building her; a common war boat made by men could answer for the purpose. I will use *Ormungandr* as she ought to be used! I am Gudrun Blackhair, and I dare to rove any sea in the nine worlds!"

The hunger for fame was a thing Felimid knew well. Singing it gave him his livelihood. He recognized it in others, though he had none himself. It burned in some men. In Gudrun it blazed.

"She suffered in the sea chase," Gudrun went on, after her men's response had ebbed. "She must be refitted, and that can't be done by men. The red dwarves who made *Ormungandr* alone have the skill. Mast, rigging, sail and oars—I'll want it all. Who's game to row north with me to ask their help?"

"Gudrun Blackhair needn't think of *asking!*" one man cried above a stormy chorus of offers. "Not while you command us. What you wish of a tribe of stunted carpenters, you have only to say—and let 'em dare refuse!"

Gudrun laughed, pleased by the bluster. "No, Hemming. I'd liefer do it in that way myself, but it cannot be. Dwarves are too stubborn for threats or torture, and they guard their homes too well, with enchantment and engines of war. The gods in their time have had to fee the avaricious little lice! Yes, and they bargain hard, as the stories tell.'' She pondered a moment, frowning. Then a new thought cheered her. ''By plundering our way north we ought to arrive with enough to content them. Again I say, who goes with me?''

Eating knives were bloodied over that. Not a man in the hall but wanted a seat on *Ormungandr*'s benches. They bragged, exchanged insults, cursed and fought. Their women urged them on, enjoying the sport.

Felimid stayed cool-headedly clear. Cradling his harp, he moved like an eddy of smoke from spot to spot as the brawl threatened to involve him. He'd taken part in enough to decide that they offered little variety, and far too likely a chance of being maimed or killed by mere ill luck—as did all mass combat. Therefore he watched, with detached perspective.

Two main factions seemed to be at the heart of the uproar, glad of the least excuse to seek each other's entrails. Blackhair and her chief henchmen had to crack heads together to restore something like peace. They did so swiftly and brutally, before men began seizing weapons from the walls and someone died. The brawlers were manhandled, beaten, cursed and flung apart, until they stood glaring at each other in two bruised, panting groups. Gudrun strode between them, impartially angry with both.

''I might have known better than to ask,'' she declared in the quiet she had just enforced, partly with her own bare hands. ''Now I'll tell you myself how it is to be. Hugibert, Ataulf, stand forward.''

A man emerged from the fore of each group. The dislike between them all but clotted the air. The blocky, coarse-haired one nearer the bard had a bleeding cheek. His sleeve had been ripped from the left shoulder. The other, tow-headed and glaring from pale blue eyes, wore a short sleeveless jacket of wolf's fur over a striped tunic. Tattoos adorned his bare limbs.

''Cast the dice, once,'' Gudrun ordered. ''High thrower comes on this voyage with me, bringing all his fellows. I'll try the dice first to be sure they are true, and see the throw made.

If one of you will not accept the result, then he must fight me.
Is that just?''

They agreed that it was, the blocky man whose hair bristled
so stiffly with a nod and an ''Aye, lady,'' the other with an expansive gesture.

''You will lose, Ataulf,'' he said, drawing the back of his
hand across a moustache now dyed crimson by a nosebleed.

''I'll surely lose if you use your own dice,'' the man with the
torn sleeve answered, ''but I'm not such a fool as to permit
that.''

They matched stares over the rattling cubes as if they would
rather have matched sword-strokes. The tow-haired man with
the reddened moustache, Hugibert, threw double fives.

''There, by Merovech's tomb!'' he yelled. ''Ten! Better that
if you can!''

Ataulf scowled. Rattling the dice in his heavy fist, he
delayed his throw for long moments, far from eager to see his
probable defeat.

''Come, let's see them dance!'' Hugibert urged. ''The summer is only so long, you know! At this rate we'll be waiting for
you to cast when the leaves fall!''

With a grunt, his rival opened his hand. The bone cubes
somersaulted. A five and a six looked up at the crowding spectators.

The blocky man bellowed joy through his mouse-colored
beard. Hugibert swore with raw inventiveness. His faction
showed anger and disappointment, too, though left it un-
voiced save for a few low grumbles. They drew sullenly
together on one side of the hall and settled to purposeful
drinking.

Felimid spoke to a swarthy man beside him. ''Now that was
the least thing strenuous; nigh as fierce as a hurley game in
Erin, and fewer broken bones in it only because it was not
allowed to last, I'd say. They were not so thirsty for each
other's blood just to gain a place on the oar benches, were
they?''

''No.'' The man turned his head as he replied. He had only
one eye. A polished agate winked in the bereft socket, brown,
with conspicuous crimson bands running through it in zigzags;
a striking gem. It turned his gaze into a disconcerting thing,
and it was brother to the stones which smoldered on Gudrun

Blackhair's sword belt. His living eye was an unremarkable dark brown.

"No," he repeated. "Those men are Franks and Goths. They love each other as the basilisk and weasel, I'll tell you. It's five years now since the Franks gave the Goths defeat in a great battle, took their lands in Gaul away from them, and drove them back across the mountains into Spain. Some of the men here fought in that war. I did myself, in Ataulf's company; he's the fellow you saw win over Hugibert at dice. We were comrades long ere we joined the lady's band." His agate eye flashed. "I'm Decius, once of Mola."

"Fel—" the bard began, and remembered his new alias. "Bragi, of nowhere in particular. I wander, and live by the harp. So, Ataulf and his Goths will be rowing north in *Ormungandr*, then?"

"You heard the lady say it. I'll be with them, belike, and I'm not pleased by that business of 'oars only.' It's only a northern superstition, forcing us to labor when we need not."

He raised his voice. "Will manmade tackle serve for this one voyage, lady? We have stores of the best rope and sail-cloth. It's a long way to go. When the wind is there, we do best to use it."

Men native to more northerly regions jeered at him.

"Work of men to rig a dwarvish ship?"

"The mast 'ud snap and the sail split before we cleared harbor!"

"As well saddle and bridle a bear, Decius!"

"A Roman's advice for you!"

"They do not lie, Decius," Gudrun told him. "*Quiet*, you starlings! What the dwarves make, none but the dwarves can equal, and nowhere south of the Baltic are any of the red breed left—that I know of. But *Ormungandr* is swift, easy rowing. We leave the dawn after tomorrow's!"

"I'd go with you, lady," Felimid said. He made his voice reach Gudrun with professional skill. To achieve even the lowest bardic rank, one had to master the art of projecting tone.

The sea-gray gaze turned toward him, direct and considering. "You would, Bragi? Why?"

"It's an adventure to my taste. These northern lands I have

never seen, but I'm told they never knew Rome's legions and
are free of the Cross worshippers now. That commends 'em to
me no matter how perilous they are. Besides, lady, I never met
a dwarf save one crippled thrall in King Cerdic's dun, and the
fancy's on me to see what they may be like in their own country.''

"Ah, Glinthi! You know him? He made my battle gear for
me. He's one of the dark dwarves, though, and these I go to
bargain with are the red kindred, who work in wood, leather
and cloth. As to what they are like, I can tell you in a word.''
Gudrun spoke cheerfully. "Bad.''

"You'd dissuade me, lady? But how am I to sing the tale of
your voyage if I do not ride your ship?''

Gudrun's eyes glimmered with amusement. "You wish to
come, ha? Tell me, Bragi, are you used to seafaring?''

"A little, lady. Mighty little, I concede. But the sea between
Erin and Britain is wild, and the Hebrides worse. I've known
them both. I travelled up the great estuary of Sabra, three
years past. Since then I never did fare on the sea until I left
London in Pascent's ship.''

"Then if you're little of a sailor, let me hear you sing, to
help me decide.'' She drank from her purple cup. Her white
throat moved. "Men must know me wherever land joins with
sea. Fame to run through the world like rivers—what else is
worth having? Sing of it, Bragi! Sing for me.''

Felimid kicked a stool forward. He'd been seeking inspira-
tion in cups, and was lightly drunk. Setting the harp Golden
Singer on his right knee, he steadied her with that arm. The
dark frame shone like silk, generations old. The golden strings
were threads of light. His left hand moved. The fine sinewy
fingers whose strength was so easy to underestimate roved
over the gold and the dark oak.

> "Tell of Gudrun the reiver, breaker of bright gold
>   rings,
> First for valor and beauty, wide in her wanderings!
> Gudrun, the raven-gorger, wearer of ravens' wings!"

The feeder of ravens and wearer of raven's wings learned
many things about herself in the next hour that she had not
known before. It appeared that she was a foundling, left by

the sea on a Frisian sandbar in a cockle boat, with a cloak of feathers wrapped around her. While a young girl, she had fought a monster beside a frozen mere, and bound together in a deadly grapple they had crashed through the ice, to finish their battle in the numbing, crusted water.

"All the fen-prowler's might was not enough to drag her down to death against her will. The strength of her arms prevailed, and the strength of her spirit which was greater. She left the evil being's slain carcass to settle in the muck."

Felimid sang more, far more, taking a foundation of things heard, seen and inferred, and building upon it freely. His account of how Gudrun Blackhair won the island of Sarnia from the wreckers who held it before her was wonderful. She had taken the narrow cliff path step by step against the resistance of an army, to hear him relate it.

The slaying of King Oisc and the capture of *Ormungandr* keystoned the tall arch of Felimid's account. It culminated in a rolling, victorious war shout from his harp's golden strings. His sweat-darkened brown head bent over the instrument, and save for echoes there was silence.

It lasted only a heartbeat. Applause echoed to the hall's end and reverberated back again. Gudrun had her own cup-bearer pour for the bard.

"Odin's ravens," she said. "You are well named, Bragi. There's a place for you in *Ormungandr* whether you can stroke an oar or not! I'd not set forth without you now. I take oath to that upon this sword of mine."

She laid the weapon naked on the table before her as she spoke, and placed her hands upon it. The polished steel had a grayer, more icy glitter than Kincaid's metal, and the blade was somewhat broader. Because it had been forged from several iron rods and strips twisted together, the final polishing had brought out a wavy pattern in the steel, distinctive as the markings down the back of a deadly serpent basking in the sun.

"Kissing Viper is its name," Gudrun said proudly. "King Cerdic's thrall Glinthi made it for me. My war shirt and helm, too."

"So?" Felimid lifted an eyebrow and obligingly prompted her to say more. "King Cerdic must hold you dear, lady, to be making you such friendship gifts."

Gudrun laughed in pleasure. "I'm not so dear to him as that. My war gear was a ransom, not a friendship gift. I carried off his son's wife in a raid, and this was my price for returning her. Who brought my head to the father or the son would be well rewarded. None the less, I mean to keep it where it is."

"And that too is a story that would make a fine song. You must tell me the full tale."

King Cerdic, his son Cynric, the British princess Vivayn and the sullen dwarf thrall Glinthi were all folk Felimid had met. He did not speak of the circumstances, however. The less he spoke of anything he'd done in Britain, the better. He was Bragi now, not Felimid mac Fal.

In certain other ways, too, he had been less than wholly frank with Gudrun Blackhair. His enthusiasm to fare into the wild north with her had been feigned. He'd left London with the purpose of crossing the Narrow Sea, and once he reached Lesser Britain, finding a ship to take him home to Erin. Instead, he found himself on the ramparted isle of a pirate's lair, and he saw clearly that he'd little hope of leaving unless Gudrun permitted it. Did he try to escape alone in a boat, he would probably drown. He was no sailor. Better to begin this reckless voyage with her, slip away from her shore camp at first chance, pick a direction, and walk.

Yet Gudrun had saved his life from Oisc. She had not intended it; the thing had simply come about while she followed her piratical trade. Even so, Felimid was alive because of her.

For that matter, she was asking little in return. She wanted him to do what he had always done in the way of *his* profession, no more. And what he loved.

It wouldn't be long, of course, until he had to fight someone, if he stayed. And the man who fared with pirates was not unlikely to hang with them. Gudrun had said it herself: "Born to trouble, as the sparks fly upward." It must follow her like the wake of her ship.

Finding the decision hard, he deferred it. There was no need to make up his mind at once. Least of all when the task came between him and sleep.

I'll wait and see. It's settled, whatever, that I begin this voyage, and meanwhile I'm guested in comfort. There's little in that to complain of.

IV
Foreshadowings

The great serpent ship had space for twenty men beside Ataulf's Goths. Each Sarnian pirate wanted to be one of them. Rowan, the Saxon youth from *Briny Kettle*, was single-mindedly eager.

"With your dam's milk still wet on your chin?" men with longer rights of precedence said. "Haw haw haw! This is a journey for proven fighting men! Learn to know one end of a sword from the other first!"

Rowan's skin flushed beneath golden fuzz. Abashed and angry together, he cried, "I'll fight any man here for his place in the ship!"

Two accepted his offer. Felimid looked at the pair of seasoned raiders and then at Rowan. Concern flickered in his restless, leaf-green eyes. Resting a hand on Rowan's shoulder, he said: "There'll be better days and stronger causes for dying, and any number of men ready to be slaying you. Needless to make the offer, just for the privilege of blisters, on your hands and elsewhere."

One of the challengers grinned. "Listen to that voice, infant. It could save your life."

"I await no danger to my life from you," Rowan answered. "You're too heavy and slow."

He made a step forward, shrugging the bard's hand away. Felimid let it fall, his concern becoming resignation. In his view any man should be free to choose his own way of dying,

46

but despite all the hero tales (and Felimid knew most of them) he had yet to learn of a better way than dying asleep after half a hundred contented years.

Gudrun Blackhair laughed with pleasure to know that men were fighting to come on the voyage; Rowan's two combats were not the only ones arranged. More practical spirits gambled or wrestled for places.

Rowan met his first adversary with spears, and gave him defeat. The second man proved the better. Driven to the limits of the marked fighting area, Rowan resisted taking the last backward step that meant losing, and twice drew blood from his seasoned opponent. Both wounds were light. However, they bled sufficiently to look worse than they were. Rowan's lack of experience led him to believe he had already won. He cut too impulsively; his blow met the other man's shield, and Rowan himself went down with his thigh sorely gashed.

Felimid was one of those who helped stop the bleeding. Gudrun was the other, for she had been watching the combat and admired Rowan's spirit. She frowned as she looked upon the wound.

"That's more than a scratch, handsome buck," she warned him. "I know wounds, and those I handle heal cleanly more often than not, but this one has ploughed you sorely. If cautery's not done, you may lose your leg and life to a mortification. . . . Can you bear it?"

Sweating, Rowan nodded.

Gudrun Blackhair did not hesitate. She had the irons heated at once, and swiftly though it was done, she vehemently cursed the delay. While Rowan waited, she poured him drink and held the cup to his mouth. When it was time, she slipped a band of thick harness-leather between his teeth, gave him her hands to grip, and nodded to the man with the red irons.

Rowan's teeth almost met through the leather. His convulsive grasp would have smashed weaker bones than Gudrun's. Beneath her wind burn, she whitened. When his grip slackened, she held him, wiped the sweat from his face, and stroked his hair. By those acts, she showed a tenderness the bard would not have looked for in her.

"I'll remember you," she said. "You are commendably skilled for such a young man."

And handsome, as you said, Felimid thought, smiling.

Pascent, *Briny Kettle*'s third survivor, was not interested in

Gudrun's plan. Not even in passing had he considered rowing
on her voyage. She was leaving the well-frequented southern
seas on a fool's venture, so far as he was concerned. Nor did
he care, save to hope she would not come back.

Unlike the bard, he did not feel grateful to her for saving
him from Oisc Hengist's son. Both were pirates; it might as
easily have been Blackhair who attacked him first, Oisc who
intervened and then spared him on impulse. Pascent's one
concern was his lack of a merchant ship. He meant to have a
new one somehow, and it struck him that the most fitting way
to get one was at Gudrun's expense.

She was foolish to take all the Gothic faction with her, leaving the disgruntled Franks. Far better to have taken half of
each contingent, while a like mixture remained on Sarnia, so
that they might watch each other closely. Thus Pascent as-
sessed it.

He would have the summer to work in. Perhaps the Franks
could be swayed against their silver-helmed captain. Their
tribe was noted for treachery—and now ruled Gaul. Pascent
tugged his earring thoughtfully. Yes. There were possibilities
here for a shrewd man.

V

The Swan's Path

Two days later, *Ormungandr* sped from the shadow of Sarnia's cliffs to begin her northern voyage.

Headstrong though she was, Gudrun would not have attempted such a journey in any other ship deprived of sail. It scarcely seemed a lack in this one. Although but thirty of the ship's half-hundred oars were in use, she ran smoothly through the water with what seemed a living awareness of the tide races and currents. Though he was no sailor, Felimid sensed it, as he had before.

Some who were sailors shared his intuition, but had less ease of mind where magic was concerned. They disliked the way *Ormungandr* flexed and breathed, with barely a creak of timber, when any natural ship made a constant racket. Ataulf ended the murmuring by making those responsible work twice as long as the others.

Sarnia fell far astern. They rounded a cape below which deadly rocks waited. Here and there a rambling timber mansion had been built high above a bay or cove.

"Wrecker lords," Decius said with contempt. The jagged red bands in his agate eye flashed unpleasantly. "A nest of them did their work from Sarnia, once. That was before the lady came. Now they lie at the bottom of the sea where they belong."

"I was hearing so," Felimid answered. "Were you with her then?"

"Not I. Ataulf and I were on the losing side five years ago,

when Clovis slew the Gothic king. Instead of returning to
Spain we turned robber, then took to the sea with Gudrun
when the chance offered. We'd have ended on crosses had we
kept to the land.''

The cape once rounded, Gudrun ordered every oar manned,
and their wonderful speed grew greater. They passed Seine-
mouth. Passing farm and forest as well, they brought terror to
the people but did not stop to plunder the shore. Nothing was
there to interest the red dwarves of the north, nor that Gudrun
Blackhair held worth her time.

Impatience and tension warred in her when she thought of
returning to northern waters. Once she had called them home,
the Limfjord especially. Memories clustered about it, some
giving her delight, others scorching her.

She looked down at the water peeling back from *Ormungandr*'s prow. Their swiftness was what some fearful ones in
her crew had called it, uncanny. A seething wave should have
lifted high as the wales. All that disturbed the sea was a glassy
twist and curl, threaded with pallor.

They went ashore that night to the fishing village at Somme-
mouth which Felimid had seen before. The long ship *Ormungandr* had covered in one day a distance of three days' sailing
for *pictae*, vessels built to be fast.

"King Oisc's body was taken to Thanet as ye commanded,
lady,'' the chief man of the village said. "The men who con-
veyed it ought to return ere long.''

"I'll not wait for them,'' Gudrun said. "At first light we
row on.''

She sat by a fire in the open, eating the same rough fare as
her men. Her mail shirt lay beside her. The silvered casque,
with a new set of raven's wings adorning it, hung on the
crosspiece of a leaning spear behind her. Someone's shield was
serving as a platter on which she cut hunks of barley bread and
cheese. Nearby a sheep roasted.

The bard thought of his home. In his mind he saw grain
lustrous as pearls, smelled applewood burning, spoke his own
language and went by his own name. He had a half-sister, a
whole family he had not seen in years. What was he doing
here? Gudrun might bury him to the waist in riches; if he
could tread Erin's earth again, some other bard was welcome
to her bounty.

The harp in his hands sighed his ache.

"Oh' fhàg mi ann am beul à bhrugh
M'eudail fhein an donngheal dhubh,
A sùil mar reul . . . "

"What is that?" Gudrun asked when he had finished. "Can you put it in a tongue I know?"

"I reckon so," Felimid said. "Umm . . . "

In a little while he repeated the song, rendered in Jutish.

"I left in the doorway of the bower
My jewel, brown-haired, white-skinned,
Her eye like a star, her lip like a berry,
Her voice like a stringed instrument.

"I left yesterday in the meadow of the kine
The brown-haired maid of sweetest kiss,
Her eye like a star, her cheek like a rose;
Her kiss has the taste of pears."

"Pretty," Gudrun said. "Is there some particular one you long for, or is she an invention, the one with all these glories about her? She sounds it."

Felimid recognized the hum of the wasp in Gudrun's tone. It amused him. He smiled at her.

"Not invented. There are several I call to mind who answer the description. But no—there is no particular one I am pining for. If anything, it's the land I miss."

"Aye. Home is an easy place to leave, and a hard one to find your way back to," Gudrun said, astonishing the bard a little. "I was born on Mors Island, in the Limfjord."

These were only names to Felimid. "Is it a fair place?"

"Heath, mostly, but with few shaws. My mother's dead these many years, and my father may be for all I know. She was a daughter of Starkad Eightarms, while my father descends from Orwendel on both sides. I'm of good lineage."

"My sorrow, lady. I can tell that more from your bearing than the names you give. I know nothing of Eightarms; of Orwendel I've heard but vaguely. And what I did hear, I reckon contradictory as to whether he was god, giant or hero."

Gudrun laughed aloud. "I too! But there's nothing I can tell you to resolve it. He's too long dead. You know, Bragi, you

have too strong a Jutish accent for me to keep in mind that
you disown Jutish blood. Remind me sometimes. It were best.
Fire and water cannot love each other less than Dane and
Jute.''

Fire leaped against invisible tethers, and subsided. Somewhere a fisher-girl laughed in a rover's arms. There was heat
on Felimid's thighs and side, a comparative chill at his back.
Beyond the fire light lay any amount of friendly darkness.
Gudrun would not dally when morning found him gone, or
mount an urgent search.

Yet morning found him on the sea again, between
Ormungandr's ribs.

The second day and night of the voyage were marked by no
memorable events. On the third day they rowed along a low
coast of brackish lagoons and marshes. The encroaching sea
had destroyed the barley fields. *Terpens*, manmade islands of
earth, brush and stone, extended the living space.

"That's Frisia," Ataulf said, pointing. "Hengist lived there
for a few years, after the burning of Finnsburg; d'you know
the story?" Felimid did. "He learned from the Frisians to
build galleys instead of rowboats, and that was the beginning
of Britain's woe.''

"Ah, no," Felimid argued. "Long before Hengist the
Romans came, and the men of Erin brought sorrow to Britain
also. But Hengist, aye, he was a successful man. Some large
fine bits of British coast are held by the Jutes now.''

Ataulf did not like being corrected. His color darkened. He
opened his mouth and might have said much, had not his captain spoken first.

"Jutish!" she said in mockery. "Hengist had, who knows,
a boatload or two of Jutish fighters when he started. Frisians,
Saxons and outlaw Franks were the rest of the force he took
into Britain. Freya knows they took the British girls where
they found them. Many Jutes came in his wake later, it is
true—and many men of other tribes with them. The leadership
was Jutish, and in their British kingdoms they all claim to be
Jutes of the true Jutish descent these days, but if it be true,
Hengist must have put out from these shores with the greatest
fleet ever to plough the sea.''

"You forget the Angles.''

"Who would think of Angles unless forced to?''

Ormungandr threaded her way slowly now, among sand-
bars and miles of salt reed. There was a tart, curious odor in

the air, as if the water had turned rancid. Gudrun Blackhair's nose twitched in disdain.

"Let's go back to open water swiftly as we can," she ordered. "Riding any storm Ran ever brewed would please me better than dawdling here."

Felimid did not like it either. A bard's eyes pierce magical illusion, and see beings invisible to most folk. Malignant spirits were taking form in the air, flocking to the ship.

He knew their like. They clustered thickly upon battlefields, battened upon blood and pain, astonishment and terror, the desperate rage of men striving to kill. They were to the ghostly sphere what crows were to the earth: scavengers. Often they appeared in the shape of crows. In Erin their unlovely host was known as the *badb*. If they appeared, it was because they expected to feast. Felimid loosened Kincaid in his sheath and opened his mouth to speak a warning.

Ormungandr lurched and shuddered as though scraping bottom. The oars were fouled. Ataulf and Felimid staggered; rowers fell from the benches. Gudrun clutched the serpent prow to save her balance, voicing an oath to the Father of Victories. Men shouted in consternation, for finned mottled shapes clung to half the oars. Others rose out of the sea, wriggling over the gunwales.

"*Nicors!*"

The sword Kincaid flickered briefly, with a dazzle like a diamond's. Then it was dulled by a nicor's thin blood. No other weapon on the ship flashed bare even an instant before Gudrun's blade, Kissing Viper. There was employment enough for both, and for all the lesser weapons aboard.

The monsters of lagoon and salt fen tore with their webbed, clawed hands. Spiny tails lashed sideways. The barbs carried filth.

Gudrun raised the war cry of a shrieking eagle. She hewed laminae of dense white muscle, clove the gristle nicors had where bone belonged. A tail whacked her calf like a heavy whip, but the fur and leather wrappings she wore below the knee kept the barbs from her flesh. She cleared the prow and sought more work.

The attack was worst amidships, where *Ormungandr*'s sides were low. The bard was working his way into the thick of it himself. His first stroke severed one ugly paw and slashed the neck behind it. The nicor dropped back into the sea. Another lunged at Felimid, gill slits opening and closing below its mouth. He cut into its head, then spitted its body. It fell but continued to move. Felimid had to chop off the lashing tail before it did him mischief.

He fought coolly, from the brain, as usual, letting distaste wait until he was ready to experience it. To Felimid's mind any mass battle was bad enough. He preferred single combat if he had to fight. *This* was like battling a pack of mad wolves in a butcher's yard at slaughtering time.

The nicors were absolutely mute. Somehow that made it worse. Mottled, sharklike skins rasped on leather and flesh. Spears rammed into mouths and sides, axes bit hungrily, and fanged jaws rilled hot human blood.

Gudrun cut a path through the monsters, yelling. She shattered a fanged face with her shield-boss, then opened a pale belly behind clutching taloned paws. She glimpsed Ataulf chopping with a short-hafted heavy axe, and Felimid slicing and thrusting to deadly effect. These clear sights flashed briefly from the background of desperate fury; then a nicor grappled the captain, trying to rend her mail. Glinthi's workmanship held. Gudrun knocked the monster sideways with her shield-rim, then beheaded it with a skilled drawing slash.

A Goth had his feet knocked from under him by a hurtling tail. Looming above him, the nicor gripped his face in its claws and quite simply stripped it from the front of his head. Another man was seized from behind, his neck sheared through by hungry teeth. The nicor's spine was instantly chopped in two by a shipmate of its victim. They slew, and they died.

"*Lir and Manannan mac Lir!*" spat Felimid, calling upon his people's sea gods. He killed a nicor which was neglecting the fight to sample a fallen cousin's meat—if nicors had cousins—and dodged a careless stroke from the man nearest him. The move brought him too close to the ship's side. A pair of dripping arms rose to clutch his waist. Turning his head and shoulders, he folded both hands on Kincaid's hilt and drove the point deeply down a voracious throat. The nicor's maw snapped instinctively on the impaling blade; flesh and gristle split around Kincaid's edges. The grip on Felimid's waist slackened, and the creature sank.

Now they were retreating, taking with them all the food they could drag or carry. To hasten their departure, the bard killed as many as possible. Some men raved at the vanishing monsters to come back so that they could destroy more.

Gudrun snapped incisive commands. Where needful she backed them with peremptory handling, till her crew was back at the oar benches. A tally showed six men missing, dragged living or dead into the sea, and ten wounded. Gudrun spoke an obscenity. Then she rapped out:

"Bend to the oars, if you love life! Look there!"

Three Frisian warships, smaller than *Ormungandr* but fully manned and unmauled, moved out from one of the *terpens* of that waterlogged coast. Taking his harp, the bard struck fierce cadenced harmonies that put strength back into aching arms and set the oars moving in quick rhythm. Gudrun watched the ships and the man-built island recede.

"When *Ormungandr* is well fitted, we'll come back and teach them manners," she said.

That, Felimid thought, after what had just happened, showed too much of an appetite for trouble. He slid the harp into her case. Controlling his breath, the skin above the arteries of his throat jumping, he intoned caustically:

"There is sea and land between you. . . . There is a great dark ocean between you, and deadly and hostile is the way there; for that wood is traversed as though there were spear points of battle under one's feet, like leaves of the forest under the feet of men. There is a luckless gulf of the sea full of dumb-mouthed beasts on this side of that immense wood. And an enormous oak forest, dense and thorny before that mountain, and a narrow path through it, and a dark house in the mysterious wood at the head of the same path, with seven hags and a bath of lead awaiting you, for your coming there has been fated."

The burlesque was wasted. Gudrun stabbed a look at him. "Are you a seer?" she demanded. "Do you prophesy?"

"On the day the gods amend me," Felimid said, and did not enlarge on that, nor laugh either. "No. I am not foretelling. It is from a hero tale I may be telling you one day, and it fits the time and place, that is all. . . . "

They rowed the rest of that day, standing well out from the Frisian coast. As night lowered, they came to a drier shore backed by dense forest. There they dragged *Ormungandr* up the beach. In spite of the best care they could give, two wounded men died that night. The others were not badly hurt and in Gudrun's judgment should recover soon.

VI
Bow, Sling and Sword

The morning was fresh when Gudrun rose from her pallet of sheepskins. Pitting muscle against muscle on their anchorage of strong bones, she worked sleep's kinks out of her body with thoroughness and relish. Then she gave attention to the fact that she was hungry.

The previous day's horror scarcely occurred to her. It was over, she had won, and the present was good. Although the air was chill, so soon after dawn. . . . She drew a lambskin vest over her kirtle before leaving the ship.

Her fast broken, she had her bows and arrows fetched ashore. The Danish one was a five-foot yew stave with a merely heavy draw. The other, a steel Byzantine siege bow, had travelled from the place of its forging to Gudrun's hands by none knew what improbable route or series of fates. Yet she prized it.

She exercised with the latter first, drawing it slowly to her ear twenty times with each hand. Then she did some actual shooting with the yew bow. For target she chose a tree eighty paces off, and sank four arrows deep in its trunk, crowding each other. The bard applauded; she felt pleased and amused.

"Your folk do not use the bow much, do they?"

"No," he admitted. "Save as a fowling weapon, mind. We have nothing like that manslayer. Maybe you can teach me."

Gudrun hooted laughter. Felimid's brows, a darker brown than his hair, drew together a little. He asked over-courteously, "Will you be telling me what's to laugh at?"

"I . . . teach you," she gasped. "Oh, Bragi! This is how my father taught *me*. When I was five he gave me a stave, a stave only, cut to my size. I held it at arm's length each day till my arm wavered and sank. When it did, he would strike me. I learned to hold out until he was pleased. Then he gave me a thicker stave.

"In time he gave me a complete bow with a cord. I practiced drawing, holding and loosing each day. I learned to care for my string, my arrows, to cut my own feathers and fletch my own shafts. I practiced shooting in calm, breeze and strong wind, at still marks, moving marks, on the flat and in the air; dropping arrows from above on sheltered targets; shooting from cover, shooting from a boat on rough water, even shooting while blindfolded at a target which rattled. I was thirteen when he said I would probably make an archer, sixteen when he allowed that I had become one.

"That's how a Danish bowman is made, Bragi. And you snap your fingers on a blue summer's morning and say, *teach me*."

"Hmm. It wasn't in my mind that you do it quite by midday. I handled a bow as a child, when the Hidden People were my playmates. I was tall as one of their men. A bow of theirs was right for me . . . then. Maybe I remember."

Gudrun handed him her weapon. "Try."

He felt an immediate, urgent desire not to fail. He drew smoothly in the recalled manner. His arm threatened to vibrate as the nock reached his ear, for Gudrun's bow was stiffer than most, but he mastered the shaking and loosed cleanly. The arrow sang past the slim tree a yard to one side.

"Well," Gudrun said, "you do know a bow is not your harp."

Nettled, the bard drew a device of thongs from his belt. "I had better training with sling and javelin. They are our distance weapons in Erin, look you."

In his wallet were a few lead ball missiles, the size of fat chestnuts. He loaded the sling. It whirled above his head, invisibly singing like bees' wings, and then was empty.

Eighty yards off, the tree shuddered as Felimid's ball smashed into the trunk, centered brutal and vehement among the suave arrows. One had been broken. Its bright fletching lay tattered in the grass.

Gudrun walked to the tree. Without speaking, she probed
with her knife for the missile sunk in the pulverized wood.
Thoughtfully she rolled it in her palm, feeling its weight. Then
she tossed it to the bard.

"Useful," she said. "The man who took one of those between his eyes would not get up."

A score of her crew had gathered to watch the shooting,
evidently with more on their minds. An air of uncomfortable
patience breathed from them, and Ataulf stood in the fore-
front.

"Lady," he said as Gudrun unstrung her bow, "how long
are we to tarry here? There's no welcome for us in these
parts."

Gudrun glanced at the men ranged behind him, then ap-
praisingly at Ataulf. "No welcome, but rich pickings, and we
have to take some plunder worth mentioning. What troubles
you?"

"Hanging troubles me," Ataulf answered. "We are in
Saxon territory, lady, and you know Edric the Fat."

"I know him. A fine merchant and a poor sort of chieftain.
He puffs on the high seat two proper men would scarcely fill,
nor lifts himself off it for war or adventure. *He* troubles you?
Ataulf, we are going to rob him blind; it's why we landed
here!"

Ataulf did not catch her enthusiasm.

"Looting Edricsburg is work for a war host. Past time it
was done, true. But with our numbers we'd be fools to try.
Better to seize a merchant ship or two."

"We cannot lurk hereabouts long, waiting for one,"
growled a second Goth. "Edric has the coast too sharply
watched."

"Right," Ataulf said. "A spy's needed, in Edricsburg itself,
who can listen to the traders talk and bring us the knowledge
later. *Ormungandr* can catch any ship afloat, if we know
where she's bound—and that her cargo makes her worth the
catching." He indicated Felimid with a brine-hardened
thumb. Contempt entered his voice, matching the casual
gesture. "He can make himself useful that way."

"Useful, is it?" Felimid said, eyes limpid. "I'm here as a
skald, to make songs. I'm no mariner, but all of you knew that
when we set out. I heard no complaint then. Why do you voice
one now?"

"Complaint?" Ataulf's glance held further scorn. "As a passenger, you've given us nothing to complain of. I doubt we can carry passengers this voyage, that's all. This is a pirate faring, and ripe with danger, and when there's pirate work to do, even singers share it. Nobody sits idle."

"Enough!" Gudrun snapped. "You're picking a quarrel. I want to know the plan you have, if there is one. Then I'll decide whether it is good or bad, and if good, who carries it out."

The burly Goth shrugged. "I've spoken the meat of it. We need a spy. Bragi here can go to Edricsburg for us. As a harper, he'll find a welcome, and all he need do then is employ his ears."

"I never heard of Edricsburg until now," Felimid said. "I take the place to be some great town or dun, but I'd know more."

Ataulf bleated like a sucking lamb.

Gudrun, at least, was prepared to be clear. "I'll tell you," she said. Straddling a large bit of driftwood, she shifted Kissing Viper forward so that she could wear him comfortably while she explained.

"It's this way. These mainland Saxons have no king, but various chieftains. Edric the Fat is the richest and strongest. His town stands at the mouth of a great river, the Elbe. It's a trading town, palisaded with strong gates and stronger men. Edric maintains four hundred picked warriors there, and he's rich enough to maintain them well."

"But too fat to lead them in war," Ataulf added. "His sister's husband Vithils does that. A wolverine of a fighter. He's smoked out pirate camps and strongholds as often as he's passed water. Fire, noose and sword, that's how he deals. I'd like to know where he is now. Find out that, too."

"I haven't agreed to find out anything. But suppose I were to go, now. What am I to say in the town? How did I reach it? Not aboard any ship now there. By walking along the coast? The coast is watched, you tell me. I might have swum ashore from a ship overwhelmed by pirates—but where and how should I join you when I'd finished my spying? I do not know these shores, and I'm no hand with a boat. You might wait a long time."

"We had better not."

Felimid glanced at the speaker. It was Ataulf, predictably.

"The plan is not a sound one," he said. "Also, it asks a less than honorable man to carry it out. Suppose I were willing to go to this Edric, become his guest, and work to his disadvantage—would I be less quick to betray you? I'm *your* guest, am I not?"

"You are over-simple," Gudrun said, "and yet there's something in what you say."

"Aye, supple-tongued evasiveness." Ataulf stood closer to the bard and above him, thumbs in his weapon belt. "You fear to go. *I've* no fear that you'd betray us, once in Edricsburg. I think you'd never dare disclose that you were sent by Gudrun Blackhair. I reckon that you are a coward."

He thrust his face aggressively close to the bard's, his jaw leading the way. "You will go, or I'll drag you through the sea at the end of a rope for an hour."

He was expecting a blow or challenge in return, yet even so the bard's hand moved too quickly for him. Catching the tip of Ataulf's nose with a finger and thumb, Felimid twisted it sharply. The gesture was impertinent, mocking and painful enough to bring water from Ataulf's eyes. Gudrun's men burst into laughter. She herself smiled broadly.

"Ahh, now," Ataulf breathed. "I'll cut out your liver for that, you half-Jutish bastard."

"*Hold*," Gudrun ordered, her smile still merry. "You will do this holmgang fashion, with sword, shield and helm and bounds marked out. The man who interferes or fouls either of you will die; is that agreed?"

The responses of "Aye" and "It's fair" were definite.

"How will you fight?" Gudrun asked. "To first blood, or to the death?"

"Death," Ataulf grunted.

"I'm for first blood, or till one of us is driven past the wands," Felimid said.

Ataulf laughed. "That is for weaklings, but I'll agree. First blood spilled is going to be your life's blood, anyhow."

"I'd be mortally cut even now, if talk was enough. Come, let's be inspecting some shields here. Are we fighting today or next year?"

Felimid preferred the small round targe which lent itself well to swift handling. As the pirates had none, he settled for a shield two feet across, rimmed and bossed with iron which smelled of the pig's fat rubbed on it to prevent rust. To ward his head he chose a four-cornered casque with a brim and upright comb.

By then the fighting area had been marked on the sand. Spears driven into the beach, points upward, emphasized the corners and halfway line of the oblong field.

Ataulf waited, a broad, ominous and now silent figure. His Gothic helm was more ornate than most; a heavy ridge above the eyes counterfeited brows, and riveted beneath that was a combined nose- and eye-guard giving the effect of a mask. A heavy spathe seemingly grew from his scarred right fist, thirty inches of killing metal.

Felimid stepped into the rectangle. Soft sand moved under his shoes, sucking away the light-footed celerity that was his greatest asset. Smiling, he drew Kincaid.

Ataulf advanced, his eyes watchful behind the hammered metal. His weapon probed the air, intended to distract. Felimid ignored them. He watched Ataulf's feet.

The pirates murmured with interest to see that the bard was left-handed. The fighters' sword and shield arms thus confronted each other instead of being diagonally opposed. Both men's blows were more likely to fall on the unshielded side.

Ataulf cut for the side of Felimid's knee. The bard parried swiftly and low with his sword, keeping the shield high. Then he rammed Ataulf with the boss. Ataulf fell back two paces, ground a heel into the sand, stood like a tree and hurled Felimid off.

Gudrun Blackhair smiled with delight. She had wondered how Felimid handled a sword. She knew he was one of three to survive the carnage on *Briny Kettle*, which argued competence, and she had received the impression that he'd done his share against the nicors—but neither time had she had real leisure to assess him. She had it now.

If Ataulf slew the bard, there would be no songs of the voyage. Still, it never entered Gudrun's mind to meddle. These were men, not house pets. Or if either did have the nature of a house pet, she wanted to know.

Ataulf feinted high, feinted again, and slashed at Felimid's leg. The bard brought his shield slanting down across his body, and though the stroke jolted him, it achieved no more than a notch in his shield-rim.

Ataulf's own shield sank a little.

Felimid sent a bright slender tongue of steel licking at his shoulder.

Now it was Ataulf's turn to use his shield very quickly. Because it lacked an iron rim, the sword cut partway into it and stuck there, at which Ataulf laughed harshly. He'd chosen a rimless shield in hopes of this thing happening. Arm braced in the grips, he turned the shield like a wheel to twist the sword from Felimid's hand. At the same time, he hewed at the younger man's side.

Felimid clung to Kincaid's hilt desperately. If he let it be taken from him, he must retreat beyond the markers or be cut down—and although he had wanted to avoid this fight, now that he was in it, he wanted as strongly to win. Slamming his shield leftward to meet Ataulf's stroke, he tried with a strong wrench to free Kincaid. The shield timber kept what it gripped.

Up whirled Ataulf's weapon, and down it sang. Felimid brought his own shield up and around, in the fashion of a trained fighter, to raise it protectively over his head and yet not block his own vision. This time he was too slow. Ataulf's edge crashed on his helmet.

Daze. A headful of burning thunder. The stroke took away half the helmet comb, screamed down to the brim and slid away across the tilted upper side of Felimid's shield, which he had raised far enough to protect his shoulder, at least. The bard's knees weakened; his sight dimmed.

Mastering his legs, he drove himself forward like a flung javelin, ramming Ataulf's shield with his own, smashing it back against the Goth's body. The point and twelve inches of Kincaid was rammed back with it. Jutting out behind Ataulf's shield, it pierced leather and flesh.

Felimid smashed his shield-rim down atop Ataulf's, simultaneously jerking his trapped sword upward. It came free in his hand. Relief and triumph rushed through him; he moved aside on recovered legs to carry on the combat.

"First blood!" Gudrun shouted, gray eyes glittering. "You bleed, Ataulf! You have lost!"

It was so, Felimid saw.

The burly Goth paid no heed. Leaping at Felimid, he hewed and slashed fiercely. The bard met him with a cool if still singing head. Having ample room, he retreated before the

Goth's onslaught and circled about. Ataulf's breath rasped.

"Stand your ground!" he snarled.

"Ah, be easy now," Felimid said. "You have lost. All you achieve is to make your blood flow the faster. It's squelching in your shoes you will be if you continue this—"

"*Fight*!"

"Have it your way."

Felimid retreated farther. Ataulf followed, panting and bleeding. Towards the other end of the fighting area, Felimid stood fast for a fierce exchange of blows. Neither man feinted now. Shield boomed on shield, sword belled on sword, sword crashed on shield. Their feet churned the sand as they strained together like battling stags.

Briefly, then, they sprang apart. Felimid seemed to flag. His shield arm fell to his side and that shoulder drooped. The watching pirates howled. Ataulf shouted as he renewed his attack. Then Felimid dropped almost flat, to send his shield skimming at the other's shins. When he seemed to falter, he had slid his arm out of the brace in preparation for the move.

Ataulf fell heavily. Instead of running him through, the bard regained his shield. As he settled it back on his arm, Ataulf rose to his hands and knees, gasping.

"I might have killed you then," Felimid said, his own breathing less than level. "Are you for agreeing the fight is over . . . or do you wish to look a greater fool . . . and bleed to death besides?"

"Aye," Ataulf croaked, lurching to his feet, one side of him crimson, all of him sand-spattered. "I give you best." Astonishingly, he grinned. "That was a good trick, but would you try it in a death fight?"

"It's yourself tried to make it a death fight. See to your hurts."

The curtness was not characteristic of Felimid, even in anger; he more often waxed talkative. But turmoil he could not explain filled him. He swept off his helmet to let soothing air flow about his head.

Ataulf's comrades rushed to take off his war gear and stop the bleeding. His wound was an odd one. Kincaid had been trapped in his shield at an angle, and the point had gone in under Ataulf's arm, sliding between the rib cage and the thick muscles of his back. It was bloody and painful, as Ataulf's swearing testified, but should not prove mortal.

Gudrun remained as she had stood to watch the fight, with the chape of her scabbard resting in the sand and her hands folded over Kissing Viper's pommel.

"Now that the play and amusement is over, hear me!" she said. "I agreed with Bragi from the beginning that Ataulf's plan was not good; but when the matter became a quarrel, I let them settle it. What? Kick our heels on some forsaken point of land, waiting for word that might never come? No! The plunder I want I am for taking here, without delay!"

Decius the Spaniard said, "We've half a hundred men able to fight."

"Enough for my purposes."

"Edric the Fat has eyes watching every yard of his coast," said someone else. "We cannot lurk here undiscovered for a trader to pass."

"True." Gudrun Blackhair laughed. "Not a gannet dives from Elbe to Weser but he hears of it, and whether or not it caught its fish. That is what I count on. Listen. . . . "

VII
Saxons

The Elbe flowed down through an immense forest to the gray sea. River trade reached from its mouth to the heart of Europe, and sea trade made it as wealthy as Thanet. Edric the Fat was the richest Saxon chieftain in Germany.

The burg which carried his name was as Gudrun had described it. Nearly two thousand lived there, every fourth soul a picked warrior, and at the great summer trading fair the numbers tripled. Beyond timber wharves, within strong palisades, lay storehouses, barrack houses, and Edric's feasting hall. Within that again stood the chieftain's seat. It too was as Gudrun had said, large enough for two ordinary men.

Movement pulsed about Edric. Envoys, traders, skippers, servants, warriors, tally-men and craftsmen came seeking his ear. He began his day early and ended it late. Gudrun had made him sound slothful; he was not.

All blinked when they first saw him. Massive was Edric, ponderous, immense. When he stood, his oxlike bones creaked. Shoulders wide as a door dropped to arms thick as other men's thighs; his belly curved far in front of him. Short legs like tree-butts supported his great mass.

A man came to him that morning, one Edric had ordered should never be kept waiting, a trusted leader of his coast watchers. Some were fighting men in fast, small vessels, some were fishermen paid to watch and report, some were landsmen burning charcoal in the forest or scanning the sea from concealed huts. The latter were provided with unobtrusive ways of signalling. Some played a double game and sold information to pirates; in most cases Edric knew who these were and allowed them to have only information he wished to be known.

Withal, he had not the flaw of being *too* suspicious. He trusted those who proved worthy. Some said that besides all this, he could understand the language of waves breaking on the shore, and perhaps he could. Certainly his shores were a place pirates rarely ventured.

That morning, Edric was heard to bellow, "*What?*" then he paid close attention to the sea-stained man by his chair. He sat still for a time, frowning from brow to chin, when the man had finished.

"Send Vithils to me," he said.

Vithils, called The Chief's Axe, duly arrived. Seven stone lighter than his brother-in-law and still a large, powerful man, conspicuously red-haired, thickly bearded, he advanced to Edric's seat. Edric had seen him walk towards a line of levelled spears with the same deliberate tread.

"*Ormungandr* is nearby," Edric said.

"King Oisc's ship?"

"King Oisc's ship that was."

Vithils nodded. His ice-blue eyes held a thoughtful look. The trading intercourse between Thanet and Edricsburg was lively; news travelled quickly from one place to the other. While Gudrun had rowed from the scene of her sea fight with Oisc, reached Sarnia, spent time there, and rowed up the Narrow Sea again, the news of Oisc's death had been spreading. Vithils and Edric knew who commanded *Ormungandr* now.

"Where?" asked The Chief's Axe. "Where do they lie?"

"In the creek mouth at the point of Cuxhaven. It's the one ship only, Vithils—so the watchers say."

"I believe them." Vithils smiled grimly. "No other could match *Ormungandr*'s pace, and Blackhair likes to travel swiftly. One ship . . . eighty men at most. I'll take a hundred."

Within the hour, Vithils had assembled a hundred thirsty spears and taken them aboard two of Edric's warships. The coast watchers who had brought the news went with him, as did skillful forest trackers and hunters.

Elbe waters divided before the two prows. They cleared the great river's mouth, then turned westward for the point of

Cuxhaven. The sun lowered ahead of them like a fiery copper ingot in a furnace's mouth. Wood creaked, water splashed. Sunset winked brassy on the spearheads. The salt sea tang mixed with scents of May growth from the vast forests that walked across the land. And the harsh, purposeful set of Vithils's face never altered.

At Cuxhaven, Felimid waited. He watched the sun go down at the rim of the sea. He listened to the creek spilling by. Once in a while he glanced at *Ormungandr*'s tall serpent head, a darker outline in the increasing dark.

Dissatisfaction sat on his shoulders. He tried to shrug it away, but could not. *Why am I here*? he asked himself.

To fight Ataulf had been stupid. He saw now what would have been best—to yield, to say he would spy. Gudrun would either have rejected the idea or agreed with it. If the former, he would have been free of an invidious task with no need of baring a sword. If the latter, why, then he might simply have gone to Edricsburg and forgotten the pirate crew, and sought a ship bound for Lesser Britain.

What in the detested name of Bricriu the trouble-stirrer had become of his wits, that he hadn't thought of that at the appropriate time?

Oh, he'd won some approval and respect among the pirates, and even from Gudrun herself. In their company, no doubt he'd have had to draw steel at some time, or grovel. Their acceptance had grown complete when he had asked—asked!—to be where he was now, as they waited for the men from Edricsburg. He and five others had the most dangerous part of all. He was acting as though he wanted their respect and acceptance enough to gamble his life, which was surely false.

Surely!

His thoughts shifted suddenly, like a veering wind. He wondered if he could have offered any improvements to Gudrun's scheme. With his powers . . . but they had not helped him aboard *Briny Kettle*. He might raise a wind, or cause the season in the creek mouth to change from warm spring to frosty autumn, veiling all in mist.

He decided that it would not be useful. Gudrun did not wish their presence hidden; she wished it to be discovered. Her plan depended on that, and the bard thought it a good plan, simple, bold and workable. He remembered the horse lord Kyle's words to him on the subject. "The sad thing about your plans is that they are always more ornate than they must be," Kyle had said.

Cein had died for that quirk of his. Her twisted husband had killed her, hoping to have Felimid accused of her death. Her fox-red hair had burned in his dreams too many times since.

Is that why I'm standing aside and letting things happen without me? A passenger, a do-nothing, Ataulf called me. He wasn't wholly unjust.

Felimid moved aft, away from the serpent head. He stumbled, cursed, and kicked what had tripped him. The pain of his toes distracted him for a while. Then he returned to that odd sense of not knowing what he was about, of having lost confidence and balance.

It's the waiting, he told himself. Restlessly he moved his fingertips over the basket-weave design carved on Kincaid's staghorn grips. *Why don't the Saxons come?*

As he left the question unspoken, it received no answer—but the true answer was that Vithils moved in his own time, not his quarry's. He had arrived, sails furled and oars muffled. Two cunning woodsmen went ashore by his orders, to prove that all was as reported. Had the bard been on land at the time, they would have been lucky to escape his notice, for he was as adroit in wildwood as useless aboard a ship; but the bard was not on land. Vithils's men scouted the creek mouth and returned to him unseen. His spear fighters, used to his discipline, kept utter silence in the meantime.

The scouts rose out of the water at last. "Aye," one whispered. "A warship is there. They have piled brush along the sides to hide it, and taken down the mast." They did not know that *Ormungandr* no longer had a mast to take down. "Meseems they are all sleeping aboard. They must be Gudrun Blackhair's men; they have not taken down the dragon head. I saw it plainly when I crept close, against the sky and the sea."

"It will be Blackhair," Vithils agreed. "She would reck little of offending the elves. All sleeping aboard?"

"It seems so. There's a watch kept. I heard one man curse another for treading on him. Then someone rose to piss over the side, and talked awhile with a guard. That went on a long time."

Vithils grinned savagely. "He'll finish pissing tonight! We

fall upon them now and spare none. Out oars, you slackers, you have rested long enough.''

The Saxon warships strode across the water like great rigid-legged centipedes. Into the shadow of the creek mouth they darted. A huge battle shout burst from the Saxons. Fire pots were broken, iron baskets of oil-drenched wood set alight and torches kindled. Noisy alarms from the pirates answered them, and a shimmer of suddenly bared weapons.

While Saxon attention was fixed on what lay ahead, a long vessel surged from hiding and bore down on them from behind.

Gudrun stood laughing in the bow, helmed and war-shirted, with Kissing Viper shining in her fist.

The Saxons scarcely had time to yell their amazement before their rearmost ship was rammed. Strongly braced within by workmanship unmatched on the ridge of the earth, *Ormungandr*'s prow shattered the Saxon vessel halfway through. It heeled far over, to sink gurgling in the murk.

The impact flung Gudrun sprawling. She regained her feet unhurt, curses boiling from her lips. Around *Ormungandr*'s sides, men in war gear struggled not to drown. Oars were raised and swung down ruthlessly like mincing blades, battering them under. Few reached the shore.

Vithils looked back, and his heart ripped across. But he shouted, "On!"

The leading vessel rushed ahead. A long narrow shape, camouflaged with brush, loomed in the light of crackling brands. The Saxons raised oars. With jarring, grinding impact, they met what they thought a ship, and discovered instead a mound of stones, hurriedly built in the rough semblance of a warship, its crudeness hidden with brush. The detachable serpent head had been raised at one end for a hunter's lure.

Tricked! Vithils thought, in fury and grief.

There were a few men on the decoy mound, to further the impression of a real, guarded ship. Now they had drawn together at one end, their shields overlapping.

"Kill those sons of mares!" Vithils roared. "You, you and you there—see to them! The rest, lock shields and hold fast!"

More easily said than done. The Saxons had no time to form a compact body and surround themselves with a shield wall. *Ormungandr* was upon them, hardly slowed by ramming the other warship. Gudrun's pirates dropped over the sides, bellowing.

With a falcon shriek of *"Here comes a Dane!"* their leader sprang recklessly from the prow. Even in the moonless night, the firelit confusion, any might know her by her silvered helm and mail. Spears boomed on her shield and one gashed her calf. She never felt it.

Her sword's edge turned red.

At the end of the mound, Felimid and his comrades strained to break past their foes. Kincaid shuttled forward and back, now flashing over the top of the bard's shield, now darting treacherously from beneath it to skewer a thigh.

Clear distinctions vanished early. The long pile of rocks gave no sure footing. Swearing men strove, trampled each other, toppled into the creek, squinted by occasional torch-light, mistook friend for foe, were themselves mistaken, and shouted identifying slogans.

"Blackhair! *Glory to Blackhair!*"

"Edricsburrrg!"

"Blackhair leads us!"

"Vithils and Edricsburg!"

Numbers were roughly even. None, however, could tell that in the circumstances. Vithils forced his way through the chaos of crashing metal and striving bodies, seeking Gudrun. *There!* Flash of a brilliant helm, glimpse of a yelling beardless face! It was she!

"Vithils!" Gudrun cried, shrill above the racket. "Where are you? Do not hide from me!"

"Turn around, you Danish bitch! I'm here!"

Wheeling to confront him, she laughed, then cursed as he killed the last men struggling between them. Mutually eager, they fought.

Vithils's strength was a thing out of legend. His first terrible axe-stroke drove Gudrun's shield down, numbing her arm. She cut murderously at his side, forgetting she had wanted him alive, forgetting all but the fierce imperative to live. She trod across something soft which flowed with gore and whimpered.

Kissing Viper bit into Vithils's byrnie. A scale or two broke, as did one short rib. Vithils braced his feet on the blood-greased rocks and slammed his shield into Gudrun's body. Thrown sprawling for the second time in moments, she saw Vithils blot out the stars with his massiveness.

She hewed at his leg from where she lay. He got his shield
there first. Rising to one knee, Gudrun hewed again, and
sheared a segment of his shield away. Her edge cut through the
iron rim in two places and flashed onward, though with
greatly lessened force, to meet Vithils's upper arm. The sword
twisted in her hand. She gashed muscle and broke bone.

Vithils grunted sharply. He whirled up his axe for what
might prove the last stroke of his life. Gudrun, knowing her
man, drove Kissing Viper hard at his throat. The same determination blazed in both fighters.

If you slay me, you shall come with me!

Felimid was nearby. Firelight blinked on metal at the periphery of his vision, as Vithils swung his axe. The bard responded with a lizard-swift reflex, in the belief that the metal
threatened *him*. He struck backhanded. His blade cut an arc
of white fire across the night.

Vithils's sound hand gripped only a length of wood. The
axe-head turned circles through the outer dark. Unheard, it
landed somewhere in the bloodied creek. Vithils lurched, off-
balance. Striking irresistibly with five pounds of steel and then
losing it in mid-stroke spun him sideways. Gudrun's sword-
thrust grated across his byrnie, missing his throat.

He tried to brain her with his shield. Too much strength had
gone out of his left arm; he failed, though he caught her by the
throat with his right hand. She battered him with shield-boss,
shield-rim and sword-hilt until he fell senseless. Even then she
had to break his thumb to drag her throat from that terrible
grip.

Panting, croaking, she extracted some of her warriors from
the melee to guard her while she stopped Vithils's blood flowing and bound his fractured arm immobile. She hoped the
swift, crude job would serve until she had more time and more
light.

One of her men winded a ram's horn to call the rest aboard
her ship. Three carried Vithils's lax weight. Gudrun and
Felimid found themselves together in the hottest rearguard
fighting. He guarded her left side, she finding her shield arm
still unresponsive, and he being left-handed. So they guarded
each other until they won their way aboard.

The Saxons hurled themselves at the ship like madmen.
Gudrun's pirates fought as hard to reach it, not wishing to be
left. Heavy poles were seized to push *Ormungandr* along. The

mighty ship moved out of the creek mouth, shedding Saxons by hard-clinging ones and twos.

At last they were clear. Gudrun cried back across the water, "Hear me, you men of Edricsburg! I am Gudrun Blackhair! I have your leader, him they call your fat chief's axe! To ransom him back, come to Forsetislund! Come prepared to pay a great price! Do you hear me? Forsetislund!"

Curses rang after her, bitter but empty. The Saxons were already considering how Edric the Fat would receive them, who had let his great henchman be captured and remained alive themselves. Their reputations would suffer.

Gudrun remembered another thing, almost too late. "Bring our serpent head!" she told them, at the top of her voice. "That is part of the ransom; I want it back! See that you bring it!"

VIII
Forseti's Temple

By dawn, *Ormungandr* was far out on the blue sea. Gudrun's famous weather luck had not turned; no more could have been asked of any summer morning. She squinted at the sunrise.

"Row due west for a time," she told her crew. "We ought to see some trace of Forsetislund by noon. If not, wake me. By Aegir the Bountiful,* I am going to sleep."

She had spent the night, what time she could spare from tending her own wounded, in treating Vithils. With careful competence she had set and splinted his arm, then watched over him lest he should bleed anew. He must live. No ransom would be paid otherwise.

As she walked yawning to her pallet, she passed the bard. He was playing fragments of music and frowning at the sea as though baffled. His music evoked the sea, but imperfectly, in scraps and flashes, like fish one might glimpse flickering through green water. His lips moved.

"Will it be a good song, Bragi?"

The frown left his face. "It will be worthy of the matter," he said cheerfully, "and worth the trouble I am taking, so."

"I'm eager to hear it." She yawned. "My thanks for last night. Vithils and I were about to take each other's lives. You merit his thanks too. But I think you will get none."

---

* *The northern sea god.*

"I'll share his ransom, then."

"Surely. You did your part, and half my share, the chieftain's share, you may have. When it is delivered, and I know what sort of price the red dwarves will demand."

"And this island that's our destination now? What kind of a place is it, lady?"

"It's holy to Forseti. Not heard of him? He's the god of laws. Men sacrifice to him when they make treaties or oaths, or would settle disputes short of war."

"A litigant's god. He must surely have begun in Erin, whatever led him to settle in the north. We're the finest lawmakers and law-expounders on the ridge of the earth, though somewhat less handy at obeying them. Do you sacrifice to this Forseti at all?"

"I've never heeded him," Gudrun said. "Little good he has done me, though I owe the Father of Victories much. Still, even Saxons should not dare treachery at Forseti's temple. I'll make him an offering this time for the sake of my good name. . . . Now I must sleep."

Lying down in her kirtle and breeches, she wasted no time about it. She had a warrior's knack for snatching sleep at any time she might. Unlike her, Felimid had slept during the night, and he had a song to complete. His fingers returned to the harp.

Guided by the flight of sea birds, they found Forsetislund about midday. The temple's carved painted pillars and gable ends could be seen for a long way. Gudrun had ordered her armor-bearer to awaken her when the isle was sighted, and he obeyed. After mumbling, swearing and trying to burrow back into her sheepskins, she shook herself like a dog springing out of the water.

"Ahh! Gods! Fetch me a bucket, Riccho, and a brush for my hair. Then bring me food. I cannot deal with the priests looking like a she-troll. They will be offended and ask twice as much. Is my armor bright?"

"Scoured and shining, Blackhair."

"What? The word is *lady*, from you to me, or I'll have your head! Go, fetch my gear."

"Aye, lady."

When *Ormungandr*'s anchor fell a little offshore from the temple, Gudrun wore her glittering mail again. Three of

Forseti's priests had come down to the water's edge. Gudrun sprang from *Ormungandr*'s bow to meet them, bare-headed, her black hair worn in the braided coronal she favored for action.

"Do you know me?" she demanded.

"I believe you must be Gudrun Blackhair, lady," said the leading priest. "This island is peace-holy to you. Welcome. I am Thrasnir."

Thrasnir was a man of late middle years, turning gray. Like his younger companions, he wore a long tunic, richly bordered.

Gudrun explained the situation swiftly.

"I'd have you do all in your power to see that the exchange is made peacefully and honorably," she finished. "Edric can come here in his full strength and fall upon us, although he will be one brother-in-law the poorer if he does. I myself will cut off his head if it comes to that! However, I think Fat Edric values him enough to pay. I'll give oaths to free Vithils unhurt when I have his ransom—well, no more hurt than he has been—and ask oaths of Edric that we may depart unhindered, you priests to witness and preside. If the ransom is not paid smoothly, this isle will run with more blood than you have seen before."

"You speak too certainly of that," Thrasnir said. "I was once a warrior, and one of King Halfdan's guardsmen before his brother slew him. I have fought in Frisia and Gaul as well as on Danish earth."

"Then you will see my point of view." Gudrun did not ask why Thrasnir had lived after his lord had been infamously slain. He would have been offended, and she wished his help. "Still, you serve Forseti now. You are committed to peace, and I too wish to see it prevail. Today." Gudrun smiled as she added that word. "So, then. Will you do as I ask?"

"Forseti dwells in a hall of silver and gold," the priest answered. "As you say, I serve him. For his honor, I may not be indifferent to silver and gold, and for yours as a chieftain, you should not be close-fisted."

"None has accused me of it, and neither shall you. But you must make this thing clear to Edric also, when he arrives . . . that a chieftain should be open-handed."

"Aye, that is fair. It is good for all concerned when folk settle their differences in peace, instead of hewing one another

apart because it is cheaper. This will increase your good name,
Gudrun Blackhair.''

"I hope it does. And what should my men do to protect my
good name while they are here?"

"Only behave as guests, lady. They should know two things
for their own welfare; the sheep of this isle belong to Forseti,
and it would bring bad luck to kill one. Also, the spring in the
temple courtyard is holy. Who draws water from it must do so
silently. If your men need water, we can fill casks for them."

"Good. Bragi, will you give the men that word and say I en-
dorse it? I think Thrasnir and I will be talking a while yet."

"Hadding, go with the minstrel," Thrasnir said to one of
the younger priests. "Answer any other questions he has."

Nettled, Felimid replied with staves in the northern manner.

"Never name me minstrel,
    minion of Forseti.
Groaning, ragged gangrels,
    grovelling by hearth fires,
Lore they lack, and learning;
    Low indeed their station.
I was trained not idly
    in the bard's profession.

"Cattle raids and courtships,
    Caves, elopements, battles,
Are among the stories
    I have mastered telling.
Call me son of Cairbre,
    Cunning scop or wordsmith;
Slight me not by saying
    such a word as minstrel."

As befitted a well-bred man, Thrasnir answered with a few
staves of his own. While he acknowledged Felimid's (or
Bragi's) status as a poet, he waxed ironical about the other's
touchy pride. Gudrun looked—briefly—like a little girl trying
not to laugh at an inappropriate moment.

Felimid resorted to more complex meter in which to relate
his ancestry and poetic distinction. It was no easy task in a
language not his own. Gudrun interrupted before he could
proceed very far.

"Bring two poets together, and they will not be content until one has made a better poem than the other. Now the greatest Saxon chief living is on his way hither, or I've misjudged him, and we have little time for contests. Bragi, Priest Hadding, will you take the word to my men concerning the sheep and water? And remind them from me to stay together."

This was done. Gudrun's warriors chewed stockfish, salt pork and tack, grousing somewhat. Felimid talked to the young priest, Hadding, finding him inquisitive and eager for news. The bard had some to tell. Apart from the stories of King Oisc's death and Vithils's capture, he had scarcely staler tidings from Britain. Then it was Hadding's turn.

The temple had been founded, he said, in the time of Gaius Julius Caesar. When Caesar had been building ships in Gaul for his expeditions to Britain, he had been hampered for a time by Frisian raiders. Finally he had trapped a dozen of their leaders alive. He had demanded why these men refused to obey Roman laws, and what their own laws were that they reckoned them so much better. The pirates could make no answer that satisfied him.

Caesar might simply have executed them. Instead, he offered them a choice; to be crucified, made slaves, or set adrift far from shore in a boat lacking oars, sail or steering paddle. They had gambled on the last.

In danger of foundering, they had cried to the gods. A thirteenth man had appeared among them, bearing a huge axe of gold on his shoulder. With his axe, he had steered their boat until they reached the island, and there he had thrown his axe ashore. Where it struck the earth, a spring gushed forth.

Then he had told them that he was Forseti, and taught them the laws they needed to know. They had remained on the island and founded the temple, descendants of theirs being the present priests, Hadding among them.

"The spring flows yet," he added, "and Forseti's axe hangs in the temple yonder, which proves it all."

"I should like to see that. Might a stranger go within?"

"That is for Thrasnir to say—but I'd wish those who enter to offer a sacrifice, to show they are not moved only by idle wonder."

"You've a mighty discreet tongue. I hazard you mean you'd rather not have thirty pirates tramping through your fane, eye-

ing such things as golden axes and thinking the kind of
thoughts pirates do entertain.''

Hadding laughed and did not deny it.

Gudrun and Thrasnir came down to the shore some time
later, to find her captive awake. Though his face was gray
from pain and loss of blood, he spoke to the point.

''Ransom?''

''Of course,'' Gudrun said.

''And this place?''

''Forseti's sacred island. Where better to handsel an agreement in peace? Your brother-in-law has no such ship as
Ormungandr. Still, by now he will have heard the news and be
preparing to sail. If the weather stays fair we should see him
tomorrow.''

''You will see him.'' Vithils's eyes glittered balefully. ''He
won't waste time. If a gale is blowing, he will be here.''

''Good.''

''It may not be good . . . for you.''

The pirates waited. As Ataulf said, ''Any pirate spends a
deal of his time in waiting, Bragi. We wait in ambush for ships
to pass by; we wait for clear weather or a suitable wind; we
wait to dicker for ransom, as now; and we wait through the
winter each year for the seafaring season to come again.''

The night passed, and some of the day. Then the lookouts
raised a shout. ''Sails on the water, to the southeast! Sails!
Saxon sails! Fat Edric is here!''

Joyful, Gudrun yelled back, ''In what strength?''

''Five sails! Five ships of war!''

Edric the Fat steered the foremost. He stood on braced legs
like short tree trunks. Despite their sturdiness, they were tested
to support his body. Thickness of muscle alone made him a
walking keg, and he was layered and slabbed with blubber
atop that.

His round, heavy-jawed face wore a scowl. Vithils, school-
ing his own face to a dispassionate mask, watched his brother-
in-law come. He knew nothing could be done at present;
therefore he hid his feelings, which had much in common with
quicklime, which sizzles at a touch.

''Chieftain!'' Gudrun cried through her cupped hands.
''Let your other war dragons lie farther out! You may approach closely and see that your fighting arm lives—but, as his

life's dear to you, keep the rest of your ships at a distance!''

"I hear you," Edric said, in a voice heavy as booming surf.

Gudrun's conditions were turned into Saxon orders and obeyed. Edric looked at his brother-in-law across a gap of sighing blue water. Mindful of the grinning pirates who would hear, Edric shut his mouth upon any relieved greeting.

Instead he said jocularly, "Well, kinsman! Each time I turn my back you get into bad company. Was it needful to sink this low?''

"I was drunk," Vithils answered. "Now that I'm sober, I wish to leave this rabble. But they expect you to pay for the carouse.''

"Doubtless. What are your terms, Blackhair?''

"We can settle those ashore," Gudrun said. "You may land with twenty men. I'll meet you before the temple with a like number. The priests will witness fair dealing, and we will take oaths to abide by their judgment if we cannot agree without help.''

"I'm content so far as that goes.''

"Then land, great lord," Gudrun said.

Felimid did not find Edric the laughable fellow Gudrun had described. Plodding ashore, he scanned Gudrun's group with shrewd, fearless eyes.

"I have ransacked my warehouses to meet the price I knew you would demand," he said. Felimid cocked one eyebrow. Surely that was an injudicious thing to say, at the beginning of such a parley? "My ships hold bundles of the best sealskins and hides, and winter furs without holes; bear, fox, marten, sable and beaver. I have casks of Gaulish wine as well. If that does not suffice, I will make up the ransom with clear candle wax you can almost see through.''

Gudrun's men were delighted with these offers. They urged her to accept at once. The mention of wine was especially welcome to them. Gudrun felt less eager, and explained why.

"Casks of wine weigh a deal. First you would break your backs loading, next you would tire yourselves rowing with such a cargo, and last you would drink yourselves senseless at the next landfall! Edric hopes to catch you fuddled and helpless, later. No, lord." Gudrun Blackhair raised two fingers. "My men deserve to celebrate, I own. They may—with two casks of your wine, no more.

"For the rest, I want goods of light bulk. Begin with the candle wax. I'll gladly take the marten and sable. Keep the hides—and what of hard coin? You must have had the foresight to bring gold with you."

Edric's gaze hardened. "I had heard that you command respect from the men you lead, woman," he said. "I cannot tell how. If you are a chieftain, show a chieftain's manners. If a fishwife, go back to skinning eels."

"Walrus," Gudrun said, unabashed. "Spearing walrus is my kind of fishing." Tall, smiling, and unencumbered by excess flesh, she looked up and down Edric's ponderous carcass. "If I visit you another day, you might show me some sport —as a chieftain, with a chieftain's manners."

"Perhaps I will visit you first."

"Send me word. I'll make sure I am home to welcome you."

"You are both chieftains of note," Thrasnir said, "and you both command men. Goading each other to anger adds to neither of your good names. Remember, lord, that your brother-in-law's life is at risk here, and you, lady, that your own men's lives depend on a peaceful conclusion to this chaffer. As said the High One:

> "Often words uttered to another
> Have reaped an ill harvest:
> Two beat one, the tongue is head's bane,
> Pockets of fur hide fists."

Finally, they agreed. Vithils's ransom was paid in gold, furs and clear wax, with two casks of red Falernian so that Gudrun's crew might make merry elsewhere. *Ormungandr*'s tall serpent head was also returned.

Both parties gave generous presents and thanks to Thrasnir. In fact they tried to outdo each other in generosity, to the priest's gain.

"As for the exchange," Gudrun said, "let you swear in the temple, upon Forseti's axe, that we may leave in peace, and give your men that command. I'll swear a like oath to set Vithils adrift in a boat once we are clear of your fleet."

"Ah, no!" Edric complained. "No! Vithils must be released here!" He waved a heavy arm at the piled ransom.

"Take it, then send Vithils to me, here on the sand."

Gudrun grew suspicious, her sea-gray eyes narrowing.
"Why? What does it matter, if you mean to honor your oath
and let us go without battle?"

"What does it cost you to oblige me, since you mean to
honor yours?"

"Meseems, lady, that the lord of Edricsburg asks nothing
unfair," Thrasnir suggested. "You and he stand here in equal
strength." He indicated the twenty Saxons and Gudrun's
twenty pirates. The ship in which Eric had landed was drawn
up on the beach, while his four others rode the sea well offshore. "If you receive the ransom, then he should receive the
one for whom he pays it, without delay."

"Agreed, then," Gudrun said. "Is there anything more?"

Edric shook his head. "I am content."

In the temple, they swore the oaths on Forseti's great golden
axe. Outside, Edric sent his ship to meet the others, with his
solemn command that no man should meddle with *Ormungandr*, or so much as set hand to weapon or oar, till the great
ship had vanished from sight. Felimid listened closely. They
were unequivocal commands, with no leeway for tricks or be-
trayal. They satisfied him and Gudrun. She set Vithils ashore,
had the ransom stowed before *Ormungandr*'s mast, and then
freed Vithils to join the Saxons. With a swagger, she led her
pirates aboard the warship.

Long ash oars swung out, shining in the sun. *Ormungandr*
swam across the waves. Then, ashore and on the sea, men
stared amazed, laughed, swore, reached for weapons or gleefully pounded each other's backs, depending on their nature
and allegiance. Edric's war dragons were converging to bar the
pirates' way.

"Lord!" the gray priest protested. "Your oath!"

"I've kept it!" Edric rasped. "By Njord of the Ships, those
men are disobeying my orders—and I never meant that they
should! Let Forseti's axe cleave my head if I lie."

At her vessel's shield rail, Gudrun watched the Saxon war
dragons drawing near. She laughed scornfully.

"So much for Fat Edric's word! This is all I expected. Now
let us see what kind of a race they give us." She grinned at the
bard. "You asked to come on this voyage, Bragi. How do you
feel about the wisdom of it now?"

He smiled back. "I haven't as yet been seasick."

Gudrun strung her bow and began to shoot, smiling still. With each arrow she slew or disabled a man, and she had a sheaf of thirty beside her. The rhythm of the oars faltered in the nearest Saxon ship.

Two thanes in scale byrnies covered the steersman with their shields. Gudrun shot for their legs, then drove a long slender arrowhead straight through one thane's byrnie. All three men fell in a tangle. The ship yawed.

"Row harder!" she said.

"You heard," Ataulf barked from his place in the stern. "Row, you sea rats! Bend! Bend! *Bend*!"

Gudrun began to pick targets on a second vessel. She wasn't afraid. Fear of ordinary physical danger was a thing she had never known. Her heart kindled, and she was borne out of herself on a vast joy.

Felimid stood at the rail, a shield on his arm but no weapon in his hand as yet. They were within spear's cast now of one Saxon war dragon. Three others were almost as close, oars combing the frothy water. It was like the game of fidchell, which begins with the quarry at the center of the board, while the pack converges from all corners. Felimid generally won at fidchell.

A spear flew at Gudrun where she nocked, drew and loosed as swiftly as she could send arrows. The bard's leaf-green eyes widened. His empty left hand flashed up. The javelin shaft smacked into his palm, the impact of that astonishing catch hauling his arm back. He spun the weapon, tossed it high and caught it above his head.

"My thanks indeed," he called. "It's a good weapon; I'll keep it."

A volley of spears answered his gibe. Felimid threw his arm around Gudrun and ducked low with her, raising his shield to cover them both. Something jarred its surface.

Gudrun had one smooth, powerful arm around him too. By nature an opportunist, the bard kissed her swiftly, so that she had no time to respond or object. Nor did she comment, but rose to her feet.

They had squeezed free by finger-widths. The outlaw ship increased its lead with each stroke. Only *Ormungandr* could have brought them out of such a trap untouched. Two Saxon vessels had even clashed together in their haste to ram the pirates. Gudrun's day was made perfect thereby.

"The right wages of treachery! Never will they catch us, even if the wind favors them! What, did you take harm, Bragi?"

The bard was sucking his hand.

"Catching yon javelin gave me a splinter," he said. "A fearful wound. I'm unlikely to live."

The Saxons pursued them hungrily, but it proved as Gudrun had said. *Ormungandr* never appeared likely to be overtaken. The Saxons turned back at last, to face their master's anger. They had broken his oath for him, and gained nothing by doing it, nor even come to grips with the pirates. They received scathing condemnation from Edric for it, and returned to the Elbe joyless.

Vithils said only, "There'll be another day."

IX
"It Requires to Be Told."

The lean serpent ship lay drawn up on a windswept, lonely beach. Fires of driftwood crackled, the flames blowing in yellow tatters. Gudrun's pirates had come ashore to carouse and brag and enjoy their triumph. But for them and the terns and plovers, the shore lay deserted for long miles.

Two Goths let a wine cask down a runway of planks, braking it with ropes. They found it gratifyingly heavy, and smacked their lips to hear it slosh.

"Praise Edric the Fat!" One of them chuckled. "Surely this is the first time he ever showed generosity to thirsty rovers."

"Aye. Even a Saxon will be generous with a spear's point at his belly."

Hemming the Saxon took exception to that and challenged the speaker to fight. Another man helped trundle the cask to the fire, where they turned it upright and broached the head with axes.

A Spanish Goth named Rasavind had a sudden unsettling thought. "If the Saxons poisoned it?"

The suggestion lessened mirth. Gudrun's pirates glanced at each other, then at the open cask which gave forth such inviting fumes. Even Gudrun hung back, wordless. She never minded an open fight, or a gamble at odds, or any kind of dangerous direct action. But poison. . . .

"I'll try it," Felimid said, dipping a pewter cup in the wine. "A double portion for me if I survive, and decent burial if I fall dead. Is that fair?'' He raised the brimming cup in an extravagant gesture. "Your name and fame, Gudrun Blackhair!''

The wine was superb, and did taste safe. He decided that he might as well have more. It became a silken glory in his blood, and presently all could see that he was not going to expire or even sicken. They jostled forward to fill their own cups, commending his nerve and pledging him. The level of wine in the cask lowered swiftly. One man's cup thudded on a solid barrier as he dipped it. He swore in puzzlement.

"It's empty," someone complained.

"Teeth of Sathanas! It is not," someone else said, trying to rock the cask. "It's heavy as your soul with sin, Giguderich. Hear it gurgle?''

"We've been cheated!'' a third man bawled. "This accursed barrel is floored partway!''

It was. They scraped and scooped the last of the wine, then broke through the false bottom. Seawater sprayed up this time. The greater part of the cask contained it.

The second cask was as false. Gudrun's pirates smashed both in their disappointment. In fact all the wine amounted to nearly a firkin, or more than a pint each, but to these angry topers it was the merest taste to the carouse they had expected. They said many furious things about Edric the Fat, and condemned his sly, niggardly deceit.

Felimid went further. Drawing music from Golden Singer like fountains of mocking, rollicking laughter, he improvised a satire which had them roaring.

"I know two ship lords, two chiefs of fighting men, the one muddy dregs, the other clear heady bright crimson wine; a walrus encased in blubber and a falcon for swiftness.

"It is strange to compare them, the ash and the stubby twisted inhospitable thorn, the tall swordswoman and the refuse of the hosting.

"Blackhair deals in pure feats of valor, Edric in sluggishness. If the foam of the bright sea were silver, and winter's dead leaves were flakes of gold, Gudrun Blackhair would give it all away; but Edric the Saxon has his paws forever in the scales.

"The one is lithe and high-leaping, her bright sword patterned like an adder's back; she sets upon strong shoulders a coat of glittering mail.

"The other is a misshapen boulder, sunk in the earth like a bad tooth in an aching jaw, by his side a blunted iron bar and on his back mildewed leather.

"I compose my verses to her of the proud hand, the captain of *Ormungandr*, Gudrun of the gray eyes, venturesome rider of the swan's path."

Gudrun smiled and offered him thanks, but in an abstracted way, and shortly she called her pirates about her.

"You may bring out the ale and finish that," she said. "We have no reason to save it, as I plan to bring you to vats of the best ale in Jutland. I'm for visiting my father in the Limfjord and finding some brisk men to strengthen our company."

There was a murmur of speculation. Gudrun waited for it to fade.

"Now I've no men with me who come from those parts," she went on, "nor have I had for all of three years. I chose not to have them. I know," she said flatteringly, "what gossip-mongering sons of mares all seamen are. I'm hoping we will spend a se'nnight or more in the Limfjord, and there will be much talking done; so much is certain. You are bound to hear what I did before I came south. I'd liefer you heard it now, truthfully from me, than in the straw from some tattling kitchen girl with bow legs and more malice than wits, or finger-wagging tosspot half-seas-over. It's my concern, no other's, but if we're to spend time in the Limfjord it requires to be told."

Gudrun Blackhair was nervous. To Felimid the signs were clear, though it would not have been believed in any place where seamen gathered. Then, seeming to take herself in hand, she spoke more concisely.

"This you must know," she said, while her cloak blew in the salt wind. "I'm outlawed in the Danish kingdom. Never trouble; where we are going it means little enough. As southerners, you may not know how it is here, but Zealand and Skania in the east are the ancient heart of the kingdom. Royal edicts do not have much force in Jutland. The chieftains are their own law."

"Good hearing," grunted one Chatheigs, a long-headed man with hollow temples and a large nose. "I had to leave Gaul because of too much law."

"And too many Franks," Giguderich added.

"I'm telling the tale," Gudrun said. "You may chatter of

your troubles in Gaul when I have finished. I spoke of independent chieftains, and my father Varek is among the greatest. He has broad acres and many ships. When I was a girl he had three sons as well, my elders, but they all died. One drowned in a storm. Sickness had the other two in the same outbreak. Our mother had already died, giving birth to me.

"Some said my father lost his understanding after that. I didn't agree. It suited me well that he raised me to hunt and fight like a son when my brothers were lost. He took me faring in ships, too.

"All this is short to relate, but was maybe eight years in the living. I was small when my brothers died. I grew tall, and I grew breasts, and my father married again. His new wife and I did not take to each other. I'd been spoiled for women's work, and liked to hunt or practice with weapons or fare on salt water. For three years we bickered and she nagged my father, and he changed towards me. Most of all did he change when she bore him twin sons.

"It no longer pleased him to see bow, sword or spear in my hands. We had fierce quarrels before I put on women's clothes. Nor did I wear them often even then. My father reckoned I ought to marry, and I wasn't eager for that. Still, I had some suitors.

"The one who mattered was a man named Ivarr from an isle north of Zealand. A mighty chieftain and a jarl under the brother kings of the Danes. I was fifteen when he asked for my hand. I asked my father to prevail upon Ivarr to wait a year for his answer. This he did, but privately he told me the match seemed good to him and that he favored it.

"I was not downhearted. Much may happen in a year. Indeed, something did. Ivarr came back before one season had passed, while my father was away with most of our fighting men.

"Ivarr had brought a shipload with him, and he made himself finely at home. Eating and swilling for three, he sat in my father's seat, drank deeply, and threw aside his agreement. He held me across his knee, handled me, swore we should bed that night, marry later, and Hel take delays."

Gudrun's men growled in anger.

"His crew nigh drank the house dry," Gudrun said. "I gave them encouragement in that. My father's brew is strong, and I myself served Ivarr as much as he'd drink. At last I begged leave to go to my bower and make it ready.

"I give my stepmother due credit, she had not taken their invasion tamely. When they began to make so free, she gave them the rough side of her tongue, and louts that they were, they locked her in a storehouse. None of the servants dared let her out or come to my aid. Not that I was liked by them.

"One friend I had, a widow with a worthless son I had saved from the hanging he deserved—don't ask me why. However, she was cunning in witchcraft, and loyal to me. She prepared a sleep-thorn. When Ivarr came reeling in, I pricked him, and he lay helpless.

"Then it was my turn to have fun. I stripped that man naked and bound him tightly. With the widow's help I dragged him to the byre. There I plastered him thickly with cow dung and rammed a pine cone up his arse. He slept through it all. I bear witness, the widow's sleep-thorn was powerful."

She paused to wet her throat. Her men were holding each other in paroxysms of laughter or seated on the sand, roaring. Felimid laughed more softly, though with no less relish, the pain under his ribs a sweet anguish. Beautiful! Oh, beautiful! Oh, what that man's reputation must have suffered!

"Last of all I stuffed him in a sack and tied the neck," Gudrun went on. "I had two carls carry it down to his longboat and stow it aboard. They were unwilling, but I had a spear by then, and I swore I'd pierce Ivarr with it unless they obeyed me. The result would be a massacre which might well include them. I'd not have done it; the girl I was would not have dared. Still, they believed it of me and the threat sufficed.

"We returned to the house. I mustered such strength as we had and sent runners to neighbor farms for help. It arrived in fair time. Early in the morning we hustled the jarl's drunken men down to his boat, saying that their master wished to leave, having got what he came for and found it indifferently pleasing. I'd have liked to be a tern hovering above when the sack was opened."

The laughter increased. One-eyed Decius, the tough, un-forthcoming Spaniard, gasped on the sand. Ataulf seesawed between the pain of his wound if he laughed and the inner torment if he did not.

"Aye, aye . . . but, Blackhair . . . " the Goth choked, "that wasn't a thing to merit outlawry, was it?"

"No," Gudrun agreed. "That came later. As I said, our neighbors backed me once they knew what had happened. Jarl Ivarr could do nothing but row away. The joke was all over Jutland in a month, Ivarr was frothing still, and everywhere known as Dungbeard. He slew a man for smiling in his presence, as I heard.

"He'd no more of a suitor's interest in me, but vengeance he did desire. He came back stealthily and captured me one day when I was hunting. He carried me back to his hall, and there I was treated as women spear-captives are. He kept me for a month, and gave me to his men when he tired of me. I did not enjoy it."

Her pirates' laughter died. Now they were quiet, awaiting her next words.

"I . . . escaped at last," she continued. "I escaped with a grimy kirtle on my hide and nothing on my feet. A stolen boat took me home."

She paused then. The telling brought back too many memories she did not wish to entertain. Indeed, she had suffered much in Ivarr's hall. They had passed her around like a platter of baked turnips before familiarity and carelessness had given her a chance for freedom. A frailer girl would have died.

When she returned home, her father Varek greeted her without sympathy. He had been angry with her, not with Jarl Ivarr. She could not believe it at first.

"See here, my she-hawk," he had growled, "I've had enough of your airs. What did you think a man like Ivarr would do, the way you shamed him? You are fortunate he did not come back to burn the house around us. Now, with this tale over the country, there can be no marrying you to a man of your own station. I'd have to give a dowry that would beggar us all before any would have you. That I will not do, by the gods. But married you had best be, quickly."

"Because I may carry a child? I do not think I do. For that matter, I do not care. I'll marry no crofter lout you bribe to have me. I'll marry no man in my life's days."

"Wild talk," Varek had said, although more softly. "It's best that you do, believe me."

"Best? You talk of Ivarr's shame and have not a word for

mine. Or your own! Were you a man, you'd gather a dozen
chieftains in a league to burn his house, not fear such action
from him! Many would take part for the plunder.''

"That would mean war with the Dane-kings. No. No more
of this. No further insults." He tried to persuade her. "It must
be, Gudrun. For you there is no other way. Shieldwomen are
fine in legends; when did you encounter one?''

"You see one now."

"Not on these acres, by Frey's prick!" her father had
bawled in renewed anger. "I'll have no daughter who lives on
my bounty talk back to me! Do as I command, or go live as
you can! Be the prey of any man who can take you! You have
caused trouble enough!''

"Agreed!" she had shouted back. "Agreed and agreed! I
will go! I'll be the prey of any man who can take me. But I
vow to Odin it is I who will do the taking from now on!''

That was her homecoming and farewell. She had left in the
same grimy kirtle she had worn when she made her escape
from Jarl Ivarr's isle. Before she quit her father's land, she
met a spear-armed herdsman of his, and true to her word, she
possessed herself of his spear and shoes, half-killing the fellow
in order to get them. He was lucky; not for many a long red
day thereafter did she stop at merely half-killing a victim
again.

Now, tall and commanding among the dunes of the neck of
Jutland, she found she did not wish to speak in detail of that;
certainly not of the last bitter quarrel with her father. That still
hurt. She did not care to recognize it.

"My father and I had words," she said at last. "I left his
house to live as I could. By the month's end I slew my first
man. He was a vagabond who thought to have sport and anticipated no trouble. I looked upon his corpse and wondered
at how easily he had died.

"My second followed quickly. An outlaw of some note, he
showed me that it is not always easy, and I resolved to be
cautious in the future—but desperation broke that resolve.
With my third slaying I ceased to care.

"I came to my full growth living hard and wild. My first
follower was a runaway thrall, hunchbacked but brawny, and
half-witted. I gathered others about me; outlaws, gangrels and
once a handful of shipwrecked pirates. My knowledge of the

country kept them alive. I led them—well, you know how I lead. If I'd kept any softness until then it did not stay with me long. I made vows to Odin, to fight and wage war while I lived, and never to flee from a foe who outnumbered me by less than three to one.'' Briefly, her grimness melted, and her laugh was unaffectedly cheerful. ''That's why any man of mine must be worth three in a fight!''

They laughed with her.

''By the time I had seen eighteen winters, I led a hundred men, and we were such a scourge to local parts I knew the chieftains would soon join to destroy us. I decided that we must leave Jutland altogether. That meant taking to the sea in at least two ships.

''Jarl Ivarr came to my mind at once. He had many more ships than two. Yes, and of all men in the north he owed me the most.

''Word came to me that he'd lately broken a pirate expedition, rowing down the Kattegat to plunder in Danish lands. By smashing it, Ivarr had added much honor to his name, but he'd taken grievous losses.

''I took advantage of that. My hundred rogues and I crossed to his island in such ramshackle boats as we could get. As Ivarr celebrated his victory, we surrounded his hall after midnight and set it aflame. Once the fire was well advanced, I let the women, children and thralls come out. At the last moment, the jarl and a score of his henchmen broke through a burning wall. We cut them down. I myself slew Ivarr, and I never knew a greater joy than when I saw him dead on the bloody ground.

''In the morning we took three of Ivarr's war boats, with loot, provisions and slaves to sell, and fared south to the Frisian lagoons. I had been a robber; that was my beginning as a pirate.''

Blown grit stung Felimid's cheek, entered his eyes. He scarcely noticed. His mind was boiling with visions of Gudrun's captivity in Ivarr's hall, and the strength of his own loathing amazed him. Not that her tale could ever have made pretty hearing, but such things did happen—only this had happened to Gudrun.

To Gudrun.

He felt violently glad that she had slain Ivarr. He wanted to

embrace her for it. No. He wanted to embrace her, never mind
reasons. He knew, now, why he had not quit her company and
gone his own way.

Felimid stood with his harp on his back, his sword beside his
leg and a wine cup in his hand, gazing at the air before him.
He looked like a man who had just been struck hard between
the eyes. In a way he had. The blow divided him within, the
detached, irreverent mind he had always believed was himself
seeing with amazement and dismay this sudden inner chaos
which was like a stranger's.

From that inner ferment, he laughed at himself. Clever
Felimid, gifted Felimid. Felimid who had the bardic sight and
could not be deceived by glamor or illusion, who saw through
such things as through thin crystal. Felimid who did not even
know when he was in love.

He'd chosen not to know. He saw that now, and he saw
why. She was a pirate, as his own father had been, and she
would die violently and young, as his own father had. If that
wasn't bad enough, she was sworn to a god he found hateful
in all ways. Odin, the northern god of battles, was known to
be implacable and faithless even among those who worshipped
him. He was, besides, a god of dark wizardry and of the
gallows tree.

No, Felimid thought. *No, sea eagle, I may love you, but we
are not for each other, you and I. Whether you could love me
or not counts for nothing. I'll not be asking you. My songs
were your price for sparing my life. I'll pay it so far as it can be
paid. I'll make you the greatest saga that has ever been
sung—and because you are a woman, no man will like it or
care to believe it, and it will not survive long. As I knew on the
deck of* Briny Kettle, *when you made a lasting fame your condition for taking me off.*

Indeed, and I'm repaid for that deceit.

He drank the last of his wine and threw down the cup. In
that hidden canyon of his soul where lived his most secret
ironies and dismays in the form of tailed, fork-tongued imps,
the whole band of them rolled and wept and kicked their legs
and pounded their fists in paroxysms of wicked joy. In their
opinion, this day was past due.

They were not without a sense of justice.

PART TWO: THE NORTH

I
Gudrun Blackhair's Homecoming

Ormungandr slid through the Limfjord in the blue summer weather. The serpent head had been taken down, so that the earth powers should not be angered. Gudrun did not usually care whether she angered them or not—the only power she sought to please was Odin—but once this place had been her home, and she wished to be tactful. A white shield had been raised on a pole amidships, as a sign of peace.

Ram's horns shouted from the shore. Armed men ran to the jetty, and one demanded through cupped hands, "Who comes?"

"Gudrun Blackhair, Varek's daughter! Gudrun, the Lady of Sarnia, slayer of King Oisc and captain of *Ormungandr*! She comes in peace!"

Felimid gazed at the long hall, outbuildings and the wide fields beyond, paying little attention to the talk which followed. He wanted to step ashore. He wanted earth under his feet again; he wanted a revel. Not a pirates' carouse, but a decent, lively feasting.

He did gather that Blackhair's father was away, buying ponies. Her stepmother Ortruda was at home, in health, and would not be tardy about greeting them. So Gudrun was assured.

"I don't doubt it," Felimid heard her mutter, nigh too low to hear. "She will come. She will do the seemly, expected thing." For her men's ears, she cried, "Let's have some sport! Who will run the oar bank with me?"

They welcomed the chance to stretch their legs. All starboard oars swung over the water, a half-fishbone, gleaming in the sunlight. Men braced the looms under thwarts. Throwing off her sword belt, Gudrun sprang to the stern oar and stepped from one to the next, moving ever more swiftly, her footing confident and sure. As she approached the bow she turned inward, so that an easy vault from the last oar took her inboard again. Her pirates whooped.

The first man to try fell in. Three others ran the bank after him, with less swagger than Gudrun, but with success.

Felimid followed. At fifteen, he'd been among Erin's finest horsemen and runners, and delighted in dancing. He ran the oars light-footedly, his balance superb. Other men tried, wobbling, throwing their arms about for balance. Gudrun made a second run, careless of her finery.

After her, Felimid ran again. His body found the method for him, a matter of rhythm and balance. All he must do with his active, meddling mind was let it go.

The other men fell one by one, with bursting silver splashes, to roars of glee from those who watched. At last only Felimid and Gudrun were left.

"Once more," Felimid told himself, as Gudrun bounded to the stern oar. "Once more, and if she does not fall then, I'll give her best."

Gudrun ran the oars this time with fists planted jauntily on her hips. The cocksure display undid her. She lost her balance, and saved herself from a ducking only by seizing an oar with both hands and throwing her knee across it. Panting, she hauled herself along the shaft to a secure footing, and met her father's second wife's disapproving gaze.

Not primness only made Ortruda view her so. She feared the trouble Gudrun Blackhair might bring with her.

"It has been long, Gudrun," she said without warmth. "Since you come in peace, I greet you in peace."

Gudrun answered as coolly. "Then I'll come ashore."

Polite nothings and lip-friendliness passed between them. The pirate's half-brothers received her better. They had been toddling when Gudrun stormed from her father's acres. Now they were nine, with Varek's heavy black hair and promise of his size. Jarnrad, the taller, had fine hazel eyes like his mother's, while his brother's were gray. Otherwise their likeness was marked. Ull, the younger, filling his gaze with Gudrun, asked: "Are *you* our sister?"

"I am that," she answered, "and had I known how well my brothers were turning out, I'd have come home sooner."

When she confronted her father, the strings of her tongue knotted. She smelled the horse sweat upon him, saw the remembered wide fan of his beard and the increase of his belly, and recalled the hot rage of her leave-taking. She said clumsily, "Well, father, I've come back. Is that good?"

Varek spoke awkwardly too. "Aye, Gudrun. It might be worse."

"I'd stay a se'nnight or two, with my men, if you permit it."

"No trouble to feed or house them. In other ways, you had better tell me. They appear a wild lot. If they forget they are my guests, I'll forget it too."

"I'll answer for their behavior," Gudrun promised. "Besides, they are no wilder than you were once, or our neighbors —unless the brother kings have tamed Jutland?"

"They have enough else to do without trying that. Oh, they will not have forgotten Jarl Ivarr, but we can talk of such things later. I'll see to lodging your men. Then I'll feast you and drink you till you reel!"

He kept his word. Few men could have been as lavish, at such short notice, as he was then. Gudrun's men conducted themselves well enough, and all weapons were left in the long hall's foreroom, the Jutlanders' as well as the strangers', to avert any deadly quarrel.

With the gods of the harp speaking to him in a glow of sweet mead, Felimid gave the hall a song of Gudrun's fresher acts.

> "She clashed with the king of the Kentishmen and slew him hand to hand,
> Then sent him stark to his kindred for a grave in his proper land.
> She has taken his dwarfmade serpent ship and rowed up the Narrow Sea
> In the teeth of the lords of the Saxon Shore and maugre their enmity,

She captured Vithils the pirates' bane on a coast where
   his word is law,
And ransomed him back to his kinsman for the pick o'
   their treasure store.
Her sail is known in the southern isles where mountains
   fume and burn,
She has raided into the dreaming west from which few
   ships return—
And when *Ormungandr* is fitted, her sorcerer's sail un-
   furled,
We go with Gudrun Blackhair beyond the wings of the
   world!''

Gudrun's men cheered this resolve and drank to it gleefully.

"It's true, father," Gudrun assured him. "Bragi sings no
more than I intend! My ship is crippled now. Only a sail
woven by dwarf women can hold the winds I need to blow me
among the nine worlds. I'll have it, but first I must have a full
crew."

"You will recruit men here?" Ortruda's voice was sharp.

"Here in Jutland, aye. Danes! Thirty ought to suffice."

"For your venture you will get nothing but wild younger
sons."

"They are the kind I like to lead! I've weapons and gear to
offer them, and the country will be calmer when I take them
across the sea. That should please you."

"No, for I see them seeking you here by the score, and
doubtless growing angry if you refuse them a place in your
crew. New slayings are too likely," Ortruda said.

"And there are old ones yet to account for," Varek added.
"Jarl Ivarr does not count for much hereabouts; it's quite a
source of pride to Mors Island that you slew him. There's a
ballad about it. Your robberies and slaying among our
neighbors are another matter, girl. Some have obligations of
vengeance against you. It's their right and they will come for
it."

"I won't deny them. Father, any man who challenges me
may have single combat, lawful and formal. I'll not involve
you, nor claim any right to be avenged by my kin. We can
declare that I have the rights of a guest here and no more."

"It's a fair offer. Gudrun, I've a friend named Thjostel

across the water—do you remember him?—who is a great lawyer, and it's been long in these parts since any judgment was thought binding unless he has a part in it. Suppose we ride to visit him tomorrow?"

"Be it so," she agreed, and pledged him.

Gudrun's homecoming thus went well enough—but, as if adders long drowsy had been stirred by the sight of this prodigal daughter's return, Felimid dreamed strangely that night. Dreaming, he returned to Erin and walked by the Shannon in autumn, in an oyster-colored mist which fingered his skin coldly. Leaves crunched as he walked. Somewhere, a stag belled a challenge. The ramparts and roofs of his home came vaguely in sight.

As he approached through the mist, those ramparts and earthworks sprouted hostile spears. The palisade turned to a wall of painted shields with his own kin behind them, men, women, and children, blood family and foster family, all shouting the same word: "*Go!*"

A rain of missiles enforced it.

In a second and worse dream, he returned to the Shannon with Gudrun and her slayers. They burned, slew and wasted, while he struck first for his own kin and then with the pirates, not knowing which side was truly his and finally turning both against him. Trapped with emptiness at his back and spear points facing him, he escaped by awaking. Sweat drenched him.

That first night on Mors was also distinguished as the last night there which Felimid spent alone. With daylight, the memory of his dreams faded like dye in running water, and he found much to distract him.

He swam while dawn was still pale. Stroking through the chill northern water, he caught a lobster with his hands and came out of the Limfjord tingling. On a whim he let the lobster go.

Walking back, he met a young woman milking cows. They chatted awhile. She enjoyed his looks, his accent, the things he could tell of distant lands, and his verses, which he invented on the spot and threw into the conversation for her pleasure. Her name was Radny; she was single although of an age to marry. When he smiled and took hold of her braids, she smiled back. The remaining cows had to wait to be milked.

After breaking his fast with porridge, cream and bacon, he
spent a couple of hours in bruising weapon practice. This was
as rare for him as rising at dawn when he did not absolutely
have to. The twins, Jarnrad and Ull, came to watch him, having—as Ull bluntly told him—nothing better to do since
Gudrun had gone with their father to call upon a neighbor
skilled in law. Clearly they saw no need for this and were impatient for her return.

With their mother's leave, Felimid saddled ponies and rode
some miles with them across the island their sire ruled—for in
effect he did rule it, the lord of Mors, an island far larger than
Gudrun's base of Sarnia. Mors was a flat place of field, shaw
and sandy purple moor. To the east lay a narrow sound either
of the boys could swim.

Gudrun and Varek returned across that strip of water in the
twilight. She was merry, he good-humored. The twins ran to
meet them. Ortruda went less impetuously, though smiling to
see the two in good spirits.

"Thjostel is coming to the feast," Varek declared. "He will
send riders tomorrow, to spread the word eastward. I'll not be
amazed if guests come from the far side of the Kattegat."

"I've already sent messengers north and south," Ortruda
said. "Our food stocks will stand it. For the feast you are
planning, though, Varek, a whale or two would be welcome."

Gudrun promptly took *Ormungandr* into the North Sea and
slew the whale her stepmother mentioned. Three days later,
the feast began. It lasted a se'nnight and tripled the numbers
under Varek's rooftree.

Seldom truly drunk, Felimid was never wholly sober in that
time, either. He rode the small northern ponies with break-
neck skill; he gambled on swimming races, foot races, dice and
the way a fly would crawl; he made staves, ballads and mirth-
ful harp music to fill the air; he practiced with weapons daily,
on firm ground and on Ormungandr's water-cradled timber;
and he lay with every fair young woman he found eager, or
could persuade. From time to time he even closed his eyes.

He saw almost nothing of Gudrun, by his own choice.

She too was active. On Thjostel's advice, she stated at the
beginning that she claimed no rights of kinship, no duty of
protection or vengeance were she slain in honest fight. She was
Varek's guest, no more, though Varek must see that status
respected for his honor's sake. None might murder her slyly

without offending her host. None might brawl with her on his land.

For her part, she was prepared to fight any local man with cause to challenge her—and she owned that such men were not few. However, the fight must be fought some distance from Varek's acres, with only assistants and judges to behold it, lest the quarrel spread.

Some were scornful of the notion of combat with a woman. Thjostel reminded them that the woman concerned had slain Jarl Ivarr and King Oisc of Kent, and made Vithils the Axe her captive. Thus it was not likely that any lesser man's honor would be hurt if he fought her, although his body might be.

A man named Kolskeggi was the first to demand that satisfaction. His brother had died in Jarl Ivarr's service on the night Gudrun avenged herself. He boasted that when he had killed her, he would hang her carcass by the heels for crows to eat, and set her head on a pole nearby so that she could watch the banquet. Those who witnessed his challenge agreed that such talk was unnecessary and ill-mannered.

Gudrun accepted blithely. They crossed the water to a meadow south of Asted for the combat. Ataulf, Sighere, two friends of Kolskeggi's, and Thjostel as witness and judge, accompanied them. Kolskeggi wondered at Gudrun's high spirits, for he did not believe her fame as a fighter had anything real in it. Doubtless the acts credited to her had all been performed by henchmen.

He discovered his mistake when she opened his belly with a drawing slash.

She gained much honor from the fight. The restless younger sons Ortruda had mentioned came flocking to find a place with Gudrun Blackhair. The restless young women of north Jutland came too, and before all was done, a score of marriages had been arranged. Varek was greatly pleased, regarding this as a sign that his feast was a success. But Gudrun chose only unmarried men.

Fighters were not hard to come by, for Jutland was in a lawless state. Most yeomen had fought against robbers, cattle thieves, overbearing neighbors and pirates. Many had gone on pirate expeditions themselves. Gudrun chose them also for skill at rowing, and some knowledge at least of North Sea water. Hunters of whale and walrus found a particularly warm welcome.

Thjostel the law-wise did his share to avoid blood-spilling.
In a subtle way, Felimid perhaps did more. He wandered
about, seeming idle, yet alert for signs of trouble, the harp
Golden Singer constantly on his arm. He would play strains
almost too low for hearing, which yet had the cooling effect of
spray from a waterfall. Somehow tempers eased and swords
remained in sheaths. Ortruda, shrewd housewife, saw that
there was always ale enough but never too much. Men did
quarrel, and there were fights, but fewer than she had awaited.

Thus Gudrun and Felimid had little occasion to speak to
each other, for both were fully occupied. One evening,
though, when Gudrun had just won an arm-wrestling contest
with a yeoman named Snat within a ring of merry spectators,
she did demand a word with the bard.

"A thousand if it pleases you, wave-shortener," he answered blithely. "You have enriched me."

He gathered a wager, while one girl laughed in the circle of
his arm and another hung over his shoulder. Gudrun had seen
him in such company before, though never the same company
for long. She drew him aside and said curtly:

"Listen, Bragi. You are a man, I take it, and not a tomcat.
Enjoy yourself as you will, but I'd liefer you chose one darling
to favor. I expect to compensate a few girls for wrongs done
this month—but Ran snare me if I pay gild to half of Jutland!"

"Now there you exaggerate."

"Bragi," she told him, honing an edge on his false name,
"I'm not the one in excess. If you have to settle with angry
fathers or brothers, I'll not protect you."

"I'll bear it in mind." Gudrun had been hoping for a
prideful bray that he needed no warding, so that she might say
to him in blazing words that he was foolish to believe it. He
cheated her. He simply took the warning as given. "Yes, I'll
remember it. True it is that I've no wish to fight duels while I
am here. I daresay I could avoid any risk of one by taking a
slave to my straw, but it seems more manly to me to chance a
woman who has the freedom to say no."

Her own story being what it was, Gudrun could not argue
with that. Besides, she sensed that upon this matter she could
too easily become foolish herself. She left the subject there.

When the feast ended, she tallied her recruits. They numbered five and thirty, seventeen of them archers even by her

standard. Eight of her original crew had not yet recovered from wounds taken on the way to Jutland; they must stay with her father, and for their sake she agreed at last to pay wergild for certain old murders when she returned, to insure against her men's being molested while she was absent. Thjostel advised it. But she declared that she would not under any circumstances pay wergild for a man who had died with Jarl Ivarr.

Her brothers had almost to be shackled to stones to make them remain in the Limfjord when she left. Felimid shifted back and forth in uncertain balance until the last hour, but when it came, he laughed and boarded *Ormungandr*. All the pretty, lightly encountered girls in the Limfjord could not draw him in the direction of his better judgement as Gudrun drew him against it.

II
The Dwarf King

Gray rain lashed the gray sea north of the Skaw. Wind blew in gusts that roughened the water to a chop. *Ormungandr* flung her prow forward into the seething waves, lurched, dropped into a trough with a smacking jolt, and raised her head to shake off water before beginning again. She rolled; she bucked. Not even an enchanted ship could ride smoothly on water like this.

Even Gudrun's fabulous weather luck could not always be good.

When the first squall hit, Felimid had reached for his harp. This time, unhappily, the winds did not listen. He saw them, boisterously happy monsters with inchoate heads and booming wings, swooping among the clouds. They roared their own songs and wanted none of his. Not on that day. Carefree, mischievous, they shook Gudrun's long war serpent like a dice box.

Felimid soon grew too miserable to care. His last responsible act was to put Golden Singer away in her leather bag. Then he clung to the wale and spewed all the food in his belly. It didn't ease his distress. His stomach went on twisting after he had emptied it. Within an hour, dizzy, retching, groaning, he was afraid he would actually die.

After a few more hours, he grew afraid that he would not.

"Unhappy, are you, Bragi?" chuckled Ataulf. "Hunger weakens a man. I'll bring you some fat bacon, nigh fresh. Or would you liefer salmon, cooked in honey and cream?''

The bard wondered what had possessed him to let this monster live.

An eternity later, the ship entered calm water. Felimid's eyes remained shut while the knowledge that the mercy of dissolution was not to be his, after all, forced itself into his resistant mind. The ship's least movement sent twinges through the nerves of his churning stomach.

"Journey's end," a nearby Dane told him, grinning.

Land was in view to left and right. The mouth of a great fjord lay ahead, with darkly forested country beyond it. Morning had broken some time ago; an entire night had passed while Felimid endured the endless static wretchedness known only to the seasick.

"Is that—"

"Aye," the Dane answered. "It's the land of the red dwarves, and their king's hall stands at the end of yon fjord. So I've been told. My mother used to tell me other things when I was a brat . . . that the dwarves would take off my skin and cover a cushion with it if I disobeyed, and the like." He broadened his grin the least bit too far. "I'm big enough to skin *them*, now."

"True for you," Felimid said. "the trouble is that the lady wants something from them which she cannot take by force. The skinning is likely to be their prerogative, in the bargain."

Ormungandr ran between the fjord's fissured sides. Winding, iron-gray water led inland like a highway. Atop the cliffs, wildwood marched in thick ranks. Somewhere an aurochs bellowed like a lur horn. Felimid breathed the green scents of land, and felt better. After shaving, washing and donning his one fresh shirt, he felt even more renewed.

In the early afternoon, they came to a long, broad tongue of land poking down the middle of the fjord, dividing it into two strait channels. An oak pillar carved with beasts and runes indicated the right-hand one. The carvings moved slowly, unsettlingly, turning to look at the strangers.

Some miles further on, they reached an island capped by a small but massively strong timber fort. As they approached it, a huge rock hurtled towards them from the verge of the cliffs, furlongs ahead. Ataulf glimpsed the boulder as it flew, spun with an awed oath to watch it, and was spattered with water as the rock fell into the fjord two ship's lengths behind *Ormun-*

gandr. Odin, Tyr, the Christian god and Thor of the lightning were freely invoked. A second rock whirled up from the cliffs on the other side of the channel, and fell even closer.

"Stop, strangers!" a deep voice bellowed from the island. "Stop and anchor where you are, lest the rock-throwers sink you!"

"Onward!" Gudrun shouted to her men. "Onward! All oars, now! Bend, you dogs! Take us to that isle!"

Ormungandr surged forward like the great sea serpent whose name she carried. Ataulf chanted an oar rhythm in his ox's voice, ever faster. *Ormungandr* grounded on a tiny crescent-shaped beach of stones with an impact that sent unprepared men toppling like skittles. Her pliant spine and ribs absorbed the shock.

"Ashore, with your weapons!" Gudrun ordered. "Swiftly now, and spread yourselves out!"

Her crew took cover among the rocks. Gudrun herself trod ashore, bare of head, her hand on Kissing Viper's hilt. She stood arrogantly poised in full view of the dwarves manning the fort.

"I am Gudrun Blackhair!" she announced. "Will you talk, or is it blood you wish?"

"I bade you anchor!" roared the same voice that had spoken before.

"And I chose not to. The pebbles you tossed had some little to do with my decision. Now I came in peace, showing a white shield, and I'm not yet here in war. Your folk built my ship. I desire to have her refitted. What is your word on that?"

"Wait!"

Gudrun waited. A yellow pennant blew above the fort ere the unseen speaker's voice had ceased to echo.

"Yellow signals the stone-throwers to pause—for the moment," the voice explained. "The ship you call yours was made for King Oisc. I know. I helped to build it. Why do you have it?"

"I slew Oisc on the Narrow Sea," Gudrun answered frankly. "His ship is now mine."

"So? Aye, then, it matters not to us. We will do the work if you pay our price, and to that end you must speak with our king."

"For that I came here. When?"

"Now, if it pleases you. One man may attend you. The rest

must bide here on the strand with your ship. We have a boat.''

Now it was Gudrun's turn to cry, ''Wait!''

Striding into the brush, she held a swift conclave with her men.

''He wishes me to go to his king, taking one companion, no more. I'm minded to do so. They are a stubborn breed, these maggots of Ymir, and I will not otherwise get what I desire.''

''Suppose we take the fort, and strengthen our power to drive bargains with a few hostages,'' Ataulf suggested. ''Its walls are none so high.''

''No,'' Gudrun said. ''I've a notion there would be evil surprises for the man who tried to scale them, high or low. Look at *Ormungandr*; recall the pillar we saw. The same magicians built this little fort.''

''Besides, there are the giants who threw the stones,'' added a Dane by the name of Crow-Eyjolf. ''Do you wish to see them wade through the fjord, reaching to crush us?''

''Aye, so.''

''I heard tales of such, and they prove true. . . .''

''We are trapped whatever we do.''

''The rocks will sink us if we fly.''

Decius spoke sardonically through the edgy murmuring. ''Giants! Pah! It looked to me like the work of great catapults, sited on the cliff. The legions had such engines in Caesar's time.'' The bizarre jewel in his eye socket flashed mockingly. ''Giants or catapults, they can sink us if we try to leave without the dwarves' consent. So much is true. You mean to go, lady?''

''I've said it. I mean to go.''

''Then I wish to go with you,'' Felimid said.

Gudrun looked at him with interest and something more. ''Why, Bragi?''

''As a witness, lady, and because this belongs in your saga. Why am I with you but to see these things? And because it is possible, just, that the king of the red dwarves may lower himself to trickery in his dealings with you. The bardic sight can pierce any glamor or false appearance cast by magic. You may find me useful, if you are willing to take my word that what seems to be a footstool is in truth a chained wolverine.''

These were reasons for Gudrun to take him as her companion. She had not meant that. She had asked why *he* wished to go with her. Her mind suddenly unclear in the mist of Feli-

mid's words, she suspected that he had answered the wrong
question deliberately—yet she decided to accept it.

"Be it so," she said with a smile. "Let's discover what the
dwarf king's hospitality is like."

Although barely eight paces square, the fort could have
resisted any human onslaught. Logs adzed square and crisscrossed between supporting posts formed the framework of its
walls. Stony rubble filled the spaces. The gate was invisible
until it swung open, and then it lifted smoothly upward and
outward by some counterweighted wooden mechanism. When
Felimid and Gudrun entered, it closed as efficiently behind
them.

Within were ten squat, manlike beings about navel-high to
their visitors. Their hair color varied from rust red to sandy to
simple brown, but each bearded face wore a similar frown of
mistrust.

"Litt and Haugspori will take you to the king," growled
one who bore an axe. He indicated the two dwarves he meant.

Without speaking, they opened a hidden shaft which led to
a cave beneath the island, a cave lapping with water. A sturdy
boat was moored there.

"Enter," Haugspori said curtly, holding the boat steady.
With a faint grind of moving stone and a somewhat louder
splashing, the cave opened at its northern end. Daylight spilled
in, revealing a round grotto five paces across and two men
high, its dome carved with wavy festoons of weed and plump
fishlike faces.

The boat moved from the grotto with neither pole nor oar to
drive it. Behind them, the opening closed in the same disconcerting way it had parted. From without, there was no sign
that any cave existed.

"All this trouble and . . ."

"Sham," Gudrun supplied.

". . . crafty concealment, not to speak of needless magic,"
Felimid went on, determined to be independent in his choice
of words, "for one little outpost? It's too much. Suspicion
and the need to be secure can become madness. The stone-
throwers alone can protect this place, and there's no approach
but by water, if that forest stretches far."

"Leagues," Litt informed him. "Aye. You would like us to
grow careless, so that you might plunder us! Never will that

befall. We're thralls to none, and those who covet our skills must pay.''

He grinned unpleasantly through his dense beard.

The boat sped on, powered by neither muscle nor wind nor tide. It was the most delightfully fashioned little craft Felimid had ever seen, wholly dry within and sporting carved wave-curls along its sides. The prow showed the likeness of a whimsical seal's head. (Dwarves expressed humor only with their hands, it seemed.) Yet for all its merry appearance, the boat was strong, well balanced, and practical as a well-forged knife.

They reached the fjord's end. It opened into a wide expanse of water, orange light from the west slanting across its mirror stillness. A gust of wind, a patter of rain, dulled the surface for a time.

Felimid's gaze flickered and darted, taking in wonders. Broad-beamed houseboats and barges, lavishly carved, floated on the water. Timber cradles housed the forming ribs of two warships. Far above, the carved beam ends and shingled roof of a noble hall threw back the honey-colored light.

"I'd heard that dwarves live in stone halls quarried from the mountains," Felimid said.

"The dark dwarves do," Gudrun answered. "Their red cousins live in forests or by hidden arms of the sea, no less hard to reach, and they work in cloth, wood and leather. Do I speak the truth, fellow?"

"You speak the truth, woman," Litt said.

"I saw fine stonework in the grotto, none the less. Your folk did that?"

Litt shook his head. "We don't understand stone or metal well. Better than any men, aye, but that means nothing. Our carpenters go to the mountains, and the black masons come here in exchange."

They climbed a trail where the cliffs were low. At the top they saw fields of barley, wheat and flax, cattle grazing in green meadows, piles of seasoning lumber, and scattered cottages which to the eyes of the strangers were curiously built. In the outside world, dwellings so small were always squalid hovels, and neither bard nor pirate had seen true chimneys before.

Around the king's hall, instead of the byres and barns they

were used to, they passed large tanneries and a building with
open sides where cloth steeped in vats of colored muck.
Elsewhere, they heard the rattle and thump of what might
have been an enormous loom.

Everything had been made for folk four feet tall, or
thereby. The strangers met them, going about their business,
but no dwarf heeded their presence save with a sardonic
glance. Men and women dressed alike, in loose belted tunics
and breeches.

Gudrun murmured aside, "Have I grown half an ell?"

"Not unless I have too."

In the anteroom of the king's hall, they were required to
change their footgear. The felt slippers their guides offered
them appeared too small, but when tried they fitted to perfection.

"You've said nothing of our weapons," Gudrun challenged. "It's ill-mannered to wear them into a host's presence."

"We're concerned with truth and hard dealing here, not
foolishness," Litt snorted. "We bargain; we don't make you
welcome. Vindalf is our king because he's our hardest
bargainer and a great leatherworker. That's how we choose
our kings, by skill. No, wear your blades, and draw them to do
harm if you like. Your suicide is nothing to us."

"Have a care," Felimid told him, spuriously grave.
"Venom loosens your tongue wonderfully. It's the most talking you have done in one breath since we met, and I'm enchanted, my dear. You'll be confiding your triumphs in love
to me next."

Haugspori said nothing, as always. Gudrun made a faint
snorting noise which might have begun as a laugh before she
muffled it. As a mighty door swung wide and the two dwarves
went on before them, she said to her companion:

"Bragi, I'm glad you are with me. I like your lightness. Now
let us see what sort of cheery fellow their king may be."

They entered the feasting hall. Polished wooden tiles re-
flected their legs as they walked on the floor, and rich tapes-
tries which slowly moved and changed color adorned the
walls. An aurochs might have roasted in the fireplace. The
long tables had individual chairs instead of benches, made
with such craftsmanship that the bard repressed a whistle. His

native land held craftsmanship, the skill to create, in such respect that craftsmen and artists had privileges even kings did not possess.

"Look upward, my friend," Gudrun said softly.

She had glanced about the hall with a warrior's eye, not a poet's. Halfway between floor and rafter beams, a gallery ran around the walls on three sides, and up there in the shadows stood silent dwarves with ready crossbows.

Draw your blades if you wish, Litt had said. *Your suicide is nothing to us.*

He reached his king's chair. Three strong men could not have budged it from its dais. Dwarvish masters had fashioned it from black oak, walrus ivory and leather; carved owls perched on the back and martens writhed sinuously along the armrests, seeming alive enough to squeal and bite at any second, while curl-tusked, swag-bellied trolls upheld the seat, grinning and grotesque.

King Vindalf sat and examined the strangers. He wore no crown, only a beautifully tooled leather band to confine his rust-colored hair, wide leather trousers, a simple tunic and a belt matching his browband. The buckle was of gold, in the form of an intricately knotted snake.

For muscle he was like a small red bull. Felimid noted his arms, his shoulders and the wide, thick-fingered hands with their layers of callus. Yes, he was a leatherworker. Felimid's British friend Gavrus the saddler had the same huge hands, his fingers similarly marked by constant use of knife, awl and waxed thread.

"Lord, these would buy," Litt said.

"So?" Vindalf considered them. "I am Vindalf, king in this place."

"I am Gudrun Blackhair, Varek's daughter," the pirate said proudly. "This is Bragi, a harper, a skald, and my guest. He accompanies me by his own wish. It's I who would buy."

"First tell me your desire; then I will name the price."

"Do you remember a ship named *Ormungandr*? She's a serpent of war, and can carry eighty men. She was built here."

"She was," Vindalf agreed, "but not for you."

"No. I took her from King Oisc when I slew him. She suffered in that sea fight. I desire mast, yard and rigging for her, two sets of each; three sails; fresh oars and to spare; ample rope and cord for any future need. Complete refitting."

"Well said. That is straightforward, but what will you give?"

"I have gold and silver. I have fine beeswax, and furs." She described them. "The gold itself is enough for the work, but I will not haggle. I wish to make the bargain swiftly."

"You spoil the pleasure of bargaining. It should not go too swiftly." Vindalf rubbed his bearded chin. "So. So. There can never be too much gold; none the less, we suffer no desperate dearth of it. Furs we have. We're cunning trappers, and again we receive them in payment. King Othgar's throne of Zealand was made here, and our fee was all the sable and ermine he could pile upon it ere he took possession.

"I will tell you what gladdens us most, if you have the courage to hear."

Gudrun laughed in his face. "King, there is nothing you can say that I lack the courage to know!"

"Then good!" Vindalf roared, suddenly and loud. "Hear! Grief for mankind, that is what we would have! Gold is fine. Hides and wool and flax we do need, more than we ourselves grow. But always we know, to our joy, that men will break faith and slay one another for the wonders we make. As you slew Oisc, woman! As he gave us twenty captured warriors long ago, to sacrifice to the earth powers. Will you match that? Will you yield us a score of your own crew to be buried quick?"

Gudrun was not disconcerted. With utter scorn she said, "No, nor even one. Be glad you have crossbows aimed at me. Now, if twenty of my *enemies* brought here in bonds will content you, I can manage it."

"Doubtless," the dwarf king answered. "Yet there would be no anguish in that for you. Let me think further."

"Why do you seek the hurt of men?" Felimid asked.

"Why?" The dwarf king glowered at him. His voice thickened. "Your race is a plague. My people were lords of all these northern lands before there were tribes called Danes, Jutes, Norse or Swedes—aye, before the Great Ice melted or metalworking was known. You slew us, robbed us, drove us into remote places, and you seek our aid still when you hunger for riches or glory! Thus we turn your need of us against you. We fight you with your own lust for our treasures, and laugh when you slay each other to possess them!

"Well, are you answered, skald?"

"I'm answered, I suppose," the bard said, "but you have still to persuade or even impress me."

"No matter." King Vandalf's little, hot blue eyes smoldered. He leaned forward, his thick fingers working. "You say you will not give me any of your men."

"I take oath in Odin's name that I will not."

Vindalf almost smiled. "Odin is not worshipped here. Do you gamble?"

"Not with dwarvish dice . . . lord," Gudrun added, the courtesy both late and less than sincere.

"I hadn't that sort of gamble in mind. I propose a game of questions. I will ask you three riddles, and if you answer them all aright, you may have what you desire for no further payment. If you make but one mistake, *one*, your skin and all it contains is forfeit to me, and I will have it flayed from your body, and the heart cut from your breast afterwards."

Seven hags and a bath of lead awaiting you . . .

"No!" Felimid shouted. His voice rang with passion in the shadowy hall. He, the lazy, carefree one, unmoved by heroics, the detached and reasonable, had gripped his sword's hilt.

"Show an inch of that blade to the light and you are dead," Vindalf told him, smiling at his distress. "Remember the crossbows."

Gudrun stared at her companion. A certain understanding showed in her sea-gray eyes, but little of patience or sympathy.

"If I want a sword drawn, I have my own," she said. "Bragi, I'll decide for myself what to say to this—I agree—wicked offer. The gods know I might have expected it." Yet she had not, and her thoughts were tumultuous. One thing was sure. Only dwarvish skills could redeem *Ormungandr* from her crippled state. "What of my crew? They must have leave to depart, whatever else happens. You have no claim at all on them. You must accept this and swear to it."

"I shall."

"Cairbre and Ogma!" the bard broke in, tormented. "Will you play his game?"

"Bragi, that's my affair."

"So it is. But, lady, do not answer him yet. Have you any notable skill in riddling?"

"Oh, fair."

She lied when she made even that modest claim. Gudrun

had no gift for conundrums or word games; she could make
verses, after a fashion, but the simplest kenning left her baffled. Although quick-witted, she was neither subtle nor
equipped by nature to resolve hidden meanings. She dealt with
complicated knots by slashing through them.

"I'm better than fair," Felimid said, knowing that he
bought an equal part of her madness by saying it. "I deal in
words; it is my kind. Why, I've been instructed in trick questions, in double and triple meanings, from the time I was a
little boy, and put to thorough examinations by masters. At
the school of Suibni the *fili*,* there were times when I would
answer in five-layered allusion, and it scanning, if someone
remarked that the weather was fine. It became habit, so. Let
me answer these questions for you, Gudrun."

Gudrun's dark brows drew together. She was hopeless at
riddling, and knew it despite the bold face she had assumed.
To accept the dwarf king's challenge in her own person would
be to kill herself. Yet to appoint Felimid her proxy would be to
place her life in another's hands, and wait passively for him to
succeed or fail.

"What say you?" she asked of the dwarf king. "May he
answer for me?"

"I'll allow it," Vindalf said, gloating, "but he must share
your fate if he loses."

"Done!" Felimid snapped. "Three riddles of your own
devising, and if I answer them all aright, your people must
refit *Ormungandr* as the Lady wishes. If I make one mistake,
we both die. The terms of this foul charade are for me to ar-
range. Is it agreed by us all?"

"Terms?" King Vindalf scowled, and leaned forward further, looking still more rapacious. "The terms have been
named and set. There is no more to say."

"Oh, lord of the red dwarves," Felimid said courteously,
"no doubt I look simple—no doubt I have become a fool—
but I am not wholly bereft of my wits. We have a deal more to
settle yet. If I may outline it . . ."

* *A combination of judge, poet and diviner.*

III
Game of Questions

The functions of a bard were many. Often he must expound the law or stand witness to a royal treaty. As yet, Felimid had attained to the third rank of bard only, the seventh rank being the highest, and his legal training was scanty, but he did have some knowledge of such matters—not that Erin's laws resembled dwarvish ones. Their one similarity seemed to be the high respect they paid to craftsmen.

This matter amounted to a treaty. Felimid dealt with it as one, demanding sureties that Vindalf would keep his macabre bargain. Gudrun's crew must be told what was happening. (That in itself almost had them storming the dwarvish town, convinced their leader had been ensorcelled.) Some must be present as witnesses; dwarves of honor and place must go aboard *Ormungandr* as hostages; Gudrun must make her crew swear to release the hostages unharmed if she did forfeit her skin and heart. The terms were not settled for two days.

On the third day, Felimid went to the dwarf king's hall again. One-eyed Decius and Sighere the Frisian accompanied him. All yielded their weapons in the anteroom, for though the dwarves were no more concerned with formal manners than they had been previously, they now saw reason to be cautious. A man who has forfeited his life and knows it has nothing to lose by fighting. Felimid thought with a certain wry pleasure that if he failed to regain Kincaid, the curse on the weapon would bring the dwarves a deal of merited grief.

"Are you prepared?" King Vindalf asked.

"Sober, unarmed and with my wits about me," Felimid replied, masking his detestation. His heart thundered. "However, I do not see the lady."

"You will see her when the game of questions is done."

Felimid flushed, grew pale, and reddened again. Sighere trod forward, voicing an obscene oath.

"Are we to trust you?" Decius demanded.

"You have small choice," Vindalf told him. "Look about you."

The Spaniard had seen the ready crossbows almost as soon as he entered.

"I know your purpose, dwarf king," Felimid said, controlling himself while he sought mental balance. "You have named the game and its forfeits, and now you show there is no advantage you will not take, however miserable. You expect me to wonder where Gudrun Blackhair is, what you may have done with her, and lose our game through fretting.

"It may befall. The lady may die, and I with her. But I tell you this. Your people are doomed far more surely than we, and the fault is their own; it does not lie with others. My ancestors the Tuatha de Danann suffered defeat with weapons from foreign tribes, and some of their leaders fled beyond the world into legend as you are doing, but others chose to remain. Because of that I am here, walking the ridge of the earth freely, with Danann and Firbolg and Milesian blood in me, and none the worse for it . . . with a Spaniard and a Frisian for comrades, and about to contest with you on a Dane's behalf.

"As for you, you will bide here, hidden in your hole until you wither, for that has been your choice and it will bring you to your dreary end at last.

"Ask your questions, dwarf king; I grow tired of beholding your face."

The dwarf king's lips worked within his beard. Felimid had stung him. Behind the bard, Decius nodded with appreciation, while Sighere smiled grimly. Neither spoke, lest they distract him.

"Two horses, swiftest travelling," Vindalf said at last, "harnessed in a pair, and grazing ever in places distant from them. Riddle me that."

"I believe I can," Felimid answered after a moment's

thought. "You will lose the game unless you ask me something more difficult. They are eyes."

"Huh!" Vindalf frowned deeply, pondering. Lines deep as incisions appeared between his brows. "A harvest sown and reaped on the same day in an unploughed field, which increases without growing, remains whole though it is eaten within and without, is useless and yet the staple of nations. Riddle me that."

Cairbre and Ogma! I would ask for something more difficult. He hasn't denied me.

Felimid smiled confidently while he sifted the words for meaning. Born in Egypt or Constantinople, he would surely have been a theatrical performer. "Harvest" was plainly a metaphor; no grain or cultivated plant could be cried useless. Useless . . . and an unploughed field . . .

"You describe to perfection, so you do, skulls on a battlefield."

The dwarf king hissed. Felimid knew wild relief.

"A red drum which sounds without being touched and grows silent when it is touched. Riddle me that."

Felimid's wits deserted him. He felt as though he was falling with nothing to grip. A silent red drum? What, what, *what*? A vision of the shaman Kisumola splashing in the Narrow Sea, his magic drum beside him, filled the bard's racing mind. Scant help was there.

Long moments went by. Red, what was red? Fire—but fire made noise, and might not be touched with impunity. The sun? He could not be touched at all. Vindalf smiled gloatingly. The long hall was so silent that Felimid heard his own blood pulsing in his ears.

Blood! The pulse of his own red blood! He had it!

"It's nothing else but a beating heart you speak of."

Nothing else but Gudrun's stake (and his) in this evil game, so simple and obvious that it had nearly escaped him.

"Now unless you can show us the Lady, unharmed, I think you will soon receive word that our hostages are dying."

"You have won the game," Vindalf conceded. "Your life is your own again, and the woman is yours to claim. You have but to recognize her." He raised his voice. "Bring Gudrun Blackhair!"

She entered through a side door beneath the gallery, her hands bound behind her, an axe-bearing dwarf escorting her.

Instead of her kirtle and breeches, she wore a long crimson gown.

Behind her came an identical figure with a different armed guard, and another, and another, until nine stood in Vindalf's hall, each with a stolid attendant.

"Name her," Vindalf said, "and she is free."

"Another cheat!" Sighere raged. "By Njord of the Ships! We'll cut our hostages limb from limb for this, you spawn of maggots!"

"Be easy," Felimid said. A cheat, yes. It was illusion, magic which cheated the mind and senses, primarily the sense of sight. Bards learned how to see the reality behind such cheats. Felimid had gained that "bardic sight" when he was fifteen, in the course of his training; he had not boasted idly to Gudrun.

His gaze moved from one tall, black-haired figure to the next. Cairbre and Ogma and Earth-Mother Danu and Angus, patron of lovers, that gown—and what it covered! Felimid had never seen velvet in his life, but if he had, the sumptuous crimson fabric cut and draped so artfully on Gudrun's body would have made velvet seem shoddy.

He felt many things at once; relief that she was alive, a freshet of desire for her, delight, pleasure, anger that she had been so clad against her will—and, an instant later, disgust with the sort of mind that would think of clothing her so splendidly in order to kill her.

His sight melted the false seeming from all the others. Their figures wavered like reflections in disturbed water. Short, chunky shapes appeared through the fading glamor. Eight dwarves stood where eight semblances of Gudrun had been, but the ninth shape was unchanged.

"Give me a knife, if you will," Felimid said. When it was in his hand, he cut her free. Gudrun sighed deeply. She made no other acknowledgement, then, of what waiting with her life in another's hands had meant to her. Nor did she deign to touch her cord-marked wrists.

"Welcome to liberty, Blackhair."

She said low, "Bragi, I'm not gifted with words. I have none. But for this you may have of me whatsoever you ask."

To Vindalf she said scornfully, "You made a bargain, you cheated and took advantage, and still you lost. Are you as false in the letter as the spirit, or do you pay?"

"We will refit your ship," Vindalf said, stroking his beard.

"It will take a se'nnight or so. You and Bragi must be my guests here while it is done."

"King Vindalf," she said, "I'd as lief be a guest in a snake pit."

"Then release your hostages. It must be one or the other."

"Ha," Gudrun muttered. "I'd forgotten about them. No, they remain with my men until the refitting is complete—and for myself, I'll agree to remain here. But Bragi makes his own decision."

"Sure, and Bragi has," Felimid said. "I'll stay."

"I'll have my own clothing and war gear, too," Gudrun added. "And Decius and Sighere may go back and forth as they please, between me and the ship."

She slowly rotated her shoulders, manifestly hating the touch of the crimson gown.

"Very well," the dwarf king conceded. "It is agreed."

IV
The Begrudged Bed

Gudrun's legs trembled as she entered the bedchamber. It was slowly becoming real to her that she was not, after all, to be flayed alive and then suffer the excision of her heart. Sitting on the large, boat-shaped bed, with its coverlet of gray fox, she paid no heed to its richness.

Felimid did, though not with unstinted enthusiasm. "I'm fond of comfort," he said, eyeing the chamber's rugs and hangings and varnished furniture, "but rushes and sheepskin would suit me better, in a place where I was welcome. Never will we sleep in a bed more thoroughly begrudged than this."

"So I think too."

Gudrun's heart hammered. She had not shared a bed with any man since the dreadful two months in Ivarr's hall. However, she had often lain awake wanting one. By killing Ivarr she had freed herself from the burden of hating him; that night of vengeful blood and flame had had an effect like the lancing of a boil. The mark remained, and itched once in a while, but it was clean.

To Gudrun, the proof of that lay in the way she felt when she looked at a handsome man. Sometimes at a man who was not so handsome. She remembered one youth who had fought gamely with a spear in a village her sea thieves had plundered. She had allowed him life and freedom, and for a moment she had wanted to lead him aside and lie down with him in the first convenient place. Then the wind had blown from him to her, bringing with it strong evidence that he had never bathed in his life. . . .

There had been others who did not stink. But always in the back of Gudrun's mind lurked the knowledge that she could not lead her men from half a yard behind a pregnant belly. She had her fingers, as everybody did, and sometimes she took pleasure with women—and for her it did not suffice.

She had never thought of the most obvious thing. Jarl Ivarr had kept her in his own bed for twenty nights, and then given her to his men for a longer time. She had borne no child to any of them, which was fairly sure evidence that she could not.

Nor had it ever occurred to her that she dreaded lying with a man more than any possible result of it. She would have taken a lover at once if it had; a male lover. Gudrun did not stomach fear, in herself or in those who followed her. But what went unrecognized did not have to be faced.

She was having to recognize a number of things now. For instance, that Felimid was clean, and that she had known for some time that he desired her. Perhaps more than just desired. And that she welcomed it.

"Why did you take the risk?" she asked. "My purposes are not yours. If *Ormungandr* broke and sank in yon fjord, you'd go your way whistling. Why?"

It was a cue if ever the bard had heard one. He kissed her. She returned the kiss.

"The dwarves are not the only ones with a use for that wild heart of yours," he said. "But it's needful, if I am to get any good from it, that it stay where it is, within your ribs and beating to keep you alive. Why else am I here?"

And did you count on that? he wondered. *When you agreed to play Vindalf's game, on his terms, were you playing your own game with me?*

Now Gudrun's mouth was on his, her waist between his hands. Perhaps she had never willingly kissed a man in her life, but she had willingly kissed *someone,* that was certain.

Despite his urgent craving, the bard would not have hurried. Gudrun was the hasty one, hasty and demanding haste. Shuddering, she drew him between her legs; her hips moved, and moved, and moved, swiftly as she might have shot arrows on some besieged hilltop.

"Oh, faster, Bragi, faster. . . ."

"Easy, acushla," he said, puzzled, moving his hands over

her shoulders, down her arms. "We have time. You cheat yourself. . . . "

"No!" She sounded frantic. "Quickly!"

He obeyed, not knowing why, only that it had import for Gudrun. When he spasmed wildly, she cried out, neither in pleasure nor pain but in raw, blind sensation. She clutched him hard until their breathing eased.

"Angus the Young," he said dazedly. "Did you—"

"No, Bragi. No. I didn't . . . seek to." She rubbed her cheek against his, speaking through a tangle of the black hair her by-name celebrated. "It's like a high leap. If you tarry, if you look at the drop and consider, you dare not. This first time, I had to be swift. You understand?"

"And now?"

"Now?" She kissed his throat. "There is a high rock at Nykøbing I used to dive from. I'd come up laughing and swim for the far shore. That is how I feel."

She looked beyond him with a sudden appalled stare. "*Bragi, beware!*"

She rolled away from him, towards the side of the huge bed where her sword Kissing Viper hung, rolled with her shift bunched about her waist and a fine sheen of sweat on her legs, reaching for the hilt. As she moved, Felimid turned his head.

King Oisc stood within the door. He was dead, gray-skinned in death and dragging his mangled leg, teeth dry in his beard. He glared menacingly at the pair. Two henchmen from the bottom of the sea followed him. More purple than gray, bloated, white-eyed, drenched, they moved like corpses under water, unhurriedly drifting and floating. Their swollen fingers reached for Gudrun.

"Odin's eye!" she whispered. "What do you here, King Oisc? I slew you, but I sent you home. You died in battle; you were buried with the proper rites. You ought to be dwelling in Odin's hall."

"Gudrun," Felimid said, "they are not ghosts or liches. This is illusion, like those Vindalf cast of you. It's more of his spite."

"You say?" Teeth bared, Gudrun sprang from the bed, sword in hand. She slashed at the semblance of Oisc. Kissing Viper cut through unresisting air. The dead king's glare did not change. Gudrun spun, striking first at the nearer drowned figure, then the other and lastly the king again, with a swift glitter of steel. Nothing happened, save that she staggered from the force of her own slashes.

As she stared in disbelief, the three horrors passed from the chamber. Other figures appeared; hanged men with runes cut on their protruding tongues, dangling in midair, turning slowly. *This awaits you*, they seemed to say mutely. *All come to this end, or a worse.*

"Enough!" Gudrun shouted. Spitting oaths, she unbarred the chamber door and hurled it wide so that the crash resounded through the hall. She rushed to the gallery rail.

"Vindalf! King Vindalf, you malignant scut! Don't trouble with sendings! Face me yourself, if you have the courage!"

Echoes answered her.

"Where are you hiding, you dog, you coward? Come out! Step up here—*and face me!*"

Felimid had followed her, a blanket kilted swiftly about his waist for the sake of dignity. Because it was somewhat large, he had tossed the long end over his shoulder like a plaid. He carried no weapons. His gaze roved the gallery and the empty hall below, seeking deadly surprises. He found none.

"I'm weary of you!" Gudrun was ranting. "Leave me in peace! I swear by the heart of Odin, if you trouble me again with your foul tricks, I will burn your hall to ashes! Tonight! You hear me? I will burn your hall around you, you filth, and slay any bearded runt who tries to stop me! *No more of your bad jokes!*"

Behind her, Felimid had begun to smile admiringly. Bluster seldom impressed him; still, he had to own the magnificence of Gudrun's rage.

"I confirm and give backing to that, King Vindalf," he declared. Less loud than Gudrun's, his voice none the less carried as far.

There was no response. The hall held only darkness and silence. Shortly, Gudrun looked at Felimid with a shrug, and they returned to the chamber. It remained empty of ghastliness.

"Why?" she asked, baffled. "What in Helheim did he want with all that?"

"I do not know. Maybe to make us miserable, just. Maybe it was in his mind to haunt us night-long, each night we spent here, and him supposing we would sicken and cower." Felimid laughed. "He's a sorry little fellow, that one."

Gudrun also laughed, her fury turning to mirth. They rolled across the bed, laughing still between kisses, stripping each other naked with many diversions and games. No further sendings appeared.

"I'm not entirely ready to love you again so soon," the bard panted. "Are you still in such desperate haste?"

"No." She nuzzled him, growling softly. "I told you. I was outrunning terror before, and he lost the race. We can play to our hearts' content now. Ah, Bragi, Bragi, how I hunger for that!"

Towards morning, Gudrun lay on her belly across the bed, asleep, cheek on her forearm. Her face was to the bard.

The lamp burned, fed by clear oil. Its light shifted on the bard's face as he looked at his new love, marvelling. Wide-shouldered for a woman, and heavy of arm, she was none the less well shaped and smoothly muscled under the soft female padding. His glance slipped down the sleek channel of her spine to her lithe, strong waist, then delighted in her buttocks and thighs. If she had a physical fault at all it was in her thick ankles and broad feet.

She turned on her side to curl against him. He looked at the sleeping face that had once belonged to a hoyden archer and huntress of the Limfjord, and was now the face of a pirate chieftain as fierce as any roving the sea. Ten years separated the two. If the girl could meet the woman, would they know each other? For that matter, ten years from this night, who would he, Felimid, be?

Then Gudrun opened her eyes, and Felimid no longer cared about the next decade.

"How long have you desired me?" she asked, some time later.

"Since I saw you. I didn't know it, however, until after we 'scaped the Saxons."

"On my father's acres, you said nothing. You chased every woman but me, as I recall—and caught a number, too. Why? Were you affrighted, Bragi?"

"Wary. Pirates die young, and often their companions share their fate."

"Ha! How fair did your prospect of dying old seem to you, that day we met? Why, Bragi, for a man who affects to hate strife, you make more enemies than I! How long did your father live?"

"Not long at all. '*He would not concede to another's rede, nor that moon or stars outshone him, and he went to his end refusing to bend, with twice twelve years upon him.*' Yes, and he was a pirate, as you know . . . Fal. But his trade was not the death of him in the end. He ran away with another man's wife, and for him it was fatal, so."

"Then you are safer with me. I'm not wed."

Felimid smiled. "I'm unhandy at sea."

"I still have need of a skald. More of your love. Beyond that, if it pleases you . . . if you must be of use . . . be my messenger, my herald, and dicker for ransoms on my behalf. You have seen it done."

"Be Ratatösk to your eagle?" Felimid asked, naming the squirrel who was said to run up and down the tree of the nine worlds, bearing messages and insults between the eagle in the topmost branches and the snake among the roots.

Gudrun chuckled. "Why not? You have the qualities, do you not? A quick, nimble body, sharp eyes and ears, and—" she moved her hand down his belly, "—a fine large tail, carried high."

The nights and days passed. The dwarves worked. Felimid and Gudrun would rise, reluctantly, from their bed at noon, to see what progress the squat artisans were making, and to confer with Decius or Ataulf.

Ormungandr's two masts were shaped, and carried down the fjord to the island. Three great square sails formed on the dwarf women's looms. Gudrun and Felimid both wished to see the work, but Vindalf refused, claiming it must be done in secret.

"Are they after planning more treachery, do you think?" Felimid asked.

"It would not astound me, but if they are, shoddy workmanship will not be part of it. They take too much pride in their skill for that. The sails will not rip in the worst storm ever to blow. Nor will a mast snap."

"I have gold. I believe I'll ask them to make me some clothes."

"You peacock!"

The bard grinned and did not deny it. However, he was practical first. He had forester's gear made for him; breeches, tunic and buskins of pliant leather, with a long green cloak, both warm and concealing, a pair of walrus-leather boots trimmed with wolf's fur, high-strapped sandals for hot weather and a couple of leather kilts.

With less pleasure, he paid another craftsman to make him a battle tunic. The dwarf listened to his requirements and in short order fashioned a tunic of lamellar armor in walrus-leather, strengthened in crucial places with whalebone plaques. Lighter than Gudrun's mail shirt, it was almost as strong, and in the company he was keeping the bard knew he needed it, to wear between his flesh and angry strangers. His own people and most northerners fought bare-headed; still, on the dwarf's advice (as Gudrun had said, they could be trusted where craftsmanship was concerned) he had a leather and whalebone helm made also.

With the last of his money, he indulged the desires of the peacock Gudrun had called him. Shirts, tunics, breeches, shoes, belts, a scarf, a short riding cape and other oddments which pleased his fancy were made in short order, with a strong wooden chest to contain it all. The dwarves demanded high payment, as always; Felimid had to break the gold arm ring King Cerdic had given him in Britain. In the end he retained not one scrap of it.

"The men are encamped ashore," Decius said, in one of his first reports to Gudrun. "Ataulf is working them stupid with weapon-drill and practice so that they have no time for mischief, and the hostages are secure. Eight of us guard them night and day."

"Beware of illusion," Felimid advised. "A glamor cast during the day cannot last beyond sunset, and cast during the hours of night, it will fade at sunrise. Watch them in some reflecting surface now and again; a reflection shows the true shape at any time. *But don't be expecting magic simply because these fellows can work magic.* Ordinary guile is often better, and if they reach the forest by any means at all, you may bid them good day. Their woodcraft will be enough for them to escape you."

"They will not get out of our camp," Decius said.

Nor did they.

Oars, cordage and spare steering paddles came out of various workshops. The finished sails were displayed for Gudrun's approval. Two were dyed a simple gray-green for camouflage, but the last was for show. A raven with open, screaming beak spread black wings across a sail crimson as the brightest blood.

"Glorious!" Gudrun whispered.

Before they departed, King Vindalf had some further words for Gudrun.

"You are a Dane . . . lady," he said from his high seat, pausing sufficiently to make his point before he uttered the courtesy. "I have intelligence you may wish to share, or for which you may care nothing. The Dane-kings are not your friends; you slew a jarl of theirs once. Now the younger, Helgi, rowed east last summer to raid the Prussians, and he has not returned."

"This I had heard."

"I know what befell him. We have ways of knowing, here. The plundering was good, so Helgi and his men wintered in the east, but as they were returning in the spring, they met a storm and were shipwrecked on the Wendish coast.* King Helgi survives, a prisoner in a Wendish temple. They will offer him to their gods by drowning him on Midsummer Day. That time is close."

"It's very close," Gudrun agreed. "Why do you tell me this? What is the fate of a Danish king to you?"

"Nothing," Vindalf answered frankly. "I tell you because, if matters are left as they stand, only the king will die. If word reached his brother Othgar, and Othgar leads a fleet to rescue or avenge him, then many men will die, both Dane and Wend, whatever the outcome. *That* will please me."

"I believe you."

Vindalf smiled at her malevolently. "If you do not wish to know where the Dane-king is held captive, I will not tell you. But the intelligence is yours for the asking, and what you do with it then—something, or nothing—is your concern. Shall I be silent?"

"Nay, tell me, lord."

The dwarf king did.

"What will you do?" Felimid asked, on their last night in what he had described as "a thoroughly begrudged bed."

"I've not decided yet," Gudrun answered slowly. "I'd be

* *Modern Poland and East Germany. "Wend" is a Scandinavian term for the Slavs of the southern Baltic coast.*

chary of saying it between these walls in any case. We have
better things to talk of, Bragi, better things to do.''

"We have that, my love.''

They embraced and ran their hands over each other.
Gudrun laughed aloud with pleasure. She had enjoyed loving
Felimid more each night, and the joy was growing yet. To kiss,
touch and hold, couple and part and join again, was like unex-
plored country to her. She had barely waded ashore to it, and
she wanted to travel a deal further.

"Bragi . . . ''

V

"To Deliver a Royal Man."

The great ship moved down the fjord on her way to the sea.
This time, a mast and yard with a furled sail cast a shadow
over the port quarter. Spares of each, with oars, ropes and
tackle of various kinds, had been neatly stowed. *Ormungandr*
was ready, fully manned, and Gudrun's heart was joyous.
When her men lowered that sail and fastened the lines, one
light puff of wind would drive them awesomely fast where
they wished to go.

She raised her gaze to the carved orbs that were the figure-
head's eyes. They did indeed seem to stare through the impalp-
able walls which held the worlds apart. There were gates which
could be found and passed. She had spoken to Bragi of that,
among many other things, and he seemed to know some little
of other worlds. Why not? Who would know better than a
poet?

Odin, perhaps, who had hung on the tree nine days and nine
nights to gain knowledge of sorcery, and bartered an eye to
Mimir for further wisdom. He might enlighten his child. If
not—there were other ways, other wizards to ask.

Her thoughts veered. *Bragi, my lover. I am greedy and glad
of it! We tore ourselves apart only this dawn, and I would I lay
in your arms again! I am not patient, but nobody has yet
starved in a single day—or I do not suppose so. I haven't
heard of it. I might be the first.*

"And I the second," Felimid said.

"Did I speak?" she asked in astonishment.

"You did, so. You almost did not have to, mind. Your face shows all that you feel, my heart. You shout when angered and laugh when joyful. I'd like to hurry the descending sun myself."

"And can you?" she asked ironically.

"Never. The sun's made of fire, and I've no gift for fire sorcery. Call upon Loki."

To utter names like that lightly was reckless, and Felimid knew it, but he was too happy to care.

Beyond the mouth of the fjord, they ran on through the night, headed south along the Geatish coast, making for the Kattegat. Gudrun and Felimid rested side by side but did not sleep; for much of the night they talked quietly.

Once, Felimid shared a nasty thought with his lover.

"Had I such mange of the spirit as Vindalf suffers, I'd warn the Wends that you may be coming for King Helgi. By sorcery, he may be able to send them word faster than even *Ormungandr* can travel."

"Hmm." Gudrun's quick mind worried the problem briefly. "We cannot stop him. Best not speak of this to the crew. I'll talk to them, on the morrow."

In the morning, ashore, Gudrun showed what she meant by "talking." Felimid could speak eloquently, sing with skill and passion of heroes, lovers, gods and demons, yet like many bards he was always aware of how much had been invented, always a little removed from what he sang, always had a part of his tongue crooked sideways into his cheek.

Not so Gudrun.

Her enthusiasm blazed. She spoke of the Wendish people with loathing, of King Helgi as the noblest of warriors, and described the Wendish temple where he lay captive. She was especially graphic anent the rich plunder it contained.

"For myself, I am a Dane," she said proudly. "So are many of you. The brother kings are not on good terms with me; they outlawed me for Jarl Ivarr's slaying, but that is a matter between them and me, and I'd think it shameful that a pack of Wends should have King Helgi's life when I might prevent it. These folk are flying too high, and it's fitting that we clip their wings."

The Danes cheered. The southern men did not look glum, for they had followed Gudrun Blackhair into many fights, but neither were they hot to rescue a man whose predicament meant nothing to them. Tiumals the Goth stood forward.

"I am game," he said, "but I'd know more. Where is this temple, lady, how is it reached, how guarded, and by how many? How strong is the demon they worship there? If we attack, we should know what to expect."

"True. I'll tell you all that the dwarf told me. Then, if any here know differently—for I'd not be amazed if the dwarf lied—let me hear it.

"This temple stands on the most northerly point of the isle of Rugen. Cape Arkona is its name. It's not even fortified, the dwarf king said. It is guarded, and by three hundred warriors, the pick of all the Wendish tribes. Not that I reckon that to be any great distinction," she added, and they laughed with her. "Wends are poor fighters for the most part, and poorly armed. Body armor they do not have, nor even shields. But these warriors will be better equipped than most. We may expect them to have the best swords and war axes their people can afford, and they will be defending their holy place, which always stiffens a man's sinews. *But they will not have bows.* We can winnow them like grain before we come to close fighting."

"Good!"

"Thresh, winnow—and then grind!"

"And the demon?" Tiumals persisted.

"Pah!" Gudrun was impatient. "Are you afraid? The temple is sacred to Svantovit, a war god—but a Wendish war god is nothing to be concerned about. They have always lost to us who worship Odin. I know what I am saying, for I swore myself to the Father of Victories before I began roving the sea. Trust *him*, Tiumals—and keep your shield high!"

"I've a query," Felimid said, when the noise had abated. "Rich as this temple may be, we may find our choice lies between looting it thoroughly and bringing out the king alive —one or the other, as we cannot overwhelm the guards with numbers. What's our first object? And might we seek his brother's support on the way?"

There was much debate on these matters, and since they affected all Gudrun's men, and they were free, she could not simply give them orders. She argued, though, with force and directness.

"Now," she announced, when all who wished to do so had

said their say, "I'll make all the noise for a time. It's agreed
that calling upon Othgar would be bootless. He may be the
milder and more careful of the brothers, but even if he did not
attack us, he'd find the source of my knowledge untrust-
worthy—and time is mightily short. Midsummer's but a few
days off. Belike no ship but *Ormungandr* can travel fast
enough to reach Helgi before the Wends sacrifice him.

"We'll go to Rugen as we are ourselves. Three hours' rest
here, then down through the Kattegat and the Great Belt. See
to your bowstrings, all. You'll require them to be sound. We
go to deliver a royal man."

She did not rest in those three hours herself. Instead she
asked among the Danes of her crew for men who knew the
waters around Zealand, and on that basis appointed a new
steersman and lookout. That done, she exercised with weapons; sword, spear and bow, the bard her partner.

"I grow soft," she complained. "I've been seven days
idle."

"But seven nights active."

"Oh, that. Much use it is when a foeman is swinging a
sword at your head." Her voice's warmth belied the disparag-
ing words. "Bragi, I want you to love me."

"Let's walk around the point and swim in the cove."

"Yes."

Gudrun had always swum when she pleased, taking reasonable care to be private but not troubling too much about it,
and demanding the same concern from her men. Now she
spoke a brief word to Ataulf, which he acknowledged with a
nod.

"They are lovers," he remarked to his sword brother. "A
lump of unshaped clay could see it."

The Spaniard smiled. "Do you begrudge them?"

"I don't begrudge *her*—but if the harper treats her lightly,
I'll split him."

Felimid had looked to find the northern water too cold for
more than a swift dip, even so nigh to midsummer. The
shallow cove proved warmer than he'd anticipated. Although
he howled like a wolf when he first ran in, he was shortly
finding it pleasant.

They romped in the spray. Gudrun ducked him, her muscles
steely under the smooth curves, and Felimid twisted supplely
from her hands. He dove like an otter, to grip her heel and

calf. Her legs waved skyward; she gulped water and rose snorting.

Felimid was halfway to some nearby rocks. She stumbled after him, slipping on streamers of weed. Turning, she put her back against blessedly kelp-mantled rock and found purchase for both her feet. The water there was about navel deep.

Felimid turned towards her. She moved into his one-armed embrace while he gripped a jut of rock for safety. After some shifting experiments with balance, they came to a better arrangement.

"Bragi," she said against his neck. "I can do this. I'm free."

Her voice sounded strange. He did not understand at first, and so he listened.

"Years ago, when I began, when I was an outlaw on the heath . . . I trusted none, and I was wise. If I went into the bushes to make water I took a spear and knife. Even then, my companions skulked after me to catch me helpless, two or three together. It's hard to fight and kill with your breeches down. I learned, though. Strike without mercy and strike on the instant.

"We were desperate with hunger the night we burned Ivarr's hall. I don't think I had washed in two years. Had you placed me in a hut with a very rank goat, the goat would have come out choking for air.

"I'd no Ataulf then, no Decius—and for certain, no Bragi. Only myself. With food in their bellies, the wolves who followed me began to think of me as something female again. I saw that in their eyes. When I said we would take Ivarr's ships and go to Frisia, none disagreed, for they were thinking that between the narrow sides of a ship, there would be ways to come at me . . . but when we reached Frisia, I gave the orders on that vessel still."

"The lagoons of Frisia are far behind you."

"Aye. I can turn my back on the henchmen I have now. The best are trusty, and even the worst know they gain because I lead them. My reputation counts for much. Respect I can enforce; I go where I will and do what pleases me; I have what few dare strive for, freedom. Why am I weeping?"

"Relief?" the bard suggested. The treacherous lap and suck of the tide made them stumble. They clung close. "It's mighty brave you are, my heart's heart."

"Bragi, call me that sometimes, but not too often. I still want you to love me; can it be done right here?"

He grinned in her eyes. "We cannot know without trying."

That night, *Ormungandr* slid through the stretch of water called the Great Belt, to the west of Zealand. Wind blew in gusts, sharp with salt and bearing smells of earth and summer leaves from both sides of the channel. Clouds tumbled silver-edged before a moon nearing the full. Somewhere a fox barked.

"Othgar's royal hall is somewhere yonder," Gudrun murmured. "It's famed throughout the north. . . . I'm told he has other troubles than his brother's vanishing. Heorot is haunted by a monster from the fens, and none can prevail against him. Well, if we bring King Helgi back, a warrior of his strength should rid the land of that pest." She chuckled softly. "If Helgi's fate is to die despite us, I may attend to that useful murder for him."

As it befell, she and King Helgi were both to be forestalled by a Geatish prince who had arrived in Zealand that day. It was doubtless well that Gudrun had not put in there, after all. The same place could not have contained them both.

While Gudrun's men rowed silently by Zealand, a black albatross landed in the courtyard of Svantovit's temple, on the isle of Rugen, to speak harshly in human words, calling for the chief of Svantovit's nine wizard-priests. It spoke with the voice of Vindalf, the dwarf king.

The next morning, *Ormungandr* reached the isle of Fehmarn. Because it lay so close to the German coast, the folk who lived there were Saxons, but they were not likely to take word of Gudrun's presence to Edricsburg; that town lay on the far side of the neck of Jutland. Besides, the fishermen and crofters of Fehmarn did not recognize *Ormungandr* as Gudrun Blackhair's ship. They ran away to hide without waiting to learn whose ship it was.

One old man with a twisted leg had not been able to run. Ataulf brought him before Gudrun. She considered his wrinkled face and toil-distorted but still tough frame.

"Do you know these waters?"

"I've fished them all my life, lady," he answered. "I know the tides, every current and rock."

"I'll have you guide this ship to Rugen, then."

The hard old fisherman flinched. Ataulf gave him some

dwarvish ale for which he had bargained while Felimid and Gudrun were concerned with other things. The fisherman's eyes glowed as he swallowed.

"Worth some risk, is it not?" Ataulf said with a grin. "Now, what is your name?"

"Tegg, lord."

"A cask of that, if you guide us."

Tegg lowered his eyes. He was thinking, Felimid guessed, that he could scarcely refuse.

"Winters are cold," the fisherman said. "Will you add fur and cloth to the ale?"

"Done," Gudrun said at once. "And a gift from the plunder of Svantovit's temple, if we take any."

"The temple!" Tegg repeated, aghast. "Faring to the island is bad enough, but the temple? Half the Wends are wizards anyhow, and the nine priests of the temple are among the worst."

"If they need fighting men to defend them, fighting men can slay them," Gudrun reasoned. "I will go there, old man, and you will guide me." She raised her voice. "Let's all drink while we may."

They broached the casks. Men praised the dwarvish ale without reserve, and in the same breath consigned its brewers to Helheim. When every throat had been soothed, Gudrun spoke again.

"It's thirty leagues to Rugen, and three days to midsummer," she said. "*Ormungandr* can take us there in one. Now, we cannot hide unseen within swift striking distance of the temple, and I have planned the raid for an hour or two before dawn, so we will leave this place at midday. Gear yourselves for fighting before we push out.

"And one thing more." She drew a tense breath. Although it was not in her nature to be coy, she did not know how her words would be received. "Bragi and I will take our rest aboard the ship. We can do without company—so well that the man who disturbs us will have an arm broken. And should one of you grin, I'll break his neck. I'm hoping you understand me."

Beside her, Felimid smiled, amused, one thumb tucked behind the buckle of his sword belt. Gudrun's raw belligerence betrayed how unsure of herself she was in such a situation. Yet looking over the crew, he saw no signs of anger or jealousy.

Some amiably knowing nods and—despite Gudrun's blustered warning—grins, marked the limits of reaction. No, not altogether. Among the Danes, who had not known Gudrun long, Felimid thought he saw a sneer or two.

"You are better at fighting speeches, my beautiful," the bard said. "Now I'll be less fierce, but equally plain. In the dwarf king's dismal hall which I am glad to have left, I became the lady's man, and she my woman. There is no hiding from any with eyes that we have fallen in love. And as we lie together, so we will fight together."

Ataulf the Visigoth stood forward, a drinking horn in his brawny hand.

"We are your men," he said. "We row and fight for you. Smooth down your feathers, raven of a hundred battles. It would be a bad business if we could not wish you joy, and drink to that, without your taking it amiss."

A great, unanimous roar of "*Skal!*" panicked the sea birds. Those pirates who happened not to have full horns or cups, filled them swiftly and repeated the toast. All then drank a third time for luck. Such was the drinking of Gudrun Blackhair's mating cup, swift and unceremonious on her way to a reckless raid—and all the wedding she desired.

VI
Battle and Sacrifice

A temple guarded by three hundred warriors and nine
wizard-priests was, to Felimid's mind, a place to approach
with more caution than they were showing. He'd have preferred for taking the place a plan less raw and swiftly invented.
To that end he would willingly have done the thing he had rejected when Ataulf proposed it, and visited the island to spy.
They had only Vindalf's word that the Dane-king Helgi was
there. The value of knowing it with certainty before they went
in would be immense.

Unhappily, there was no time. When they reached the
island, midsummer would be two days off. Besides, the people
of Rugen spoke a Slavic language the bard did not know even
slightly.

Differences of spoken language were no bar to the air elementals. They had not devised speech—men had done that—
but air carried it. Felimid had often heard tidings from those
beings and would have questioned them now, save that it was
useless. Rugen, scene of the events which concerned him, lay
thirty leagues to the east, yet the wind at present blew con-
sistently from the west. News from the neck of Jutland was of
no tactical use to him.

In blowing towards Rugen, of course, the wind would carry
Ormungandr there like a winged dragon, but it might also bear
tidings to the nine wizard-priests of Svantovit, if they knew
how to hear and interpret its message.

Felimid wished he knew clearly what sort of magic these Slavic wizards practiced. Did it derive from fire, earth, air or water? Were they shamans like Kisumola, skilled in divination and in evoking spirits? Were they perhaps the darkest kind of sorcerers, drawing their power from unnatural, monstrous acts? Did they revere sun, wind, rain and trees, like the Druids—and could they, like the Druids, summon fire, mist or madness to confound their enemies? Or did they practice another kind of magic of which he was wholly ignorant?

Lacking a way of discovering these things, he did not harrow his companions by talking about them. He clad himself in his walrus-leather tunic, instead, and chose a few slender, narrow-headed javelins for the nearing fight.

One came sooner than he had expected it.

They were sailing with the west wind behind them, a wide bay to starboard and the isles of the central Danish realm to port. On that course, they met two large war boats coming from the northeast. They had no sails; like all manmade vessels then in use on the Baltic, they were flat-bottomed and powered by oars alone.

Hailed by the strangers, Gudrun answered with courtesy through her spokesman and approached them. With an expert's eye she appraised the two ships, their arrangement of strakes and rowlocks and the way their crews handled them.

"What men are you?" she asked, assessing their strength at half a hundred men in each ship. This was professional habit on her part, no more, as she did not wish to fight; she was saving her strength for Svantovit's temple.

"We are Saxons," answered a big man with a mouse-colored beard, from the nearer vessel. "You are some mighty chieftain, I see, perhaps a king."

Gudrun corrected his mistake anent her sex. "I am Gudrun Blackhair, once of the Limfjord in Jutland. I see by your shields and the red wounds among you that you have lately fought, and since you come from the east you must have been plundering. I'll not ask what you have won—"

"Ask if you will," the big man interrupted, with a laugh. "I do not fear to tell you. I, Withhad Engwal's son, count myself well able to hold what I have won."

"That is good to hear," Gudrun answered, "for if you have not taken so much plunder that your ships can hold no more, you may care to join me in a venture of mine. I'd never extend such an invitation to one I thought a timid man."

"I received a blow on the skull in the fighting," Withhad said. "My head buzzes with it yet. I'll draw nearer, by your leave, so that I can hear you better."

Ataulf snorted. "Here's trouble, my bucks. Spit on your hands. Butter in his mouth and treachery in his heart, or I don't know Saxons."

"Draw nearer, by all means," Gudrun agreed. "I ask whether you are determined to pass on, or whether you would care to join me in a raid—and you will have to decide quickly, for time presses."

"I'll not force you to wait, bitch," Withhad told her. "*Attack!*"

Saxon oars dipped, and the two ships rushed at *Ormungandr*. Her crew had been expecting it for two hundred heart-beats or more. Danish and Gothic bowmen sent a hissing volley among Withhad's rowers even as their own heaved on the oars, grunting with effort. Gliding through the blue sea like a shark, *Ormungandr* swam out of the closing trap and turned back before the Saxons could respond.

A second flight of arrows sang almost straight up, to drop like a sleet of death among Withhad's men. One rower stared briefly at fletching which vibrated before his eyes, and died before he comprehended that the shaft was buried at a narrow angle in his chest. Another man toppled with his bare head transfixed, and thrashed violently—for a while. A third flight followed closely.

Ataulf chanted instructions to Gudrun's rowers. They bent their backs, making the great ship fly. She rushed against the quarter of the other Saxon ship, struck, and smashed its steering oar. Strakes broke apart; the ship lurched. Men were hurled over the port wale like toys.

Felimid cast two of his javelins with care. Each found a mark. Then he heard Gudrun's voice give an order, and her pirates pushed clear of the damaged ship. Now the long serpent named *Ormungandr* turned upon Withhad's vessel.

They were too close now for bows. The ships exchanged volleys of spears. Grappling hooks flew. The bard threw his last javelin and drew Kincaid.

Gudrun screamed, "*Odinnn! Hai, Victory Father!*"

"*Erin!*" Felimid shouted. It was the first battle cry that sprang to his mind, and like many a man before him, he found

that a lusty bellow gave him power. He was among the first
dozen to board the Saxon.

A din of clashing metal spread across the sea. Shields
boomed. Felimid leaned into the Saxon line, feet braced and
shield high, moving it just enough to ward him from thrusts
and cuts. Kincaid shuttled around the shield's edge, mostly
working above it or on the sinister side, but occasionally darting from beneath it to hamstring a foeman's thigh.

Gudrun fought with reckless savagery, shrieking like a
falcon, smashing knees and faces with her shield even as she
smote with Kissing Viper. One-eyed Decius plied his own
sword as Rome's Spanish legionaries had done in former
times; skillfully, with stubborn valor, his teeth bared in a ruth-
less grin. Ataulf swung the long axe he favored for such work.

The Saxon shield wall held firm along their ship's side.
Felimid drove Kincaid into a bearded throat, and as that
Saxon fell, two more thrust their spears at him. The bard
crouched behind his shield; he had no space to do anything
else. One spearhead thudded into the double thickness of
linden wood. The other flashed by his head. While the first
spear remained embedded, he chopped through the shaft and
lunged, extended, ramming Kincaid's point into the yelling
face of the man before him. He toppled backwards, now yelling louder.

An axe came down on Felimid's shoulder. The dwarvish
war coat saved it from breaking, and he hardly felt the blow in
his fighting heat.

He buried his sword in another Saxon neck, laid open an
arm which spurted red, and engaged the Saxons who pressed
forward to close the battle line. Legs braced against the
bulwark, he sent Kincaid flashing across the rail. His unusual
practice of thrusting served him well, as always. Men never expected the point of a sword, only the edge.

On *Ormungandr*'s far side, Gudrun's archers continued to
shoot at the damaged Saxon craft so that the men in it might
not come to their comrades' aid. The Saxons were no bowmen, and swiftly learned to regret it.

Their line weakened suddenly. Decius slew a Saxon, and as
that man slumped across the rails, the one beside him swung a
blade at the Spaniard, but his blow never landed. Felimid,
leaning far over in an extended lunge, drove Kincaid through
the Saxon's leather-clad side. He sprang over the rails into that

breach, striking with his shield-rim as he went to break the neck of one man who resisted him, and sliding his sword downward through the throat of a second. A third cut at him as he dropped into the Saxon ship. Ataulf's long axe spoiled the fellow's aim and broke his spine besides.

Seeing her men breach the Saxon shield wall some yards away, Gudrun fought with doubled fury. She slew a man, sent him lurching back against a comrade with his face a ruin and a terrible, gurgling shriek bubbling past the remnant of his jaw, and then fought the man who replaced him. Waddico the Goth thrust and stabbed at her left; chestnut-haired Sigar, who had come to challenge her over the death of a kinsman and ended by swearing to follow her, handled another pike at her right.

Now the Saxon line was breached in two places. Gudrun's men rolled it up ruthlessly. Sigar, his pike broken, drew a heavy seventeen-inch knife and used it with wicked skill. In the confused press of the infighting that followed, it served him better than a sword.

Felimid had been trapped with a knot of other men near the Saxon stern. His shield, battered and chopped to pieces, was of no more use. He cast the fragments at his nearest foe, ran the man through the belly when he slipped in a stream of blood, and found himself holding a small axe in his right hand a moment later. Where he had found it he did not know. He did not remember snatching it, but he had it.

He used it. In the bloody confusion, he fought until he lost the axe, fell sprawling across a fallen man who was not yet dead, and felt other men trample them both to come to grips —which belike was all that saved him from being skewered where he lay. Struggling to his knees, he saw a mangled arm dangling from a thwart, and hanging on that arm an intact shield. He seized it, pulled it free. The owner of the ruined arm shrieked like a demon.

A spear in two hairy hands was driven at his chest. He struck it aside with Kincaid and punched the conical shield-boss into his attacker's belly. The man staggered, gasping, and Felimid cut across the proffered neck.

The ship was less congested now. He had space to move, and his agility served him better. A badly wounded Saxon lumbered after him with an axe, but Felimid saw him from the corner of an eye and spun, his whole body behind Kincaid's scything arc. The rising axe continued to rise, the Saxon's severed hand still on the handle. He died before he had time to understand his loss.

The other Saxons were surrendering now. Their weapons fell to the deck as they called for quarter. Few remained standing.

"Bind them," Gudrun ordered. "Swiftly! Then follow the other ship. It cannot flee far, and I crave the plunder of both."

She was right; the ship did not flee far. With its steering oar smashed, its planks sprung and *Ormungandr* in pursuit, it had no chance. The crew had been reduced by arrow fire to thirty hale men; Gudrun's archers reduced it further, then grappled, boarded and dealt briskly with those who still resisted.

Thirty-three Saxons survived the battle altogether. Withhad was not among them.

"He didn't lie when he said they had won booty," Ataulf declared. "Look! Women! There is gold and slaves! A deal of gold!"

"Gold!"

"The best loot of all!"

"And women with it!"

"They must have raided Bornholm," Crow-Eyjolf opined. "That island has gold in plenty. It's well defended, though. I'll wager they rowed there in greater strength than they came away."

The plunder was thirteen score *solidi*, gold coins received in trade from the south, six of the round pendants called bracteates, and a number of sword-rings, brooches and pins. There were also eight captive women who had huddled under thwarts during the battle. The pirates whooped to see them, and called out the greetings of their choice as they were herded aboard *Ormungandr*.

Gudrun's men counted the gold while she tallied their losses. Eight were slain, thirteen hurt so sorely that they could not fight. A spear had gashed Felimid's thigh.

"Make for land," Gudrun said. "Bring the Saxons."

Land, by then, lay a couple of miles to the south. It was forty to their destination of Arkona on the isle of Rugen. The bard scarcely wondered why his lover chose to turn aside at such a time; he assumed, without thinking deeply about it, that she intended to set the Saxons ashore alive instead of drowning them. It was what he would have done. His mind was more upon having his wound cleaned and his thigh bandaged, and it hurt.

The pirates who remained hale were dicing for order of precedence with the already battered women. They might revere Gudrun and make her almost a goddess, but clearly they did not extend that regard to others, and Gudrun did not require it—for she would not have remained their leader long if she had.

This, and the recent slaughter, made the bard feel sick. Jutland had been more to his taste, and even the malice of the dwarves, because he had had the pleasure of outwitting it. Now the crimson truth of the pirate life which he had been foolish enough to forget had been hammered home to him again. He did not like it.

He was about to hear a thing he would like far less.

They sailed on a reach till they came to a deserted strand. Behind it stretched the ancient, untouched forest, all but impenetrable. However, Gudrun had no need to go deeply into it.

"Take the Saxons ashore," she said, "and find me an ash tree, great and tall."

Felimid heard her say the words. His head whipped towards her as though turned by a violent blow. "Gudrun, what will you do?"

She looked at him. She might have been, not a different woman to the one who had held him in the sea or embraced him in the dwarf king's begrudged guest bed, but some wholly different order of being. Her face was like a carving, her sea-gray eyes fixed on some unalterable purpose. She stood with blood clotted darkly on her mail, her shoes and arms, and seemed not to perceive him as someone in the same world as herself.

"What I swore to do long since," she answered. "I took these men in battle, and they belong to Odin. I will give them to him."

Felimid whitened. When King Oisc hunted him down, he had been moved to satire and mockery, though death had stalked very close, and when the nicors swarmed out of the sea, revulsion had only nerved him to fight better. But he whitened now.

"Gudrun, you cannot!"

"Stay aboard, if you have no stomach for it. I will not think the less of you for that. But there is the Wendish temple to take, and instead of gaining allies I have lost men. I will need Odin's favor as I never have before."

"By the gods my people swear by!" Felimid burst out. "I will think considerably the less of you if you do this thing!"

"Be quiet, you whimpering pup," Ataulf said, striding stiff-legged to face him. "This is not to my taste either, but Blackhair is my chieftain, come fair, come foul. If you are not prepared to be her lover on those terms, then you chose the wrong woman—and chose her knowing it! Stay aboard, as she says. You will not sway her."

"Do not meddle, if you please, Ataulf." The bard thrust Ataulf aside and went to Gudrun. He said passionately, "Gudrun, if you do this thing, all that's between us will end when it has barely begun. It must. Had you wiped out these men when they attacked us, I would not shudder, but this—making them a sacrifice to a god worse, more foul than any other—I cannot stomach it."

"You knew from the beginning that he's *my* god," she said. "Bragi, I'll talk of this to you later . . . I see that I must."

"After it is done, there will be no purpose to talk," he said in anguish. "Set them free, Gudrun."

She shook her head.

The Saxons went ashore to their deaths unafraid. They too were children of the one-eyed god, of the rider on the eight-legged horse, lord of the spear and the gallows. Such sacrifices as this were common in war, or after sea battles, and made in various ways.

Beneath a huge ash tree, Gudrun unsheathed her sword, holding it aloft in both hands.

"Father of Victories, I give you these men. Let me win the fight I go to, whether I live or die. All those spirits my sword casts out of their bodies I dedicate to you. And mine, when you appoint the time and place I must fall."

Her men made nooses and hanged the Saxons. Most were ritually speared as well, while they dangled in the wind. The great ash creaked with the weight of its fruit. Gudrun scattered her share of the gold among its roots, and led the way back to *Ormungandr*.

Despite Gudrun's promise to talk to him, neither of them, Felimid nor Gudrun, said anything more. The west wind filled

Ormungandr's sea-colored sail again, speeding them to Rugen. The sky had clouded, and to the bard the water was the color of curdled blood, foul with the stink of death, where sluggish monsters wallowed. This was not the bardic sight, a perception of the truth behind a deliberately cast glamor, but the reverse, a fanciful vision of what was in his own heart. Felimid knew it.

But blood there had been, and blood was to come.

VII
Out of the Sea

Dcheko had not trusted the words of the black albatross which had flapped into the temple courtyard in the night. A wizard himself, he had known the bird for a spirit sent out of another wizard's body, even before it had declared as much. He listened to its warning, and while he did not believe it at once, he sought his own auspices.

In the morning he summoned his subordinate wizard-priests. All wore flowing hair and beards, long full-sleeved tunics worked with zigzag patterns, figures of gods, horsemen, beasts, birds, warriors, fires and trees in lavish profusion, headbands and cinctures still more richly embroidered, and certain talismans of power. Yet their faces were the surest badge of power drawn from sources other than human. These men had spoken with demons and reached into the dark, devouring belly of the earth. Among the darkest wizards in the Baltic lands, they were also reckoned powerful.

They gathered below the carved beams of their temple, facing the towering statue of their god. Svantovit's four grim faces looked in four directions. He held a bull's horn filled with wine in his right hand. Beside him hung an enormous sword, a jewelled saddle and bridle, and a rich battle banner. Behind him a sacred white horse stamped in a stable which was part of the temple.

Ranged in a semicircle, the lesser priests raised their arms and bowed their heads before the statue, chanting. Dcheko

146

bowed low three times, his beard brushing the temple floor. Moving forward, he lifted the bull's horn from Svantovit's carved hand, and looked within.

The wine had turned dark and thick. It stank like decaying blood.

Dcheko's face might have been hewn from the same timber as the god's. "Now, my brothers, ill fortune hangs over us," he said, "but lead out the divine steed, and have our company of heroes set spears in the earth, and we will take other tokens."

In a forest-girdled meadow by the temple, the warriors planted their spears in long rows. Two of the wizard-priests led Svantovit's sacred horse from the temple. White as new milk, he belonged to none but the god and had killed a bear with his hoofs.

Trotting between the spears, he cleared them easily for part of the course. Then, for no manifest reason, he kicked out with his heels and fouled two spears, knocking them awry. Further on, his white shoulder brushed a third, and near the end of the course, his near front hoof caught another. As he returned, one of the leaning spears he had touched fell nearer the ground, then tore out of the turf completely, to lie flat.

"Indeed, we are threatened," Dcheko said bleakly. "I believe the black albatross now. Yea, but trouble cannot come if those who would bring it perish in the sea. My brothers, let us join our power and make a *bogatyr* of fishes to destroy the woman Blackhair and her ship."

The ship in question was then at Fehmarn. The master priest and his "brothers" were a full day in making their magic, and before it was complete, Gudrun had met and fought the Saxons. That delayed her; the sacrifice to Odin delayed her more. The nine wizard-priests might have lacked the time to weave their sorcery else.

But Fate granted them the time.

Ormungandr's crew rowed her across a sea brilliantly lit by a yellow moon. In the nearly landlocked Baltic, the farther east they travelled, the less salt grew the water beneath them. Accustomed to the brine of the wide ocean, the serpent ship grew fretful; she creaked her timbers in protest for the first time that any man aboard her remembered.

The fisherman Tegg squinted at the stars. "Lady, you will not reach the temple before dawn, however your men row," he predicted. "Not in this ship nor any other."

"How if a strong west wind rises for us again?"

"You know your ship better than I," Tegg said dubiously. "It's nine or maybe ten leagues to Rugen yet. That's my best guess."

"And sixty hale men to fight three hundred when we reach it. I reckon three of my rovers to one lubberly Wend, but that is still heavy odds. They may even know I am coming to raid them. I need a new plan."

The same thought was in Felimid's mind. Shaken and bruised by Gudrun's blood sacrifice to Odin, it was a mind which none the less must be active. The west wind had died. That had prevented him from asking news of the east from the air elementals. Now the night was stirred by breezes so slight and contradictory that even for *Ormungandr* they constituted a calm.

Felimid undid the buckle of his sword belt and put the weapon aside. He drew the harp Golden Singer from her bag. Her strings shone yellow as the moon, and when he plucked them with his nails, they sang like fine steel. None who heard the sound ever believed those strings could truly be gold. The art and the sorcery of working pure gold to that tensile strength had gone from Erin. Nowhere else had it even been discovered.

His fingers leaped, plucking, striking, making music for swift wild dancers not shackled to the weight of a fleshly form. They heard and drew close. Only the bard saw them as they danced on shifting currents of air. Like huge dragonflies, they dipped and hovered, or skimmed the wave-tops like insects on a river.

Felimid spoke to them in the secret language of bards. The sylphs answered from the sheer pleasure they took in words; answered in riddles, ornate figures of speech, which would have been maddening to any normal, practical man working against time. They did not madden Felimid. He unravelled the spider-web intricacies, spun others of his own in response, and took pleasure in the game. But always he held to his object of learning what he wanted to know.

He harped; the sylphs danced, flickering and swift.

At last one dipped close to him. It had altered from the shape of a gauzy insect to a mask centered in a mass of streaming hair. The mask was blank but for delicately pared eyeholes and mouth. It spoke to him with the fleshless clarity of a flute blown from glass.

Then it abandoned the form it had briefly held and gusted about the ship in exuberance, stippling the sea. Felimid slowed the pace of his intricate music with relief. For all his skill, he was made of flesh and bone. His hands pained him.

Air elementals never allowed for the limitations of solid matter. One met them on their terms or not at all. That meant a mental and oral dance sustained at the speed of the wind, and if one could not sustain it—if one bored them—they were apt to vanish.

For a pensive while he harped something desultory and slow. He had the knowledge he sought, but had not decided whether or not to share it. Suppose he lied, and said there was no foreign captive on Rugen? Gudrun trusted him. Like as not there would be no raid.

He replaced the harp in her bag. Gazing across the brilliantly moonlit water, he mulled over the notion. The stranger in the temple was nothing to him, and if the raid was not carried out, lives would be saved, perhaps including his own. Gudron's reckless blood-spilling wearied him, and he owed her nothing.

Untrue. He owed her honesty, if no more than that.

His musing was suddenly broken. Barely a spear's cast ahead, something made a hero's leap out of the sea. *Whale!* Felimid thought, for at first he could conceive of no other fish so huge. Then, while still it rose through the moonlight, his brain accepted what his eyes had seen; the lean, compact body, long as the ship, the distinctive head with its ramlike snout, the mottled sides and powerful tail—a fish's ribbed tail, not the horizontal flukes of a whale.

And still it was there, before him. Only now had it reached the full height of its hero's leap. Streaks of water hissed by, hurled by the whipping tail. Some drops of spray which struck Felimid's arm stung like hail.

The monster dropped, its savage jaw snapping at the sea which received it. A watery blossom of mellow gold bloomed three men high in the moonlight. The tail lashed, driving the great fish deep.

All in a moment, all in a year.

"*Pike!*" Felimid shouted. "*Ware pike!*"

It rose under the ship's keel and virtually shouldered

Ormungandr aside. The ship lurched far over, to gulp water across her shield rail. Crewmen toppled into the sea, roaring. Some of the wounded were among them. Hemming the steersman bore down on the tiller of the huge rudder oar, raising the blade high, and in a display of presence of mind and astonishing strength both, brought its edge smashing down on the monster's head. Felimid glimpsed the distinctive snout again.

No use to declare it impossible; a pike it was. A fish of lake and stream at large in the sea. The most ferocious of all fish, and a monster in size.

He clutched the shield rail as the pike's tail slammed *Ormungandr* aft. Eyes wide, he saw it turn towards a byrnied man struggling in the sea, saw the great jaw snap and half an arm fall away while the rest of the hapless pirate—was gone, taken at a gulp.

"Spear me that child of Hel!" Gudrun cried. She herself had taken a bow, her seldom-used siege bow of Byzantine steel. In her anger she drew it with ease. A long arrow flew. Its narrow iron head, made for piercing body armor, sank into the monster's backbone, and Gudrun shot twice more as quickly as she could loose. The Gothic and Danish bowmen followed her example.

Bending like a bow itself, the pike rushed at *Ormungandr*, two dozen arrows sprouting from its back. All the violent driving power of its tail hurled it onward.

Men threw spears of several kinds. A narrow-headed javelin pierced the pike's left eye, to lodge in the bony socket. Its armored snout rammed the ship, and her sides groaned as with a living voice. Foul splintering noises smote the men's ears.

Gudrun failed to hear. She had been steadily firing with one knee braced on the gunwale, and the impact toppled her over. She struck the water heavily; her prized siege bow dropped from her hand.

Ataulf gave a yell and sprang into the sea himself, gripping an axe. Seizing a spear, the bard followed him.

Gudrun floundered on the surface in two and a half stone of silvered mail. The pike rushed at her. She ceased kicking, and let her war shirt take her down, out of the path of the voracious jaws.

The pike turned, seeking her. Ataulf caught a fin, held it for his life and chopped into the mottled side with his axe. The armor of scales gave way slowly. Ataulf, half drowned, clung grimly with one tough hand and smote with his weapon. Now he had cut through the steely scales, and layers of dense muscles were splitting under the blunted edge of his axe.

Gudrun kicked strongly to the surface. She found herself beside the monster's head. Felimid was nowhere in sight, for he had dived, to stab at the softer belly with his spear. A strong swimmer with ample breath for the dive, he did not rise again quickly, but rammed his spear deeper and twisted it in the monster's bowels.

Gudrun too was attacking it, with all the ferocity of her nature. Atop the pike's skull was a plate of bony armor, ridged at the back and above the eyes. She found a grip there. The lucky javelin still jutted from one eye socket, its shaft broken; Gudrun crooked her knee over that for purchase and drew Kissing Viper. Her men raised a rapturous shout to see her.

The pike's tail thrashed. Water foamed white. Ataulf lost his grip on the monster's fin and rolled aside, into a gape of horrible teeth. The pike bit him in half.

Gudrun remained on her slippery perch. Twisting around, she swung Kissing Viper with both hands, chopping time after time into the fish's spine. Meanwhile, Felimid had risen gasping to the surface, bringing his spear. Supple as an eel, he drove the point into the monster's gill slit and worked it forward, seeking to jam it fast in some vulnerable spot.

Gudrun, perched above, shouted Odin's name and struck yet again. Chips of muscle and bone flew high. Her edge reached the white marrow of the pike's spine.

The monster fish dove. It surfaced, and leaped high over *Ormungandr*'s stern, shedding the man and woman as if they were wet leaves, but Gudrun fell gripping her sword. The pike returned to the sea with a tremendous splash.

Then it was gone. Men awaited it with poised spears and drawn bows. Gudrun dove, looking for it, and when she did not find it she sheathed Kissing Viper beneath the sea. To swim to the surface again in her war shirt was hard work for her. Felimid found her and upheld her until they could be taken aboard. She needed his help by then; she neared exhaustion, and his leather tunic was lighter than her mail.

She did not accept his help graciously, however. Splashing

and coughing, she choked, "Leave me, you fool! The pike . . . the pike . . . will have us both . . . in one bite . . . if . . . we're this—*ulp!*—close. . . ."

"Toss us a rope!" the bard cried. Her objection had reason in it; he saw a red vision of his legs bitten off at the hip, and voided his bladder into the sea. Time to think was, on occasion, the worst of gifts.

"Here!" Decius answered, and flung half a coil through the glowing moonlight. Catching the end, Gudrun pulled herself aboard. While she kicked along, Felimid dove once more, lest the pike rise unseen to the attack. His spear was lost. Still, he might do some harm with the fifteen-inch knife at his waist.

Eyesight was all but useless. His ears and his skin must serve to warn him. No warning came, no sudden surge of displaced water, and sound carried well in the pulsing sea.

Nothing.

Reaching a trailing oar, he hauled himself up the shaft at a rate which would have won him prizes at any spring fair in his home province.

He lay gasping in the ship, streaming seawater. "The pike?" he managed to ask.

"No sign," Waddico said. "We're watching closely, my oath to that."

The bard nodded, sneezed seawater, indulged in spasms of coughing and finally felt better.

Decius did not feel better about anything. The man whose company pleased him best had died in the incarnadined sea. Tears ran from his living eye. The jewel in his other socket shone a malevolent red.

"What damage to the ship?" Gudrun demanded, for she was the captain, and for all she knew *Ormungandr* might be sinking under them.

"Four smashed oars," Hemming said. "Some harm to the side yon demon rammed . . . we are taking water, but not much. I'll swear any other ship had been holed and sunk."

"Will this one sink?"

"No danger of it."

"Seven men are dead, Ataulf among 'em," Decius said harshly. "The pike swallowed two and smashed five with his tail."

Men muttered at that. Some declared that their venture was

unlucky, and should be abandoned. Louder, more numerous voices called for persistence and revenge.

Gudrun agreed with the latter. "Luck is with us! We were victorious against the Saxons, and won fine booty. We met a monster fish which might have destroyed us, yet by our own courage and Odin's favor we have driven it off. I believe myself it was a sending of the wizards of Rugen, which shows their magic is nothing that cannot be defeated."

"They may do better next time," grunted a morose Goth. "Seven men slain, and Ataulf among 'em, as Decius says, and the ship almost sunk—if that is how the wizards fail, I've no wish to be nearby when they are successful."

"Wait," Felimid said, and heads turned towards him. "It's in my mind that this failure cost them dear. I saw the monster, and I too think the Wendish wizards sent it. More, I think they *made* it!

"Consider. A pike, e'en if it could be so huge, is a sweet-water fish. It's not natural to find one in the bitter sea. Less natural yet, it cast no shadow and had no blood, or if it had, my spear and Gudrun's sword drew none. I'll wager Ataulf's axe drew none either, though that I did not observe. I was somewhat busy."

Men chuckled at that, and listened.

"So," Felimid went on, speaking with his entire body, hands moving in quick gestures. "Bloodless and shadowless, yet able to strike like a thunderbolt. To be hurt, and to flee from hurt. Real, and not real. I believe it was a sending of all nine wizards in concert, sharing their power, for no one man —even a strong wizard—could create such a monster.

"If I'm right, we hurt them when we hurt their long sea-death. They could not give it such power to harm unless they filled it with their own vitality—so they must have suffered from the harm we gave it. My head upon it, they are in no state now to work the least magic—and they will not recover by dawn."

"Then, if the cursed wizard-priests are out of the game, I'm for raiding their temple," Decius said, his tone and look vengeful. "Yes, and slaying them all. No games of honor, no concern for glory. Strike where they are weakest. If the fighting men come to meet us in boats, we'll burn or ram the boats, sink them without giving their numbers a chance to tell.

If they wait for us ashore, let's trick them into massing in a body, then shoot them with arrows. I've counted them. We have a long thousand left.''

"Who else wishes to speak?" Gudrun asked.

"I'm with Decius," someone said.

"And I."

Shouts of agreement rang from bow to stern. Gudrun's men cared far less for danger than for the (in their eyes) impertinent offense the nine wizards had committed against them. They were pirates; it was their proper trade, and the proper function of such people as Wends was to be their victims, not to resist. To resist by means of sorcery was even less decent. Gudrun scarcely had to exhort them to stand by their original purpose.

"I know something else," Felimid declared. "I was told it but shortly before the pike appeared. The dwarf king seemingly did not lie; there is a captive in Svantovit's temple, a Dane of noble bearing. What's more, he is a tall, strong man. It's not wholly certain that he is King Helgi, I suppose. However, it's likely."

"How did you learn this, Bragi?" Gudrun asked, in wonder but not incredulously.

"The wind told me. The wind told me, and I trust what it said. Now, Gudrun, you have lost men to the Saxons and the pike, and should go craftily. The Wends may cut this Helgi's throat rather than let us rescue him."

"True."

"What if I go ashore with twenty men, a mile or so from the temple, and lead them through the forest? We've hunted together, you and I; you know my quality as a woodsman. Allow us time to gain the back of the temple ere you land. We can break in unseen while the Wends are occupied with you. With luck we will find the temple poorly guarded. We can free the king and rejoin you. Hmm . . . that will be the difficult part. One of us should take a horn and wind three blasts if we have the king. Then you can help us open a path to the ship."

"It's a fine ploy. Better than simple frontal attack! Yes, Bragi." Gudrun laughed with delight as the plan's possibilities unrolled before her. "Wind three blasts if you have the king, and one if he is dead or not there."

"Be it so. Who wishes to take the gamble with me?"

More than the twenty men he wanted were ready to go; Felimid had to select.

Later, Gudrun said to him quietly, "I never know what you are about. You cursed me for giving the Saxons to Odin, and sulked in the stern saying not a word thereafter. Tonight you helped me defeat that fish from the rivers of Helheim. Now you are helping this raid you mislike to go smoothly—"

"Smoothly?" Felimid echoed. "Gudrun, it's as hastily cobbled a botch as I've had the ill luck to partake of. What planning you did do has gone all awry. We'll arrive in the morning, not in the darkness before dawn, and with three score men able to fight, not eighty . . . or have I miscounted? No matter. If we escape disaster, it will be by fool's luck. But because of my own folly I'm a part of this misbegotten voyage." He spoke lightly, his wide, flexible mouth smiling, his tone at odds with the scathing content of his words. "I prefer that you do not get quite all your men slain while I'm in their company."

Gudrun swore a blistering oath. "You—! You are not angered with yourself. You should be, maybe, but you're not. You are angry with me. You have been angry since I gave the Saxons to the One-eyed. Why do you not say so?"

"Angry?" The bard's mobile face altered expression again. "It's sick to the heart I am—for you, not for them! But I'll not be talking of it now. I'll find dry trews, and grease this leather before the brine rots it away. Anything else I leave until we have rescued the king."

Gudrun looked at him for a moment. He dripped water still. It darkened his hair and shone on his face in the brilliant night like a drenching of tears. Whatever was amiss, she wished it did not exist, and that he would take her in his arms before the fighting began. But the anger and pain she sensed in him was nothing an embrace could dispel, and as he said, time was short. Its relentless tread would not slow for love or death or the gods.

"Until we have rescued the king, Bragi."

VIII
Svantovit's Temple

Rugen lay wooded and fair in the early daylight. An island of some size, ten leagues from north to south, it sustained many more folk than the priests and temple soldiers. They raised grain, flax, hemp and beasts, fished the sea, hunted in the forest, observed the rites of their gods and other powers.

The temple stood on the northern point of Arkona. Vindalf had said as much, Tegg had confirmed it, and one of the captured women taken from Withhad's Saxons had added to that sketchy knowledge. A Wend herself, she had been born on Rugen and taken into bondage on the rich isle of Bornholm later, in time to be abducted thence by the Saxon raiders. She was having a varied succession of masters.

Felimid and his score of men made their way through the forest. It grew wild and tangled, uncut and unpastured since time began. A few winding trails led through its green dimness.

The bard, leading, was aware of an enchantment about the wood such as he had scarcely known since leaving Erin. He had trodden British earth for years; ancient and holy though that was, its magic had in the main retreated from human sight in the generations of Roman rule. Driven into the waste places and taught a fearful caution, faerie beings hid themselves even from Felimid's senses. Here they observed no such constraint.

He heard water make music as it seeped through the black soil, and leaves whisper in a language close to human. Something gnarled and tufted, with pop eyes and hands of manlike shape, squatted among the roots of a willow and fearlessly watched them file by.

The bard guided his men well. Although as much a stranger to the island as they, he was no stranger to forest paths. Bent low, he slid through the undergrowth like a questing fox, knowing by long practice and innate awareness where to step. His clever, sensitive feet told him where mud sinkholes lay under the innocent-looking mold, and he never stumbled on the half-buried logs in their shrouds of moss and fungus, despite the dimness under the forest roof. The pirates learned swiftly to take any advice or warning he uttered, without questioning it. They found him as adroit in the woods as they had found him lubberly aboard a ship.

They had less than two miles to cover. Soon enough they heard hundreds of voices roaring a war chant, diffused through brush and leaves.

"That'll be the Wends greeting *Ormungandr*," Sighere muttered. "Can we not move faster?"

"I can, but I'd be leaving you all behind and have to face the Wends myself, unsupported and alone," Felimid said, "and I haven't such a hunger for glory. In this tangle, we are moving as swiftly as twenty of us can, and stay together. But it's in my mind we will not be late to the feast."

He used the last word ironically. He knew stories of champions and heroes who ran to battle as to a banquet, but for himself, he was thoroughly glutted. He rather enjoyed the notion of snatching the captive king from the temple while a frontal attack was achieving only noise and carnage—but his appreciation was mental, while the bloody frontal attack would leave numbers of real corpses on the ground. Besides, he had never even approached believing that the Danish king's rescue was worth the slaughter it would cost.

The deep-voiced battle chant of the Wends thundered in his ears. He imagined them standing in a stubborn mass before their temple, the rage of their god filling them. Then a louder shout and a briefer cut across the chant. "Our archers loosing," Sighere opined, and the shout was repeated. Felimid envisioned a sleet of arrows. The pirates would sustain it while they had shafts and targets.

Felimid and his band came to the forest's edge. The temple by the shore was unmistakably itself, a huge circular building with many pillars and a fantastically shingled roof. Long barrack houses for the temple warriors stood a distance away.

Ormungandr lay on chest-deep green water, with Wendish bodies floating between her and the shore. Apparently the Wends had tried to wade or swim to her and swarm aboard. Arrows were still flying towards the beach.

"So," Sighere grunted. "Hear the Wends bellow! Not even the lady will land with such odds against her."

"Let's to work, then, while she holds their attention," the bard said. "The temple wasn't made for a fortress, and yon gate looks promising."

He led them across the open ground at a run. His leather cuirass made no sound but a slight creaking, and he kept the temple between himself and the shore. Reaching the gate, he flattened himself against the wall, noting the smell which came to his nostrils from within. A horse was stabled beyond that gate, and a horse stabled in a temple could only be a sacred animal. He hardly needed to think to reach that conclusion. The sacred horse was a familiar concept to any Celt, even a Christian one, which Felimid decidedly was not.

Someone had barred the heavy gate. That delayed Felimid perhaps three heartbeats. He slid Kincaid's fine blade between the jamb and the gate, raised the bar, pushed and entered. A great white horse reared in his stall.

Beyond the stable lay the temple proper. Gudrun's twenty pirates rushed sacrilegiously in, to be received by twenty Wendish guards. Big, powerful men armed with spears, they rushed the strangers at once. Felimid and the pirates locked shields together, standing fast across the wide entrance to the stable, while behind them the white horse attempted in a frenzy to kick his stall to pieces. The temple resounded like the inside of a drum.

Bare-headed, lacking armor, the Wends held the way with brute strength for long minutes. A few pirates died before their surving comrades broke the Wendish resistance. Then the struggle became a brawl, raging throughout the temple from wall to wall under the baleful four-faced regard of Svantovit, fight as one could, triumph or die.

Felimid slew three Wends with the leaping, flickering point of Kincaid. The pirates cut down the rest, paying almost half of their depleted number to achieve it. The nine survivors then

looked to their wounds or, if they had none worth urgent concern, ransacked the temple.

"Helgi! King Helgi!" Sighere bawled. "We be friends come
to rescue you!"

"I am Helgi Dane-king," answered a steady voice.

The speaker was shackled to a pillar by a set of crudely
forged manacles. To break and then pry open a link of chain
did not take long. The pirates had come prepared.

"The gyves must stay, King Helgi, till we can take you
aboard our ship and set a file to them," Felimid said.
"There's need for haste. Will you let explanation wait until
there's time for it?"

"Aye!" Helgi answered, as most men would have. Tall,
lean-hipped and long-legged, with heavy shoulders and arms,
he smiled broadly through an untrimmed flaxen beard. "But
whose men are you?"

"Gudrun Blackhair's, lord."

*And I'm Gudrun's man in another sense, though not for
much longer.* The thought went swiftly through Felimid's
mind, hurting as it passed. His companions had seized the
silver lamps and shaken their oil about, and were now striking
sparks to tinder; they needed neither orders nor counsel to
commit efficient arson. The precious hangings smoldered,
grew fingers of flame. Sighere had opened the temple portals
sufficiently to let in the wind, and to see what was happening
outside.

"The lady feigned an attempt to land, and provoked a
charge from these boulder-headed Wends," he reported.
"Our lads fed them arrows and then drew back from the
beach. They haven't come to hand-grips."

"What of the wizard-priests?"

"I see one, holding their war banner. No sign of sorcery
thus far. You were right, Bragi; they have spent their power."

"For now, perhaps," King Helgi answered. He slammed his
manacled hands against a pillar, stretching the chain between
them. "Here, fellow, break this with your axe; I cannot endure waiting for a file. I must be able to hold a weapon, and
you will need every fighter. Strike!" he ordered, in a king's
voice.

The pirate obeyed, though his axe-edge suffered badly. The
flames took a surer hold, speaking in hisses and crackles. Men

stowed the silver lamps in improvised sacks, with other temple
treasures small enough to carry.

Felimid had run to the sacred horse's stall. Seizing his mane,
he dragged the furious beast's head down, a display of
strength unexpected to the men who rushed to aid him.

"They won't harm the horse," Felimid panted. "He belongs . . . to the god. His trappings are yonder. I saw them.
Saddle him quickly, and give me the bridle."

The white horse's harness included the richest objects in the
temple. Each belt and strap was covered wtih plates of gold.
The rings and cruciform spacers in the harness were of gold,
finely worked. Rhomboid plates of embossed gold edged the
saddlecloth; there were many looped chains and chiming bells
of the same precious metal; even the bit, necessarily of iron,
was gilded. A thick spiral ring of wrought and jewelled gold
was evidently meant to encircle the horse's tail, but Sighere
thrust that into his byrnie.

Swiftly, Felimid checked the saddle and made adjustments,
giving the maddened horse an impious knee to the belly so that
he could tighten the girths as the beast abruptly exhaled. His
eyes watered in the thickening smoke. He coughed from a
tightening throat.

"They see the smoke!" someone shouted. "The Wends do!
Some are rushing here!"

"What of the ship?"

"Aye, the lady sees too! They are coming ashore from
Ormungandr, shields locked; no deceit this time, a true landing! Their arrows are spent, I think."

"Out of here with us, then! Out through the stable and
around the side to the shore! Open the stall!"

As he spoke, Felimid mounted the white horse which only
the god should dare to bestride. It screamed in outrage—or
dread of the growing flames. When the stall opened, it dashed
for the sunlight, and once outside, Felimid needed all his
riding skill to stay in the saddle. The great horse plunged and
kicked. Felimid, his legs gripping the horse with steely power,
drew its head remorselessly about and struck its haunches.
With a scream, it rounded the temple and rushed down the
beach.

Outnumbered six to one, despite the slaughter they had
done with their bows, Gudrun's pirates found the distraction
caused by the burning temple most welcome. Some thirty

Wends had rushed into it, and blinded by smoke, wasted precious time before they were sure the desecrators had left. By then the roof had caught fire.

Wildly bucking, the huge milk-white horse with Felimid on its back crashed into the Wendish force. He had never been trained for war, or for any merely human purpose, and his flying back hooves knocked down two warriors by chance only. A third man was knocked sprawling by the horse's chest, and trampled.

None of the temple warriors struck a blow at their god's sacred horse. Thus the bard too was immune, and fortunately for him, since he could never have defended himself from the saddle as his frantic mount plunged and curvetted.

The Wends scattered before him. They hadn't fought in any disciplined order to begin with; although strong fighters, stubborn and enduring, they were ill-organized to the point of heedlessness. The pirates' crescent of interlocked shields cut through them like a coulter through sand.

King Helgi and the nine men from the burning temple sped through the gap Felimid had opened in the loose Wendish ranks. Staying together in a tight knot, they fought their way to the main body of pirates.

Dcheko the arch-priest, hands clenched like talons on the pole of his god's war banner, glanced wildly about him. Three of his fellow priests lay dead with arrows piercing them; a fourth had fallen to some unknown pirate's sword. Now he saw his holy place ablaze.

Maddened, he uttered a long wordless scream. The flesh writhed on his bones, beginning to seethe and flow into a dreadful form. His howl went on and on, rising to a note of dire pain. Clearly this attempt to transform himself to . . . something *other* . . . cost him immense effort.

Felimid glimpsed him from the raging horse's back. He turned the beast's head with gentle but irresistible hands. Perhaps Dcheko could complete his grisly alteration of shape, perhaps not. The bard was not so insatiably curious that he wished to know.

He drew Kincaid humming from his sheath, and urged the white horse forward. Dcheko never saw him coming. The point slid through the tall wizard-priest's neck from side to side. As he fell, the white horse stamped and stamped upon him in a frenzy of loathing. He died, still but half-trans-

formed, the flesh of his torso and one leg like cords and bulbs
of melted, re-congealed wax. One arm had acquired blue-
black scales and ended in a straight, yard-long claw. The head
as yet was wholly a man's.

Svantovit's war banner had gone down, to be trampled in
the bloody sand.

Gudrun's pirates retreated into the surging water. Wheeling
the horse, kicking it to a run, Felimid followed. Cold water
shocked his legs; spray rose. Gripping the horse's barrel hard
with his knees, he sheathed Kincaid.

As he swam the horse to the ship's side, he drew his knife.
Some of his companions had reached the ship, and were
spending their last few arrows to discourage attack. The rest,
shoulder-deep in the sea, held together and guarded each other
as they climbed aboard.

The Wends are truly stupid, Felimid thought. *In their position, and blessed with their numbers, I'd have sent a hundred
men to take and burn* Ormungandr *once the pirates had quit
it! Then we'd have been trapped here*.

Slipping the bridle from the white horse's splendid head, he
shouted, "Catch!" Then he sliced the saddle girths with his
knife and slid from the horse's back. Ready hands dragged the
precious saddle and saddlecloth into the ship, then hauled
Felimid after. A Wendish spear thudded into timber close to
his thigh.

Gasping, he rolled among the thwarts while men bent to
their oars, pulling for the open sea. In their outrage, Wendish
fighters swarmed after them, clawing at strakes and oars, forcing their way to grips with the pirates. They died for their
determination.

Felimid looked back. Fed by the brisk sea wind, fire was
devouring the temple for all its guardians' efforts to quench it.
The smoke was long visible, and its smell clung to Felimid for
longer yet, but it pleased him to see that the sacred horse had
regained the shore.

IX
A Love Song

"Whither?" the steersman asked.

"To the nearest land that is not a part of Rugen!" Gudrun laughed. "Umm, yes, the wind is from the northwest. There is plenty of wilderness coast where that will take us, and we need time to lick our wounds. Raise sail, Decius."

"Aye, lady."

Chisel and file were at work on King Helgi's wrist shackles as they spoke. Felimid sat by, his leather cuirass discarded, more comfortable in his light tunic.

"Dwarfmade or not, ye should grease that again," a Dane advised him. "Seawater has touched it more than once of late."

"It doesn't matter," the bard said indifferently. "I'll not be requiring it again, so have it as a gift and grease it your own self, if you like."

"*What?*" The man's jaw slackened. "Why, Bragi, that's a prince's gift! You paid gold to get it, and now you toss it aside like a tuft of grass you have used to wipe your bum! What ails you?"

Felimid laughed ironically. "Only that my bum has been adequately wiped, indeed, and from now on I'll be using goose down."

Before the mast, Gudrun walked to the king as rivets split with a muted clank and Helgi's second shackle sprang open.

163

He rubbed his abraded wrist and spoke a word of thanks to the smith.

Gudrun's mail rustled as she faced the king. Bloody, sweating and soaked to the breasts with salt water, her helmet laid aside but armored else, she looked magnificent still.

"Well, King Helgi, you should find my hospitality better than theirs."

"You are Gudrun, Varek's daughter, the one called Gudrun Blackhair."

"That am I, lord. The woman who slew your jarl, Ivarr, years ago. I did it in single fight, no man aiding me, whatever you may have heard. I've long known that the man who brought my head to you would be rewarded. One or two have tried. It should gladden you now that they failed."

"Of that I'm not yet sure," the king replied. His craggy, leather-hued face showed lively interest. "But your intentions towards me would have to be foul indeed for me to prefer that Wendish temple to your ship. Ransom?"

"It's not in my mind to demand any. We have paid ourselves with plunder from the temple. No, I mean to restore you to your people and to your brother, lord. In return I'd have what I did long ago forgotten, and be no more an outlaw in your kingdom."

"Ah. You wish to come home?"

"Jutland is my home," Gudrun said proudly, "and no Jutlander has asked a king's leave or paid him scot this hundred years. However, I'd be free of the harbors in Scania and Zealand, able to come and go in friendship—and it does not suit me that Wends should believe they can sacrifice Danes to their four-faced god. They needed a lesson. You were not saved so that I might beg you for anything, lord."

"You make that plain. Mmm, I and not you must sweeten Ivarr's kin. Suppose we both think the matter over. I'll hold no grudge if you choose to ransom me, though for my honor's sake I'm bound to demand that you make the ransom a high one."

Gudrun shook her head. "I don't want that. But you are right, this is not the time to settle it. Will you pledge me your royal word that whether my sentence of outlawry is lifted or not, I may take my ship out of the Kattegat in peace after I bring you home?"

"May my own sword turn against me otherwise!" King Helgi said. "And I'll not be so niggard as to give you no better gift than a safe conduct. But you, my friend, you say little, and it was you who broke me from that foul prison the Wends called a temple. By Odin! I joyed to see it burn and the priests die! Who are you?"

"Like all the others, I'm one who left the Limfjord with eighty companions, and now has but thirty." Felimid's voice was bitter. "Odin gave you your victory, Gudrun, but he's an avid god, indeed. It seems the Saxons you offered him were not enough."

"All men die," Gudrun said, puzzled. "*We carried the thing off*, against three hundred Wends, and that's worth telling! I don't understand you. See the rest of the men. Are their spirits low?"

They were not. The pirates bragged and joked among themselves, none caring much for their hideous losses. Those with wounds flaunted them.

Felimid did not speak his answer. He touched his harp. Under his fingers she wept molten tears of grief and anger, and the tears were all for Gudrun Blackhair. The tall woman's throat rippled, once, in a tremor of nameless emotion. With a sharp gesture, she left the bard to himself.

"He's unhappy, it seems," Helgi observed.

"He's a poet, and has his moods," Gudrun said. "I hope this one passes soon."

They landed at dusk near the mouths of the Oder, a river which compared well in length and size to the mighty Elbe. Gudrun had *Ormungandr* drawn ashore. Were they attacked, they could use the ship as a fortress, or launch her quickly if they had time; not that Gudrun expected it. After all, they would be stretching their legs here for one night only.

The captive women cooked a meal for the surviving pirates. For them, it was a blessing that so many had died. The fewer men's lusts they had to appease, the better—and they now had grounds to hope they would be given to the Dane-kings, and so better their situation.

Felimid ate a large portion of the food. He was hungry, and the meal might have to last him some time. Then he sought Gudrun, who sat with King Helgi near a dancing fire.

"I suppose I should be telling you, Gudrun, if you haven't

discerned it," he said, standing jauntily, his tone a gay mantle tossed over scalded flesh, "I'll remain here when you depart on the morrow."

Gudrun rose at once, furious. "I should take you at your word and abandon you! It's what your folly deserves! Have sense, Bragi!"

"Not I, Gudrun. I haven't any sense at all, or I'd have gone my way when the chance offered in Gaul, and again at Edricsburg, and a third time in Jutland. Because I've no sense at all, I let myself forget that you worship Odin, until I was reminded most harshly. My fault, not yours. And having come so far, I was too stubborn to desert you before you had fetched the king out of Svantovit's temple. Well, it ends here."

"You did all that for love of me, you said. You change your mind quickly!"

"Yes. I love you. But not enough to swim through more seas of blood beside you, and too much to watch when your master Odin gives you your last reward."

His harp cried out like a creature in pain.

> "Blackhair, beloved, I sailed in your ship,
> And sang in your praise for a smile from your lip,
> More than for dowers of gold I might grip.
>
> "The fire of the hawk's land* means little to me.
> It is mine for the asking where'er I may be.
> *Then I saw you hang men on the battle god's tree.*
>
> "The ash branches creak where a staring corpse swings,
> Companioned in death by the men he gave rings,
> And the ravens do blacken the sky with their wings.
>
> "You wear the dark wings of death on your helm,
> And the God of the Ash has you fast in his realm,
> For you turned in disgust from your mother the elm.
>
> "I stood by your side when the sharp arrows sang
> And fought in your cause when the sword-iron rang—
> But I will not be there when it's your turn to hang."

* gold.

The harp music seemed to burn like fire. Golden Singer's frame glowed like red-brown embers; the strings blazed, and King Helgi's flaxen hair shone in the fire glow. By contrast, Gudrun's figure was shadowed, and the hollow noise of surf thundered at her back.

Past a bitter tautness in her throat, she said, "Aye, those who are sworn to the Spear-wielder do not live long, but you knew that when you—you—oh, fool, you cannot bide here! The Obodrites live by yon river, a strong Wendish tribe. Isn't that so, King Helgi? You have no word of their language and would not live a day!"

"I've had difficulties of that sort before. I have Golden Singer to smooth my way, and where there are horses I can make myself useful. Who's likely to know that I helped sack Svantovit's temple? I can dwell in the forest if all else fails."

He offered his arguments from a habit of debate, not because he expected—or cared—to convince. His professional control of his voice sifted all trace of stress from his words, though the effort was great, for his own throat too was tight and burning. He added lightly, "And since I'm determined to go, you cannot force me to remain, can you, Gudrun?"

"With thirty men I'm very sure I can. You will not kill over a thing like this. Not you. No, Bragi, you will sail with us as far as Zealand if we must take you in a wrapping of sailor's knots, for your own silly sake. Then you are your own man once more. You hear me, fool?" she shouted. "You may go where you please from Zealand—but you may not stay here!"

"Do you tell me?" Felimid's voice was as soft as hers was loud. Then, suddenly, it lifted to a yell matching hers. "No. Gudrun!"

His left hand swept across the harp on his knee. His nails shifted, plucked, struck, ran smoothly as coursing dogs the width of the strings and doubled back. He knew three strains to compel mortal feeling, and now he played the third, the sleep strain.

Rarely, very rarely, did Felimid use it as a weapon, or for advantage. The reasons lay within himself, not in the nature of magic; he enjoyed using his wits and preferred to triumph by them. But scruple and vanity now went under in a torrent of bursting, contradictory feeling, like flimsy bridges in a storm-fed river. The notes of the sleep strain flowed out.

Gudrun swayed as though partly stunned. King Helgi, rising

to one knee, halted in mid-motion with a puzzled gesture and then fell slowly sideways. Gudrun's jaw and knees slackened. She toppled across him.

Felimid played on. The music carried irresistible power, but instead of lulling those who heard it into easy, dreamless slumber, it bludgeoned them senseless, as Felimid's pain and fury throbbed from the harp strings. His victims lay twitching. They moaned softly as foul dreams assailed them.

A man by another fire sprawled among the coals. Felimid saw the pirate's clothes catch fire, and clenched his hand, quelling the urge to harp on. He dragged the smoldering man from the fire and smothered the flames in sand before he suffered much.

Fewer than a dozen had heard the bard's enchanted music. Others came to see what was amiss, and Felimid, hearing them come, seized his gear and vanished into the forest. He had no wish to harp these men asleep as well, leaving the whole band helpless until morning on this alien shore. Besides, if he tried, someone might well be swift enough to hurl a spear through him before succumbing.

I'm fading on the wind, as always, he thought, *and again I leave unfriends behind me.*

With one difference. This time he was not pleased to be travelling on his way. This time, it hurt.

PART THREE:
THE EAST

I
The Trader With Two Families

The river Oder was greater than any in Erin. Like the rivers of Erin, it had its own power, life and mystery, but while the rivers of Erin were goddesses, the Oder was male.

Felimid walked beside it. Through the soles of his feet, he felt the wild ancient magic of earth and water; primitive magic of the senses and feelings, far different from the magic of air that was governed by the mind. All around him stretched the forest. Tangled it grew, wholly untamed.

The faerie life of that wilderness shared its nature. Tree spirits walked free. A slender white birch-woman passed him with madness and death in her long-fingered hands if she chose to touch him, and Felimid did not trouble to step aside. Once, something ponderous and uncouth made of moving stone blundered by at a distance. Felimid heard a huge tree topple and saw light break through the forest roof.

The crackling, crushing noises ceased. At the end of a swathe of flattened bushes, Felimid came upon a boulder thrice his height, roughly shapen like a crouching, six-limbed beast. Why it moved and why it had stopped he would never know. Perhaps earth would rise up its sides and grass sprout over it and the forest weave tightly about it until, in a dozen or twenty generations of men, for its own insensate reasons, it moved again. Or perhaps it would remain as it was forever.

He shut Gudrun out of his mind. But his mind was the least of the territory she had captured. From the corner of an eye he *saw* her, walking with her bold swagger, and turned in a joy almost unbearable with her name on his tongue—to see nothing but shadows and fancy. The pain was like having his heart torn out, twisted and wrung and thrown away.

He stood still a long time before he moved on.

What sense he retained kept him close to the river. When it occurred to him, he drank the Oder's clear water to keep himself alive. He caught fish with his hands, gathered herbs and used other familiar skills. To survive in high summer in a land so fertile was easy for one who had known the forest from childhood. The difficult thing would have been to starve.

None the less, Felimid was not as he had been. He'd become dangerously unwary, knew it and did not care. Once he trod into a sinkhole of mud and was nearly engulfed. Another time, a green-haired, pop-eyed forest spirit led him astray, feigning the strident laughter of an excited woman. Had the being not abandoned its game on a whim, Felimid might not have been seen by human eyes again.

The narrow escape sobered him—not a great deal, but enough. He returned to the river bank with far more trouble than it had taken him to leave it, and took counsel with himself. What to do next?

That happened spontaneously. With Gudrun's vital, square-jawed face in his mind's eye, he wept until his whole body was agonized, choking and coughing like a man spewing poison.

When it was over, he felt somehow more free. He knew where he was and saw where he might go.

One way led back to Gudrun. He still loved her. But he saw the men hanging from the branches of the sacred ash, some pierced by spears according to the rites of the One-eyed, and knew that was no path for him. He'd more happily share her with a dozen other lovers than with that god.

Well, then, he would not turn back. Best to continue upstream, away from the sea. The more distance between him and the coast, the less chance that any would connect him with the raiders of Svantovit's temple. A lone wanderer with a harp on his back was not likely to be suspected of pillage, even if he did wear a sword in addition. His music should gain him a welcome, and failing that, Felimid knew he was worth his keep at any place there were horses. He did not require to speak the region's language to prove it.

He sighed. Gudrun's invitation to be her lover, herald, poet and negotiator in one had seemed wonderful, for a little while. It would have suited his talents and kept him beside her—and atop her, and between her, and behind her, and under her, and —*no, by Cairbre and Ogma! None of that!*

He stripped off his clothes and swam, using the fine river sand to scour himself free of grime, and took the trouble to shave his neglected jaw. Having given himself the attention, he felt better.

Because the day was warm, he put on kilt and sandals only. He pushed his other garments into the sack he had carried so far. He was still sunning himself on the bank when the boats came by.

Someone hailed him affably, in a language unknown to him. Raising his head, he saw two flat-bottomed river boats like oared barges, probably trading vessels. Despite his meager knowledge of the region, he had heard that most river traders in these parts were foreign.

Taking a risk, he answered in the Jutish dialect, with a good attempt at Danish inflection and accent.

"Good day! Have you space for a passenger who is not averse to work?"

"I may," the same man bawled, this time in a tongue which held meaning for Felimid. "By Frey! You sound like a Jutlander!"

"No, you're in error there, though I've had dealings with some."

"So? No matter, I'll not hold it against you, and since you ask I'll take you aboard. But hear this! Should you be the lure for a band of thieves in the brush behind you, they'll find they have bitten into harder meat than their snags can chew, and the first to find a spear through his brisket will be you." He spoke with confident good humor rather than threateningly. "Now, what do you say?"

"Row in, chieftain; your terms are fair."

The boat slanted across the current, its wide-bladed oars shining. It was not unlike the Saxon war craft, though broader and partly decked. The second vessel stayed in midstream. Felimid settled his harp bag on his back, balanced the leather sack on his shoulder and stepped adroitly up the plank the strangers thrust ashore for him.

"I see you have done that before," the leader commented. Big-bellied and strong, he went bare-headed, showing a bald crown fringed by a V-shaped yellow mane which fell to his shoulders. "I'm Beigadh of Gotland. Trader. But I have a family in these parts too."

"I—" The bard barely hesitated. For over a month he had answered to the false name of Bragi; now he abandoned it. "I am Felimid of Erin, the isle west of Britain. By trade I'm a bard; you would say skald."

"You've come far."

"True for you, chieftain. I like to roam. I wintered in Jutland and then went with a raiding band to rob the Prussians. The voyage was a fine success, but alas, on our way back the leader took offense at some staves of mine and had me put ashore with what I carry. I don't think myself, the staves were as provoking as all that, and I'd like to see that captain again and discuss the matter with him—between wands."*

Beigadh chuckled. "I'd like to hear these staves. I'll be truthful. When I saw you by the river I wondered if you were a gangrel I might sell as a slave, but if you are a poet, then for me you are sacrosanct."

Felimid lifted an eyebrow. His long-jawed, snub-nosed face expressed pure innocent astonishment as spurious as his tale of raiding the Prussian tribes. "I'm relieved to hear it."

Later he invented a leader for his fictitious pirate expedition, and declaimed the staves which had allegedly given such offense, composing them offhand as he went. Beigadh enjoyed them. He seemed to accept Felimid's tale with no more than reasonable reservations, taking it for granted that some embroidery had been done; he knew poets.

"These parts are strange to you, eh, Felimid?" he said. "You were stranded here lacking a word of the language. Huh! Well, the Obodrites are the strong tribe hereabouts. They live by the river, and take their name from it, too. Oder, Ob-Oderites, Obodrites. They're a Wendish tribe. I've been wed to the daughter of their prince these ten years. It betters trade to have relatives. She's a good wife, what's more. I've another in Gotland, and children in both places. I'm on my way to visit my second family now. I stay until autumn, go back to Gotland for the winter, and return here in the spring."

"Which has the milder winters, Gotland or these parts?"

"Gotland, because of the sea."

* On ground formally marked out for single combat.

Felimid was not ready to decide his course as far in advance as the onset of winter. However, that was a thing worth knowing, and so was the language of the Obodrites. Beigadh had a number among his boatmen, so Felimid set himself to learn their tongue and customs. He might be with them long enough to master it and find it of use.

The trader's boats moved up the shining river.

II
"I Rule Now!"

They stopped overnight in a Wendish village. The folk lived crudely, in log houses roofed with sod-covered planks on either side of a dirt thoroughfare. However, they were tall, strong and evidently well fed.

"I see no weapons," Felimid remarked to a bulky Swede named Koll.

"They have none, save spears and bows. I have never seen a people who know so little of arms. It's scarcely decent. They don't know how to make even the poorest shields—but by the gods, they can drink!"

They did not seem lively to Felimid, but a dull-eyed, heavy, drably clad lot in general. The women wore long skirts and woollen jackets, the men tight trousers and knee-length shirts of thick linen. Dyeing seemed unknown to them, and tailoring nearly so.

"You had better dress more as we do, my buck," Beigadh warned his passenger from the corner of his mouth. "You're scarcely decent."

Felimid had noticed before that these northerners were prudish about skin. True, display was not considered seemly in Erin either, but there a man's bare knees and chest were not a hanging matter. With a shrug, he returned to the boats and changed to the only other garments he had, his forester's buckskins (which smelled somewhat gamey.)

"Frey's manhood, but they were strange," Beigadh opined

later, as they rowed farther upstream. "They chattered like jays about nothing and would rather look at the ground than my face—or any speaker's. Did you mark it?"

"Not I, chieftain. But that's not astounding, as I know neither them nor their language."

"True. Aye, well, it may be bogies or trolls have unsettled them. They are yokels . . . and they do live in a haunted land. There are beings in yon forest I'd not care to meet myself."

They camped on the river bank for two nights, and then stayed at the steading of a minor chief, and last of all were guests in a second village. The tensions Beigadh had sensed were the same in these places too, and the reluctance to speak of more than the weather.

"Something is far wrong," Beigadh muttered to Koll. "When I ask them how my father-in-law fares, they all but slaver to tell me he does well, his acres are fertile, his health a wonder—tcha! He's gouty and his guts are always in disorder, as all men know. D'you suppose he can have become tyrannical as well, in less than half a year?"

"Maybe," Koll said unhelpfully.

"Aye. Maybe." Beigadh scowled. "I've an urge to shake these lackwits till their eyeballs wobble, and they share what they are not telling. Still, we will reach Kustrin tomorrow, and should hear sense there . . . whether or not of a kind that's pleasing. Best we look to our weapons."

Felimid heard this exchange, for the boat was not large, his hearing excellent, and the speech in Swedish. Letting a judicious amount of time lapse, he asked Beigadh about his second family, particularly the father-in-law.

"Old Hervet is more than a chieftain," the trader said. "He's the prince of the Obodrites—*voivode*, they call it. He's ailing, but then, he will be fifty in a few more years, unless he dies. Then the people may choose a new prince, or decide they can do better without one."

"Hervet?" Felimid repeated. "That has the sound of a German name."

"It's Gothic. He has Gothic blood; the Goths ruled over the Wends for long, and then the Huns conquered both. Oh, it's a tangled story, and I'm not certain it was told to me right. The present is what concerns me. Something is far wrong! At least, every village and holding along the river believes there is. All fear to speak. I've seen protective signs made, and heard the word *zŭlo* uttered more than once, though in whispers."

"*Zŭlo*? What is that, now?"

"Evil."

On the morning of the sixth day they reached the place called Kustrin, at the Oder's junction with another great river, the Warta. As they approached, the trader chieftain and his men stared, thunderstruck.

The prince's settlement, secure within a stockade in the fork of the rivers, provided with many ways of escape should they be required, had vanished. In its place a vast mansion rose on foundations of cut, polished stone. Each of its three stories was smaller than the one beneath, and yet even the roof, its alternating gables and domes all shingled with ornate parings of poplar wood, dominated by one great central dome—even the bizarre confection of a roof covered three acres.

The mansion boasted no palisade or outer fortifications, only a courtyard enclosed by long walls, one of them pierced by a wide, arched entrance. There were no gates. Access was a matter of walking in, which chilled the bard more than sentried ramparts would have done. This certainly was not the abode of some half-savage Wendish princelet.

Docks of banded gray, white and apple-green stone offered moorings. They too were a new sight to Beigadh, Felimid felt sure. So, perhaps, was the row of upright metal spikes on which severed heads were displayed. Felimid's stomach twisted. Despite the month and more with Gudrun, he had not become inured to seeing such things suddenly.

Beigadh stared in disbelief. Then, with agility which belied his heavy build, he vaulted to the quay and looked closely at the hideous row.

"It's Hervet!" he raved, of one head in particular. "It's Ludovena's father! It's the *voivode*, and these others were among his chieftains!" He mastered himself. "Come," he said, turning to his boatmen. "Out of this; it's a trap! By Njord of the Ships, and by Frey, I'll raise a fleet and come back for my wife and children. . . ."

"Beigadh!" Felimid said sharply. "Be careful, one comes."

The trader turned about. A figure had emerged from the courtyard of the mansion and now approached the stone quay with a gait of utter, disconcerting confidence. Save for this one man, all appeared deserted, yet Felimid felt sure it was not.

The stranger had a dreadful presence, even a furlong off. His appearance as he drew nearer became no more soothing. Taller than Beigadh or any man in the trader's party, long-limbed and powerfully muscled, he radiated vitality like a great, scorching fire. He went richly clad in a brocade caftan, silk sash, tall brimless felt hat and boots of Persian leather sewn with pearls, yet his grooming was sluttishly careless. Black hair, tangled and rank, spilled over his shoulders and chest to mingle with a beard equally unkempt. He stank remarkably at close range.

His large-featured face, broad of cheekbone and heavy of mouth, was astonishing—and tragic. Once, perhaps, it had been attractive as well as strong, a thousand years ago as vice and madness were reckoned. Now the flesh lay seamed and eroded above the prominent bones. Grayish-purple sacks of skin hung empty beneath the dark, intensely burning eyes, and broken veins twisted redly across his cheeks. The gaze he bent upon the newcomers was not quite sane.

His bony hands gripped a two-foot metal cudgel, the striking end shaped like a bull's head lowered to gore, and his manner said loudly that it was both scepter and weapon to him.

"BOW!" he thundered. "BOW AND TOUCH YOUR HEADS TO THE DECK!"

None obeyed. Beigadh said thickly, "You! Did you slay Hervet? What of my wife?"

The giant seized Beigadh's arm and flung him sprawling. "BOW!"

Beigadh sprang upright, disregarding the order, and advanced holding his axe in a businesslike fashion. The man he threatened loosed a bellow of laughter, let his cudgel-hand fall indifferently to his side, and with the other tore open his priceless caftan.

"Strike, then! I give you leave!"

He spoke some archaic German which Felimid comprehended only because the giant's utterances thus far had been brief and simple.

Beigadh took him at his word, and struck a sundering blow at the naked belly so blithely offered. The axe glanced off, as from an iron wall. The giant took one backward pace at the impact, venting a deep grunt, and Beigadh almost split his own shin as his axe rebounded.

"So!" The giant roared. "Now I, Koschei, will strike *you*!"

With a laugh, he swung his cudgel almost negligently in
what was plainly a love tap to the blow he might have dealt.
None the less, it shattered Beigadh's shoulder and knocked
him flat.

"The puppy has had his one permitted bite," Koschei said.
A malevolent scowl replaced his former mirth. "Now hear me,
dogs! If a second hand is raised against me, none of you will
be alive tomorrow. And the strongest of you will howl for
death before he releases you from torment. BOW TO ME!"
he yelled, his vehemence casting specks of froth into his beard.
"I WILL IMPALE THE LAST TO OBEY, AND THE
FOUR NEAREST TO HIM!"

Before the sheer volume of that demented cry, the boat
crews stood stunned for a moment. Felimid too was shocked,
but resilient as ever—and as lacking in awe—he felt a per-
versely amused smile threaten to cover his face. He was first to
prostrate himself in order to hide it.

While he pressed his brow to the deck, he smoothed the dangerous quirk from his lips. This Koschei was a madman, it appeared, and invulnerable besides. Kincaid might disprove that,
but on such short acquaintance Felimid thought he would be
cautious.

"Remain," Koschei ordered. Unseen by the prostrate boat
crews, he raised his cudgel high and shouted, "Attend me,
pikemen!"

Twenty men in red lacquered leather cuirasses ran down to
the quay in a line, bearing pikes slanted across their chests. At
a gesture from Koschei, they formed a semicircle facing the
trader's boats.

The giant boarded the nearer of the two, his caftan hem
brushing prostrate forms. His dark smoldering gaze roved
from bow to stern, weighing the casks and bundles.

"Rise," he bade the men at last.

Standing, they looked at him indecisively, awed by what
they had seen, and by the confidence that had not even
ordered them to cast aside their weapons.

Koschei's gaze fell upon Felimid. He confronted the bard,
standing close, and dropped a hand to Kincaid's hilt.

"This sword is enchanted," he announced. "I know such
things. With this you might slay many beings immune to common steel—and there is a curse upon it. I feel, I know! I know

also that it cannot cut or pierce *me*, though its metal came from beyond the sky.

"I boast, you think? Then draw and strike, if you dare! But if I survive I will have you sewn in a deer's hide and torn by hounds!" He glared into the bard's eyes. "Well?"

Felimid shook his head. "I am content, my great lord."

"Ha!" Koschei cried. "Now hear me, strangers! Hervet of the Obodrites is dead. He would not own me his master, and died for his insolence. His fortress I swept from the earth like trash from a floor; my mansion stands there in its place. I rule now! I rule, and you serve me. Therefore you must know that I will be obeyed. For the rest, these men will teach you my law."

He went ashore, pausing on the quay to nudge the groaning Beigadh with his toe. "Have the surgeon attend this man."

"Yea, sovereign mighty one," answered the olive-skinned, black-moustached leader of the pikemen, with no manifest trace of satire. The northern barbarians were plain men who addressed even their kings simply as "lord," yet none of the boatmen sniggered.

"Who is he?" asked one.

"Koschei the Deathless," answered the chief pikeman. "If he wishes you to know more than that, doubtless he will tell you. If you gossip or question, you are likely to be whipped with scourges. He commands, and others obey. If you remember that you will do well enough.

"My name is Nikolai. Leave your weapons and come with us to the mansion. I warn you, for your lives do not venture above the lowest story, and pray to your heathen gods that *he* never commands your presence on the third. Be wise, and fear him. This is wholly well meant advice."

"On the other hand," Felimid said thoughtfully, "now that your invulnerable lord has taken himself back to his mansion, we might slay as many of you as we find needful, and depart."

"I'd die pitying you," Nikolai assured him. "Fool, do you suppose our twenty pikes maintain *his* power? 'Tis the other way about. You would not reach the sea."

"Beigadh?" Felimid asked. "What say you?"

"I half believe this cur," Beigadh rasped. His face was gray. "Besides, I've a wife and children here. I must know how they fare. I stay until I know."

"Then I stay too," said Koll.

"And I," Felimid affirmed. He felt alight with a strange, lucid excitement, the thrill of danger mixed with the strong urge of curiosity. Behind it all he had a sense of being on familiar ground at last. For him, the tumult and vulnerability of loving had been like a river sweeping him away; this was a matter to which he could apply his wits, and act as his wits dictated without favor or regret. He was very sure that he stood in no danger of loving Koschei.

Leaving his ancestor's sword in the boat, he helped carry Beigadh in a makeshift litter. He doubted that any would engage in theft on Koschei's quay. Besides, the man who stole Kincaid in any circumstances was a dead man; when Koschei sensed a curse on the weapon he had not been mistaken.

The half-Oriental air of the mansion held no associations for Felimid. The only styles of architecture he knew were Celtic, northern and Roman. Still, the strangeness and dazzling opulence of Koschei's audience chamber impressed him. From the glazed tiles (alternately white and sky-blue) and Persian rugs beneath his feet to the painted ceiling, the room was rich past reasonable meaning. He gathered a swift impression of recesses of sculptured stucco, of silk couches and cushions, of gold, ivory and twinkling gems, but took no detailed notice. He had seen the outside of the mansion and declined to boggle further. No doubt there were many more wonders in the place. The question, for him, and the greatest wonder, was how it had been built in the midst of a land sparsely populated by folk whose arts were rude by any standard.

The answer, of course, was sorcery—of exceptional power.

Koschei flung himself into a gilded chair, thrust out his long horseman's legs and shouted for wine. A black-haired youth fetched cup and flagon at once, and poured. Koschei gulped a prodigious amount and flung the precious vessel across the room to strike the wall; as it rebounded, a gem burst from a cracked setting.

"Listen!" he said to the boatmen. "You are my slaves now. Serve me well and you shall be greater than kings in other lands. Serve me other than well and you will long for death. That is my word. Nikolai!"

The captain bowed low. "Sovereign mighty one?"

Koschei pointed out five of Beigadh's crew. "Impale them."

"Ye howling madman!" Koll bawled, and sprang at a nearby guard. His attempt to seize the man's pike failed. He twisted strongly and skillfully, to send Koll sprawling.

Lifting his hands, Koschei spoke in yet another tongue. The words fell from his lips like burning ash.

A globe of emerald fire formed in the air above the prostrate Koll. It crackled and seethed. Felimid, on a premonition, shut his eyes and turned his head aside.

The searing greenish-white flare dazzled him even through closed eyelids. Heat scorched him. A roasting stench filled his nose.

When he opened his eyes, Koll lay charred and twisted on a smoldering rug. His slowly contracting tendons made him writhe and curl gradually, although he was dead.

Fire magic, Felimid thought numbly, and fought a horrified urge to vomit.

Destroyed like a beetle . . . as were the five men Koschei chose to punish for failing to grovel quickly enough at his command. Nikolai's pike-bearers impaled them on greased stakes, transfixing them quickly by hauling on their legs, so that their end, although terrible, was at least not prolonged.

Koschei drew a long, sighing breath as the last man expired.

"I rule now," he said. "Let all of you remember it."

III
By Forest Ways

Gudrun sprang ashore. The Oder's several mouths opened into the sea, unchanged since she had left this spot, not so long before. Standing above her in *Ormungandr*'s bows, Decius waxed more darkly mordant than his wont.

"You are a fool, Blackhair," he said bluntly. "May I be damned if I address you with respect when your acts deserve it so little. God's eyes! You were wise enough, barely, to guest with the Dane-kings awhile and thus avoid giving them offense a second time. But how do you conceive you will find a man as woodwise as Bragi, in that wilderness yonder, if he does not care to be found?"

Gudrun was not offended. "I'm woodwise too. I may find him alone—by the sound of his music if nothing else. Did I take *Ormungandr* up the river, he'd see us coming a league off. What he may say to me when we meet is his affair, and mine. Ah, Decius, we have argued this too many times. Go. Take the ship and do some plundering in the east. Come back in forty days. I'll either be here or I will not, and if I am not, assume I've died."

"At this rate you will return to Sarnia with a crew of Danes only—if you return at all—and find that a Frank has usurped your leadership."

"Then I'll knock him out of the way and take it back," she said. "Fare you well."

Decius waved sardonically. Having strengthened the crew of

Ormungandr to fifty men in Zealand, he looked forward to some good looting among the Prussians. With him leading, there would be no rash forays to rescue captive kings.

Gudrun walked along the strand, tall in a kirtle, cowhide jerkin and breeches of linden green. She wore her treasured sword at her left hip, a heavy knife at the other, and carried her bow and a quiver of hunting arrows. Her only other burden was a satchel; to overtake the bard, she knew she must travel lightly laden.

"Bragi, I'm surely as mad as you," she said aloud, "and maybe our quarrel cannot be mended—but if I find you again, I'll try."

She vanished into the forest's green shadows. A lone magpie insulted her. In the treetops, a pair of noisy squirrels skirmished. Gudrun trod springily on crackling leaves. Despite her announced conviction that she must be mad, she felt blithe at heart.

The welcome she received on Zealand had been one to remember. Helgi's return, as it happened, had been the one thing his brother needed to complete his joy, for the monster Grendel has just been slain by a stranger from across the sea. Then he had finished the work by slaying the monster's terrible dam, who laired in a cave behind a waterfall. Gudrun's rescue of Helgi had faded somewhat by comparison. She had grown restless within days, and at last owned to herself that she wanted to seek her estranged lover.

Two things were certain; he would travel upriver, and he would not recede into bashful hiding. A harper so skilled was sure to become a subject of talk. Although Gudrun had scarcely a word of the Wendish language, she knew that Swedish traders dealt with them. She would contrive; she would find ways. In her thick pied jerkin, she could pass as a young man. That was why she wore it. If none recognized her as a woman, then none would know her as Gudrun Blackhair, who had sacked Svantovit's temple.

I must cut my hair, she thought, not without a pang.

Before doing so, she hunted, and in time her bow twanged death to a fallow stag. Her shot was true, and the beast did not run far. Kneeling beside the body, a foreleg in one hand and her knife in the other, Gudrun was suddenly aware of a presence. She rose, her skin turning unaccountably cold. A stranger stood in the trail.

"Who are you?" she demanded.

In her surprise she had forgotten that they were not likely to have a language in common. However, he answered her in Danish.

"Do you not know me, Gudrun Blackhair? You ought to. Then call me Grim."

The deep-toned voice rang. Gudrun saw him clearly, even in the forest dimness, save for the face a wide-brimmed hat cast into blacker shadow. His gray beard fell to his chest. The glitter of a huge spear he held matched the glitter of his lone eye.

"I see, at least, that you know me," she said from a dry throat.

"Aye. Well enough to give you sound rede. Turn back. This path will prove unlucky for you, should you not find the one you seek, and worse if you do encounter him again. He will bring you to your weird. Look no more for him. Return to the sea and all else you desire shall be yours, riches and lasting fame."

"I have those things. My hall in Sarnia is piled with wealth, and many know my name. This man is all I lack."

"This man has spoken ill words to you," the stranger rasped. "He has spurned you before your warriors, used magic against you to the hurt of your honor, and you chase him like a foolish, wanton girl. You should wish to slay him. Where is your pride?"

Gudrun's men, had they witnessed the scene, would have awaited a response of fury from their captain. But awe humbled her for once, because she had guessed who the stranger was.

"Pride does not trouble me—lord—where he is concerned. He may need aid. I'd have died at least twice were it not for him. However, in full truth, I do not follow him because I owe him debts."

"No," retorted the graybeard. "One of Freya's cats has clawed you. Such scratches heal. Once more, turn back."

Gudrun shook her stubborn head. "I go on."

Grim's eye flashed like a malignant star. "You hold me lightly, to spurn my rede! You are enamored of a weakling. His love will take strength from your sword arm and bring you soon to your end. Gudrun Blackhair, you have too many foes to afford softness."

"I've done more than I can afford all my life, and always

prevailed," she answered. "Lord, I intend no affront, for I think I do know you. But I will not turn back."

"From this decision you will get bitter woe." The old man's voice was cold as a wind from the realm of Hel. "Your vows are severed; call yourself no longer mine, nor invoke my name. Pass on, fool. Rush to your fate."

Gusts of air whirled in the forest, striking Gudrun like blows. She fancied she saw Grim mounting a death-gray horse with more than the ordinary number of legs. Then a clap of wind struck her directly in the face. Her eyes and teeth were spiked with blinding agony, such was the cold. When she could see again, the game trail was open before her. Rime dusted her jerkin and hair; frost, in high summer.

Gudrun shivered, though not with cold. Some time passed before she dressed the neglected carcass of the stag, and even then her thoughts remained a jumble. Odin . . . she had met Odin. Met him and had him disown her.

His prediction of doom troubled her only a little. Death had long been a close companion of hers; she had never ignored the truth that she was mortal. Other things about her meeting with the One-eyed jarred upon her.

To Gudrun, he had ever been the patron of warriors, who gave or witheld victory, and received the brave with honor when they died in war. However, he was the god of the gibbet as well, the lord of dark sorcery, and notorious for deceit. His particular children were the berserks, foul madmen who knew no restraint and often emerged from their fits of rage to find themselves crippled or dying from wounds they had not noticed in their frenzy.

His eight-legged horse was simply a poet's way of saying *death*. A man rode to his grave on an eight-legged horse—a pall with four bearers. An image, a fancy. Then the many-legged horse she had actually seen was an illusion, cast by Odin.

Gudrun had learned something of illusion in the dwarf king's hall. Besides, she knew that Odin was deeply crafty, and given to wandering the world in disguise. What if the one-eyed graybeard with the spear were only another fancy of poets—one Odin found convenient? And if he had appeared to Gudrun in his true shape, what would she have seen?

Sudden revulsion crawled through her heart like a snake, like the venom-fanged Nidhogg who gnaws forever at the roots of Yggdrasil. With sudden insight she comprehended *why* her vanished lover loathed Odin so dearly.

The more reason to find him and tell him so.

Wrapping part of the stag's bloody liver in his own hide and stowing it in her satchel, she threw his hindquarters over her shoulders and went on for a winding league. By then, strong though she was, she was glad to hang the venison from a tree. The liver cooked quickly, though not too quickly to suit her ravenous hunger.

She passed the night in a huge oak's branches. Starlings awoke her. Venison and herbs formed her breakfast. Having eaten, she cut her hair short with her knife, then threw the tresses into the forest.

"Now I'll pass as a man," she said, trying out a deeper tone, "or at any rate a tall youth—so long as none feels my ribs!"

She scouted several winding trails, climbed the tallest tree she could find and observed the country. She had strayed from the near vicinity of the river since her meeting with "Grim." It lay over a mile to the east now.

She took the trail most likely to remedy that, and carried a single haunch of meat with her. It proved heavy enough. Still, over two days she reduced it to a well-gnawed bone.

The forest did not swarm with supernatural beings to her senses as it did to Felimid's. Gudrun could not see them plainly unless they wished it; none the less, she saw and heard disconcerting things.

When she found her path stopped by a stream tributary to the Oder, she followed it, seeking a ford, and in time she came to one. The village beside it looked like a good place to inquire after a wandering harper. Perhaps he had even been here.

The stocky, coarsely clad villagers seemed friendly. Her mime of plucking harpstrings produced no result, though. Thinking that the local chieftain might have more to tell, she asked, "*Voivode?*"

The bearded men in their loose shirts responded with shrugs. Maybe *voivode* was the wrong word; what other term for chieftain or noble had that silly Wendish woman taught her?

"*Zhupan?*" she hazarded.

Their brows cleared wonderfully. Ah! *Zhupan!* They indicated that she must travel farther upstream to find him. She decided to do so. If the visit yielded no information, she would retrace her steps to the Oder.

This smaller river was kept navigable by many men's labor. Gudrun saw earthen levees in places, and once a gang of Wends destroying a snag in midstream. In one spot where the water ran too shallow for boats to pass, its level was raised by a brushwood dam which had to be torn down and then remade whenever water traffic went by. It showed that the local chieftain was diligent, Gudrun thought—and in a household of any size, there should be someone to translate for her.

The *zhupan*'s farmstead stood within a log palisade and two encircling ditches for defense, amid cleared fields of flax and barley. A large boathouse stood by the stream, and some way above it, a growling water mill was fed from a fine timber dam, no crude brushwood weir.

Water mills were nigh unheard of in the north. Folk milled their grain by hand in stone querns, were they Danes, Swedes or Norse. The Wends were a ruder people yet. The man who had built this structure must come from the south, or the west. Thus he was almost sure to speak some language in common with Gudrun, who knew both east and west German dialects and could tackle Latin.

She strode boldly to the gates and asked the guard for leave to enter as a guest. Men looked at her in wonder, for in these parts her clothes, travel-stained though they were, counted as finery. Her sword marked her as someone of rank. She had no difficulty in meeting the *zhupan*.

He oozed water over the juniper-strewn floor of his eating hall when she first saw him. The sluice gate of his prized dam had suffered harm, and he was fresh from working on it.

"Good day, lord," she said, in the Frankish dialect—an impulsively loosed shaft which hit the mark.

"What?" the *zhupan* said, astonished. A small, robust man whose baldness displayed the round shape of his skull, he spoke quickly, the words crowding each other. "Are you Frankish, young sir? Can you tell so easily that I am also? Or perhaps you came seeking me, Leubast? No matter, you are welcome, whatever your errand. Come in. Drink with me."

"Thanks," Gudrun said. "I'm, er, but half Frankish, and Skanian born; still, it's good to meet kindred. My name is, is Warinar."

She said this to explain her accent, which was not that of

one born in Gaul. Further explanation she did not offer, and
would not unless asked for it; she disliked even the deceit
of giving a false name, when she was so fiercely proud of
her own, and of concealing her sex, of which she was not
ashamed. But caution demanded it.

After spending a little more time with Leubast, she felt less
sorry that she had deceived him. He did not impress her as
truthworthy. The jerky swiftness of his speech irritated her.
He appeared to look straight at her when he spoke, but stared
too fixedly, or focused his gaze some way beyond her. For all
his effusive chatter, she discerned no warmth in him.

"Once I lived near Colonia,* on the Rhine, a king's vicar,"
he hiccuped, when drink had made him maudlin. "A king's
vicar, honored . . . aye, but I had a rival, and the king favored
him above me. We fought, and he prevailed, the . . . " Gudrun
waited out Leubast's curses on his former rival. "I fled for my
life to the land of the Thurings, to their king's court. Before
long I discovered that he planned to send me back to torture
and death at my own king's hands. I fled farther still, through
leagues of wilderness. Now I am here and have not done so ill.
Not so ill. Ah, but I miss the cultivated, civilized life I had."

He made an unpleasant noise and staggered to the wall to
spew.

When he returned, Gudrun asked if he or any of his folk
had heard of a green-eyed harper, explaining her interest by
saying that he was a friend of hers, once outlawed but with his
sentence now lifted, whom she wished to find and tell that he
was free—but she might as well have saved her breath, for
Leubast was too drunk to understand.

"No, I'm not free," he muttered. "Not I. My sentence
still stands."

With an impatient hiss, Gudrun gave up. She would ask
Leubast again when he was sober; his wives and children
spoke only Wendish, so there was nothing to be gained from
them. The same applied to his workmen and slaves.

She slept fully clothed in straw that night. She had slept in
worse places by far, and with worse noises than snoring in her
ears. Maybe she had grown too used to command since then,
and to giving orders which were obeyed, for when she awoke
with rough hands on her limbs, she reached for her weapon

* *Cologne.*

too slowly. A couple of brawny laborers held her fast.

While she struggled, cursing, a third man opened her jerkin and rent her shirt. Her breasts were not apparent to sight in the dark; none the less, when the lout gripped them, there was no hiding her sex. He announced his discovery with a roar of laughter.

The others, surprisingly, made no effort to handle her. One spoke to the fellow who still mauled her breasts, and spoke in curt reproof. Although she heard it, Gudrun did not conceive at once that she was molested for any reason but the obvious one. She continued to struggle, but with less than her full strength, so that they might underestimate her. They could not attempt rape without exposing themselves to her attack. One chance was all she required—to sink her teeth in a nose, to gouge an eye, to smash genitals, and then to seize a knife. If they dragged her aside to enjoy some semblance of privacy, so much the better.

She was not afraid and had nothing in her mind but tactics, no thought of surrender.

When her ox-muscled captors thrust her towards the door, she went, her arms twisted behind her. When they dragged her across the yard, out of the steading altogether, and down the hill, she yelled in her loudest voice for the *zhupan*. When her abductors made no attempt to silence her, she began to wonder if this was a simple matter of rape.

Whatever it was, she had let it proceed far enough.

They hustled her toward the water mill, which she also found puzzling. Why there? Well, it was unimportant. Clumsy louts that they were, her captors stumbled on the way. Gudrun moved like lightning, ramming her shoulder against one before he recovered balance, then driving her knee into the other's belly as his mate went sprawling. She struck him violently in the throat to ensure that he did not recover his breath.

In a heartbeat-long search at his belt, she found and possessed his knife.

The first laborer had not yet regained his feet. Gudrun almost broke his neck with a savage kick. Once again, he went down. The third man, following them, only then began to draw a weapon. Gudrun's ears told her so; she knew that soft grating slide of metal very well.

A long blade glimmered faintly. Moving in leafy darkness, on uneven ground, she closed with him—sank the knife in his belly—dragged it across—drew it up and around. The man's attempt at a scream came out as a long, ghastly whistling. Gudrun cut his throat as he toppled.

The weapon he had carried was her sword, Kissing Viper. With it, she killed the last carl.

Hotly furious, in no humor to let matters stand as they were, she trod forward. The trio had been taking her to the mill-pond for some reason. She intended to know what it was.

Her huntress's ears caught the noise of a man pacing by the marge. He, too, heard her. Turning, he called a query in an impatient tone, and she knew Leubast's voice. The *zhupan*, here, waiting for his underlings to fetch her. No wonder they had not cared when she shouted his name.

"Dog!" she greeted him. "The saying is true; a Dane for courage, a Saxon for niggardliness, and a Frank for treachery."

"You! Where are Bod and Orik and Pechen?"

"Lying yonder, dead. I gave them no chance to say any last words, but I'll hear yours if you wish, since I can understand them."

"Bitch!"

"Then try my teeth," Gudrun invited, and came on.

Leubast bore a spear. His weapon had more range than the pirate's sword, and he used it to full advantage. Thus the fight was somewhat long. Plainly Leubast's maudlin drunkenness had been feigned, for he proved active and skillful.

They surged back and forth along the starlit marge, each intent upon nothing less than the other's death. Once Leubast's spear-tip grated along Gudrun's ribs, and once it drew blood from her thigh. At last her quickness prevailed. She dodged a thrust, responded with a short chopping stroke which cut fingers from one of his hands, and a moment later opened his belly. Panting, she stood above him as he weltered, with her back to the starlit water.

"Fool!" she laughed. "Greater men than you have tried to conquer Gudrun Blackhair!"

"Blackhair?" Leubast croaked. "You?"

His body spasmed in its last movements. He never spoke again.

"But why?" she asked the corpse, fruitlessly. "Even treachery must have a reason, if only a fancied reason."

Behind her, the placid water erupted. Spray scattered in the starlight. Wheeling, Gudrun glimpsed lithe, dripping shapes with eyes like lanterns. Slender arms twined about her, many of them, enfolding her waist, legs, shoulders, clasping her sword-arm and drawing her into the pond. Water like cold silk closed over her. Bubbles erupted silver.

The many arms pulled her down.

IV
A Horse of Fire

In the meantime, this had been happening elsewhere:

Koschei the Deathless pursed his heavy lips and moved a gamepiece to the seventh rank. Felimid studied the new situation. The pieces were carved rubies and diamonds; at first, it had so intrigued him to handle them that the game held less interest. Now he treated them as casually as pebbles.

He shifted a piece three squares. Koschei nodded approval.

"You have surprised me. Ha! I had thought to capture your king in four moves! Now I believe I cannot do it in fewer than seven."

Felimid had played this game enough to gain some skill, becoming quicker each time, more aware of patterns and possibilities. He had never approached winning, but now the sorcerer required as many as twenty moves to defeat him, and favored him above other opponents.

"Whence comes this game, sovereign one?"

"I learned it in Persia," the other answered, "where I dwelt for generations of your mortal kind. I was at Ctesiphon when the Romans burned the royal palace, and I have followed the Silk Road east of the Aral Sea. I studied with the magi, the fire priests, and learned things unknown even to their leaders. Yea, and long before that, I had made myself ageless, proof against all harm from anything upon this earth—or beyond. Koschei the Deathless I am called, and not lightly. Yet I was born a savage in a howling wilderness where the wolves are black and the trees sweat lakes of honey. My mother squatted on the naked earth to whelp me. *This* land is a terraced, cultivated garden to the land where I grew to manhood. I say it.''

"Yet rude to Persia or East Rome," Felimid said.

"It will blossom!" Koschei brought up the piece Felimid called a "tower," gripping it hard in his black-nailed fingers. The bard saw no sense to the move. "No longer ago than yesterday's dawn, all this was a Hunnic domain. Their khagan, Attila, ruled from the Rhine to the Caspian, from the Baltic to the Danube. *Attila*! I lived in his court and advised him for a time. He knew how to conquer and had even some notion of how to build; Huns, Germans, Sarmatians and Slavs he welded into an empire.

"Then he died. His empire rotted apart like ice in the spring sun, but had he been immortal . . . " Koschei glared at Felimid. "You doubt me! You would smile if you dared!"

"I await instruction," the bard said calmly, "if my great lord is pleased to give it."

He dared bandy words with Koschei in this frame of mind. Despite his bluster, the magician was lucid and wholly within his own control—for the moment. He was even expansive. In the next moment, he might hurl the chessboard aside, demand music, and shed copious tears at its beauty. On the other hand, a transport of utter, ungoverned rage was just as likely. In Koschei's presence, one gambled with each breath one drew on being embraced rather than throttled.

Yet Koschei was no mere demented braggart. He spoke with ease in Greek, Persian, Latin, several German and Asiatic tongues, a kind of Old Slavic which might well be his mother language, the current form of it spoken by the Obodrites, Swedish and even Finnish, and switched among them without warning. Nor was he patient with those who did not comprehend him. He would shout, "Then learn!"

It was best to do so.

Quickly.

Koschei, no matter how mad, was swift and acute himself and demanded it in others. Some things he said suggested to Felimid that he was sowing the seeds of a multilingual court in this place. Perhaps Koschei himself knew why, perhaps not. But the bard had never met a more powerful wizard—or one with powers more varied. Svantovit's nine priests were like children to him.

Felimid had noted some of those powers. Koschei could summon lightning in the form of fireballs which consumed what they touched, or in devastating flashes. He appeared invulnerable to all physical harm. His ramblings when he grew garrulous showed that he had indeed lived hundreds of years. The bard suspected that this strange tyrant jumbled together events which had occurred generations apart and in different lands. His brain held memories as vivid as they were random.

Felimid believed Koschei's mind had begun to topple because of his centuries. One mortal life extended so far was surely more than a mortal brain could govern. If he founded an empire he would do it as he played chess, for amusement. An ancient, terrible child working to distract a mind crumbling to ruin.

"I have mastered demons," the magician said once, during a drinking bout. "They serve me. Many. Who built this mansion in a night? Demons! They are my slaves, as you are. Demons are far safer slaves than men, for to control them one need not be wise, but only rigorous."

"It's little I know of demons," Felimid said. "Elves and sheehans, spirits, elementals, ghosts, shapeshifters, fetches and even gods—these I do know, but what is a demon?"

"Ha ha! Does not your puling church inform you?"

"My church it is not, sovereign one. I have never listened to its priests since I discovered their views of women. If they are unsound concerning beings they have all seen, should I take their word concerning demons?"

"They are mingled of four elements, like you, but they are immortal. I have become so; it is their nature. They can assume any shape they please, however strange, by willing it at the time of sunrise or sunset. Again, this is their nature and calls for no learned sorcery. Although they can be killed, time, hunger nor sickness will not achieve it.

"Fear they do not know, yet they can be ruled by a word, a sign or a talisman of power. And woe to the mortal who rules them if they should regain their autonomy." Koschei's mouth warped into the approximate shape of a smile. "Dawn is near. Demons are unknown to you? Come. You shall see one, child!"

He emptied his cup of the resinous Greek wine. "Phrates, I have an errand for you."

The Persian youth who was his cup-bearer bowed mutely.

Koschei led the way to the lavish stables behind the mansion as the eastern sky grew lighter.

"The *zhupan* Tverets, who dwells four days' journey by boat upstream, defies me," Koschei said. "He will not send levies to be trained as pikemen. He says he will bow to no wizardly dog. *He says that!*" Koschei roared. "Go! Rend his family, slay all to the youngest babe, and hither bring him living for me to punish!"

The slender youth bowed again. The first rays of light flashed across the land like hurled spears.

Phrates grew larger. Within a score of the bard's hammering heartbeats, the cup-bearer towered four yards high in a manlike, feathered form with taloned feet and the head of a vast hawk. Spines crested his head, grew from his backbone and forearms.

Spreading crimson-feathered wings the width of the stable yard, he beat the air so that straw went whirling. With muscle-cracking labor he fought his way aloft. A few hundred feet above their heads, he caught a rising wind and soared.

Felimid saw and vaguely noted that as Phrates grew, the dungheap beside him had diminished, turning to streams of murky vapor which flowed into the demon's form. Even for a being confined to no particular physical shape, bone and flesh had to come from somewhere. But though Felimid saw and even noted this, he did not ponder it; he was too shaken.

"Behold another demon," Koschei said, treading like some great cat to a stall richer than most royal tombs. Within stood a glorious horse, tawny as lions, its mane and tail made of living yellow fire. "This good heroic steed can carry me nine nights and days at a gallop while I wear full cataphract's armor, if it be needful. I will ride him in war against the river *zhupans* if nothing else will cause them to bend the knee. If! Ha! When they see how I deal with Tverets they will own that they may not govern save in my name! I rule now!"

It was his favorite saying, and he was making it true.

"Yet demons can be slain, sovereign one," Felimid said. "Have you many at your command?"

"Upwards of twenty," Koschei answered. "I shall use them. They are potent instruments of fear. Pikemen and mounted archers shall serve that purpose too. None shall disobey the laws of my empire!"

"I fancy I can ride this demon, sovereign one," Felimid

said, indicating the horse. "Is that against your law?"

"You! Your hand shall be cut off if you touch him!" Then Koschei suddenly laughed. "No. I unsay that. If you touch him he will bite off your arm. My justice will be needless once Ogon here has imposed his own. Did you attain to his back, he would pluck your kneecaps as if they were apples. He would stamp and rend you—" Koschei bit the sentence short, with froth beginning to speckle his beard. "Enough!"

Felimid also thought it enough. Koschei had begun to enjoy his visions of the demon Ogon dismembering the bard, and might have taken the sudden whim to make those visions actual. It was a pleasure to see him depart to the upper story of his mansion. Yawning after a sleepless night, Felimid applied his wits to the knowledge he had gained.

Upwards of twenty demons were at Koschei's beck. If Felimid were to leave, attempt an escape from this barless cage, one or more would pursue him. Perhaps he could slay it—or them—with Kincaid. The ancient sword was deadly even to beings which could not be harmed with common steel, although not to Koschei. Felimid would test the magician's boast of utter invulnerability if he must. It might be no more than that, a boast. Yet Felimid tended to credit it.

He still wore the sword because Koschei was at least wary of the curse attached thereto, which fell upon any who possessed Kincaid unless they were of Ogma the Champion's blood. Not even Koschei the Deathless could be sure of warding himself against a god's curse. He had sensed at once that it was there, locked in the sword steel. It was matter for regret that he had not chosen to defy it and plunder Felimid of the weapon. His life would have come to an end within a nine-night.

But Koschei had been too wise.

Nor did Ogma's sword make the wielder invincible, or fight by himself, or guide the wielder's hand. If Felimid did face a demon, it would be for him, with his own quickness, skill and courage, to send Kincaid's point to a vital spot before the demon plucked him apart.

To free the demons from Koschei's dominance would be far neater. He mastered them by some—what had he said?— "word, sign or talisman of power." The bull-headed iron mace he carried like a scepter might well be the talisman in question, or it might be something else. Perhaps it could be nullified somehow, and if so, the results for Koschei would not be pleasant. If he survived, he should be too beset to concern himself with one absconding bard.

Yes. There was one possible way of escape.

Another was to steal the demon horse and use it to outdistance demon pursuit. Koschei's lurid warning did not frighten Felimid. If a creature had a mane and tail and four undivided hoofs, he was confident he could ride it.

He had walked by the river while he considered these things. Returning by way of the courtyard, he watched the captain, Nikolai, drill his pikemen. They numbered eighty now: the Byzantine veterans and three score recruits levied from Obodrite villages. Once Koschei had made an example of the recalcitrant *zhupan*, no doubt the levies would increase.

Nikolai said as much, later. "I'll have hundreds to train, as I now have tens," he predicted, "and in due time, thousands. Other officers of the Empire will join me here. Some fine ones lose favor because of intrigue every year. What *he* wishes to achieve is a task for armies, not demons."

"Indeed. His ambition's known to you, then—and that he deals with demons?"

"He does not deal with them, harper. He bids them hunt, heel and bite, like dogs. I say it's for him to settle his own account with their dark Lord." Nikolai crossed himself. "I am a soldier." Seeing Felimid smile, he snapped, "What amuses you?"

"That you are so very sure. There is Earth, Heaven and Hell —nothing else. There is this life, and one beyond, which lasts forever—nothing else. I had a tutor named Fintan the Ancient who might have argued that, so. Koschei too could instruct you."

"I'd not care to ask him," Nikolai said grimly. "*He* might instruct me in that which I would rather not learn, as he does the merchant."

"Beigadh?" Felimid had not seen the Gotlander for days. "What has become of him? I'd supposed. . . ."

He paused there. He had supposed nothing, or more than carelessly taken notice that Beigadh was gone. His henchmen had been put to work; his wife Ludovena, elder daughter of the luckless Hervet, had done little in the bard's sight save hide in shadowed corners.

Nikolai refused to say more. Whatever he knew or surmised of Beigadh's fate, he considered it unwise to discuss.

When the demon Phrates returned with the chieftain who
had defied Koschei, that wretched man met a fate none had to
conjecture. His doom was public, witnessed by a dozen other
zhupans whom demon messengers had summoned to observe
the lesson. Two demons also attended the execution, flanking
Koschei's throne in the form of winged, man-headed Assyrian
bulls. The victim lingered more than a day; the other *zhupans*
then swore oaths of subjection and kissed Koschei's foot.
They went away convinced that uncountable hosts of demons
obeyed the magician.

Phrates himself had resumed the form of a handsome boy,
and his duties as Koschei's cup-bearer; and shortly after the
defiant *zhupan* had the good sense to expire, Beigadh the
trader was seen again.

He appeared, neither announced nor expected, at a banquet. He tottered like an old man, leaning on a burly attendant. The muscles and the whole set of his countenance had
slackened into defeat. Seeing him thus, Felimid heard Nikolai's warning again in his mind: "Do not venture above the
lowest story, and pray to your heathen gods that *he* never
commands your presence on the third." Had Beigadh received
such a command?

Startled and horrified by the change in a strong man, Felimid moved swiftly to support him on his other side. Beigadh
accepted his arm, and could be felt to tremble as he lowered
himself to a couch. The Beigadh Felimid had first met, even an
ill Beigadh, would have told him with forceful good humor to
stop fussing.

"Cairbre and Ogma!" Felimid swore, pouring wine. Beigadh drank it, his teeth clicking against the vessel's rim.
"What befell, chieftain? Were you tortured?"

"Torture?" Beigadh echoed, looking at the bard from
sunken, shifting eyes. "Nothing so cleanly. Nothing so . . . decent. I'd ha' laughed at red irons and spat in the torturer's
face. Ah, gods!"

He noticed the bard's cloak of brocade, flashing with silver
thread and tissue, the tunic, the silk trousers, the soft half-
boots of Persian leather. "I see you are in some favor," he
said. "I'll tell you, then. You may require to know, and when
you do . . . you may decide you'd liefer die than bide here.

"There's a Byzantine surgeon, above," he went on,
breathing jerkily, indicating the upper stories of the mansion

with a thumb. "One of those gelded things a real man should not have to look at. A magician himself, in his way. He cast a spell on me . . . so that I felt nothing and my blood ceased to flow . . . yet I lived. He took out, took out, took out everything inside me . . . lights, liver, heart, guts . . . and sealed them in a split, hollowed log he had prepared. It's up there now"—Beigadh made the gesture with his thumb again—"held shut by three steel bands. Man, I'm hollow as a seashell, and yet I live. The wonder is that I'm not mad!"

He reached for more wine with a shuddering hand.

"*Why*?" Felimid asked.

"*He* wants trade. I'm to serve him as a merchant, he says, and for that . . . he must let me out of his sight. He thought Ludovena and our children might not suffice as hostages. I've another family in Gotland, as you know, and if I left I might choose to remain there. Now . . . he holds my living vitals hostage, and however far I go I must come back. Do you see?"

"I see indeed," Felimid answered, dry-tongued. Hardly a nuance of meaning was hidden. His hand pressed Beigadh's shoulder. "Courage. This banded chest, or log, or what you said, belongs to you, and you can steal it back, even from Koschei. Tonight I counsel you, drink deeply; drink yourself unconscious! Or if Koschei doesn't call me, let me harp to you, and give you peaceful sleep."

"Ha! You think you can?"

"I know I can," Felimid answered; and did.

V

The Palace of the Vodyanek

Gudrun struggled fiercely as the pale figures drew her under the surface. Fighting proved useless; they moved like fish, and she could get no purchase to use her greater strength. Water pressed cold and heavy on her ribs. Desperately, she held her breath.

The dark lake glowed red before her eyes. Intolerable pain filled her chest. With a sob of surrender, she sucked in a breath—and instead of choking, knew sweet relief. She breathed beneath the lake. Cool fingers held each wrist and leg.

As her vision cleared, the pressure on her chest relaxed. Hands thrust and pushed her out of . . . a pool? She lay dripping on a floor of rippled limestone, where nothing should exist but the mud at the bottom of the millpond.

Raising herself, she saw fluted columns, curtains of lacy stone, spires and domes of millennial growth, archways leading to other caverns—and she saw the beings who had captured her.

They were slender young women in robes of shining mist. Their blank, luminescent eyes seemed blind.

Gasping an oath, Gudrun raised Kissing Viper. She had held the sword firmly throughout her brief ordeal. Its weight heartened her.

"What are you?" she snarled, her ready anger flaring. "I'll

202

cut you apart if you touch me again! Or unless you answer! Speak!"

"We wish you no harm," said one, in a voice soulless as rippling water. "You have avenged us. Living men and women call us *rusalki*."

"Living! What are you—ghosts?" Gudrun's voice continued raw with danger. "Move back from me!"

"We are *rusalki*. Aforetime we were women, young and alive. Leubast drowned us in his dam as sacrifices to the *vodyanek*, the water godling. But for such offerings, he would have broken the dam and set the stream free . . . yea, and shattered the mill. The latest sacrifice was to have been you."

"Niflheim!" Gudrun spat, naming the realm of Hel. "How long has he done this?"

"One of us perished each year," answered another of the beings.

"Nine of you," Gudrun said, glancing from one to the next around the daunting semicircle of them. "So, then. A tenth there will not be! You say I have avenged you and that you wish me no harm. If that is true, why am I here? What do you want of me? And what place is this?"

"You stand in the *vodyanek*'s palace," a third ghostly woman said. Anything she might have added was forestalled by the hasty Gudrun.

"*Vodyanek*? The water demon? What is he, a nicor of some sort? Is he close at hand?"

"No." It might have been the first speaker who replied; Gudrun was not sure. Their common eeriness made it difficult to tell them apart. "He is away from his palace now, but he will return. We wish you to slay him when he does."

A susurant chorus of agreement rose from her sisters.

"Why should I?" Gudrun demanded. "It's nothing to me."

"It is much to you. When the *vodyanek* comes, he will destroy you for trespass if you do not destroy him. You must slay him to live."

"You might guide me whence I came."

"Not before you slay the *vodyanek*. Nor can you threaten us. Being dead, we are beyond your power. The *vodyanek* is not."

"You ghostly bitches!" Gudrun raged. Profitlessly. Realizing it, she uttered a short laugh, void of humor. "So, then, curse you! Let me know the full tale, and be sure to include the reason, why and wherefore, you wish this stream god dead."

"That is soon told." The speaker drew near, a veil of luminescent mist swirling about her. "The *vodyanek* is lord of the stream and dislikes having it fettered. When Leubast made his dam, the *vodyanek* broke it down by night as quickly as it was built by day, until Leubast began sacrificing girls to him by drowning. Then the *vodyanek* was pleased and allowed the dam to stand.

"Now a girl who drowns, whether by murder, self-murder or mischance, becomes a *rusalka*, such as we. Being dead, we must inhabit the dark, cold waters in winter, but when Dazhbog* enters the road of summer and warms the lakes and rivers, our nature is to leave the water and go into the forest where the leaves and shadows are dense.

"Yet we were offered to the *vodyanek*, and his might holds us here for all the yearly round, to be his slave doxies. We would be free. The live water of summer is hateful to us."

"Hateful!" echoed another.

"Yea!"

"You needn't clamor so! I believe you!" Gudrun said. "If I slay this *vodyanek*, you will be free, and hie to the dim forest? And show me the way out of here?"

"Yes!"

"Yes!"

"This is only the truth!"

Gudrun shivered suddenly, a tall, strapping woman still dripping water in a dankly cold place, surrounded by the dead . . . by drowned victims. *What if I had to confront men of my own slaying?*

She wrenched her mind away from that possibility and thought of her immediate situation.

"Your offer's acceptable," she said, "but not yet enough. I seek a man. He's travelling somewhere in this land. You must aid me to find him. If you will promise to do that . . . I'll slay your cursed *vodyanek*!"

"You must slay him in any case," one of the *rusalki* said,

---

* the Sun; literally, ''the god who gives.''

ingenuously. "If you do not, he will slay you."

Gudrun smiled rather cruelly. "You have all met death only once. I know him well, babe in arms. I do not forget that you caught me like a fish and offered me a poor sort of choice. I'll not let you coerce me!

"Yes, I'd fight your *vodyanek* if I met him. I always fight when I must, and at times for the sport . . . but if I slew myself? Where would I leave you?" She drew her knife and studied the point. Her expression grew dreamy. "You may not impose your will on me so easily, little ones. I think we must bargain."

"We will do as you wish."

"Good." Gudrun sheathed her knife. Her bullhide shoes squelched as she moved her feet. "Now show me the rest of the palace."

The nine *rusalki* formed an eerie escort, moving softly on bare white feet. Gudrun glanced at them as often as at the fantastic chambers and grottoes of the *vodyanek*'s dwelling. Ghosts. No, not ghosts as the stories of her home described them, but beings peculiar to this land, part ghost, part water sprite, part forest nymph. She felt her fancy caught by them even as she trod in a realm of danger—as it had always been caught by the new, the wonderful, the unknown.

They led her by ponds with thin discs of stone growing across their surfaces, by spires and spines and chandeliers of dainty oolite, through water-fretted archways, passages, and chambers like the interiors of ornate shells. Startling wealth lay piled or scattered in some of them. Her pirate's eye recognized amber, pearl, opals, jade, gold, tarnished silver from sunken river hoards, and more obscure treasures—some magical in nature—mingled with curious rubbish. Skeletons sprawled. Leather erupted with lurid fungi. Spearheads rusted or tarnished. A sunken barge lay rotting apart. Within it, a nine-foot water dragon lazed on a bed of piled weed, indolently turning its head to watch Gudrun and her guides pass. Its color slowly changed from beige to a smoldering purple.

"He will not attack you," a *rusalka* said. "He eats only fish."

Gudrun wondered how the ghost-girl knew the dragon's sex, and briefly entertained some bawdy, grotesque speculation.

"I've seen enough," she declared. "What of your lord? Where should I await him? What is he like? Is he vulnerable in the same places as a man?"

"You can slay him as you would a man," came the soft, multiple reply. "None the less, you must give him his death with one stroke. If the first is not mortal, or if you deal a second in mercy, he will be invulnerable forever after to any attack of yours. You must slay him with one blow or not at all."

"I'll remember," Gudrun promised. "I'll not strike him by stealth, mark me. It's my way to face those I challenge. Even demons."

She smiled with ferocious good humor.

"Then you need but wait," she was told.

While she waited, Gudrun shed her sodden clothing and wrung it as dry as possible, lest she shiver and chill until she was useless. That done, she drew on her breeches, cursing the clammy way they stuck to her, belted them and fastened her shoes. She moved about, swinging her arms, leaping and kicking to stir her blood.

"Make haste, demon," she muttered, feeling warmer. "I am Gudrun Blackhair, and I am not known for patience."

The *vodyanek* did not make haste for her, but in time, he did arrive. Two of his drowned playthings ran into the chamber where Gudrun waited, their pale hair drifting, blank eyes alight with dread.

"The *vodyanek* is here!"

Gudrun had found a serviceable shield among the water-corroded litter; a bronze target aged green as summer, with a central spike. Her allies pointed the way through a passage, rimed and sparkling with a million pinpoints of light, and fled the other way as she went to the combat.

"*Vodyanek!*" she cried.

He turned a splendid head to view her. His eyes had less in common with humanity than those of a wolf or hawk, or the *rusalki* themselves, who had once been human. His seven-foot body was that of a magnificently formed man, clad in a scale tunic of some emerald-green metal. Almost carelessly, he held a pike taller than himself.

"Mortals do not come to this place unbidden and live, shield woman," he said.

"Then I must kill you in order to depart," she answered.

"Come and fight, or must I come to you?"

Matching the act to her words, she closed the distance between them with a leopard's spring. The pike whirled in her adversary's hands. It jarred on her shield, threatened her face and then her breast. She struck it aside with Kissing Viper.

Flat-footed she retreated, knees slightly bent, her naked torso and arms gleaming in the cavern light. The black hair she had hacked short clung to her neck in damp rat's tails.

She thought, *I must give him death at one stroke.*

The most likely places to strike fatally with a sword were the belly and throat. The *vodyanek's* belly was covered, his throat a smaller target, and hard to reach past the jabbing pike. Against a foe so much larger and stronger than herself—and she met very few—she would ordinarily have tried to disable him, negate his advantage, before she struck to kill. Now it was precisely what she must not do.

Slice his throat or cleave his skull. Or, perhaps, cut his thigh so terribly that he bled to death—but that would not be certain.

The pike hissed at her ribs. Gudrun straightened a knee and moved aside. She chopped at the tough pike-shaft, but failed to halve it. The *vodyanek* reversed his weapon, smiling through his smooth black beard. The pike-butt boomed on Gudrun's shield. She cut at the shaft a second time.

They struck and parried in a lethal dance amid the marvels of shining stone. The *vodyanek* seemed tireless. In motion he was somewhat deliberate, almost ponderous, slower than the pirate—yet always he moved smoothly, with flawless grace and a fighting skill which made him appear to draw Gudrun's movements obediently after his.

The nine *rusalki* had crept back to watch. They eddied about the fighters like curls of foam on troubled water. Gudrun backed into a many-spired grotto floored with yellow sand virtually as coarse as gravel. She left barely an imprint as she moved across it, but the *vodyanek's* weight was such that he made distinct tracks two inches deep. It slowed him.

Gudrun attacked. She knew she must strike her one permitted blow before she grew too weary. Unlike the *vodyanek*, she did not have endless stamina.

She hewed, feinted and struck. The pike-shaft intercepted Kissing Viper's blade, and flew in two parts. The stream lord

struck at Gudrun's face with his shortened weapon. She might
have slashed his offered arm with ease, but a mere wound was
not a death blow, and she dared commit herself to nothing
else.

To refrain was hard. In the instant's confusion it caused
her, the *vodyanek* struck her shoulder a numbing blow with
the butt half of his pike, making it hum in the air like a willow
switch. Kissing Viper flew from Gudrun's hand.

The *vodyanek* laughed.

In the next moment he paid for his mockery. Gudrun leaped
at his face, raising a yell of fury and striking with her shield.
Startled, the *vodyanek* turned his face aside, as concerned for
his eyes as any mortal. Gudrun slanted her shield by instinct,
and added every pound of impetus her arm could supply.

The princely head moved perhaps a hand's width, and Gudrun struck the massive body as though slamming into a pillar.
Rebounding, she dropped at his feet, rolled aside, breathless,
and glanced upward.

His inhuman gaze lowered to regard her. He appeared puzzled. She saw, briefly, a flash of ruddy bronze among the hair
of his temple, a flash centered in green corrosion. She made
the connection without conscious thought; a glance at the
shield on her arm showed her that the central spike was missing, broken off, its stub showing a similar glitter of clean
metal.

The *vodyanek* fell, spiked through the temple.

As Gudrun retrieved her sword, his form altered. When she
looked again, something hairless lay there, something with
variegated white and indigo skin, its webbed clawed feet
drawn up beneath a huge paunch. It smelled, to a faint ap-
proximation, like frog spawn mingled with oil. Worst was the
wholly human shape its head retained. Bands and blotches of
color gave its face the appearance of a mask.

The *rusalki* danced their glee.

"Stay with us," they pleaded later. "You shall be our elder
sister and roam the forest with us in summer. In winter, you
shall rule this palace."

Gudrun felt inexplicably moved by their wish. Looking into
her heart, she searched for rancor against them and found
none. A sudden, aching sadness for their fate rose in her; a
knot below her larynx loosened, and Gudrun Blackhair astounded herself by weeping.

"No, little sisters," she said at last, having left the cave where the *vodyanek*'s body lay. "I cannot stay. I told you why; I seek a man whom you must aid me to find. We agreed to this."

"Then we will go."

One of the *rusalki* left, to return some time later with a pair of intricately stitched boots.

"Wear these, elder sister; you will find them useful. When you stamp three times with the right, a bridge will appear to span any chasm, river or other barrier to your journey. After you have crossed, stamp three times with the left boot and the bridge will vanish."

"You say so?" Gudrun accepted the boots. "Why, useful's a tame word; these could save my life if I'm pursued! I thank you! Now, let us inflict some fear on the kin of this swinish Leubast, long may he rot."

The sudden haunting of their house by nine ghostly women did indeed terrify the Wends. They never saw Gudrun recover her bow and other gear while they scattered in panic. By morning, she was far away in her enchanted boots. The sisters she had adopted had no need of such things to travel swiftly.

VI
A Horse of Flesh

Felimid did not know Gudrun had followed him. Although he might have asked any wind elemental for news of her, he would not. He told himself that it was over and best forgotten, with nothing but useless pain to be had from any such tidings. Her face continued to trouble his sleep for all that, and his waking eye would leap to any tall, black-haired figure an instant before his mind recognized the mistake.

However, he'd little safe leisure for mooning. In Koschei's mansion one had to give full attention to the present. Felimid spent one morning as a witness to Koschei's justice. The magician rose at dawn, and for hours after breaking fast he displayed a clear wisdom which would not have shamed the legendary king, Cormac mac Art.

That same afternoon, while watching a trained bear perform, Koschei demanded that it fall prostrate before him. It had not been trained for that. When it failed to obey, Koschei ordered it crucified—and the thing was done.

To Felimid it was worse in some ways than seeing a man die foully. Worse, because of the beast's innocence, and the insane caprice of the command. It might be the bard's turn next. Koschei's delight in his music did not reliably protect him.

He thought again of Koschei's demon horse. His initial urge to steal and ride it had never quite left him; he lusted to do the thing for its own sake, because it challenged his prowess as a rider. Often, he had gone to the stables and looked at the demon. The desire of achievement aside, he'd require such a mount to take him out of Koschei's reach. No other could—

Ah, wait! There was another, the black mare he knew as Myfanwy, The Rare One. In Britain he had delivered her from bondage to a man who had become her master by learning her true name. A daughter of the horse goddess Epona, she thought and spoke, and had the power to move among the worlds, through foreign dimensions—the power Gudrun ascribed to the ship *Ormungandr*, and had hoped to exploit.

No. Forget Gudrun!

"When you are desperate and have need of a fast horse, call me by the name you gave me. I'll hear and come, Felimid."

So Myfanwy had promised. *That* name was not her true name and could not compel her, but she had said that she would answer it. Felimid smiled broadly, delighted. To vanish, leaving Koschei baffled and raging, was all he could desire. If Myfanwy did not appear, he would stand in no more danger for trying.

Indeed, the fate of an inoffensive bear offered proof that nothing involved greater danger than to bide in Koschei's mansion.

He ran to the apartment Koschei had allowed him, snatched harp and sword, spun about and left, indifferent to the couches, the rugs, the confections of carved silver-gilt wood, and the many cool-hued silks. For a heartbeat his eye rested on a chessboard of pale and dark wood, on which he had been testing endgame variations; and he almost scattered the pieces —but that had been a pointless, peevish gesture of rebellion, the sort of thing Koschei performed on a larger scale because immortality had not, after all, fulfilled his desires by making him godlike. Felimid left with the weapon belted at his right hip and the harp bagged in leather on his back, as he had travelled in Britain for fifty-odd cycles of the moon.

The occasional guard did not challenge him. Felimid was privileged to a degree; to come and go as he pleased, within the limits of Koschei's specific orders, and to wear Kincaid— though never to draw him, on pain of whatever punishment Koschei cared to inflict. He needed no excuse to wander into the forest. There, in the dense shade of a birch grove, he called the black mare.

"Mare with the grace of a gliding swan,
  Once we met where a dim sun shone—
  Here I stand and I'd fain be gone,
  Myfanwy, O Myfanwy!

"Remember the lord with his hunting pack,
  Who dared to saddle your silken back
  And rubbed you raw on his quarry's track,
  Myfanwy, O Myfanwy!

"The honor a goddess's daughter is due
  Was something less than he paid to you,
  And mine was the sword that pierced him through,
  Myfanwy, O Myfanwy!

"You said that day you would come to me
  If I should ever have cause to flee
  A hard pursuit or captivity,
  Myfanwy, O Myfanwy!

"Goddess's daughter, recall your vow!
  Wind-swift hooves and sagacious brow,
  My need is strong and my need is now,
  Myfanwy, O Myfanwy!"

He waited, hopeful yet wary of hoping. Perhaps something prevented her hearing. Perhaps, even if she heard him, she would not come.

Cool, shadowed air shimmered between the birch trunks. She appeared, beautiful as a steed of the Tuatha de Danann, her hide gleaming, jet black, sin black, midnight black, yet with a mane and tail like two flurries of snow.

"Welcome, lady," Felimid said. "As always, your beauty causes me to regret I was not born a horse—and you prove as true to your word as lovely."

"As always, you would pause for pretty words with a hundred blood enemies behind you," she answered, the words coming from deep in her throat with the burring vibration Felimid remembered. Her horse's mouth played small part in her speech. "Who pursues, Felimid mac Fal?"

"Oh, none," he said. "I'm a captive within bounds, lady; a slave, so the master of this land assures me, but I'm not after sharing his opinion. Still, he's a magician of mighty power, and violent to madness when the humor's on him, as it is two hours in seven. I'd rather take my leave than contradict him to his face."

"How mighty a magician?"

"He commands twenty demons and can summon lightning. He's lived hundreds of years and made himself invulnerable to all weapons, or so he boasts—even Kincaid." Felimid touched his sword's silver pommel. "I truly believe him. He came near Kincaid and knew at once this is a weapon of power, and it bearing a curse. Yet he invited me to strike at him and was not afraid."

"Then he may well sense that I am here." Myfanwy lowered her fine head to crop a mouthful or two of grass. "He would be a mad magician indeed who dared my mother's wrath by harming me. . . . But I see by your glances back and forth, and the anxious way you finger your sword-hilt, that you would depart."

"I would, indeed, lady," Felimid replied. "Had you lived for a month at Koschei's whim, you would understand why; the Lord Avraig was gentle and restrained beside him."

"Come, then."

Felimid caught her mane and bestrode her in a lithe, continuous motion which looked too easy to be called a leap. He knew better than to suggest or even think that she submit to a bridle or saddle; she would toss him into the grass and disappear. He would manage without.

Riding by the river, a mile on the other side of his mansion, Koschei suddenly drew rein, glaring about him. Fed and sharpened by sorcery for hundreds of years, his senses warned him that some being of power was nearby. The demon horse between his thighs reared and snorted, more strongly aware of such things than even its master.

"So!" Koschei growled. "You scent evil, do you, sorry nag?" His magnificent, ravaged head turned slowly, scanning, seeking. "Yea, so do I! Yonder . . . go swiftly, swiftly!"

The demon horse raced in a wide halfcircle around Koschei's mansion, its fiery mane and tail streaming. Unlike Myfanwy, it did not speak, but like her it thought and understood. Before long, its unpupilled yellow eyes and Koschei's dark ones were scanning the ground among the birches.

"A man was here, and an unshod horse which neither approached nor departed upon the earth," Koschei said. "He trod like a young man. The ground bespeaks it. Who but the bard? Who but my eunuch-surgeon and he would deal with magic unafraid, of all my slaves? Was it the bard, sorry nag?"

His horse stamped a forehoof, thrice. It knew Felimid's scent well.

"And he has gone, the faithless, the empty of truth." Koschei's voice held pain. "He that I gave rare gifts and favored with company and speech has gone. Evil! Evil! Evil! Yet I will bring him back." His fingers tightened on his metal cudgel. "You and I will do so. If I waited to sow a field with barley, grow the crop, reap it, thresh it, malt it, brew drink with it, get drunk, and sleep off the drunkenness, and then set out—by Dazhbog and Fire his son, I would still catch them!"

Felimid did not hear that impassioned boast. He was riding through a blue twilight which dissolved vision in a blur a few hundred paces off. The growth Myfanwy's hooves dinted looked more like swansdown than grass, while here and there leafy hemispheres of shrub grew high as her knees. A rich, lascivious odor emanated from them.

"This was the simplest place for me to enter," Myfanwy said. "The pattern of the worlds is like a maze with many gates, avenues and blank walls. To return to your world, we must tread a path intricate as the design on your shirtsleeves. More than one is open to us, Felimid. Where would you go?"

"Can you reach Erin?"

Myfanwy gazed at vistas her rider could not perceive. "Not with ease. We would have to ride through worlds where time runs differently; you would come to Erin eight or nine generations after leaving it, though for you only days would have passed on the journey. Can you endure this?"

"No," Felimid said emphatically. "No, and no. Let me return to the earth I know in the year that I left it, lady—and that stipulated, let it be where in Gaul, Spain or Britain you choose."

"Lesser Britain abounds in circles and gates; I can take you there in twenty ways."

"One is enough! Lesser Britain let it be; I was bound there when all this trouble began."

Myfanwy's hooves moved without sound on the white growth which covered the soil. They passed copses of trees with white, fuzzy leaves. To Felimid it looked like a land of snow, yet the air was mild. While his eyes might tell him white herbage surrounded him, and his mind might accept it, his body still expected to shiver.

At a spot which looked to Felimid like a hundred others, the black mare halted.

"We must go swiftly through this next world," she said. "There is no air to breathe. For a moment or two you must bear it. Breathe deeply and swiftly, as you would before diving. Then, when I give the word, open your mouth and empty your lungs, and as you love life, cling fast to my back. Are you prepared?"

"I soon shall be."

Felimid exhaled as the blurred blue vista disappeared. Before him lay a circle of yellow dust like a lake, contained within a ring of abraded beige and saffron rock. Myfanwy stood on the inner slope of the ring. Above them a hundred thousand many-hued stars covered the sky, as leaves cover a forest's roof.

As she had warned him, there was no air. His skin prickled painfully; gas rumbled in his bowels. Remembering Myfanwy's caution, he clamped his knees to her sides.

She descended the slope at a sliding, scrambling run. Neither her feet nor the rocks she sent tumbling made any sound. They bounced and spun with a curious slowness. Felimid had a dreamlike sense of floating.

The mare raced across the lake of dust, her hooves throwing silent sulfur-colored arcs. A stone's cast away, a dark notch in the rock showed plainly. Myfanwy rushed at it and sped through.

Sweet, breathable air struck them. Blinking his dry eyes, Felimid looked upon blue sky and a forest of larch and poplar. The ground between the trees was fairly open.

"That hilltop is our goal," Myfanwy said, gazing at a rugged crest knee-deep in bracken. "Will you go there now, or rest?"

"Now," Felimid said, though dazed by marvel. "How many more worlds are we to traverse, lady? And are any peopled by men?"

"By men and others," Myfanwy answered. "Why so astounded? You have travelled on my back before."

"Not so swiftly. Let's on, lady. I'll own that the more

worlds lie between Koschei and me, the better I'll be pleased.''

Myfanwy laughed, a gently amused nickering. "He must be fearsome, if you fear him. You were bold before Avraig and his hunting pack, and you dared mock Tosti Fenrir's-get. *They* did not trouble you greatly.''

"Tosti most surely did. None the less, he was only a berserk and skin-turning manwolf. This Koschei is worse. He's as mad and ferocious as Tosti was, with far greater powers—and withal, he has a mind I must admire, when he's not frothing at the lips. Never could I say that of Tosti.''

"Then, as you say, let's on.''

They left the forest for the hill's lower slopes as the afternoon died. Felimid dismounted for the last steep climb to the top; that final slope remained sunlit, though dusk had covered the forest below. Looking back, he saw a double light which shifted.

"A firebrand!" he cried. "No, two, close together, and those who carry them ride swiftly! Wait.'' His tone of interest became one of dismay. "No brands are they. It's Koschei's demon horse, with burning mane and tail. He follows us.''

"He's reckless to do that," Myfanwy said. "By my mother, I will make him regret it. Mount!''

On her back, Felimid gained the hilltop, where the last of the coppery sunlight touched them. A heartbeat later, the hill was a mountain, and Felimid smelled the breath of a million pines. Lake, bog and plain stretched from the mountain's foot to the horizon, and vast black mosquito swarms hummed across it in living clouds.

"If we went down there, we would both soon go mad,'' the black mare said. "If Koschei does not cross it, he must wait until sunrise in the world we departed. That gate lies open at dawn and dusk only. If he's as mighty in fire magic as you think, Felimid, he can force the gate, and if his own nature is fiery, he will choose to—but it will cost him great effort. That must be our plan; to save our own strength and lure him to waste his.''

"He won't be content to blunder along after us like a bear cub after his mother,'' Felimid opined. "Not he! If there are twenty ways we can reach our destination, there must be twenty for him to anticipate and forestall us. True?''

"If he has the skill, yes.''

As in a chess game, the bard thought. He could not help

remembering that he had yet to win a chess game with Koschei. However, he was not the player in this game; Myfanwy was. She displayed no anxiety.

They passed swiftly through a number of worlds, of which the bard received brief, vivid impressions.

A desert of crimson gravel, utterly flat, with variegated sand dunes, pink and black, in the distance, and scorching heat in the air . . .

A lake among green trees, where beavers the size of small bears worked on their dams and lodges . . .

A valley of rich growth and warm steaming air, where mud bubbled in pits like porridge and brown-skinned people prepared a feast of lizards larger than themselves . . .

A place where islands and uprooted mountains drifted aimlessly in a pearly void, with fan-propelled ships plying between them like immense moths . . .

An empty snowfield below a trembling aurora . . .

Yellow fire burned on the snow. Koschei derided them, laughing wildly over his horse's flaming mane. He had emerged from the Gate Myfanwy meant to use.

"Check," Felimid said with mordant irony.

Myfanwy wheeled, to leap again through the Gate which had given her ingress to that world. Felimid was almost thrown. Strange skies, caverns, hues, and once a city thronging with three-quarters naked people (four quarters, some of them) decorated with carmine tattoos, tumbled in swift variety before the bard's eyes.

Koschei confronted them again, quaking with dreadful laughter.

This time Myfanwy led him a chase through the paved streets, slipping nimbly down alleys, leaping thoroughfares from roof to roof, and finally bursting into a temple which was sacred precisely because it contained a Gate. For the daughter of a goddess, she was irreverent, but Felimid had wondered from time to time whether gods might not be the worst unbelievers of all.

He'd little time or attention to spare for theological musing, in any case. Keeping his seat on Myfanwy's naked back while she scrambled, soared and dashed had taxed his horsemanship. He dripped sweat. His backside and thighs felt like steak clubbed tender.

"Can you not take us to a . . . world . . . where we'd be

welcome and he would not?'' Felimid asked, as a warm spiced
breeze carried butterflies (or were they winged seeds?) past
him. "The isles of the Tuatha de Danann, now? Mag-Mell and
Tir-nan-Og?''

"I'm trying to reach such places,'' Myfanwy answered.
"He forestalls me each time. He's cunning, this one. His
demon horse is slower than I, less agile, but more powerful
and able to endure longer. We must lead him into danger and
let him trap himself, I think—which means daring it ourselves.
Are you willing?''

"And ready, lady,'' he answered, "for indeed, he is coming
in anger. He has the bleeding heads of his enemies with him in
the chariot, and wild stags are bound to it, and white birds are
bearing him company.''

The sky turned red. Then a filtered green twilight replaced
it. Mile-high trees rose above them, their foliage screening the
sunlight. On the forest floor, plants doggedly strangled each
other in efforts to reach the light. Fungi erupted, red, gray and
hectic orange.

Myfanwy stood on a slimy, fallen trunk which stretched a
third of a mile through vine-festooned gloom. Trotting along
it, she crushed a beetle large as a lobster beneath her hoof; the
stink which filled her nose and Felimid's set them both gag-
ging.

A twisted branch, rising like a bridge, had a pit of decay
eaten into its junction with the trunk. Slimy muck with scum
thick on its surface filled the pit. Myfanwy neighed like a
melodious bugle and kicked a mass of fungi into the noisome
pool.

Light flared, the light of a demon's burning mane. Behind
them, Koschei galloped his steed wildly along the sloping
trunk. Before them, the surface of the pool surged; through
the scum rose a soft, pulsing, bear-sized bulk centered in a
mass of tentacles. Myfanwy sprang across the pit. A tentacle
whipped about her near hind leg. Turning, Felimid saw thorn-
like claws emerge from sockets of dilating muscle on the tentacle's inner side. He drew Kincaid and sliced the tentacle apart
as Koschei, unable to stop his mounted rush, blundered into
the pit, steed and all, in a racket of neighs and infuriated
roars. Vileness spattered.

Myfanwy struggled up the curving branch beyond the pit.

An abandoned nest of sticks, adorned with the husks and bones of some predator's victims, marked the Gate she desired. She favored her leg as they approached it.

They passed through. Before them stretched a vast flat plain, gray-brown in hue, dotted by countless tussocks and shimmering in haze.

"Ah-ha-ha!" Myfanwy breathed. "Too dangerous! I'm in your debt, Felimid mac Fal."

"Scarcely. It's on my account you are here at all," Felimid panted. "Your leg bleeds, lady."

"That boggart wrenched it," she said, stepping gingerly. "No matter; I can take you as far as you must go."

"Are we to cross this fire of a plain?"

"Most of it, my friend. I confess it will help me if you dismount."

Felimid lighted down, and they began walking. Dust devils thrice his height danced across the plain, playful air elementals feeding on the sun's heat. The bard's skin dried, then baked. He frequently glanced behind him.

Koschei appeared.

He and his horse Ogon were blurred together by their coating of unspeakable muck. The fiery yellow mane was nigh invisible in the scorching sunlight, and heat haze obscured the pair further. None the less, Felimid recognized them. Koschei flogged the demon mercilessly with his long reins.

"They slew your surprise between them," Felimid said.

"Clearly. I'm sorry, Felimid. I have failed you."

"No. The fault's mine. I underestimated Koschei and his demons, and now it appears I'll pay for it. Make you for the Gate, lady. I'll hold him back as well as I can. Ah, go!" he exclaimed in exasperation, when she hesitated. "Bathe in the sea and comb your mane with a clean wind! Can you fight Ogon, do you suppose? For all you have done and risked, I do thank you, lady, but stay you must not."

"I will go. But . . . Felimid, if Koschei harms you, I will bring all the Horses of Epona to trample the seeds of his empire before they have sprouted!"

"Fare you well."

Felimid did not watch her depart. It was in his mind that if he turned his head, he might lose his courage and shriek at her to come back. He watched Koschei and Ogon instead. They

drew steadily nearer, the demon horse beslimed from pastern
to shoulder, his head almost as thoroughly caked with filth,
while Koschei looked as if he had been immersed in a cesspit.
The gritty dust of the plain was rapidly coating them both.

A fine pair, Felimid thought dryly. *Demon and maniac!
Come for me, then. And believe as you come that my courage
has broken.*

He made his knees tremble, then bend. He sank to his
haunches in a supplicating pose. Koschei drew nearer, dark
eyes terrible in the dust-caked mask of his face. Felimid
lowered his own gaze, lest Koschei meet it and discern the
resolution there. He had come too far and dared too much to
surrender tamely now—and Koschei surely could not hear a
man's thoughts, else he would have had Felimid scourged
within a day of meeting him.

Koschei said nothing. Now he was a spear's length away.
Rocking backward to bring his feet beneath his body, Felimid
leaped a sudden half-yard in the air, the sword Kincaid leaping into his hand. Blue steel travelled sleekly across and
through the demon horse's throat. Fire, not blood, spurted
forth. Skimming, bending, turning like a dancer, Felimid had
already shifted aside, and struck with the point at a spot which
ought to prove mortal if Ogon had faithfully copied a horse's
anatomy when he assumed the form of one.

Demons might live indefinitely, but they were not unkillable. As for horses, Felimid had killed them before—badly in-
jured ones for whom it was a mercy. Being large beasts and
strong, they did not die easily. He knew where to strike in
order to end their suffering at once. He had never struck more
deeply or surely than now.

Ogon, twice mortally hurt, sank down slowly. Fire gushed
from his throat, welled from behind his shoulder. Koschei
stared in disbelief.

"Now, sovereign mighty one!" Felimid taunted him. "*Now*
how will you return to the Oder? By Earth-Mother Danu and
all Danu's children, if I rot on this forsaken plain, so shall
you! My ancestors were lords of magic, lords of Erin, and you
would enslave me?"

"I eat your heart!" Koschei rasped. "I drink your blood!"

He had become, again, the savage he admitted having been
born. With a bestial roar, he swung his bull-headed mace.

Felimid shifted his balance, moving aside from the crude bash as a fish moves in water; with a seemingly negligent flash of tail and fins, it is suddenly somewhere else. Yet the iron horns of Kincaid's mace grazed a rib.

His own blow, its force unabsorbed, threw Koschei to his knees. Felimid ran him through the body, driving Kincaid with all his power. Koschei knocked the bard several yards with a clumsy cuff, and then rose slowly to his full towering height while Felimid stared disbelievingly. Kincaid still transfixed the bemired, gritty giant, the hilt protruding from his ribs on one side, towards the back, while the point emerged at an angle on the other side, a hand's length from the breastbone.

With another animal roar, Koschei threw away his mace and rushed at the bard, apparently filled with a craving to destroy him with naked hands and eschewing any weapon as insufficiently gratifying. The bard was enclosed and lifted in a terrifying hug. Growling and foaming, Koschei butted his brow with the top of his unkempt head until the smaller man hung helpless and three-quarters stunned in his arms. Koschei dropped him in a heap, gasping like a bellows.

Finding that he could not remove Kincaid from his body by any feat of contortion—the hilt was impossible to grasp effectively—and that magic was useless to budge the weapon, Koschei left it in his unnatural trunk. While the magician strove, Felimid began to recover. Koschei rendered him helpless again with a kick, and bound him immovably to the fallen demon. Then he possessed himself of the long reins, cutting them loose from the bridle with the metal bit rings attached. As he whirled them through the hot, dusty air and listened to them hum, he even smiled. It was not an engaging smile.

Felimid regained his full senses with the distinct impression that he had passed through a wolverine's entrails. Gore from his battered, pulpy forehead clotted his eyes shut. The pain was intense, and the after effects of Koschei's bear hug and kick announced themselves to him in their respective degrees.

He lay stretched along the dusty, slimy, rapidly drying side of Koschei's demon horse. The magician had bound his arms about its neck; passed his, Felimid's, belt through the saddle girth and buckled it anew about his waist; and lashed his legs to the demon's back legs, making him entirely helpless. The demon breathed yet, in slow, faltering respiration. Felimid felt it do so. However, he did not think it would continue breathing for long. Nor, probably, would he.

Koschei tore Felimid's clothing from his body.

Stretched on the equine carcass, sweat drawing lines through the dirt on his flesh, his brown hair made pale and drab by dust, the long, lithe dimensions of his body pulled taut, his face turned sideways on Ogon's neck with the engaging disproportion of snub nose and long jaw manifest in profile, Felimid received Koschei's first blow.

The metal-studded reins ending in heavy bit rings cut through his skin at once. Blood jumped forth. Koschei lifted, whirled and brought down his makeshift scourge, and again. At the third blow, Felimid turned his head and hid his face in Ogon's tawny neck, on which the fire of the demon's mane had almost ceased to smolder.

As the reins whistled and thudded, the bard's eyelids clenched at each stroke. His body spasmed from neck to heels. Impaled hamperingly through the trunk, Koschei could not employ his full strength or his right hand, else he might have cut Felimid's spine in two. Still, the punishment was dire enough.

Before long, pain eroded pride and drew a gasp, which in time became the first, choking cry. A long time later, Felimid no longer had breath or strength for sound, and much too long after that, Koschei ceased plying his scourge. He sank panting against his slain demon's saddle as Felimid sank into unconsciousness.

He thought, *This is how and where I die. . . .*

VII
"Uncut and Unturned by Metal."

The narrow bridge had appeared from nowhere, sprouting across the river as Gudrun stamped three times. Nothing creaked or vibrated as she ran across; the structure stood firm as a boulder. On the far bank, she turned about and stamped her left foot. As her sole touched the ground for the third time, the bridge vanished.

Gudrun shook her head in wonder. Thrice now she had made use of her enchanted boots. She felt an impulse to create the bridge again, and destroy it, to see the marvel—but she suspected that to do so lightly would bring bad luck. The scruple showed either her resilience or the shortness of her memory. She had displeased Odin; any other bad luck was trifling to that. But nothing had ever made her downhearted for long.

"Where are you, Bragi?" she asked the sky and the water. "Did you continue south, up this river, or follow one of the lesser streams that feed it? Or maybe think again and return to the sea? You are so changeable you well may have done! I think I must visit another village and ask."

She had grown leaner, and more deeply travel-stained, with marks of thorn and rock and hard sleeping in the wilderness plain upon her. *He will laugh at me if I do find him. No! If he laughs, I'll take his head! No, and no again . . . I'll not do that, but I'll strike him. . . . Oh ho, listen to me!*

She laughed aloud, there by the great river. "Gudrun Black-hair," she jeered, "you're a fool!"

"Elder sister."

Gudrun spun about, flushing. The title sounded more familiar than the speaker looked. Gone was the robe of floating
mist, gone the pale hair, changed the blankly glowing eyes.
This was not one of the *rusalki*.

Wait. They had told her. It was their nature to leave the
water and dwell among the forest shadows in summer, as a
stoat wore white fur in the snow and brown fur in the season
of growth.

"Are you one of the nine? I hardly know you."

"I know you, elder sister, *vodyanek* slayer."

The *rusalka*'s hair had thickened and become green as moss.
She wore a tunic of overlapping leaves which fitted closely as
an integument. Her fingers had become a joint or two longer
(or such was Gudrun's impression). Her skin had gained an
apricot tint and her eyes were now dark. Something very like
gray bark had grown over her feet. Only her voice was
familiar.

"Welcome, little sister. You have changed!"

"Yea, thanks to you. We no longer endure the scalding of
summer water. I bring a companion, and we have tidings for
you. . . . come out of your thicket, *ljeschi*!" she said. "Let my
sister see you directly!"

What shambled forth, grumbling, had none of the *rusalka*'s
grace. His gray-green skin sprouted tufts and mats of hair like
unkempt grass, his feet resembled roots, and his corrugated,
bearded facial features included pop eyes which rolled in independent directions. He carried a wooden spade and a leather
drawstring sack.

"He dislikes being seen," Gudrun's "little sister" explained. "Even so, he has been free of the land all the while I
was in bondage. He knows more of events than I. Therefore I
forced him to come to you, by threatening to pluck out his
beard."

"Oh, little sister, how hideous," Gudrun said gravely.
"What drove you to such lengths as that?"

"Tidings. A mighty magician has come into this land; his
mansion stands yonder. You cannot see it, but if you travel
another day or two you will reach it, where the Oder joins the
Warta—and then you may wish you had not, for he is a
tyrant. His purpose here is to make a kingdom for himself to
rule. His own powers aside—and he's deathless and invul-

nerable, for a beginning—he gained power over a band of demons on Kupala's Night.''

"I'm baffled already. What is Kupala's Night?"

"One of the enchanted times. You call it midsummer. Kupala is a god, a young, beautiful god whose rites are most pleasant. . . . '' The *rusalka* sighed, remembering. "He belongs to the living. One night of the year, in the most secret place in the forest, a fern sacred to the god blossoms at midnight, with a flower of pure white fire. The man or woman who can pluck this flower and bear it away has gained the world! It shows where hidden treasure lies, gives access to all beautiful women and handsome men, and luck in winning them withal—and more than this, endows who has it with mastery over demons.''

"So? If this be true, little sister, your fire-blossom is a thing worth having. How is it got?''

"By finding the sacred fern before the night of its flowering and learning to know the place well, so that you can go there even in darkness. Then, on Kupala's Night, you must draw a protective circle about the fern and yourself, and keep vigil until it blossoms.'' The *rusalka*'s delicate hands moved expressively as she spoke, cupping and unfolding as she described the fern's magical blooming. Her arms, her entire body, undulated upward. "That is a perilous watch to keep. Demons love their freedom; it does not please them to see the flower possessed by a mortal. On Kupala's Night they gather quickly as moths, waiting for the fern to blossom, working with all their guile and power to lure the seeker from his protective circle. If they succeed, they make an end of him. To listen to their voices, or only to look at them, is to be lost—unless you are a strong magician, used to the wiles of demons. Koschei is such a one, and he obtained the flower. Now he is more powerful than he was.''

"I believe you, little sister," Gudrun said. "Yet what has any of this to do with me? I am not here to meddle with magicians who rule demons, but to find a lover who quarrelled with me. Were Bragi trapped under this Koschei's hand . . .''

"We do not know.'' The spirit laid her hand on the crouching *ljeschi*'s shoulder. "You travel in his land, though, and may find yourself in his house whether or not you desire it. The fire-blossom is there as well. Smother it out, and Koschei's dominance of his demons ends. They will desert him—

even slay him if they can, which is unsure. It is unsure that any power can. He's known as Koschei the Deathless."

Gudrun laughed scornfully. "To his bootlickers! If he crosses me, I am ready to test that distinction of his. But tell me more. Knowing how to turn his own demons against him could save me trouble."

The *ljeschi* barked and grumbled. He waved the objects he held.

"The blossom is made of fire," the *rusalka* said. "It flames white, with no smoke or fuel, and is as large as your two cupped hands. Loose earth can stifle it out. The earth must be dug with a stick, or your hands. It must, elder sister, *must* be uncut and unturned by metal. Soil from a field which has once been ploughed or hoed will not do. It must be earth which metal has never divided. Failing that, use water from a clear spring or a running stream, but earth is simpler to carry. We bring you the means."

Her gnarled companion held out the spade and sack to Gudrun.

"Thanks, little sister," the pirate said, "and you, my little sister's friend." Somewhat puzzled, she glanced from the ghostly forest sprite to the uncouth *ljeschi*, as much a spirit of the wild forest as she; no familiar of the tamed, cultivated earth, Gudrun Blackhair was sure. "How did you come by these things?"

"A farm laborer had them. He walked too carelessly in the forest, and I waylaid him. Thereafter he had no need of tools, or breath either."

"You slew him for this trash?" Gudrun demanded.

"He died kindly, elder sister; no, in ecstasy. When a mortal man embraces a *rusalka*, his life is destroyed. Nothing else is possible."

Her matter-of-factness caused Gudrun's hot blood to run briefly cold. She almost shouted phrases of loathing, of repudiation, at her "little sister." Human the *rusalki* might once have been; human they were no longer, in any degree.

Then she remembered the hanged men turning in the wind, and her meeting with Odin. Why should the *rusalka*'s deed offend her? Gudrun had slain many men, and not kindly, not in ecstasy! It was the part of a hypocrite to be appalled.

"I'll take your gift, and I thank you," she said. "But if I am your elder sister, accept my authority; bring me no more gifts you slay men to obtain. The news and the warning were enough, and I'd know whatever else you can tell me of this Koschei. *Deathless*, is he? That's a dangerous boast.''

"He has trapped a band of men from beyond the sea. They came from Oder-mouth in two boats not long since."

"Merchants?"

"I cannot tell what they were."

"Not long" in the *rusalka*'s mouth might mean one day or one year. She did not understand time as the living did. But if her "not long" meant "within the past month," it was possible that the bard had joined the foreign band of which she spoke. Even if he had not, he might well have reached the magician's mansion by himself. It stood at the junction of two great rivers by which many travelled.

"Besides," Gudrun said, "as you tell it, the mansion of this Koschei is the worst of places to be. I think I'll find Bragi there. He was mired to the shoulders in the rankest predicament for a hundred mile when I met him, and that is where he will be here, as a salmon finds the right river for spawning. I'll go and see."

VIII
The Flower That Enslaves Demons

Felimid was alive. As he slowly became conscious, a knife of fear invaded his heart; he knew intolerable pain waited for him, out there beyond the murk wherein he drifted. He tasted it apprehensively, as he might have tongued a painful tooth. Not a nerve responded. The agony no longer lurked in ambush.

His skin touched silk. Both skin and silk were clean. His back, the back Koschei had lacerated to the white wicker of his ribs, felt whole and did not hurt. Pain was a fading memory in his flesh. Although he felt languid and weak as a slug, the relief was blissful.

It could not be true. He was dreaming, in the last few breaths of his life. Koschei had scourged him to the black edge of extinction.

Felimid opened his eyes. The burning lamps suggested night. The clear flame, the lack of smoke, more than suggested Koschei's house. The bed's brocade, fur and gilt confirmed the location, for there could be nowhere else so rich in all the land of the Obodrites.

Koschei's mansion—and someone had healed him, somehow. At Koschei's orders? Manifestly. Why?

His mind surrendered and gave up the work.

"Ah. Your senses are your own again. Do you know me?"

The creature was beardless, soft-voiced and plump. His

beautifully kept hands lacked rings, though jewels flashed in his ears. Felimid did not like him. Despite his courteous, even servile manner, he wore the cruelly playful smile of a cat about to display claws and teeth to a broken-winged sparrow.

"I never saw you before," Felimid whispered.

"Sad. I was told you had wit." The creature smiled more broadly. "Do you *know* me?"

Eunuch, the bard suddenly guessed. *One of those gelded things a real man should not have to see.* Beigadh had said something like that. This was the surgeon who had sealed Beigadh's vitals in a hollow log without killing him. He must also have healed Felimid's back.

"Surgeon," he breathed.

"Surgeon, as you say—and much more." The eunuch drew back the brocade coverlet. "Your back was mangled meat when I first saw you, fellow. I think you were less than an hour from death." His hand, surprisingly firm for its soft-skinned, pudgy appearance, slid across Felimid's shoulders and down to the tuft of hair at the base of his spine. No ridged or roughened areas caused any friction; there were no scars.

"My salves and enchantments aided your body to heal," the eunuch purred. "I learned long ago that most of those who vaunt themselves as physicians and surgeons are fools who know nothing, and that I must practice magic if I wished to leave their ranks. I did. However, your body is weakened. You will not walk for days yet. Lie quiet, eat and drink."

"What else will you do with me?"

"See that you recover fully, since the Mighty Sovereign One has ordered it." The eunuch's voice grew unctuous as he declaimed the title. "This is wondrous clemency from him. What makes you worthy of it is not for me to conjecture. I hope, myself, that he regrets it and alters his mind. Then he might permit me to play with you more interestingly. Ah!" Small white teeth glittered again in what some might have named a smile. "I find little gratification in mending injuries, even to perfection. It is like stitching an ordinary, simple seam when one has the skill to embroider a royal robe. In Constantinople I altered the bodies of infants so that they provided wondrous merriment for the court nobles; for my inventiveness in the profession I was named Procrustes." The bard did not understand the joke. "You are too old for that," Pro-

crustes added regretfully. "The Sovereign Mighty One may
wish me to do no more than blind you. That would cure you of
running, and yet you could harp."

To Felimid's disgust, a tear of weakness and frustration ran
down his cheek. All the striving and danger had not brought
him freedom. Koschei had returned to his inchoate kingdom
(how?) and was perhaps giving thought to the bard's punishment at that moment. As Procrustes said, he might decide
upon blinding. Discouraged beyond words, Felimid shut his
eyes.

Two demons in the shape of women served him strength-
giving broth. Lithe, black-haired, voluptuous, they moved
with inhuman ease and lightness. No wonder Koschei had
nothing to do with mortals sexually. His demons could
become man, woman, beast or any amalgamation of the three.

A day later, Koschei visited the bard's sickbed. Felimid
smelled him before he entered the chamber, and formed the
opinion upon seeing him that drops of blood from his scourging were still clotted in Koschei's stinking hair.

"Dog!" the magician greeted him. "Slayer of my good
heroic steed! I did you nothing but good, and like all, you con-
spired me evil! I would rid this land of robbers, and the chieftains defy me! Robbers themselves! Slayers! Bandits! But
you . . ."

"Why then am I here?" Felimid asked. "I was about to die,
what last I remember. You have burdened yourself with my
wickedness anew."

Koschei's eyes burned like black lamps. "You jest with
me?"

He hurled the couch over with a splintering crash. Felimid
rolled on the floor, striking his elbow and shoulder. Pain
blazed along his arm. Koschei towered above him, glaring.

"Dog! Cur! Scion of curs! You thought to entrap me far
from this realm I have chosen. You believed me helpless if my
heroic steed died! I, Koschei! Know that I can walk between
worlds as freely as any demon or godling, though a deal less
swiftly. As for you . . ."

Felimid rose unsteadily from the floor.

"You!" Koschei repeated. "None desert me, none disobey
me. Not even I can decide at once how to punish you. I
brought you here to await my justice, and ordered you healed
in the meantime; that I thrashed you was a bare inkling of my

displeasure. I promise this. You will have time to recover your
full strength, and you will require it all.''

If Felimid lacked strength yet, he had at least recovered his
wits. Koschei's words did not ring true; were he sincere, he
would be more . . . frenzied. His present manner, for Koschei,
ranked as mere peevishness and boasting.

Felimid did not think that Koschei could travel between
worlds unaided. In that, he lied. Therefore Myfanwy must
have aided him. She had returned, in time to stop Koschei's
beating Felimid to death, and bargained with him. She had offered to carry him back to the banks of the Oder in exchange
for his oath, an oath sworn in terms it would cost him all his
magician's power and knowledge to break, to spare and heal
the then unconscious bard. Felimid could conceive of nothing
else that might explain it.

And Koschei must have ridden home with the sword still
transfixing him. He was deathless, indeed; that much was no
boast. Yet even he could not compel Myfanwy. For that, he
would have to know the black mare's true name.

"Now go!" Koschei rasped. "The upper level of this house
is barred to you again. Tonight you shall play for me.''

As the bard left, Koschei flung himself into a chair and lowered his brow into his hand. He sat thinking with fierce con-
centration for hours.

Felimid's thinking was more desultory. Having tried to escape his self-proclaimed master and failed, and received a
scourging he flinched from remembering, he could think of no
valid action to take. To be sure, if he couldn't escape, then on
the face of it he must destroy Koschei before Koschei destroyed him . . . except that Koschei could not be destroyed.

If any moves remained (queen taken, both his knights removed from the board, and mate seemingly two moves away)
they must take place on the forbidden third story of the mansion, which demons guarded. *Someone* must have a notion of
what was there!

Sunning himself beside Beigadh in the courtyard next day,
Felimid questioned the trader.

"What is on the third story?" Beigadh echoed. "Why,
you've been there, lad." He rubbed his bald crown. "*His*
private quarters." *His* uttered in that tone called for no finer
definition. "That dung-eating capon surgeon's apartment and
cutting room. I hope fate allows me to strangle him one day.''

Even that was said too mildly. Beigadh had been reduced to a
bland acceptance of the intolerable which Felimid began to
fear was true of himself. "Demons. A mort o' those, in different forms each day and night. Above . . . " He shrugged.
"The great dome. Many a gable, tower and little dome. What
is in those, the gods know."

Felimid turned his head to study the central dome. From
without, it was just that, a great bulbous pointed shape with a
skin of poplar shingles, visible for a league. Koschei would
store anything crucial to himself there, flaunting it before his
subjects and enemies alike. It was appropriate, it was like him.
It felt like the sort of thing he would do.

Felimid had learned something of the Obodritian tongue.
Though he spoke it but haltingly, he could now converse in
simple phrases, and understand it fairly well. His chief teacher
aside from Koschei himself was Orya, the younger sister of
Beigadh's wife. A certain friendship had grown between them;
Orya, Felimid knew, was inclined to more than friendship.
But Felimid did not want a lover.

Do you not? he asked himself derisively, and answered, *I
do, indeed, but she is not here.*

In Jutland, he had once tried to ease his passion for her with
a succession of light bedmates. He hadn't succeeded, and
knew now that he would not. Only time would free him from
Gudrun Blackhair—or death, if time was denied him. Yet he
liked Orya well. Stocky, brown-haired and outspoken, she
hated Koschei with a fierce, utter loathing.

"Thing!" she muttered as she kneaded Felimid's muscles in
the bathhouse. (It was one place Koschei never approached.)
"Child of Chernobog! May Moist Mother Earth engulf him in
pits!"

"Be cautious," Felimid warned her. "He hears . . . you die.
If demons hear, too. Why do they obey him?"

Orya lowered her voice. "Lord, do you not know? All the
river knows! He appeared with his demons after Kupala's
Night. The other women and I had performed the rites, which
are not for repeating to a man, but I can say this: everything
was wrong that night. Trees moved about and spoke mysterious words. Fish went mad and flew through the air until they
died thrashing. Garlands sank instead of floating. And it is
known that the fern blossoms on that one night of the year
with a flower that enslaves demons."

"So," Felimid said, on a long breath, while the muscles showed clearly through the skin of his magically unmarked back. "Orya? Say more of this flower."

She did. She said enough more, and eagerly, to assure him that this was the talisman Koschei had found, by which he ruled his entourage of demons. And it was Felimid's not especially difficult guess that Koschei kept the flower in the forbidden dome. Koschei's demons would revolt if it was destroyed —but Orya knew nothing of how to destroy it.

Later, seated by Koschei's bed, Felimid harped the magical sleep strain which eased the violent, corroding mind and allowed it rest. The giant lay still, sleeping as he would sleep until dawn, free of spasms and nightmares. Felimid studied the seamed, fissured map of furious debauch that was Koschei's face for some time, hatred, fascination, fear and compassion mingling in his heart.

Koschei might have resisted even the sleep strain, had he so chosen. That he willingly succumbed to it in order to enjoy a night of ease proved his confidence. He must be entirely certain that he was unkillable. Nor did Felimid doubt it any longer.

"But I do not at all fancy being ruled by you, Mighty Sovereign One," he mused, sitting by the immense bed. "In any case, you have promised to slay me before long. With nothing to lose, I'd as soon die seeking to be free, so."

IX
Seven Deaths

Gudrun limped, having wrenched her leg slightly. Lines of crusted blood marked her face, for she had forced her way through a thicket. Now she paused, knife in hand, longbow on her back, to rest and view the scene.

The mansion's ornate roof rose above the trees at the juncture of two rivers. Gudrun looked at it, marvelling. Then she heard the harp.

She knew at once who played it. The music spoke of loss. The notes were light and strict, weaving intricately together, drawing her heart.

"Bragi," she whispered.

He sat by the river, watching it flow, the harp on his knee. Golden strings gleamed in the sunlight. She barely saw the costly wool and embroidered Byzantine linen he wore. The smooth brown hair, the fine hands and well-muscled body she remembered blazed upon her sight through the unfamiliar garments. She would have known him in a tunic of reeds.

"Bragi," she repeated, louder.

He had never dropped the harp Golden Singer before. Now she jangled in outrage as she slid down the bank, to stop against the roots of a dog-willow. Gudrun saw the amazement and the growing joy in his face. It mirrored what she felt. Then she was in his arms and he was drinking from her mouth like a man who had existed for ten years in the heart of a fire. She requited the kiss with equal thirst.

234

"Gudrun," he said at last, gasping for the breath to utter it. "You glorious, high-hearted fool! Oh, my love, my love, I'm glad past measure to see you. . . . But all gods be my witnesses, it grieves me to see you *here!*"

"You were always of a double mind. I'm only glad to see you."

Again they were kissing, holding, intertwining as they sank towards the ground (and clumsily, with laughter and curses, ridding each other of clothes they discovered they hated). For some time their only talk was babble. Neither tried to explain or excuse anything. They tried, in their coupling, to exchange hearts and set them beating in each other's bodies—and to them it was as though they briefly succeeded.

Then time demanded his scot. They had had their hour and a little more. They had intelligence to exchange and plans to make. And when their plans were made, a woman in forester's garb came to the court of Koschei's mansion, bearing herself quickly in spite of a tiny limp, and asked if a certain green-eyed harper was known in the region.

The pikemen on guard mocked her cropped hair and sword. She taught three of them manners, one after the other, despite her game leg, and then she repeated her question. At that dangerous point the bard happened to appear, as they had arranged beforehand. Those present were treated to a meeting of parted lovers which belonged in a story.

Not long afterwards, Gudrun faced Koschei. She told him the essential truth, including her name, her lover's quarrel with Felimid, and her raid on Svantovit's temple. The latter interested Koschei most. Indeed, it delighted him.

"So. You burned the place? You, with one ship and half a hundred men! Good! Good! I should have had to kill those priests myself, some day. They would have fought me. You have the friendship of the Dane-kings, you say? Better and better! When your ship returns, you may tell your men you have found worthy service for them."

"You honor me, Mighty Sovereign One," Gudrun said; and to Felimid, for one, that magniloquent title in Gudrun's mouth had the cloying, transparent stickiness of honey poured over a knife-edge. "My men shall know. For myself, I came here to find this man. We were lovers until we quarrelled, and I would we were lovers again."

"Why afflict your lord with trifles? Whom you love and

whether that love is returned is your affair. Be concerned with
this instead; if you have lied to gain a hearing, and are not the
captain of *Ormungandr*, I shall have you crushed like a frog
between two boulders."

Koschei's harsh voice reverberated with menace, and his
dark eyes gleamed avidly, as they often did when he talked of
such things. However, the pirate did not whiten; she reddened
considerably, and kept her anger behind her teeth with effort.

"My lord, he dared to call himself," she hissed in Felimid's
ear later. "I never had any lord but Odin, and even that is finished now. He brags that he's a lord of demons, too—where
are they?"

"I can show you one, no farther off than the stable,"
Felimid told her. "I slew his predecessor, and as Koschei
wanted another steed, he had one of his surviving demons
assume the shape of a horse to replace him. A dozen more, or
thereby, have become giants with gills and scales, and are slav-
ing in the depths of the river to make it navigable. When they
have finished, it will be for you to enforce Koschei's law on
the Oder. I surmise that's in his mind."

"It's not in mine, Bragi! I said to him plainly enough why I
came here."

"True for you . . . and you saw how much weight he gave it.
He has ordered Beigadh to Gotland, and his boats are loading
now. I must warn him; Beigadh, that is. I cannot unleash
demons without letting him know what may happen. He has a
wife and children here, and he dealt well with me."

Gudrun made a sound of disgust. "He will rush to the magician and betray you, Bragi! Not everyone is as foolishly high-
minded as you are! As you say, this Beigadh has a wife and
children to consider—and his own heart, lungs and guts held
hostage! Did you not say so? Brrr, that's foul!"

"He may have his surgeon do the same to you."

"Not while I live."

Beigadh proved more than dubious.

"I want no part of it," he growled. "You are mad, Felimid.
I'll take Ludovena and the children to the village, lest the
magician take their lives, too, when he learns what you have
been trying to do. But that's all. You are bound to fail."

"Will you tell him?"

Beigadh rubbed his bald crown in angry distress. "I will say nothing. I heard nothing. You said nothing. By my advice you'll forget this crack-brained intent. Wasn't it enough, what *he* did the last time you defied him?"

Felimid waved a languid hand. "Beigadh, you make yourself entirely plain. He has broken you to harness and obedience. I'm fortunate . . . all he means to do with me is kill me when he has devised a way sufficiently foul. That, or when the whim strikes him. My respects to your wife."

Koschei had saddled his new demon steed and announced that he would be absent a day or two—which none dared question. Nor was anybody amazed. He had done things far more sudden and arbitrary than that.

Yet Felimid was moved to sudden suspicion upon hearing it. This was too . . . convenient. Gudrun's arrival, her acceptance by Koschei, Beigadh's impending departure, the majority of Koschei's demons set to labor in the river's depths, and now Koschei's choice of such an opportune time to remove himself, all suited Felimid's purpose too neatly.

He said as much to his lover.

"It's luck," she assured him. "Yours has been bad; now it has turned. Seize it! Bragi . . . Felimid . . . we will see his mansion torn down tonight, by the demons who built it, and then we'll away! I have even a pair of enchanted boots my "little sisters" gave me, by which we can cross any river or chasm. I hid them before I came here, with the bag of virgin earth. All will be well if we only dare. Do not lose courage now!"

"Enchanted boots?" Felimid gave her a startled look. "I wish you had told me sooner. What virtue do they have?"

Gudrun shrugged, but when he had persuaded her the question was of moment, she answered in detail.

"Cairbre and Ogma," he swore. "Did you use these boots to cross the river when you came here?"

"Yes," she said, puzzled. "You needn't fear that I was seen. I retraced my steps far downstream, and crossed in the moonless dark. I'd have been here days earlier else."

"Night or day, it's the same to Koschei. When a deed of magic is done within leagues, he knows of it. If the boots you hid are enchanted, he'll be nosing them out like a pig hunting truffles, so he will. He'd find your sack of virgin earth beside them, know at once what we planned, and . . . confront us?

No. I think not. More likely he's waiting at the spot even now, intending to blast us with lightning when we appear."

"How he has changed you."

"You don't know him. Maybe he'd replace the virgin earth with field soil, many times ploughed and spaded—useless— and allow us to make our futile attempt to crush out his fire blossom. Then he'd split his sides laughing at the joke. Aye, and the punishment he'd award us would be more hilarious still."

Gudrun gripped his shoulders and shook him. "Bragi. I know what that monster has done to you, but do not turn white-livered now!"

Her angry concern made him smile. He ran his hands up her arms in a caress of reassurance. "I haven't lost courage, Gudrun. I'm thinking, that is all. I know for a certain fact that Koschei can sense magic, whether proximate or far away. He sensed the curse on Kincaid, and he knew when Myfanwy entered his land, though he was nowhere near. I must be supposing he has found your boots and the sack of earth. We cannot use them if that is so—but is there another way?"

Gudrun snapped her fingers. "Water! My 'little sisters' told me that water from a clear flowing stream has the same strength against the fire-blossom as virgin earth."

"Wonderful!" Felimid laughed softly, exultantly. "We can choose either of two mighty rivers. . . . Water's more easily spilled and less easily gathered again than earth, but it's our one option. We'll fill a flask each. I'm for climbing to the roof and breaking through the dome, rather than trying from within; Koschei may have gone away, but I'll vow he left instructions with someone. He's like a great ugly cat with two mice. But tonight he will learn how far we can scamper."

"Yes." Her smile matched his. "Now you talk like my man. Bragi, I fought seven men and a water godling, and wrenched my leg, to find you again. It was worth it."

"Then kiss me."

A number of kisses and some more serious preparation later, they began their invasion of Koschei's sanctum. The sun had scarcely set. With swords, targes, a heavy single-edged knife each, candles (Koschei's house was luxurious in the extreme, with wax tapers by the hundred available to pilfer), flint, rope and their precious flasks of water, they gained a terrace and began to scale the mansion's outer walls. As always, the bard carried Golden Singer on his back.

He went first. The carved, interlocking ends of logs formed a ladder to the second story. Gaining a secure perch on the back of a stone bear whose mouth spouted rainwater in wet weather, he shook down a rope to Gudrun. She made somewhat harder work of climbing than he; her leg still troubled her.

The walls of the third story were smoother, more difficult to scale. Felimid went up barefoot, seeking crevices with his fingers and toes like a four-limbed wingless fly. Once, in desperation, he drove his knife deep in wood for a handhold while he sought with exquisite care for purchase elsewhere, and at last he straddled a gable ridge in a certain amount of safety. Moments later, Gudrun was beside him, breathing deeply.

"By the gods my people swear by," his soft voice greeted her, "you wheeze like a granddam of forty winters. Now we have all this roof to cross before we gain the dome, and as you see, it's of fair size."

He understated. The mansion's roof covered two acres or more of bizarre wooden confections; gables, lesser domes, galleries, watchtowers, a ring-shaped catchment feeding cisterns, and at last, within all these, the huge central dome with its intricate shingles, fitted closely as a fish's scales.

Linking themselves together with a length of rope, they moved towards it. Felimid had regained his agility and grace after the beating, but not much more than half of his endurance as yet. But although he wasted no strength in flourishes, he was light-hearted. He felt joyous and confident.

That Gudrun had abandoned her pirate expedition to find him again meant more than the wrath of all the wizards in creation. His own overwhelming joy at seeing her meant more than his detestation of anything she had done in the service of any god. Partnered like one pair of hands, they approached the dome.

At the base, they went to work with their knives, splitting, prying, removing. Even in the circumstances, it cost Felimid a pang to wreck such superb joinery. He told himself that it was the work of Koschei's demons, and thus without human meaning, and widened the hole.

Clouds covered the sky by the time the opening was large

enough for ingress. Felimid shed every burden save his knife
and crawled inside. Gudrun passed him flint, punk and a candle, covering the hole with her back so that none should see
the light from the watchtowers.

In a little while, he patted her shoulder. She passed his
sword and his harp through the hole and then joined him. The
candle illuminated a wide, curving passage, the shingles and
adzed beams of the outer dome on one side, a surface of cool
greasy stone on the other.

"It's a shell," Felimid marvelled, gazing into the murk beyond the flickering candlelight, "all of one piece and polished
smooth!"

"His demons are powerful. Well, we cannot break through
that with knives, and axes would not serve either." Gudrun
studied the floor of the passage. "It's jointed timber, and
stout as Orwendel's arm. Perhaps there is a weak place somewhere. If there is not, we will have to labor like demons ourselves to break through before midnight."

They moved forward, testing the footing and finding it solid
as bedrock. Shortly they came to a disc of stone set in the
floor. A collar of oak surrounded the disc as an iron tire grips
a wheel, and from the collar heavy wooden rods rose vertically.

"This might be a giant's quern," Gudrun said.

"Yes, or part of the same giant's butterchurn."

"I'm reminded more of a siege engine."

They examined the timber uprights and collar without gaining any insight into their purpose. The disc extended beyond
the narrow passage on both sides; they would have to step on
it if they were to proceed.

Felimid did.

It dropped from beneath him, suddenly and sickeningly. He
fell atop it through perhaps two fathoms of air. It struck a
tiled floor with a monstrous crash that set the dome resound-
ing. Air gusted about him, blowing out his candle. Shaken, he
crouched in the dark, his fingers pressing grooves in the useless taper.

"Bragi!" Gudrun called, through the thundering echoes.

"I'm alive."

He waited for pikemen or demons to rush into the dark
place where he found himself. An apparent eternity passed,

with no such intrusion. It was inconceivable that none had heard; the mansion must have boomed like a drum from roof to foundations. Therefore Koschei's inflexible command that the dome be shunned was being observed. None willingly went near it, whatever sounds might originate there; a disadvantage of too much terror.

Gudrun lowered herself by rope to Felimid's side. Much later, they had contribed to light their candle again. They were in a little round antechamber of some kind, with two stretches of corridor leading away from it at angles. The stone disc—all of a foot thick, with curiously grooved sides, now that they could see the whole of it—had dropped from above when Felimid had triggered its sensitive release by stepping on it.

"A deadfall," Felimid said from a suddenly dry mouth. "Light of the Worshipped Sun! I was better above this stone than beneath it! I remember now . . . Koschei boasted to me once when he was drunk, and I was drunker, that he guarded his sanctum against trespassers with seven deaths. It's in my mind that this was one."

"None will disturb us," Gudrun said pragmatically, urgent with the need for action. "The guardsmen would be here now if they were coming at all. There is the corridor, and we have only six more deaths to evade—supposing that Koschei did not lie."

Felimid stared at her. "Yes," he agreed at last. "Always supposing that. Gudrun, I love you chiefly for this cause, that nothing deters you. Nothing! Ah, Koschei, for once you have misjudged your slaves! They are not cattle, but the wild deer of the dark places of Slieve Fuad. Yes, let's proceed. As you say, there is only the trifle of six more deaths in our way."

He recovered the rope and coiled it neatly.

"Forward or back?" he asked.

"The way we face pleases me."

Lamps were bracketed to the walls. Boldly, Felimid lit them as he advanced, candle in one hand, Kincaid in the other. Awkward though it was, he wore his shield on the same arm with which he carried the light; his right arm, nearest the wall. Gudrun reversed that arrangement, being right-handed.

"H'm," Felimid said. "Another little antechamber lies ahead, and maybe another trap."

"Of what sort?"

"I cannot see the ceiling clearly, but I do not think it will be a deadfall again. There are spears hanging in alcoves. . . . "

The spears hung ornamentally crossed on the walls in groups of three; two oblique, and one upright in the center. Nothing appeared suspicious. Felimid took a light, wary step into the antechamber, and instantly the spears darted at his flesh.

He deflected one with his targe, and two more with quick, economical flickers of Kincaid, standing fast long enough for Gudrun to join him and protect his back. He did the same for her. Together they backed out of the antechamber into the next stretch of corridor. The half-dozen spears pursued them.

Hanging in the air, they danced and thrust. The pair retreated into dimness, for the lamps in this length of the passage remained unlit, and the candle had fallen somewhere. The darker the passage, the less effective grew their defense.

"Odin!" Gudrun yelled, reverting to habit. "Look behind us!"

Something huge awaited them. Felimid received the swift impression of a triple-jawed yellow beast bulking like an aurochs, completely blocking their way. It was evidently mute. The trap was a neat one: Felimid and Gudrun must always retreat to escape the tireless enchanted spears, but if they retreated farther they would withdraw into the beast's teeth.

"I'll go under, and draw its attention," Gudrun said. "Then you go over. Give me the word."

"Now!"

Gudrun flung herself sliding beneath the beast's belly. Her targe scraped harshly on the floor. Felimid whirled Kincaid in a blindingly swift figure eight, to counter a simultaneous attack high and low by the darting spears. At the same time he covered his throat with his targe. Gudrun, on the beast's other side now, shouted "Come!" By kicking the beast's shoulder, she made the abnormal head turn towards her—more in surprise than pain, for the kick was weak because of her wrenched leg muscle. Felimid sprang to the beast's sloping haunch in an instant, and thence launched himself into the corridor beyond, with his back prickling in anticipation of spear thrusts.

None eventuated.

"Meseems this stretch of passage is forbidden them," Gudrun said thoughtfully. "Are you hurt, Bragi?"

"I think not. Quickly! Let's make some light! I tell you, there should be better illumination than candles and fire-brands, and a swifter means of making fire."

"There ought to be a less clumsy way of bearing children, too. Ask Karilva. But there is not and never can be. I have flint and punk here. . . . Suppose you grope your way to a lamp."

After a nerve-twisting interval, they could see again. The yellow beast eyed them malevolently, though it remained silent. A massive chain and staple restricted it to an ante-chamber of similar size to the others they had passed, and which the beast almost filled. It was there to bar the passage only, not to prowl it.

"Where did Koschei find such a thing?" Gudrun wondered.

"Nowhere in this world. Ah! Look."

One of the spears had gashed the beast's side. Black blood dripped from a superficial wound. Where it fell, it ate smok-ing pits in the tiles.

"Well for us we did not attempt to slay it."

"Indeed," Gudrun said savagely. "Let us get on. Bragi, my water flask was smashed when I rolled under the beast, or maybe by a spear, so be careful of your own."

All appeared quiet in the next antechamber. Here, the walls were carved with grotesque wooden faces of goblins, were-wolves, dragons and *ljeschi*. Felimid did not believe it was solely for decoration. The chamber of the spears and that of the beast had contained no such ornaments. Koschei must have had a reason for placing them here.

Gudrun fidgeted. She wished to move. However, the bard was contemplating something he seemed to find significant, and his arcane thought processes had saved her life in King Vindalf's hall. She waited.

"They are discolored, those faces, about the lips and mouth," Felimid said at last. "You see?" He moved his can-dle forward and back. "It might almost be soot, but it has a green tint. Yet this mansion hasn't existed longer than two months. Even the cookhouses are not sooty yet."

"Wizards do burn unhealthy fires when they conjure."

Felimid scanned the wooden faces again, more closely. "Were it only that, the discoloration would be the same across the entire wall, and darker in the crevices, like the wrinkles in the brow of that face. Smoke works more evenly. Smoke . . . I wonder, now. . . . ''

"Best you not wonder all night," Gudrun said. "Bragi, if you have a notion, act!"

"Yes. I've a notion, and I'll test it. Gudrun, fill your lungs deeply. Then hold your breath. I'll go first, and if I cross this chamber safely, then follow me fast! But do not breathe."

"I think I see."

Felimid inflated his lungs several times. Then he dashed forward. The carved mouths vented thick green vapor, making it impossible to see within a heartbeat. Gudrun rushed blindly after Felimid, caught him, and moved down the next length of corridor. The vapor billowed after them.

In the next round antechamber, vines growing on a trellis reached for them, to bind and strangle; but here Koschei had overestimated the deadliness of the trap he set, or else the vines had weakened away from their native environment. Felimid and Gudrun cut their way through the clutching tendrils without any formidable difficulty.

With their flesh swelling painfully where the vines had gripped them, they halted to breathe and to revile Koschei the Deathless.

"He promised intruders . . . seven deaths . . . the son of a mare," Gudrun gasped. "How many have we passed?"

"Hmm. The deadfall, the spears, the beast . . . ''

"The killing vapors."

"Right; the vapors, and then the plants. We've two more to thwart yet. Gudrun, this corridor bends at angles, with an antechamber at each angle. I believe it surrounds Koschei's sanctum—a hexagon—and that no matter where you begin, you must walk the full distance and come back to your starting place before you can enter. If I guess aright, two more obstacles ought to bring us to the deadfall again."

"Joy," Gudrun said ironically.

As it happened, Felimid's guess was correct, though his geometry was lamentable. In speaking of a hexagon he had meant a seven-sided figure; and by sheerest chance, his mistake with that foreign term had led him to accuracy, for the polygonal corridor did bend through six angles only.

They trod warily along the next stretch of corridor. Like the others, it had ornately panelled walls and a vaulted ceiling above. The sixth antechamber, too, was essentially like the others; circular, with a floor of costly tile, and about three yards across.

"If all's as usual, something unpleasant will happen the instant one of us treads upon this floor," Felimid said. "May I have your jerkin, now?"

Gudrun handed it to him wordlessly. He tossed it on the tiles. Nothing happened. Lightly, experimentally, he rapped with the rim of his shield upon the floor, assessing the sound it made. He studied the walls and the groined ceiling above. At last, frowning, he rapped the tiles again, made a sudden vehement noise of comprehension, and struck harder.

The pattern cracked like ice between the tiles. Something moist and gritty welled out of the fracture.

"Quicksand, the bastard," Felimid said, grinning. "A cistern abrim with a smothering morass, and it sealed over with pretty tilework no stronger than eggshells. He didn't waste the time he spent in East Rome and Persia."

"It's good that you admire him so. I would enjoy showing him what his own heart looks like. How does *he* pass these traps untouched?"

"I'd say they ignore him. Watchdogs do not bark at their master. How are *we* to pass this one?"

Gudrun's fingers were forming a bowline in their length of rope as she answered. "I'll go first this time. On my belly, with my arms and legs well spread. If the tile gives way, this loop will be around my body and you will have the other end. If I escape a bath in muck, it will be your turn, my harper."

They did it in that way. Despite ominous noises, the fragile, treacherous surface held together. On the far side of the trap, they performed the now-familiar task of lighting the lamps.

"Why, there's the deadfall!" Felimid said. "We have come the full way. Did I miscount? No, we've escaped six deaths, and Koschei threatened seven. There is another yet."

"Look," Gudrun suggested, in an odd tone. On the inner side of the final length of passage, a portal of vivid colors had appeared. On its surface, an artist had depicted every kind of fire elemental in metal and jewels. A phoenix rising from its pyre dominated all, its plumage umber, orange and gold. At the periphery, pale will-o'-the-wisps drifted and ruby-scaled salamanders crawled. Beneath the pyre, sparks of garnet and topaz fell upon a blazing demon as he coupled with a she-

dragon. Burning lamps which smelled faintly of sulphur out-
lined the doorway.

"Koschei's sanctum."

"Surely. It's too garish to be anything else, and the seventh
death must wait inside."

Gudrun slid her sword through the fretted bronze latch,
lifted and pushed. She had learned too much that night to
touch the portal with her bare hands. It swung wide. Within
lay a great hexagonal chamber, the domed ceiling rising into
shadowy distance, all of it lit by the pure white light of a
supernal fire-blossom.

Deadly serpents seethed and crawled on every surface. They
clustered, hissing, upon ledges. They writhed four deep on the
floor, a living carpet. They covered tables, chairs, a footstool;
coiled about the legs of an iron tripod; stared from compart-
mented shelves. Some fat, black and sluggish, with blunt tri-
angular heads, others yellow and worm-tiny, rapidly darting,
still others copper-colored, with pale bellies and tomb breath,
they filled the air with their sibilance and the chamber with
Koschei's seventh form of death.

"Is it illusion?" Gudrun asked.

"I fear not. I'd know if it was."

They stood outside the door, baffled.

X
White Flame and Black

"Helheim!" Gudrun swore. "The fire-blossom is there, we see it burning! Here we stand with water to drown it! I haven't come this far, past all Koschei's dirty traps, to stop now for a few serpents! I'll pad my legs and run over that floor if I must. If I'm bitten, I will not die before I reach the flower. I may not die at all."

"Easy!" Felimid said sharply, catching her by the arm, anxious to stop her before she turned her words to actions; he knew her rashness. "Most of the snakes are of no kind I know. It's sure I am that Koschei would choose inordinately deadly ones."

"Well, nothing less than magic will keep their fangs quiet. Bragi, why not harp them asleep? I know you can do that, for you did it to me, burn you."

"You and some of your men." Felimid gazed at the writhing mass with fascination. "Those who escaped were only those beyond hearing distance. You would have to block your own ears to the sleep strain most thoroughly, my love, or what happened to you before would happen again—and I'd be needing you to guard my back while I harped. Besides, it's by no means certain I am whether snakes can hear at all, and if they cannot, I might harp until morning and not charm one of them into slumber."

"It's nothing to me what you do, so that you do it quickly!"

Felimid smiled. "Guard my back, then . . . and you need
not block your ears."

He drew the enchanted harp from her bag. As he knelt in
the doorway to play, Gudrun turned to watch the corridor.

The first notes rang fine and thin, chiming like ice. That
sharp melody sang on, into a waterlogged valley of darkness
and cold which Felimid mapped about it with the thicker
strings. Then, as his nails leaped and struck, the imagined
bogs froze. His music spoke of forming ice, hard, brittle and
exact. He harped frost in growing, delicate patterns, precise
snowflakes whirling in multitudes, and sudden cracks like the
splitting of cold-tortured trees. Felimid harped winter.

Summer's warmth departed the dome. The bard's breath
fumed white. Cold sent skewers into his ears and teeth, and
threatened to stiffen his fingers. He mastered that and harped
on. Winter chill invaded the sanctum.

Rime formed on the walls. The writhing snakes sank into
torpor, stupefied by cold. Felimid stepped through the doorway and partly descended the short stair leading to the chamber's sunken floor. Gudrun followed in something of a daze,
thinking, *He can do these things. Then what kind of man is
he?*

Felimid said prosaically, "Padding your legs was a fine
idea, but let you do it to mine instead."

Gudrun complied, drawing off her kirtle and shirt and rip-
ping both in half with her knife, according her lover's thick
tunic the same treatment. With aching fingers she wrapped
them about each of his calves in layers, then fastened them
with turns of rope.

"Now go," she said through clicking teeth, "before we
freeze or the water turns to ice!"

Felimid made himself step into the tangle of half-dead
snakes. He harped as he walked, sliding his feet delicately
among the gelid bodies. Most slithered weakly aside; even
through the leather of his Persian boots, the contact made
Felimid's jaw clamp reflexively. A few struck feebly, but their
fangs did not penetrate his leg wrappings.

After the longest walk of his life, he reached the table where
the fire-blossom burned in its metal bowl. He looked down at
it, into its softly radiant heart, a white glory surrounded by
ring after ring of trembling, ever-changing flame petals. Even

its heat was only a pleasant warmth, delectable and welcoming, not the raw dry scorching of ordinary fire. It was the most beautiful thing he had ever seen.

He would almost as soon have destroyed Myfanwy.

Slowly, he unstoppered the flask, his fascinated gaze never leaving the flower. He needed all the resolution he could gather to pour water into its luminous center.

With the first splash, the flower divided in two, its fiery petals extending, their symmetry gone. The flask gulped air and gurgled forth water, once, twice, thrice more. All that remained of the fire-blossom then was a glimmer and a memory.

The sanctum grew dark.

Koschei kept vigil in the forest with red laughter in his heart. The laughter ended when his new demon horse quivered beneath him, neighed gleefully in violation of his command to observe silence, and threw him headlong. He crashed into a tree and rebounded. The demon charged him.

With a mad dog's snarl, Koschei met its rush. His iron mace sank through the demon's skull even to the horns, driving its head to the ground and breaking its neck. Yet even that appalling blow did not stop it. The demon hurtled tail over shattered head atop its erstwhile master.

Groaning with fury, Koschei strained against the enormous weight pinning him down. Half-lifting the carcass, he squirmed from beneath it. Grunting, crawling on his knees, he groped until he found his bull-headed mace, spattered with brains.

Shaken, enraged beyond his ability to show it, Koschei did not have to wonder what had occurred. He knew. No demon of his could have attacked him unless the talisman by which he ruled them had been destroyed. His playfulness had betrayed him. While he, like a scarred ancient cat, had watched the wrong mousehole, his mice had scurried behind him and tied his tail to a wolfhound's nose.

His demons were free.

Slavering in his beard, making inarticulate sounds, Koschei walked towards his mansion. Balls of green lightning formed in the air above him; at his command, one consumed a tree which barred his way, but such acts did not make a mile one step shorter. His newest demon steed had rebelled and died, and in consequence Koschei must walk like anybody else.

In the mansion, Gudrun had entered the darkened sanctum with a lamp to light her lover's way out. The air felt like knives in her lungs. The serpents beneath their feet were comatose or dead, and did not stir.

As Felimid and Gudrun gained the stair, a hideous noise came from the roof. The dome began to shake under repeated impacts.

"I'd say the demons have discovered they are free," Felimid said.

"I would say you are right, and that we should leave."

"I will. To find Procrustes. The fat cruel slug has something of Beigadh's, and I mean to restore it to him."

Behind them, the dome burst like a robin's egg and fell in fragments. Gudrun laughed. "Our master, was he? Koschei will not forget us, whatever betide."

They left through a splintered, gaping wall of the corridor. The demon on the roof continued to smash the jagged remnants of the dome, yowling with glee. Felimid and Gudrun moved with light-headed, lethal haste through the maze of doomed tapestry, carpets, wrought silver, scent, lacquer, and colored stucco, triumphant, yet aghast at what they had achieved. Gudrun did not even remember that she was bare to the waist.

In a hallway they met the surgeon, who looked ridiculous in his silk night garments, eyes popping, sucking air like a desperate chub. Felimid halted him with an uncompromising grip on his fat arm.

"Good e'en, Procrustes," he said, misleadingly gentle. "The racket you hear is your master's demons unleashed. They have discovered they need obey him no longer, so they have, and my advice is to save yourself if you can—but not before you have shown me where Beigadh's vitals are kept."

"I will cut out yours if you do not," Gudrun said, more succinctly, pressing her knife against his round belly.

"You are mad," he croaked. "The Mighty Sovereign One will—"

He flinched and cried out as Gudrun pressed harder with the knife.

"He's rather less mighty than he was, and by sunrise he may not even be sovereign. I've said to you that his demons are free. Can you not *hear*, gelding? The mansion is falling.

Time's short, and you may not go your way before you oblige us. Remember, I'm the man you talked of blinding. Do not tempt me."

Gudrun cut into Procrustes's fat. He squealed in pain. Then he led them to the hidden niche where a log, long as a man's torso and triply sealed with steel bands, was kept. Procrustes sank against the wall, gripping his belly as if to hold in the intestines Gudrun's knife had not even approached.

"Stop whimpering and go," she commanded. "I hope you meet a demon who will give you cause to squeal. Bragi, can you carry the log?"

He held it clumsily under one arm. "It's awkward, but not over-weighty. I can lug it as far as the stables."

As they retreated down the hallway, its ceiling cracked open and a rain of serpents cascaded through. The sinuous creatures lay on the floor and began to revive in the comparative warmth.

Descending a stair to the second story, the pair met a demon, more or less manlike in form, slouching, heavily muscled, green-furred and wolf-headed. It blew a gout of lightless black flame which began to consume the wall, without smoke or heat. Then it regarded the man and the woman with a baleful stare.

"We too were between Koschei's stinking hands," Felimid said, dropping the log and letting it roll to the foot of the stair, "and we destroyed his power over you tonight. Maybe you can discern it."

"Am I to thank you?" the semilupine demon bayed.

Felimid showed a hand's length of his sword; Gudrun moved away from the wall to draw the being's attention. "Koschei will return yet," the bard said. "Let there be comity among former slaves, if the notion does not offend you."

"Peace, then," the demon answered, looking at the silver-inscribed blade.

As they departed, it vomited a hissing gush of black fire over the stair. In moments it was impassable by anything mortal.

Between them, Felimid and Gudrun manhandled the log into the stable yard. In passing, Felimid let out the horses, to scatter where they would. A murky shape was still systematically breaking the roof apart, high above.

They found two frightened stable boys in the yard. Felimid spoke them fair in his halting Wendish, and suggested that they leg it for the forest together, since Koschei's demons had plainly grown disobedient. He offered to let them carry the log so that he could fight unburdened if self-defense were necessary.

"It contains treasure," he added.

Beigadh would not have disagreed with him. Besides, his assertion drew the two Obodrites' full attention to the torso-sized log in time (barely) to save them from having their heads broken by Gudrun for goggling at her breasts.

As they crossed the fields where the harvest had lately begun, they saw immense dripping shapes rise from the river to advance upon the mansion. Koschei's other demon slaves, freed from bondage in the Oder's depths, had come to take part in the destruction. The white flame of Kupala's flower had gone out; the black flame of the demon's breath burned for many hours.

It still burned in the morning, consuming the stone foundations and the stone quay where Beigadh's boats had once been moored. Felimid watched in wonder as the granite fed the lightless, inexorable fire, corroding like blocks of salt. All the treasure, all the mansion's opulence, gone in a night as it had appeared. Nothing would remain, not the smallest trace.

"And here we sit, you and I, with one shirt between us," Felimid said. He loosened its neck cords. "You had better have it."

Gudrun put it on. "What do you suppose the demons will do now?"

"H'm. It's past sunrise, and by the look, they have already taken shapes which please them, not those which suited Koschei's ends. It's in my mind that they won't tarry long. Were I a demon, I'd have only one further thing I wanted to do here. By Cairbre's fingers, I see it now!"

Koschei stalked from the forest.

"If I had my bow—" Gudrun breathed.

"Yours will not be needed. Look."

A demon in the form of a black steel statue was bending a steel bow. The arrow passed through Koschei's throat. He staggered, spat a large clot of blood, then gave his characteristic wild roar of laughter. Throwing his arms wide, he bellowed, "Try again!"

Three demons who had become black and orange dragons sprang into the air, their webbed wings beating. As they rushed upon him, Koschei thundered an incantation. Green lightning crackled from the sky, striking the dragons dead. They fell like ragged leaves. Koschei laughed again, furiously, and strode onward.

Felimid had provided himself with a sling and some round stones. Now he sprinted after Koschei, whirling his weapon, and shouted the giant's name. Koschei turned. Felimid hurled the stone, which struck Koschei in the pit of the belly with terrible force. Unlike the arrow, which had passed through him, the blunt missile expended all its force on Koschei's body. A normal man would have been instantly killed. Koschei was knocked on his back, writhing.

As he struggled to his knees, a fourth dragon descended on him. He was lifted in scaly claws, beaten by the gusts of wind from thrashing wings, carried high into the air and let fall. Spread-eagled and howling, he dropped hundreds of feet into a millet patch. The other demons converged upon it. Felimid and Gudrun joined them.

Koschei was merely stunned by a fall that ought to have shattered all his bones. The demons swarmed over him, fanged, taloned, steel-handed, mauling him with preternatural force, yet when they drew back at last, he remained unmarked.

"Obstinate," hissed a dragon.

"As he's disinclined to die," the steel demon said in tones of belling metal, "let him live as long as he wishes, but tightly enclosed and deprived of power, sight and hearing."

His fellows cachinnated, hissed and screeched their approval. They knew far more of the method for immobilizing a fire magician than any mortal. They wrapped Koschei in a linen shroud well sprinkled with salt, and wound iron chains about him from neck to heels, forging the links together to stay. Then they placed an iron helmet on his head. For beings who had built a mansion in one night, it was simple to fashion or obtain these things.

The steel demon and others had meanwhile excavated a pit nearby. A gray, six-limbed monster unceremoniously felled and trimmed an oak, seasoned the trunk to the hardness of flint by breathing on it, and in moments adzed a coffin from the timber thus treated—with its nails. Koschei recovered his senses before these latter preparations were complete.

"*Why?*" he demanded of the bard. "I dealt well with you."

That he truly believed it made an answer difficult. Felimid tried.

"You laid claim to my life," he said. "You told me that I might not come or go save at your bidding, and breathe only because you suffered it. I'm an indolent man who loves wine, music and dancing better than strife, my great lord; but if a god told me that, a god with the sun in his right hand and the moon in his left, I would dispute him."

"You think this ends it?" Koschei snarled. "Beware, betrayer! And you, pirate! I cannot die. You will see Koschei again, if not in this life then in some other, and Koschei the Deathless will remember you and know you. *Fear that day!*" he shouted, shatteringly loud.

The demons had restrained him with iron, and now they shut him in his oak coffin, and last they lowered him into the pit which they had lined with massive boulders, and heaped more boulders over him. Throughout the day they labored at their last task for him, raising a mound above his living grave, raising an artificial hill of gravel, clay, brushwood and stones. They strengthened it with vertically driven logs and wove others in crisscrossed layers, until the mound was finished. It measured eighty feet high and three hundred long.

The black fire had long since consumed every trace of foundation and quay. That done, its fuel exhausted, it died. Koschei's only visible monument was the one beneath which he lay buried.

Crowing with satisfaction, the demons departed.

When Beigadh the trader returned to the ruined mansion with a force of a hundred Wends, there was nothing for him to do but receive the gift of his encased vitals which the bard had entrusted to the captain, Nikolai. Nikolai and many of his pikemen had escaped the burning mansion alive, and in the circumstances he was not inclined to be bumptious. Of Procrustes there was no sign. Beigadh sat with his arm around the squat log in which his vitals were sealed, fondling it and shaking his head in wonder.

Koschei's incipient empire had joined all the unborn or forgotten empires the earth had devoured.

The bard was free.

Of everything but Gudrun Blackhair.

Epilogue

The Oder poured into the sea through its several mouths. Gulls rode the wind. Redshank, eider and oyestercatcher trod the shore, seeking food. Felimid and Gudrun walked through the dunes.

"Odin has disowned me, you see," Gudrun said, "and those eerie deathlings named me their sister. A weird is on me. . . . I think I am fey."

"Not unless it is your fate to be," Felimid argued. "I was told you northerners believe even Odin cannot change that, for good or ill."

"And neither can he. My meeting him was a strong sign, though. If I'm not soon to die, a change almost as great is in the wind for me."

"Now that's more the right sort of talk," Felimid said enthusiastically. "Why should there not be? Do you still intend to fare beyond the world in *Ormungandr*?"

Gudrun fisted him in the ribs. "I have given it small thought of late. I was tracing an inconstant rogue I know through a wilderness—and when I found him I had to help him out of trouble. I suppose I do."

"That inconstant rogue thanks you and loves you. But you are not such steady stuff either. Remember how you hurried north, leaving more than half your pirates to their own devices on Sarnia? Wagered your life on a whim with Vindalf? Bade Decius take your ship and amuse himself as he liked while you tracked me down? I wonder if you have not been growing weary of the pirate life, for it's eager you seem to throw your captaincy away."

She was silent for a space, turning that over in her mind. At last she said, "I'll answer you when we have reached Sarnia again. Decius for one would agree with you, that I have treated my captaincy like an old cloak. . . . But he will return for us. I know him." She frowned. "When he does, I will have to discard *Ormungandr*'s red sail. The bird of Odin can be my emblem no longer."

"You needn't do that. We have battle goddesses in Erin whose bird is the crow, and Morrigu the greatest. Call upon her instead. For that matter, you might even go to Erin and there head a king's bodyguard. We do not look upon fighting women as unnatural, Gudrun. The foster mother who taught me weapon use is a famous one."

"Erin," Gudrun mused. "Yes, even Odin's curse might have too short an arm to reach me at the western edge of the world. The thought is a fine one. Maybe . . ."

"Manannan! See yonder!" Felimid exclaimed. "That's *Ormungandr*!"

Gudrun scanned the sea. "It is. Decius is days early. Back to the boats with us; quickly. If Beigadh and his men return and meet *Ormungandr*, and we are not there, it will come to weapon-bathing. *And I'll be there before you!*" she challenged.

Her heels threw up sand. Felimid crested the dune a yard behind her. In a moment the sandhills were empty; Gudrun and the bard had reached the shore while *Ormungandr* was still a long spear's cast beyond the mild Baltic surf.

Before the sun had set they were sailing west.

AFTERWORD

As a setting for fantasy, the Dark Ages have the advantage of being free from detailed records. The contemporary histories, regnal lists and letters can often be interpreted in more than one way, dated in several, or shown to be outright mistaken in the light of modern archaeological discoveries. (And modern archaeological discoveries aren't necessarily the last word either.)

None the less, far more hard information about these centuries is available now than when I went to high school. It used to be assumed that history stopped between the fall of the Roman Empire and the rise of the Middle Ages. I have used the new information to make the background to this novel as accurate as I can, but I'm not reckless enough to vouch for any one incident's being correct. For instance, Nennius describes King Oisc of Kent as Hengist's grandson, while the Anglo-Saxon Chronicle spells his name Aesc and calls him Hengist's son. Which is right? The Chronicle indicates that he did indeed die in the year of this story, after a reign of twenty-four years, but as Sportin' Life observed, "It ain't necessarily so."

Bard II is set, specifically, in northern Europe in the summer of 512 A.D. A century before, give or take a decade, the last Roman legions had been withdrawn from Britain and the province was left to defend itself against hungry barbarians. From the British resistance (which continued fiercely long

after other provinces like Gaul and Spain, and for that matter
Italy itself, had been taken over by various German tribes)
grew the legend of King Arthur.

In 512 the British position looked stronger than it had for a
hundred years. The recent defeat of a combined Saxon and
Jutish war-host at Badon had led to the destruction of Saxon
settlements in the Thames Valley as far east as London. The
invaders still held coastal realms from modern Essex to
southern Hampshire and Wight, but their inland gains had
been torn from them and they, not the British, were then on
the defensive.

In Gaul, the Frankish conqueror Clovis had died the year
before, dividing his kingdom like a private estate among his
four sons according to the Frankish law of inheritance. The
standard fratricidal process of elimination had not yet begun,
but the knives would come out soon enough. Armorica had
become known as Lesser Britain for the numbers of British
who had settled there, and would in the future be called Brittany.

The English Channel (Narrow Sea) was as pirate-infested as
this novel describes it. The pirates were mostly Celts—including and particularly the Irish!—or Germans from the North
Sea coasts. Gudrun Blackhair is a fictional exception. The
Viking Age had not begun, and the Scandinavians had not yet
learned how to build the famous Viking longships. (*Ormungandr* is very like one—but *Ormungandr* was made by the
dwarves, the master artisans and engineers of Norse legend.
It's a matter of mythological record that the dwarves built enchanted ships for the gods. I have assumed that they would
sometimes do so for mortals if the price were tempting
enough.)

The Danish brother-kings Othgar and Helgi appear in early
epics. Othgar, or Hrothgar, is the king on whose behalf the
hero kills the monster Grendel in *Beowulf*, and both brothers
play a part in *Hrolf Kraki's Saga*, which has been retold by
Poul Anderson. If they really lived, it must have been in the
early sixth century. They would have been ruling at the time of
this story.

The temples of Forseti and Svantovit existed, as and where
described. Forsetislund is the island we know as Heligoland—
but in the Dark Ages it was far larger than it is today. Wave

attack and rising sea levels had reduced its periphery from 120 miles to about eight by the mid-seventeenth century. The temple of Svantovit, with its wizard-priests, sacred white horse, rites and divinations, can be found in Saxo Grammaticus along with an early version of *Hamlet*. I've assumed that they would have changed little in hundreds of years.

Odin was worshipped in the north then and much earlier. His sinister, implacable nature as a god of death and the gallows is no slander invented by Christian missionaries. Human sacrifice was part of his cult, offered by hanging, burning or spearing, and sometimes by drowning. Prisoners taken in battle were often dedicated to him en masse. He inspired the mad frenzy of the berserkers, and even his most ardent followers were aware that he could not be trusted. He knew the way to Niflheim, the realm of Hel, which he reached on an eight-legged horse . . . a poetic image for a funeral bier, as Gudrun Blackhair realizes. The picture of him as a noble, dignified all-father belongs to later centuries and was probably an invention of poets, like his marriage to the ancient mother-goddess Freya. (The death-goddess Hel would actually have been a more fitting mate for him.)

Bragi, Felimid's alias among the pirates, is the name of another northern god, the god of poetry. I'm not suggesting that Felimid was the original, and I hope no reader would take the idea seriously if I did. But I enjoyed hinting that Bragi—rather a vague figure among the Aesir—might have begun as the memory of a foreign bard. In one later poem, Loki taunts Bragi for his dislike of battle, which does sound like Felimid. Although for a man who dislikes battle, he has a suspicious knack of failing to avoid it.

The Obodrites were a real Slavic tribe. All the creatures of Slavic folklore, the *vodyanek*, the *rusalki*, and others, are authentic. So are the rites of Kupala's Night, and the powers ascribed to the magical flower which blooms only then. Koschei the Deathless may be found in Russian folk tales, although I haven't borrowed much more than his name from the original sources.

His chess-playing is an anachronism, even allowing for the fact that he says he learned the game in Persia. I've preferred the many colorful legends of the game's origin to mundane fact. The Persians, Jews, Arabs, Egyptians, Romans, Irish and many others have been credited with inventing chess. It has suited me to assume that the Persians did, at about the time of Trajan.

Finally, the bard and his powers are described according to the beliefs of his culture. Bards in the Celtic world were a special class with special and extraordinary privileges. The "three strains" for mirth, sorrow and sleep are attested in Irish myth. The enchanted harp to whose music the seasons came and went is the property of the Dagda in the stories. I've taken it from him and given it instead to Felimid's supposed ancestor, Cairbre, the bard of the half-divine Tuatha de Danann. I say "supposed" ancestor because I don't wish to imply that Felimid knows everything, or that all he believes is necessarily true. Even in a world of printed records, it's easy to be mistaken about one's lineage.

Felimid's magical powers are chiefly "airy" in nature; that is, they have their source in the reasoning mind, and are given form and effect by means of speech, poetry and music. His ability to see through illusions which deceive most people (the bardic sight) was gained when he was initiated into the third rank of bards, the rank he still holds at the time of *Bard II*. To go beyond it, he would have to return to Erin and resume his interrupted training. He'd readily learn to create illusions as well as see the reality behind them, if he stayed in one place with the right teacher for long enough—but, perhaps luckily for everybody he meets, he can't create illusions yet.

He loses the magical powers he does have whenever he enters a Roman town, city or other structure, and also within a Christian church or monastery, because these things represent ways of life and thought completely at odds with his own. The Church is continuing what Rome began, and magic is slowly being choked out of Felimid's world.

But it won't vanish in his time.

MAGICQUEST™

A new fantasy series featuring the best in Young Adult Fantasy— classic titles of magic and adventure by the top authors in the fantasy field, in paperback for the very first time!

THE THROME OF THE ERRIL OF SHERILL
by World Fantasy Award Winner
Patricia A. McKillip   _____ 80839-5/$2.25

THE PERILOUS GARD
A Newbery Honor Winner by
Elizabeth Marie Pope   _____ 65956-X/$2.25

THE ASH STAFF
first of the Ash Staff series by
Paul R. Fisher   _____ 03115-3/$2.25

TULKU
An A.L.A. Notable Book by
Peter Dickinson   _____ 82630-X/$2.25

THE DRAGON HOARD
by the popular and acclaimed fantasist
Tanith Lee   _____ 16621-0/$2.25

Prices may be slightly higher in Canada.

Available at your local bookstore or return this form to:

TEMPO
Book Mailing Service
P.O. Box 690, Rockville Centre, NY 11571

Please send me the titles checked above. I enclose _____. Include 75¢ for postage and handling if one book is ordered; 25¢ per book for two or more not to exceed $1.75. California, Illinois, New York and Tennessee residents please add sales tax.

NAME_____

ADDRESS_____

CITY_____ STATE/ZIP_____
(allow six weeks for delivery)

T13

You
decide . . .

HOW TO SURVIVE in the streets of *Thieves' World's* Sanctuary.

HOW TO DEFEND a collapsar planet during Joe Haldeman's *Forever War*.

HOW TO STOP the Union as Mazian in **The Company War**, based upon *Downbelow Station*.

HOW TO BECOME the dominant Weyr in **Dragonriders of Pern**.

HOW TO EMERGE from dank Dungeons rich and renown with **Role Aids.™**

You make the decisions with exciting games from Mayfair.

For more information write:

MAYFAIR GAMES INC.
P.O. Box 5987
Chicago, IL 60680